BORNE RISING

Beyond the Shadows

MATTHEW CALLAHAN

Roguish Creations

First published by Roguish Creations 2020

This novel is entirely a work of fiction. The names, characters and incidents portrayed in it are the work of the author's imagination. Any resemblance to actual persons, living or dead, events or localities is entirely coincidental.

Matthew Callahan asserts the moral right to be identified as the author of this work.

Matthew Callahan has no responsibility for the persistence or accuracy of URLs for external or third-party Internet Websites referred to in this publication and does not guarantee that any content on such Websites is, or will remain, accurate or appropriate.

First edition

ISBN: 978-1-7329222-1-1

Cover art by Patrick Knowles

Editing by Meredith Tennant

❀ Created with Vellum

CONTENTS

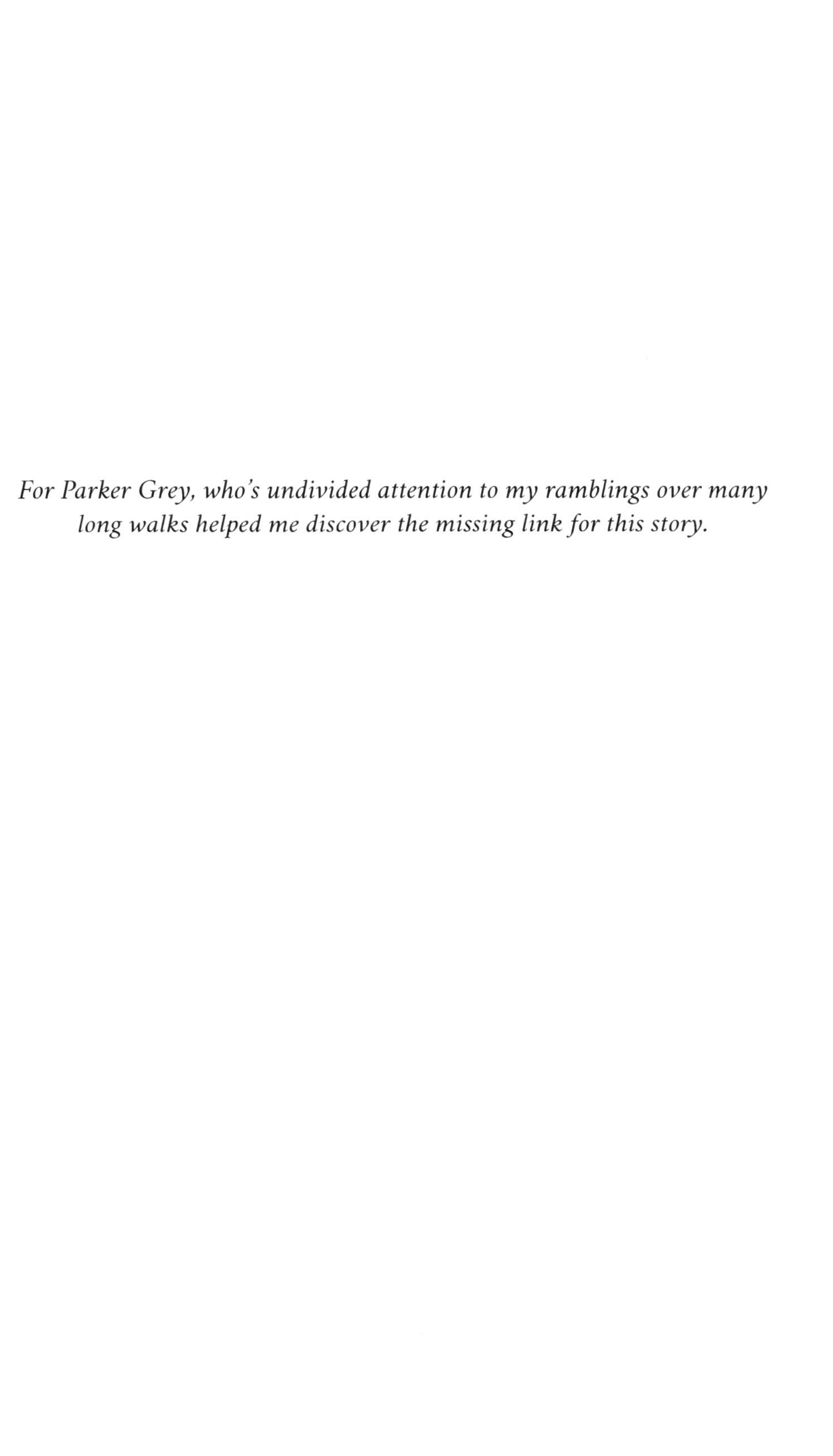

For Parker Grey, who's undivided attention to my ramblings over many long walks helped me discover the missing link for this story.

PROLOGUE

Sitting in the pool of darkness, the Crow watched his seneschal conclude her business of the day. She was efficient and earnest. Eager, even. Overall, she had been a good replacement for the last one. That man had been problematic for more years than the Crow cared to admit. Yes, the man's loyalty to the Nordoth, to the Crow, had been unwavering, but the Crow did not regret removing him from his position. There could be no denying that all reason had escaped him by the end, the pressures of his job too demanding. The event with Thorne's descendants proved that.

Bringers of change, that pair.

The audience having ended, the Crow turned silently. Masked in darkness, he lurched into his personal office where he poured himself a glass of wine and eyed the measure on the far wall. It had been active lately, far more active than he'd seen it in decades. Darkness billowed against the bright white, smoke-like substance although there was still no variance of control. He'd thought there had been a surge of darkness briefly a few months prior, a flux, but it had gone quickly. Still, an active measure merited careful consideration.

Bringers of change, indeed. The Borne always upset the status quo.

He sipped at his wine and considered. Perhaps it was time for change.

There had been no reports of the brothers nor word from their Seeker guide in some time, too long for the Crow's liking. There had been a sharp uptick in cultist activities in both the borderlands and central control. The Necrothanians were growing bolder, no longer simply a mild inconvenience but burgeoning to a problem that would soon require attention. He did not believe the timing coincidental. Nor did he believe that the horrendous crack in the heavens that had appeared around the same period was coincidence. Many things the Crow may be, but a fool was not among them.

The pieces are moving on the board and the world is falling in their wake.

There was a sharp rap at the door.

"Enter," the Crow said and collapsed into his seat. He sipped at the wine once more before placing it on the table. The door opened and Shifter, commander of his personal patrols, stepped within. The lean man removed his helm and the Crow frowned slightly. The man's weapons and armor were worn and cracked. *Resupply. Another item that demands attention.* The Crow beckoned the hawk-nosed man toward him. Shifter gave a slight bow and approached.

"Lord Crow."

The Crow eyed the man. "You work fast. Report."

"Yes, my lord. The roads leading into the city have seen an increase in activity, particularly those peoples from the lands north of Theravane. Havenfjord and Tavernal have also reported population influxes given the aggressor activity stemming from their outer territories. There have been no attempts to infiltrate any of the major hubs yet. The roads beyond Letchbrook continue to bear the brunt of cultist attentions."

A continued focus on Theravane and Letchbrook? Interesting. "What of Stormvale?"

"Additional watches on the pass, but overall no change."

Yes, as ever they think that Umbriferum acts as their protector, even in death. "Carry on."

"The gazers have maintained a constant watch on the heavens since the event. The crack in the sky has continued to be a cause of concern for the general populace. While its brilliance is unwavering, the reports of size fluctuation were exaggerated. It remains static. The gazers have no new information at this time. Given that, the stockpiles of the Nordoth have been filled according to plan. The armies are being amassed.

"Sir." The commander took another step forward and leaned down, speaking in a quiet tone. "If I may, troubling rumors are spreading. An upset, as it were, where none was expected."

The Crow smiled thinly, hiding his disappointment at the gazers' inability to explain the rent in the sky. That Shifter grew troubled at rumors, however, took precedence. *Ripples, then.* "Explain."

"Your request to bolster the defenses of the Nordoth was passed through the ranks and active recruitment has begun. The Undermyrian people are hesitant, as expected, as are the people of the surrounding territories. It has been some time since the last faction war, and few are willing to believe that another may be upon us. Nonetheless, recruitment has been steady these past months."

"Good." The Crow nodded. *Yes, sheep seldom believe a wolf approaches until it is already tearing them apart.* "Go on."

"Thank you, my lord. Some time ago, you expressed a need for readily trained soldiers of . . . special qualifications. I gathered the Thirteen and made your will known to them. A small contingent set out to find such mercenaries and engage their services.

Contact has been successful with many of the regional bands and I've sent additional men to the lands beyond the Daurhi Wastes. However, there has yet to be any contact with the Shale."

Shifter paused and the Crow raised an eyebrow. *And now we come to it.* "That is hardly news, Commander," he said. "The Shale have ever been notoriously difficult to contact."

"Agreed, my lord. This instance is of particular note, however. The problem stems from the usual liaisons. We have made contact with them, established terms and brokered costs. It is they, sir, who have had no contact with the Shale."

The Crow did not let the surprise show on his face.

"It appears," Shifter went on, dropping his voice ever further, "that there has been no sign of the Shale for some time now. Reports indicate the last official contact via their sources coincided with"—the commander paused a moment, searching for words—"with the arrival of the Blademaster's descendants."

The Crow's mind worked quickly, connecting the dots and filling in the blanks before the commander had finished speaking. He saw the entire story plain as day, though he had difficulty believing it despite everything he had seen in his long life. *Changes. Yes.*

The commander, receiving nothing from the Crow, continued. "As difficult as it is to believe, sir, our contacts believe that the Shale have fallen."

"And you think that the young Shadowborne did such a thing?" The Crow watched as the commander wrestled with the absurdity of the notion before finally nodding.

"My lord, I do."

The Crow laughed. "Your concerns are noted, Commander, although I do not share them. The Shadowborne was young and inexperienced." He sipped his wine and considered a moment. *Not the boy, but another.* "Do your contacts know of the boy? What rumors spread of the Shadowborne's coming?"

"None, my lord. The channels are ignorant on this matter, it seems. As ordered, no word of the Shadowborne left the citadel following his arrival. In the city there is the usual fear that arises any time cultist activity increases, but I have heard no rumors regarding the Borne that bear acknowledgment, sir."

"What do the people believe then?"

The commander did not hesitate. "Sir, they believe it has something to do with the shattered sky."

They're more right than they know. The Crow steepled his fingers and smiled at the commander. "Very interesting. And do they have any theories to back this belief up?"

"No, Lord Crow. Merely superstitious conjecture."

"Indeed. Is there anything else, Commander?"

"No, my lord."

The Crow waved him away. "Very well. Well done, Commander. One cycle's reprieve before your next assignment."

"Sir." Shifter saluted and turned, making for the door. Before he could reach it, another knock came. The commander paused and glanced back at the Crow. The dark man nodded and gestured for him to leave before calling for the other party to enter.

A short, inconspicuous form entered—Calen, one of the Crow's personal messengers. He slipped past the departing Shifter and hurried over to the Crow.

"My Lord Crow," the thin man said, bowing. He handed over a small, folded piece of paper. "A Seeker delegate from Greygarde has arrived. She wishes to see you. She said you would be expecting her."

The Crow knew who it was before he opened the missive. The parchment was unadorned, the plain script saying only *I have news.* The Crow snickered at the brief, useless message but folded it nonetheless and tucked it delicately into a nearby drawer. "Send Cephora in."

Calen turned and promptly exited the room. In the brief interlude of silence, the Crow sipped at his wine and worked through the many details his web of spies had collected since his last meeting with the Seeker's Prime. He analyzed every angle and smiled. *Yes, this should be interesting indeed.*

The tall, dark-skinned woman entered. It had been just over a year since he had last seen her. Nothing had changed—she appeared exactly the same and bore the same manner, although he supposed that was to be expected. Even if something had changed, this ancient one had long since adapted to not letting it show. She was armed, as was customary of the Seekers when they met with him. The Nordoth guards had protested for years, but the Crow brushed their concerns aside. Weapons or no, a Seeker was dangerous, this one particularly so. But the Crow held no fear of them or her.

Cephora scanned the room quickly and then crossed to him. Her face was impassive, but the Crow noticed a slight hesitation when her eyes found the measure. He studied her while she analyzed it, suddenly growing even more interested in whatever she had to report. What had his spies missed?

The Seeker gave a small shake of her head while reading the device then, without a word, moved on and surveyed the entire room. Spying the decanter, she crossed and poured herself a humble serving of wine. Only then did she acknowledge the Crow's presence, raising the glass to him in a greeting before politely sipping at its contents. Unbidden, she sat opposite him and placed the glass on his desk. Then, with a casual sigh, she clasped her hands and leaned back.

"You look well," she said.

The Crow smiled a genuine smile, a rarity for him, and tipped his own glass in salutation. "I feel well." A moment passed where neither spoke further. The Crow let it stand. The silence began to stretch and he chuckled to himself. *Very well, then.* "I expected you sooner."

"Complications arose."

"That, my friend, is why I sent a Seeker."

"Complications beyond my own capacity."

This brief, bold statement shocked the Crow, another rarity for him. Still, he did not let it show. "Well then, hmm. Complications, you say?" He raised his eyebrows. "What do we know now that we didn't before?"

"Dorian Valmont is alive."

Two-thirds of the calculated potential outcomes of this meeting immediately dropped by the wayside. He dismissed them without a second thought. "That is hardly the shock you make it out to be. Nor do I imagine that the knowledge of his survival is beyond your capacity to comprehend."

Cephora cursed. The Crow smiled, watching her frustration boiling just beneath the surface. She took a measured breath, regaining her composure. "I should have presumed you would have known of his survival."

The Crow spread his hands, as if to express that all his cards were on the table. "It is in my best interest to plan for all potentialities. Go on."

The Seeker frowned. "Jero din'Dael is alive also. Alive and free. It was he whom your information led us to. He had been imprisoned deep within the Shale. The Davis boys released him. The Revenant destroyed both the Shale prison and army upon his release. The Shale are no more. I assume you knew that as well."

The Crow nodded. He had expected as much, given Shifter's reports, but confirmation was always welcome. He motioned for her to continue.

"The celestial anomaly that has lingered in the heavens was a direct result of din'Dael's act."

That would interest the gazers. The Crow stroked his chin and sipped his wine. "Continue."

"Valmont did not come alone. His army has already risen in force."

Of course he has his force with him. But if she saw them then . . .

The Crow raised an eyebrow. "You saw him, then?" Cephora nodded. The Crow's features stretched into a knowing, toothy grin. "Complications, indeed."

Cephora held his gaze unwavering, no warmth in her expression. "The first contract we agreed upon was to guard the assets in their journey to the Shale."

"I recall."

"The second contract was contingent upon their success within the Shale," Cephora continued. "In the event of successful retrieval of the assets, the Nordoth entered an agreement with Greygarde to guide said assets to Umbriferum in order to retrieve any records from the ancient halls. The assets did not reach Umbriferum."

The Crow did not allow his expression to change, but he mentally crossed off another significant percentage of his remaining potentialities. "And why not?"

"Valmont. Immediately following the destruction of the Shale, he made his presence known to us. *Immediately*. I do not know how. I only had time to recall myself and the Shadowborne to the nearest Greygarde haven. The extraction from the Shale was . . . difficult. The Casc needed time to recover, but he was understandably irate at the loss of his brother. It was some time before we set out once more. I do not know what became of din'Dael or the other Casc."

The Crow had already dismissed them. Madigan Davis had had promise of a potential leadership position within the guard, given his ancestry and training. The loss was a blow, but only a minor one. The whereabouts of the young man and din'Dael was an issue for another time. "Time, yes. But upon the boy's recovery, you did not set out for Umbriferum."

"We did not. When Valmont was last active, he set out to destroy the Umbriferum. Taking the Shadowborne there would have been a tactical error. Valmont would have expected such an action. Instead, other measures had to be taken."

"Such as?"

"I took the asset to Greygarde. We remained there for some time while the Shadowborne pored over the resources we maintain. Following that, we departed for Undermyre to report."

"It would have been preferable had you come here immediately."

Cephora cocked her head to the side. "The Seekers do as they will, Crow."

The Crow conceded the point and turned his attention to his wine. "And where is the young Davis now?"

"He is in a location where Valmont will not find him. He should be safe." Cephora's hesitation was almost unnoticeable. Almost.

The Crow snapped his eyes to her, his casual demeanor dropping away as more of his plans fell by the wayside. "He did not accompany you to the Nordoth?"

"The first contract was to get him to the Shale and, should he survive, to extract him. That having been completed, the secondary, conditional contract calling for travel to the Umbriferum was unfortunately cancelled. You know the clause of which I speak."

The Crow did not let the scowl cross his face. He knew the clause. *Formal recitation of terms does not excuse your actions, my dear Seeker.*

"My contract having therefore ended, the obligation of Greygarde to the Nordoth had also reached its conclusion."

The dark-clothed man leaned back in his seat and steepled his fingers, staring intently at the Seeker. "Contracts, yes. And yet there is more to the young Shadowborne's absence. Elaborate."

Cephora met his eyes and did not flinch. "After our time in Greygarde, we departed for Undermyre. En route, the asset discovered an opportunity for additional training. Or, rather, I should say that the opportunity found him."

The Crow frowned.

"The opportunity was another Borne. She demonstrated her skills in Shadow and, despite my protestations, the asset chose to go with her."

Her. The Crow did not blink, did not flinch nor even exhale out of the norm, but as soon as Cephora said that word, his plans came crashing down till only two options remained. "He did not trust you."

Cephora's previously stoic expression cracked, giving the Crow a brief glimpse of her pain. "After the separation from his brother, he grew . . . distant. He did not approve of my decision at the Shale."

"This Shadowborne," the Crow said. "What did you make of her? How old was she? What further information can you provide?"

Cephora's armor returned. She met his gaze unwaveringly. "If you're asking if it was *her,* then I do not know the answer. She always was excellent with disguises, even before she went into deep hiding. After she destroyed the Order of Umbriferum, well"—Cephora shrugged—"I can hardly believe she's become anything but a master at masking herself."

"Fine. Did she appear of proper age?"

The Seeker nodded.

The Crow's brows narrowed in anger. "You sent that child off with an unknown Shadowborne. A female of the correct age. One whose history you did not know."

"I sent no one away." Cephora leaned back and folded her hands. "The Casc is headstrong and impulsive, yes, but he is strong and capable as well. He chose to go with her."

The Crow rose. "She enticed him, you mean to say." He moved to the decanter and refilled his glass. "You saw her Shade then?"

"I did."

"And?"

"As I said before, Crow, I do not know if it was her."

The glass trembled in the Crow's hands briefly. He steadied it but knew that Cephora had seen the brief evidence of his frustration. *A different tack, then.* "She was just as dangerous as her father, Cephora."

"Worse. Dorian was at least predictable."

"And now he's back and that boy may have walked right into his trap."

"Madigan Davis has chosen his own path. That is his right."

Madigan Davis . . . The Crow's mouth went dry. He drained the glass and moved back to his chair. He did not speak for a moment, only steepled his hands and stared at the measure. So, there had been a flux. *Minor adjustments necessary, but this may work out for the better in the long run.* Cephora waited. Despite all his efforts, when at last he spoke there was the faintest waver in his voice.

"What of the other boy? The younger brother."

Cephora looked at him intently. "I do not know. As I previously said, when we faced Valmont, he stood alone before him. I could not rescue them both."

"Pity." The Crow swallowed more wine and was thankful to see that the tremor had left his hand. "That boy had potential."

"It is possible that Jero din'Dael got him out."

The Crow laughed humorlessly. He turned his dark eyes upon the Seeker. "And why would din'Dael have done anything of the sort?"

Cephora cocked her head and stared at the Crow. Her mouth turned up in the hint of a smile. "You did not know? Truly?"

Suddenly interested, the Crow raised his bushy eyebrows and leaned back. "Know what, Cephora?"

"The boy is Lightborne."

The Crow stared at her wordlessly as his final two plans became ash. "Is he, now?"

Cephora nodded, smiling fully. "He and his brother stood before Valmont together, Shadowborne and Lightborne. I witnessed it with my own eyes."

"I believe you." *The bonds of brotherhood . . . interesting.* "Perhaps din'Dael did save him then." There was a brief silence while the Crow considered what she had told him and Cephora's own place within the story. He returned her smile, allowing it to stretch wolfishly across his face. He could not help but enjoy how the act unnerved her. "That is all, Cephora."

Cephora did not move.

"Was there something else?" He raised an eyebrow and did not allow his smile to falter.

"You claimed that the boy had potential," she said cautiously. "Yet you did not know that he was Lightborne."

The Crow did not respond immediately. From the look on the Seeker's face, he had obviously given her something. *Involuntary dilation of the pupils, most likely. I shall have to amend that.*

Cephora waited. Her face resumed its casual, presumptuous air. "What is it that you *do* know?"

The Crow leaned forward, the unnerving smile plastered upon his face. *And now I've got you.* "I know that Madigan Davis is Shadowborne. I know that he was left as your charge. I know that he is now in an unknown location with an unknown woman with unknown motives. And I know that there was one surviving Shadowborne unaccounted for, a woman, in fact. And I know that if that woman has Madigan Davis, Undermyre will fall."

He saw the gravity of the words wash over her.

"It may not have been her," Cephora said quickly.

"No, it may not have been," the Crow agreed. "But you asked for what I *know*." He watched while she wrestled with her desire to press him further, to obtain more information for her organization.

The two faced each other that way for a time, neither speaking. Finally, Cephora drained the last of her wine and stood. She gave him a perfunctory nod and made for the door. Before it closed completely behind her, the Crow called out.

"And you shall be awaiting orders from me where, then?"

He heard the sharp intake of breath that cut off the nearly silent curse flowing from her lips. She cracked the door just enough that he could see the cowed look on her face. *Good.*

"Use the Street of Ash," she said finally. "Clarice will know how to find me."

She closed the door, no doubt preparing to leave the Nordoth and touch base with her contacts in Greygarde. The world of the Seekers had just grown far more complicated than it had been in years, and the Crow knew she must itch to make a full report. The organization were notoriously hard to control, but Cephora had left herself wide open and the Crow had seized the advantage. That was as it should be.

He sipped the last of his wine and turned to the measure once more. The swirling vapors twisted in their typical hypnotic fashion, but he did not allow himself to become distracted; the Davis brothers had suddenly returned to the forefront of his mind.

The elder had manifested as Shadowborne, that was good. But the younger boy . . . that was problematic. The Crow had seen many things in his long years, had heard many rumors, but for any Borne—particularly one of such strength—to reverse alignments was unprecedented. It simply did not happen.

That meant the careful guidance of his maturation was of utmost importance. More important than Valmont's undertaking. More dire than the potential return of the madman. The younger Davis was paramount, an anomaly in the game.

He stepped closer to the measure, leaning toward the intricate face.

Yes, he mused. *Change is most certainly coming.*

I
DESTINY CALLS

Will spat another mouthful of blood and coughed. One of his molars was loose and his constantly probing tongue didn't help. *Focus.* His spinning head drooped. His split lips burned. Another wave of nausea surged through his stomach and he felt the bile rising. *Dammit, Will, keep your head. Don't lose focus. Just hold on.*

Mad's voice. Or, at least, the fading ghost of its memory.

Wish I could, buddy. Will forced the bile down and immediately broke out in a clammy sweat. The air surrounding him—a dry and scorching, nearly physical thing—burned his lungs when he drew in fresh air. It was sour, but he had grown used to it. It complemented the lingering acrid taste of vomit and blood. *Don't lose focus. You can do this.*

He could bear the pain, stomach the foul air, but it was the electricity that called to him most. There was a near-humming static upon the air. He yearned for it, that promise of power, but knew that he must not reach for it.

His wrists were bound tight, the rough ropes biting into his skin significantly less painful than they once had been. For that, he was grateful for the buildup of scar tissue. Still, it was far from comfortable, even with the thick skin to help him ignore the chafing. *Not important, Mad would say. Focus.*

Will pushed the discomfort from his mind and tried to do just that. *My surroundings, right. Focus on those. What am I working with?* The chair he was bound to was solid, not something he could easily break. His arms and torso were bound tight, but his legs were not secured to the chair's frame in any way. He groaned inwardly—it wasn't an oversight. They had plans for his legs today. They needed them flexible and mobile. The last time they'd focused on his legs, he hadn't been able to walk for weeks.

Along with his arms, they had taken his eyes. His world was darkness, but it held none of the comfort it once had. *Those days are long behind me.* At least their attempts at taking his hearing had failed, despite their best efforts. The blows still rang, but short of puncturing his eardrums they couldn't dull it entirely. They wouldn't go that far; he knew that much.

The thick blindfold covering his eyes passed over his ears, muffling sound but not so well that he couldn't make out at least something of his surroundings. He could feel the presence of other bodies in the room, three of them this time. He could sense their eyes upon him, could hear the shifting sand on the stone floor when they moved restlessly.

That's a lie. Not his brother, Jero din'Dael this time. *This world is filled with lies. See them for what they are and be free of them. Elevate yourself.*

Right, a lie. These individuals were far from restless, Will knew that. So why hadn't they started on him yet? He tongued at the loose tooth. *Psychological. The threat of pain can be more terrifying than the pain itself.* Whoever they were, they were patient and would wait as long as they had to. They would wait until he broke. Until he gave up.

They were going to be sorely disappointed.

Will quickly worked through the various possible outcomes

of the situation before he found one to his liking. He focused on it and suppressed all others; they no longer mattered. He had committed to one course of action and would see it through.

Decide, din'Dael's voice echoed in his mind. *Decide and push all other potentialities from your mind. Do not dwell on them once you have moved past them. They are only a distraction and will lead you to second-guess yourself. Decide and then act.*

Will did as his mentor instructed.

Time passed, an hour perhaps, Will had no way of knowing. *Not that it matters.* Will sat and waited. He kept his breathing smooth and controlled. He did not fidget. He did not twist and worry at the ropes binding his wrists. The trickle of time grated on him, but nevertheless he forced himself to focus. The moment was coming soon.

"You're quite the quiet one, when you want to be."

Nearly there. Will held back a smirk. *Show them nothing.*

"He is awake still, isn't he?" said another voice.

"Of course he is. Look at him, he's listening to everything we say," came the first voice once more.

Dammit, they know. Will forced himself not to hold his breath. *Dammit.*

"You don't know that."

"Damn me to Theros if I'm wrong."

"He's Casc, who knows what they're like?"

Will's shoulders relaxed and he chastised himself for the slip. They didn't notice. That, coupled with the brief turn of his jailers' conversation, meant that the tables had turned. He would be free soon. There was only one unknown to overcome. The third person had neither spoken nor moved; he could not place them. It was infuriating. *Know your opponents and act on their weaknesses.* This one had given Will nothing to go on.

"He's got to be asleep. I'm checking."

Footsteps approached. Will kept his head down and waited, bracing himself. He'd planned to have all the information by this point, but that silent third was an outlier. Din'Dael's words came to him once more. *Plans will only get you so far. In the end, action and reaction are all that are required.* He'd just have to take his chances with the unknown variable.

One of the unseen individuals approached, their feet nearly brushing against Will's own. Will kept his body loose and fought the urge to act. *Not yet.*

A large hand slapped his face. It stung, but the thick blindfold absorbed much of the blow. Will felt the loose tooth rattle but did not allow himself to react to the strike. Hard fingers dug into his jaw while the person's other hand gripped the back of his skull. Will was momentarily appreciative of his roughly shorn hair, taken down nearly to the scalp early on in this endeavor. *One less handhold for them.* His head was forced upward.

"He's barely breathing. What the hell did they do to him this morning?" The voice's cadence had changed, signaling that the source had turned back to his companions.

Will struck.

He drove his feet into the ground and thrust upward. Tightening his neck, he slammed his skull into his captor's head when the man turned back. He heard the crunch of bone and stumbling steps as the figure fell. Will pushed backward, turning his back to his captors. Right on cue, the air split as the chair was shattered by a surge of lightning.

Will grunted, thrown forward by the force of the blast. The splintered shards of the chair ripped through his shirt and buried themselves in his skin. He grimaced. *Don't get distracted.* His arms were still bound and the blindfold was still securely attached, but he could stand and move freely. *Focus.* He did not hesitate.

He darted back the direction he had come, instinctively dodging another crack of white fire that shot toward him. Will stepped expertly, avoiding the writhing figure on the ground. He lunged at the source of the blasts, leaping forward and crashing into the Lightborne. At the same instant, he drove his knees into their abdomen. A sharp, choking gurgle came when breath unexpectedly vacated their body. Will forced them to the ground. Another sharp strike from his knee and the figure was still.

The third individual had neither moved nor stirred. Will tried to shake the blindfold off, to no avail. He took a wide stance and crouched slightly, cocking his head to the side and listening for any change in the room. *Just like Mad used to with my Shade.* He pushed the thought from his mind.

He grunted. Something biting drove into his stomach. A split-second later Will's nerves fired. Burning pain. He screamed at the blade in his gut. He dropped to a knee, feeling hot blood flowing from the wound. His body cried at the intrusion, railed against it. He curled over but somehow managed to keep from collapsing to the ground.

Stomach wound. Lower right quadrant. Not near the liver, just guts. His mind raced. *That's right, isn't it?* He fought to suppress the thought of complications from bowel lacerations. *Keep your head, Will, don't pass out. It hurts, but you can handle it.* His breath came in short bursts. *The knife is still in, it's slowing the blood flow. You've got time.*

Quiet, light footsteps approached. The other two were still down, so it could only be the third. They knelt directly across from Will and placed a hand on his shoulder. The other hand gripped the knife in his body and even the brief contact sent him screaming—*Jesus, Mom*—before the blade was pulled free.

Will wanted to vomit. Blood flowed onto his lap. He felt whoever was holding him tense and knew that a second strike was coming. It didn't matter; without medical attention he was dead already.

He drove forward and threw his body into the blade. Pain seared across his chest as the knife collided with one of his ribs and skidded off the bone—they had missed. Collapsing onto the assailant, Will struck with the only weapon available to him. His teeth bit into the soft flesh of his captor's neck and held fast. Will clenched his jaw and jerked his face away. Flesh and blood followed him.

He was forgotten. The figure pushed away, screaming. Will felt blood hitting him in gushing spurts. Realization dawned. *I must have hit the carotid artery. Shit.*

Forcing his own pain aside, he rolled off the writhing figure. Scrambling with bound hands, he searched for the fallen blade. He found it, slicing his fingers when he turned the blade over. Still, he managed to cut into the cords that bound him. His head was spinning—*no time for that*—and he slashed furiously at the rope. Freeing himself, he ripped the blindfold off before doubling over and vomiting from the pain.

He glanced over at the gasping figure gurgling and choking on their own blood. *No, no no no.* He grabbed the thick blindfold and forced it onto their neck to stem the bleeding. It was soaked though in no time. The eyes, so familiar, stared at him in pleading terror.

To hell with this.

Will's fist glowed with the white-hot fire of Radiance. He cupped his palm around the wound. The smell of searing flesh filled his nostrils.

Within moments, he was thrown aside. People crowded him and the dying girl on the floor, immobilizing them and working in a controlled chaos. Will's shirt was cut away. His body was burned over and over. But his eyes never left the face of the blood-soaked girl next to him.

WHEN WILL CAME TO, JERO DIN'DAEL WAS LOUNGING ON THE bunk next to him. The Revenant's hands were clasped behind his head and he was staring at the stony ceiling. His eyes were fixed beneath their dark brows and his mouth was set in a thin line, yet his face was utterly relaxed. The entire thing was a mask. *This isn't going to go well.*

"How's Rienne?" Will's voice was a hoarse croak.

"You had one job, William."

Will was quiet for a moment to see if din'Dael would continue. He didn't. "Jero, how—"

"*One* job, William. One job and one rule."

"I'm very aware of that but—"

"What was the job, William?" Jero rose and stood over the bed.

Will forced down the frustration building in him. He hated being patronized. "To escape by any means necessary. Except—"

"And what was the rule?"

Will rolled his eyes and inhaled deeply. The wounds in his stomach and ribs ached. "To escape by any means necessary. But under no circumstances should I call—"

"Upon the powers of Radiance by which you are Borne. You must escape without the use of your Flare," Jero finished for him with a sneer. "You failed to follow orders."

"The situation changed, Jero, it evolved. I changed with it."

"You deliberately disobeyed orders then? I would have preferred ignorance over insubordination."

"She was dying, Jero," Will snapped. He looked up at the man. "Rienne was dying."

"In battle you will see many friends die. This is something you must accept. You were to overcome the enemy and finish the job. You should have let her die."

"If she had been an enemy," Will said, meticulously enunciating each syllable, "I would have let her die. If it were combat and I couldn't help, I would have let her die." He leveled a stern gaze at din'Dael. "This was neither."

"Still, you didn't follow orders."

"Did you want me to let her die?"

Jero's face brightened in a wide smile. He laughed, loud and cheerfully. "Not at all, William. Rienne is a very gifted Lightborne. A bit soft, maybe, but gifted nonetheless."

Will eyed the man. Soft was not a word he would ever have used to describe Rienne. Efficient, calculated, deadly? Yes, but never soft. "Given her knife-throwing skills, let's agree to disagree on that point."

Jero laughed again and wiped his eyes. "Yes, she stuck you rather well, didn't she? It was quite amusing."

Amusing? Will looked at the man next to him. His mentor. His teacher. His only connection to a life before the Sapholux. Jero din'Dael's madness had largely left him since their arrival in the citadel of the Lightborne, the years of torture undone by years of safety and recovery. Yet still, there were traces of it. There was a wildness in the large man's eyes, something feral. There was a piece of him that Will couldn't understand, did not want to understand.

"Jero, please. We can debrief later. I'll report on every action I took and my reasoning behind it if you like but, please, is Rienne alright?"

Din'Dael's chuckling ceased. His expression darkened. "Why ask me? You inflicted the wound. You're rather familiar with them by this point. What do you think?"

Will clenched his fists, forcing himself to stay calm. "I know the severity of the wound. I'm asking if cauterizing it helped at all. Did Nelle and the rest get to her in time?"

"I would hardly say that she is alright, William." Din'Dael spread his hands and leaned back onto the bed behind him, lounging like a cat. "But I believe she's still alive for the time."

For the time. The words echoed in Will's mind. He swung his legs off the bed and fought back the waves of nausea that came when he twisted his abdomen. "May I go to her?"

"For what purpose?"

"To offer my aid."

Jero's eyes darkened. "William, we've been through this. You must purge all traces of your old life in order to become a Blade." Will said nothing. He met din'Dael's gaze with determination.

Finally, the large man rolled his eyes and shook his head. "All this time, they still function?"

Will nodded. "Last time I checked."

Jero shook his head and returned to his feet. "You are an enigma, William Davis. Go to her, then. Offer what help you may. But do not be surprised when your methodology is poorly received."

"Yes, sir."

Will pushed to his feet, wincing and momentarily reminiscing about the regenerative properties of the Shadowborne. Cauterizing from Radiance held its own relief, though it was a far cry from the comforts of a Shade. He forced the thought down, burying it amongst the rest of his former life. *Stop it. That's behind you now.* He could fight through the pain. He controlled that part of him, not the other way around.

"William."

Will paused and turned back to din'Dael.

"You did well today."

The praise came as a surprise but Will said nothing, only nodded.

"Compassion is not a weakness, but it does not always have its place. Today, however, you were correct in your course of action. Return to your quarters and retrieve what is necessary, but before you see her, head to the larder. You yourself are in need of rejuvenation."

Will smiled and inclined his head. "Yes, sir."

WILL KEPT HIS CHAMBER AS SPARTAN AS THE DAY HE FIRST ENTERED the Sapholux. His sleeping pad was on the ground on a pallet. At the foot of it sat the small trunk that contained all his worldly possessions. When he arrived at the Sapholux, ragged and battered after weeks in the desert following din'Dael and his blasted eagle, most of his belongings had been burned. But his blood fangs, his key, those he had been permitted to keep. *Mementos of a dead man,* din'Dael had said. *And I do not mean your grandfather.*

Will had certainly felt dead, then, a corpse walking. His skin had reddened and cracked before shriveling into a dry, leathery tan. There had been no food, no water, but he had survived. He knew now that the fires of Radiance had fueled him when he should have died, the fires that scorched and parched his insides. No drink could quench the thirst from Radiant flames. The constant thirst had driven him to near madness. *What a pair din'-Dael and I must have made in those weeks of travel.*

The decrepit exterior of the Sapholux had looked like a tomb, the final resting place where he would collapse in death. But when the gates beyond the terrifying entry tunnel opened and he stepped within the protective walls of the Sapholux, the terrible thirst began to abate almost instantly. It had shocked him by its absence. But more shocking still had been what he found on the interior of those ancient walls.

The legends had been wrong. The histories, the records, everything had been wrong. The Lightborne, supposedly culled following the Wars of Dawning, were massed in force. For them, the Wars had never ended; they merely employed a new strategy. For hundreds of years, they shut themselves off from the world. Only their herald, Jero din'Dael of the Maddened Flame, Revenant of Radiance, dared venture out into Aeril. He'd sought out the straggling remnants of the Order, brought them together, hidden them from the world. Until the Shale caught up to him, that is.

That was all before. After the Shale, din'Dael had taken Will under his wing and trained him, taught him to embrace the brilliant fire within him. *The Flare, so different from a Shade and yet so similar.* Din'Dael taught him to leave the trappings of his old life and fuel the blaze within himself, stoke the coals. But Will had told din'Dael, told him right at the start of everything, that he would never leave it all behind, that there would always be a part of him that was still the same William Davis.

He'd kept the bit about being Shadowborne to himself as well.

Will grimaced in pain and removed the blood fangs from the trunk. He could still sense the power within them, though their stones were much diminished. But it was there. He fit the belt around his waist and stood, wincing when the wound in his stomach bit him. Coupling the fires of Radiance with the resources at the Sapholux was a boon toward healing, and their medicines were second to none, but it would still be days before his body felt right once more.

Except that wasn't the case. Not anymore. He had been permitted his blood fangs. They could undo the damage in no time at all, given proper fuel. He smiled at that. It felt right to be wearing them again. They were a part of him, as much a part of him as his Shade had once been—as much as the Flare that burned within him now. And, to din'Dael's voiced amazement, the fangs still responded to Will.

To the larder, then, Will mused. He closed the trunk and shoved it back against the bed. Will would recover. Rienne would survive. And din'Dael, well, din'Dael had relented on the fangs for the first time. That meant something had changed. Will smiled, sensing that his time within the confines of the Sapholux would soon be coming to an end.

I'll see you soon, Mad. Wherever you are.

2

ABSOLUTION

Will's hands were stained red by the time he left the larder. It was messy work and brought back far too many unpleasant memories, but the stones needed fuel. Steeling himself against the scent of fresh blood, he'd done his job delicately, cleaning the game under Quintel's guidance in order to most effectively use the animals after. The Lightborne had sniffed disdainfully when he saw the blades Will intended to use, but he said nothing.

I'd forgotten how much the smell lingers, Will thought. He coughed and grimaced, hands instinctively clutching at his stomach. He looked down and eyed his trembling, dark-stained fingers. *Rienne isn't the only one who needs healing.*

Leaning against a wall and sliding to the ground, Will reached for the flows of the bloodstones. He'd never felt them so alive before. He pulled at them and guided them over his stomach and set about knitting his broken flesh. The relief was almost instantaneous.

And yet, the flow felt strange maneuvering through his body, manipulating and mending his cells. His nerves were firing, setting his skin alive with tingling. Old scars from the recent years of training burned with new pain before fading away. Will shuddered. *Am I doing something wrong?* It was so long since he last wielded the power, maybe things *had* changed.

No, the familiarity was there. It was as if . . . as if the blades were fixing *everything,* not just the most recent wounds. What had Cephora said when she'd shown him their power? *The power of the fang comes through my connection with it. Binding myself to it.*

Perhaps there was more to these things than he'd known. *Surprise, surprise.* It had all seemed so simple, then. He'd been healing mostly aches and blisters from travel. Mostly.

Except for when it was worse. Except for the Shale.

Memories of weapons protruding from flesh appeared in his mind's eye. Images of Madigan, leg broken and body rent by wounds. Of Morella's screams.

No, not going there.

Will tried to shake off the dark memories, but they clung. It had seemed like one big adventure in the beginning, filled with magic and mystery. Where had they gone wrong? He could still feel his arm go dead when the Shale's weapon bit through it, could still feel the weapons piercing his body when he fell to the ground. When he slept, if he rolled over and cut the circulation off in his arm, he would wake in a state of panic. The nightmare of everything that had happened after, the rampant murder of Shale and prisoner alike, still haunted him.

But we survived. He raised his bloodstained hands and stared at them. *Most of us, anyway.*

He could still hear Morella's screams. His stomach tightened, the sharp pain of loss a wound that the bloodstones could do nothing for. Valmont's sudden appearance—the strange inevitability of it all—and then Will's world being ripped away. Madigan was alive somewhere, Will still believed that. Cephora had gotten him out just like din'Dael had gotten Will out. But Morella . . . Will didn't know.

How had Valmont's army, dead and twisted, been so silent in its approach? How had he gotten the drop on them? *Me and Mad, sure, I'll take that. But the Revenant of Radiance? The Prime of the Seekers*? And throughout all that came after, the dark sorcerer Valmont had sneered.

Bastard.

That man was the root cause of all Will's suffering. That man murdered his grandfather and destroyed his home. That man separated him from his brother and the woman he—*loved?* —cared for.

Will closed his eyes and let his head fall between his knees. Morella was most likely dead, he knew. Abandoned at the end by Cephora and Madigan. Abandoned by himself and Jero din'Dael. Alone amidst the undead hordes of Valmont's warriors and the sorcerer's maddened power. Even if she had somehow escaped, she'd been weeks away from any sense of civilization, trapped in the Daurhi Wastes without food or water.

And if she survived all that, she's alone again. I abandoned her.

The sting of tears wrinkled his nose. Will glowered and shoved the emotion down, suppressing the memory with all the rest. Someday, he knew, there would be a reckoning for so much suppression, but for now he needed to focus on the living. He stood and took a deep breath to quell his shaking. He could not undo what had been done to Morella, he could not salvage that loss, but he could at least help Rienne.

Will arrived at the infirmary and paused just long enough to knock before pushing the door open and stepping into the large, bright room. There were enough beds for at least fifty occupants in this particular infirmary and there were at least a dozen others like it located within the Sapholux—a sign of the Order's former strength. Now, however, only a single bed was occupied.

"Rienne," Will called out and stepped forward tentatively. "May I come in?"

The woman raised a weak hand that Will took as an okay. He

approached and took in the battered form of the young woman. Her tan skin was pale and had a gray tinge to it. Blood had pooled beneath her eyes, making her look as though she had been severely beaten. Her hair was hidden beneath a wrap that kept it free of her neck. The neck and wound itself were wrapped in bandages heavy with the strange salve used in the Sapholux to aid healing and prevent infection. The bandages also meant the wound was worse than Will feared.

"Up and moving already?" Rienne's voice was strained and she winced when she spoke. "Guess I didn't get you as close as I thought."

"Oh, you got me well enough." Will gave her a pained smile. He pulled over a stool and sat next to her. "You, though"—he shook his head—"I hope it's not as bad as it looks."

"That bad, is it?" Rienne laughed briefly before her body seized in pain. Tears welled in her eyes, but she forced herself to return his smile. "A bit closer than I would like, that's certain."

"Rienne." Will thumbed the blood fangs. "I'm sorry. Jero din'-Dael allowed me to come here, permitted me to help if I may. May I?"

She raised an eyebrow. "Help?" One corner of her mouth turned up in a weak smile. "You broke it. If din'Dael thinks you can fix it, be my guest."

Will inhaled and tried to calm his nerves. *I can do this.*

He held out a hand and, raising an eyebrow at him, Rienne took it. He withdrew the left blood fang and gripped it tight in his hand. Rienne's eyes grew wide at the sight of it and she recoiled from him—*Of course she knows what they are*—but he held her hand tight. He felt the bloodstone's power, felt it cascading and entwining his hand, and guided it toward Rienne.

He focused on her neck, uncertain of the extent of the damage and how much energy it would require to repair. His thoughts drifted to Morella, of the wound on her side when he met her on the road. He thought of his brother and the broken body he had suffered at the hands of the Shale while saving Will. He thought of himself, battered and bleeding on the stone floor after his Flare and the sudden power of Radiance had manifested within din'Dael's prison chamber. Compared to the latter two, this wound was slight—Will knew that Rienne would be alright.

She gave a sudden gasp and squeezed his hand, a grimace of pain crossing her face. Suddenly, she screamed, recoiling and pulling away, but Will held her. Her hands crackled with lightning, the Flare of Radiance burning defensively, and still he held on. She cried out again and again while he restored her broken flesh and replenished her body to a healthy state.

He stopped, sensing that he had done all he could. Rienne was panting heavily, her eyes wide with shock and fear. He couldn't understand the pain of the process for her; he had never seen it before.

"Rienne, I—"

"What the hell was that?" Her voice was sharp, angry, but strong and tinged with awe.

Will was silent for a moment. "That was the art of the blood fang."

"I know *what* it was." She reached a hand up to the bandage at her neck and tentatively pressed on it. Will hadn't thought it possible for her eyes to grow any wider, but they did. She tore at the bandage and ripped it off, her fingers delicately touching the smooth, unblemished skin. "How? How did you . . .?"

Will smiled. The pools of blood were gone from her eyes. The gray cast to her skin had faded, returning it to its natural deep tan. He sheathed the blood fang. "It's a long story."

"Only Blades of Shadow are capable of wielding the blood fang."

"And Disciples," Will corrected. "But I am neither." He did not offer any further explanation. Rienne stared at him, questions clear upon her face. "I'm sorry for the pain it caused. I . . . I didn't expect that."

"Lightborne cannot wield blood fangs." She was distant, defensive.

Will held up his hands in front of her and met her eyes. Ripples of lightning danced across them. He smiled, trying to put her at ease.

"Apparently, they can."

"Of course it hurt her. What did you expect?"

Will stared at Jero din'Dael, deep in concentration while maneuvering the claymore through the air. The sheer size of the blade seemed impossible. Holding it aloft seemed to defy physics, let alone being able to move it with the grace that din'Dael managed. *Yet another commonality between din'Dael and Madigan.*

"It never hurt anyone before. It heals, not hurts."

Din'Dael did not break from the fluid motions of his form as he spun the blade. "Clearly your memory of our brief time together at the Shale has slipped your mind."

Will scoffed. The pain of whatever ritual din'Dael had performed upon him, coupled with the massive destruction, was not likely to ever be forgotten. "Hardly."

"Then you will no doubt recall your own actions against me there."

My actions against *him?* Will closed his eyes and rubbed his temples. "Apparently, you and I have differing opinions on what happened that day, Jero."

"You are an enigma, William." Din'Dael spoke as if he had not heard Will at all. "You wield what you should not. You are capable of the impossible. The impossible seems to be, with you, possible. Your existence defies logic."

"Yeah, well, your logic is skewed," Will muttered. *I don't know why I even bother with him half the time.*

Din'Dael finally halted the motion of his blade and leveled it at Will, his gaze hard. "You are Lightborne, William. You burn with a primal fire that has made you the envy of many within these walls." Din'Dael cracked a smile. "Not the least bit being because of the aid I gave you for freeing me."

Yeah, I wouldn't exactly call this place welcoming. Despite the huge sword pointed at him, Will couldn't help but roll his eyes. "Your rhetoric rarely changes these days, Jero."

The smile on din'Dael's face faded. "You are *Lightborne,* William. And yet you manage to manipulate the weapons of a Blade of *Shadow.* You control an element that is the very antithesis of everything you are, of everything I am. Everything that Rienne is."

"The blood fangs are neither, though. Cephora told me they were something more ancient than that. Why should it affect anyone any differently?"

His mentor's face split into a wide, humorless grin. Lightning erupted from din'Dael and coursed through the massive sword, flickering and biting at the air. Will leapt backward.

"Radiance and Shadow are opposites, William. You know this. Radiance is ever in flux while Shadow is consistently"—he smirked—"boring. You understand, William, that we are the superior."

Having known both, I'd disagree. And you didn't answer my question. Will opened his mouth to say as much but closed it when din'Dael raised an eyebrow at him.

"And yet you still fail to understand." Din'Dael closed the distance between them. Will scrambled backward, the glowing, spitting claymore tracking his every move. "You heal with a power that should destroy you, should leave you in agony. And yet, heal you do. Moreover, you manage to heal others, Lightborne and Shadowborne alike. That is something unknown, and, in this world, anything unknown is valuable."

Will backed into a wall and froze. *What the hell has gotten into him?* His eyes darted down to the sword and back to the man wielding it. "So, that's what this has all been, then? You find me, what, a curiosity? A valuable secret to be unlocked and used?"

Din'Dael laughed and released the power coursing through the claymore before resting the blade upon his shoulder. "Oh, William, your naiveté never ceases to amuse me."

Will couldn't help the embarrassing sigh of relief that escaped his lips. He pushed away from the wall and straightened his clothes, trying to regain some sense of composure. "Very much appreciated, Jero."

"You recall what you witnessed at the Shale, yes? The sheer magnitude of such power?" Jero paused, waiting for Will to nod before continuing. "Yes, hard to forget, I would imagine. I had been imprisoned for so long that the force of the power within me . . ." He took a deep breath and exhaled exultantly. "It was exquisite, Will. The transference barely touched me. The mighty Shale were ants beneath my boot heel. I touched the heavens and felt them tremble in my wake. You bore witness."

"Oh, I saw alright." *You ripped the bloody sky open.* "I saw the slaughter."

"The stores were barely tapped even then. My brief lapse, the recovery." He shook his head and smiled. "It was astounding how quickly it all came flooding back. Radiance *grows,* William. With time, with training, it grows exponentially."

"Can you please just be frank, for once?" Will was growing impatient with the man's addled mind. "You constantly speak *around* a topic but never *about* a topic."

Jero din'Dael chuckled and looked at Will through patronizing eyes. "William, dear William. Fluctuation is a part of Radiance, is ingrained within it like an inhalation and exhalation of breath."

Will considered the words. "So, the more power you expend, the longer it takes to recover?"

"Precisely."

"Then it's like you said. We're in flux. We wax and wane." His mind drifted to Madigan battling within the Shale, his Shade controlled and measured as he fought. "Shadow is consistent. Doesn't that give them the advantage in the long term?"

Jero stared at him, an amused smirk on his face. "No Shadowborne could ever be capable of what you witnessed that day, William."

"Then what makes Valmont so formidable?" Will said quietly.

The humor left din'Dael's face. "As I said, the unknown is valuable."

"Fine." Will could leave the question of Valmont alone. But din'Dael being so open was a rarity. He decided to press on. "Does Radiance have limits, then? I mean a lower limit. Is it possible to ever run out?" He considered his fangs and their bloodstones. "To tap the entirety of the power and be unable to access any more?"

Din'Dael sighed and shook his head. "Lightborne recover quickly. None could expend themselves to such an extent that they would be left devoid of any power, William."

Will eyed him. *That wasn't a real no. Any power, even the faintest trickle of current, is more than none.* "And Shadowborne, they don't, right? Like you said, constant." *Just imagine running dry right when Valmont shows up.* "I hardly see how that creates a superior force."

"Consider this, William. Where are we? Do you recall what you felt the first day you stepped within these walls? The Sapholux is a fount of power. A primordial flow of Radiance, a bastion of raw energy." The smile returned to his face, but it was different, twisted, bordering on cruel. "And our people, William, our people have been absorbing infinitely more power than they have been expending for years. Hundreds of years."

The implication of his words finally dawned on Will. Cold fear trickled down his spine. What would happen to the world if hundreds of Lightborne, wielding as much power as din'Dael had that day in the Shale, were unleashed upon it? *The Necrothanians, Valmont, they'd be obliterated in a breath.*

Din'Dael cocked his head to the side and appraised Will. The man chuckled and nodded, agreeing with himself about something that Will had no insight on. He mounted the claymore on the wall and turned back to Will, smiling. "Come, William. Walk with me."

Will felt the hairs on the back of his neck rise. *He's up to something.* He hesitated. "Where to?"

The Lightborne smiled at Will and crossed his arms. "You passed your tests today. It is time."

An inkling of old curiosity tickled Will's mind. He met din'-Dael's smile with one of his own. "Time for what?"

Jero din'Dael's left hand glowed emerald green. In the distance, somewhere deep within the massive expanse of the Sapholux, shrieked an eagle. "Time for you to enter the Halls of Legend."

3

THE HALLS OF LEGEND

The pair ventured deep underground, farther down in the Sapholux catacombs than Will had ever been. Jero hummed to himself all the while, a simple tune that Will found strangely forbidding. He first heard it on the day he followed the mad Jero through the desert after the encounter with Valmont. Often as they traversed the Wastes, din'Dael hummed the short, haunting tune. He'd never told Will where it came from. *But there's something about it. Something primal I can't explain.*

Dahla, the magnificent golden bird perched on din'Dael's left shoulder, was as much a curiosity as any that Will had come across since arriving in Aeril. Something about her transcended reality, as though she existed on the fringe of waking; a dream made reality. Will had never uncovered the connection between the bird and din'Dael; yet another question that was never answered. *Too many of those.* Will frowned. *And I'm no closer to getting answers than I was the day I arrived.*

They paused at a large stone door, twice as tall as din'Dael and black as the Crow's robes. Still humming, din'Dael placed his right palm against a small, carved section of the black mass, his fingers splayed. Lightning danced across his fingers as he Flared against the door. Will gaped. An infinite number of cracks appeared on the dark stone, glowing blue and white, lightning against a night sky, before the door suddenly shattered in front of Will.

He recoiled, holding up a hand to shield his eyes from the countless shards of rock that blasted outward. Only, there was no impact. Will risked a glance and dropped his arm. He took a tentative step forward, mouth still open in awe. The shards were all frozen in air, suspended in space. They had separated and extended outward, allowing a tall, narrow passage through the stone. Din'Dael passed through wordlessly while Dahla turned her golden eyes back to Will.

Will followed. Of course. He was intrigued. Passing through the separated stones, he could see that each one was crystalline, almost glasslike. Where the stones had separated sparkled beautiful rainbows of color, like the sun reflecting through a prism, only more vivid, more intense. He paused beneath the massive stonework that still rippled with the force of Radiance, stricken by the beauty of the impossible structure.

"I wouldn't linger," din'Dael called back in a musical tone while striding into the chamber beyond. "You won't want to be standing there when the ward resets."

Snapping his attention back to din'Dael, Will rushed across the threshold and took a few steps into the room. He turned back just in time to see the stones begin to quiver. Suddenly, as if in a vacuum, the shards reformed into their original door formation, blocking the passage. He stared for a moment, imagining the beautiful crystals impaling and crushing him where he had been standing.

"Thanks for the warning."

Turning back to din'Dael, Will saw a large, dimly lit room. Bright alcoves were set amongst the walls, spaced only a short distance from one another. He closed the distance to his mentor quickly, noticing that Dahla's eyes never left him. They were the unblinking, unyielding eyes of a predator. Despite his time with the eagle, there was still something about her that eluded him. Something familiar, even comforting, but simultaneously destructive and terrible. *I really don't understand that bird.*

"These are the Halls of Legend, William." Jero din'Dael spread his hands and held them out. Dahla flew from his shoulder and soundlessly landed on a frieze high above. "This is where the most treasured artifacts of the Order are kept. This is where the magnificent history of the Sapholux is made real. This is what we fight for."

He seemed to be waiting for Will to say something. Will shifted his weight and glanced around. "It, uh, it's great."

Din'Dael beamed and admired the room. "It is, isn't it?"

Uncertain of what to say, Will stepped away from din'Dael. The hall extended for quite some distance, bright and silent. He approached the nearest alcove and, with an approving nod from din'Dael, stepped inside. Within was a small square table and three chairs. Upon the table was a single book, ancient and weathered, as well as a drinking glass that appeared to be made from obsidian and lined with gems.

There was no barrier of entry, no museum glass or gate cordoning off the area. Will's eyes fixed on the book. He could not make out the letters that formed the title. The script was unfamiliar, ancient. The letters were burned onto the leather binding and worn from age. It called to him. Will reached out for the book, then hesitated.

Glancing back at din'Dael to make sure he was permitted, Will gingerly picked up the book and opened it. The scrawl of writing within was the same script as the cover and flowed together, page after page with no breaks and no punctuation. It reminded him of the ancient epics he had studied with his brother and grandfather. How, in their original forms, the poetic texts flowed together, in the absence of modern formatting.

Epics . . . Will's heart leapt in his chest. *It couldn't be.* His hands began to tremble. *Surely it can't be . . .* He stared, wondering at the possibility of such a delicate treasure of indescribable value. "Jero, is this . . .?"

"*The Veleriat.*" Din'Dael nodded. "Yes. What you hold is the oldest known complete copy of the work."

Will's face split in a wide grin. *What Mad would give to see this. What Morella would have. This thing has got to be thousands of years old.*

He froze. He couldn't believe that din'Dael would let him touch something so ancient, so delicate, without any kind of protection. Just the oils from his skin would be enough to damage the ancient pages. Feeling strangely lightheaded, he set the book back down on the table and steadied himself on a nearby chair.

"Do not worry, William. The book has survived far worse than the touch of a youth. There is an enchantment upon it that protects it from all harm."

More magic. Awestruck, Will looked back at the book and traced his fingers across the etched writing again. "An enchantment? Really?"

Jero din'Dael burst out laughing, wild peals of hilarity that echoed back to his madness within the Daurhi Wastes. "Of course not, William. It is only a book."

Will tensed at the outburst but sighed and shook his head. There was a time when he had almost grown accustomed to din'Dael's maddened wit. Almost. He looked back at *The Veleriat* and cocked his head. "It seems . . . denser than the other copy I've seen."

Din'Dael stepped forward and peered over Will's shoulder. "Because it is. This one contains the original writing's notes.

Interviews, perhaps. Traces of the full amount of research that went into the writing of *The Veleriat.*"

Will's head snapped around to face him. "Wait, this copy has the foundational research?"

Din'Dael rolled his eyes and flicked Will on the forehead. "Do you plan to reword and repeat everything I say, William? Have you learned nothing?"

Will didn't bother to hide his annoyance at the flick but didn't comment on it. "Are copies such as this common?"

Jero stared at him levelly. "William, do you really think that if this book was in any way commonplace or ordinary, it would be held within this vault?"

Will chided himself for the foolish question. "It's only"—Morella's face danced across his mind and the smile faded from his face—"I knew someone who would have been quite interested in those notes, once upon a time."

"There are many who would be interested in them. After all, within them lie the most detailed descriptions of the Relics of Antiquity known. That, William, is why this copy is so well guarded, so well preserved."

The Relics. It had been so long since he'd heard anything about them that he'd nearly written them off. *And this book may hold the key to finding them.* Eyeing it, Will glanced around for any signs of security beyond the entrance. He saw none. *Just the door. But any Lightborne could open that. Any one of them could make off with it.*

But they wouldn't. The Lightborne he'd met since his arrival were too devout, too zealous to consider anything of the sort. Nearly all of them had kept him at arm's length, considering him an outsider. Only Rienne had opened up and welcomed him. The rest of them would probably die before they'd let anyone get this close to the book. *And no one wants to see them mobilized like that.*

He traced *The Veleriat*'s marked cover again. "So, if it isn't magic keeping it around, how is it so well preserved?"

"It is vellum, William. Specifically, etched dragon hide. You'd be hard pressed to find a more resilient material for record keeping. The hide is nearly indestructible. That anyone successfully managed to burn any amount of text onto it is impressive."

"So a work of this magnitude . . ." Will flipped the book open and leafed through the pages. He couldn't make out a single word, wouldn't even have known where to begin, but he knew that before him lay a more thorough story than the telling he had been given by his grandfather. "This took someone some time."

"Precisely."

"What does it say, though? Can you read it?"

Jero frowned at him. "It is *The Veleriat,* Will. It tells the story of Velier and the Thorns of the Rose aboard the *Crimson Twilight* as they seek to prevent the end times." He stepped forward and snapped the book shut. "Really, William, it's as though you don't listen at all."

Will bit back a retort. "My apologies," he said sarcastically. "I should have been more specific. I mean, what does it say *beyond* the common knowledge of the story?"

This time, din'Dael chuckled. "Many things, William, many things." He turned and began to walk away, farther into the room.

"Wait," Will called after him. Jero turned back and raised an eyebrow. Will pointed to the ornate drinking glass. "What about that? What is that for?"

Din'Dael's mouth tightened in a grim line. "That is for drinking out of, William."

The man strode away, moving with purpose. Will followed, feeling extremely small and foolish. After the promising start, he had the distinct feeling that he was now continuously disappointing his mentor. *Not everything needs to be part of a fairy tale, Will. Get that through your head.*

At the next alcove, din'Dael paused and gestured for Will to approach. Within was another small table with a drinking glass on it. But behind it rested an axe head of such proportions that Will's jaw dropped. It stood as tall as he, and the metal was unlike any he had ever seen. It appeared to have been blued after its forging, but upon closer inspection Will realized that the coloring was not the finish of the blade but rather a quality of the metal itself. The head seemed to vibrate, pulsing lightly beneath his fingertips when he touched it. It was warm and, when he brought his gaze closer, he could see countless tiny rivets within the metal in a constant state of expansion and contraction.

"The axe of Polathanion," din'Dael said reverently. Will's hand froze and trembled inches above the axe. "The very blade that shattered the *Crimson Twilight*. When the Thorns of the Rose stood before Polathanion, he struck down many of Velier's companions and destroyed their way home. Unafraid, they held their ground, accepting the death that was to come. Ellianor alone brought the creature down, striking out again and again while he battered her. Her blade did little against his armor, but, nevertheless, she persisted. By her patience and cunning, the giant eventually fell before her, dying upon its own snapped blade." Din'Dael smiled. "While Polathanion lay dying, she severed the creature's tongue, impaling it against its own forehead for the insults it had given her."

Will stood transfixed before the ancient weapon. He knew the story, had heard it from his grandfather countless times. But even knowing that so many of his grandfather's tales had been true, even with Morella's insistence, he had never really expected *The Veleriat* to be so rooted in truth. If this truly was Polathanion's axe, then it was an artifact that predated Aeril itself, predated the unmaking of the world. It existed outside of time.

But what does that even mean in a realm where time stands still?

"This metal," Will said, hearing the tremor in his voice and not bothering to mask it. "I've never seen anything like it."

"No, you have not. This is all that remains of it. In the early days following the Sundering, attempts were made to forge weapons that could compare, but all were a pale reflection of what once had been."

Will had heard that before. The words echoed Morella's when they had stopped at the bladesmith's en route to the Shale. "Aerilite?"

"Ah, so you can use that brain up there." Din'Dael began to sway, stretching his arms above his head. "Yes, William, aerilite was this world's attempt to master"—he broke away from the stretch and gestured to the axe—"whatever that is."

"I'd heard that aerilite was the greatest metalworking the mortal races had ever achieved." The metalwork danced before Will's eyes. *It's almost like my key.*

"It was," din'Dael conceded. "But this axe was not the work of the mortal races. Plus, Gren'al was a proud fool and took the secrets of its manufacture to his grave. Had he passed them on, well, who knows what might have unfolded? Come."

Din'Dael moved again without waiting. Will whirled and chased after his mentor, his imagination racing with what else the vault may hold. They passed more alcoves, each relatively spartan in decor but obviously highlighting a single piece. Some contained books; some contained armor. One contained something Will immediately recognized: a measure, but one different than the Crow's. It was larger, more ornate, and the swirling face bore different colors. Yet, somehow, the colors themselves seemed hollow, void of brilliance.

Will wanted to ask about each piece but forced himself to keep his mouth shut. Din'Dael was moving with intent now, toward the back of the hall where another of the dark stone doors stood. A shiver of excitement coursed through Will. *If all this is out here, what would they keep even more secure?* Before they reached the passage, however, din'Dael turned abruptly.

The alcove they entered held nothing of interest, only the same small table with the same drinking cup of all the previous alcoves. Only this time, two cups were upon the table instead of one. Din'Dael picked them both up, admired them, and then handed one to Will. Standing in silence, the man raised a conspiratorial eyebrow and waited.

Will looked down at the glass. It was empty. He looked back at din'Dael. The man's face was unchanged. *Dammit, he's testing me.* Will waited a moment, just in case din'Dael was going to offer anything more. Nothing came. *And that's all I'm going to get then. Fantastic.*

He looked around for a carafe or bottle or anything that might hold something to drink. He saw none. Din'Dael stood patiently, barely blinking. *A test then, but not the one that it seems to be.* If din'Dael had expected a drink, he would have said so. So, why this alcove then? What was it about this particular one that made it special?

He scanned the small room but saw nothing that bore closer inspection. He looked back at the cup. It was beautiful, he had to admit, but there were no hints on its surface. It was different than the one din'Dael held, simpler, with no gems adorning it, but other than that it was unremarkable. The finish was smooth, the polished obsidian unmarred except for a small chip at the base. He thumbed the chip absentmindedly and turned back to the room.

Ten minutes passed. Din'Dael neither moved nor spoke. The only sound was the distant ruffling of feathers as Dahla flew to a new perch. Finally, Will sighed and shook his head. "Alright, what is it?"

"You nearly had it, mighty William Davis." Will rolled his eyes; din'Dael only used the title when he was gloating. "Return to the chip. Begin there."

Obviously, the chip was key to whatever puzzle din'Dael had going, but how was it relevant? Will scanned his memory, thinking back to games and stories of hidden puzzles. Anytime something was broken, the stories all said that the object had to be restored, right? Will smiled. *Seems straightforward enough.*

He set the glass on the table and began searching the alcove for the tiny shard of obsidian. He checked the table and the vacant sconce. He turned the chair and scanned every inch of its surface. He combed the floor on hands and knees, determined not to miss an inch. All the while, din'Dael stared at him with an expression of bemusement.

Will found nothing. Finally, he stood and dusted himself off. "I'm sorry, Jero. I can't seem to find it. It is in this room, right?"

Din'Dael cocked his head to the side and smirked. "Is what in this room?"

"The chip. The piece that will repair the chip in the glass."

There was a brief moment of silence that was shattered by din'Dael's roaring, maddened laughter. It burst out of him so suddenly Will was taken aback, startled by the sudden ferocity. Din'Dael put a hand out against the wall to brace himself and doubled over, tears streaming down his face.

"Oh, William," he struggled through gasps of air. "How did I ever exist before you entered my life?"

Will shifted uneasily. "I take it you know something I don't."

The comment only sent din'Dael into more peals of laughter. Will waited, feeling increasingly foolish. With no break in his laughing, din'Dael snatched the glass off the table and placed his thumb against the small chip. His hand glowed white and, from the small chip, the glass exploded into countless tiny pieces, just like the door at the entrance to the Hall.

Will groaned, which only caused din'Dael to double over in laughter once more. Bent over, he casually flung the floating shards of the glass to the vacant sconce. Retaining their shattered form even in flight, the fragments landed within the sconce. A low rumble came from beneath their feet. Wiping tears from his eyes, din'Dael took a step backward from the alcove. The stone floor seemed to melt away, revealing a wide passage.

"Oh," was all Will said.

"By the Hesperawn," din'Dael said, recovering himself,

"William, sometimes I wonder if I am correct to place so much faith in you."

"I just—"

Din'Dael held up a hand to silence him. His face changed rapidly, growing serious and stern. "No, William. Do not feel the need to defend your actions. You did well. You are exactly what the Lightborne need."

Will paused, glancing at the hole in the ground. "What do you mean, 'what the Lightborne need'?"

Jero din'Dael smiled. Within that smile Will saw the same maddened fury he had seen on their first night together, the blazing fire of righteous belief. Lightning danced across the Revenant's eyes as he gestured to the darkened stair within the hole. "Come below and I shall explain everything."

4
THE FIRES OF SAPHOLUX

Vertigo overwhelmed Will's senses the moment he stepped into the passage. The darkness was such a contrast to the illuminated stone of the Sapholux that Will fell heavily against the wall to brace himself. A momentary fit of panic constricted his throat—when was the last time he'd been in such absolute darkness? *Years.*

Will steadied himself and focused on his breathing. After a moment, feeling a bit more at ease, he inched forward and found the edge of the stair. Taking a cautious step, he made his way down the steep steps. The air felt heavy, cold. He cursed when his forehead met slick rock. He could hear nothing of din'Dael ahead of him, nor the cries of Dahla from the rear. *Where are we going?*

The passage abruptly brightened, sending Will slamming against the low ceiling again. He cursed and clenched his eyes shut against the flash of discomfort.

"What the hell, Jero?" Will rubbed his forehead and blinked his eyes rapidly, trying to get them to adjust. "Give me at least *some* warning here."

"Didn't I?" din'Dael quipped. "Ah, well. You must be prepared for anything, William."

Yeah, right. Will blinked again, his eyes finally adjusting. His breath caught in his chest. *Holy shit.*

Before him was a large, brilliantly lit chamber. Everywhere Will looked were heaps of arms and armor. Filled near to bursting, every spare surface was covered. Stacks of crates covered the floor, filled with what Will could only imagine to be more arms. Axes, swords, maces, daggers, spears, weapons of every shape and size surrounded him. The armors were much the same, sized from some that could nearly match Polathanion's axe to others that would fit a toddler.

"Wow." Will walked over to a sword mounted nearby on the wall and held it aloft. It was light and nimble, perfectly balanced with just the right amount of blade mass. Holding the blade before his eyes, Will discovered metalwork he had never seen before. *No, not entirely. It's almost like Polathanion's axe.* In fact, the only difference he could see was the axe had been dark blue, whereas this metal was streaked with a bright, almost electric blue that was brilliant to behold.

He returned the blade and lifted an armored bracer from the table next to it. The metal was the same. Will spun around, quickly taking in every bit of armor that he could see. Every piece he saw bore the same characteristics.

"Aerilite," he said softly.

"Very good, William."

The brilliant blue streaks caught the light and almost seemed to glow. Will was entranced. "There are so many pieces . . . I thought they had all been lost or destroyed."

Din'Dael smiled. "You said much the same of the Lightborne when you first arrived here."

Will reached for the nearest piece, a cutlass, and inspected the edge while his mind stretched back to his arrival at the Sapholux. He had been haggard, thin, and delirious. When he'd seen the monolith of the Sapholux, when they'd passed beneath its killing gates, he'd never felt so small and alone. And then, when the great doors had opened, he had been shocked to find nearly an entire city, hidden from the world.

"Your people did a good job of secreting themselves away, Jero. I'd always thought them wiped out after the Wars of Dawning."

His mentor's mouth tightened. "*Our* people, William. Our people." He sighed and eyed the cutlass Will held. "A good weapon. Keep it." Before Will could reply, din'Dael turned away. "Still, you are not wrong. The remnants of our people that I was able to save"—he shook his head—"they were a fraction of what we had been. A broken force facing annihilation."

Will knew the story well. The Guardian of Radiance, Shigei O'Saq, had been driven to madness long before his death during the Wars of Dawning. The Blades of Shadow, emboldened by their victory, had set out on a mission to cull the tainted Lightborne from Aeril. The Lightborne themselves, lost without their Guardian, scrambled to survive. Will had heard both sides of the story, but one thing remained constant: It had been a slaughter. There had been no mercy for the Lightborne. As far as the rest of the world knew, only Jero din'Dael had survived.

"I fought for years to find what survivors I could." Din'Dael's voice held a quiet pain Will had never heard from him before. "There were not many, not compared to what there had been. I was a fugitive in my own lands. All because my people had been led astray by the madness of O'Saq." He clenched his fists. "The madness that touches us all when we leave these walls. It is said that all are driven to it, eventually. Do you understand, William?"

Will shifted slightly. "I've seen . . . hints of it, before."

"Another of the fallen god's gifts for us." Voice grim, Jero din'Dael turned and walked through the great armory. "I found them, William. I found every survivor I could and I brought them home, where they would be safe. I killed everyone who discovered our secret. I guaranteed that my people would live, that no word of their existence would pass into the lands. Once they were home"—he paused and picked up a large round shield—"I set about ensuring their survival."

"You collected this?" Will's stared incredulously at the vast hoard. "You brought all this back here?"

"The finest weapons and armor that anyone living has ever seen. Yes, William. I brought it home to them."

"To rebuild," Will said quietly.

"To rebuild our people's strength, yes." Din'Dael picked up a long sword that matched the shield. "To regain our power within Aeril and guarantee our survival. I brought them everything they would need."

Everything . . . Will's eyes darted over the equipment in the armory. It was enough to outfit the entire population of the Sapholux five times over. *There's not even close to enough Lightborne here.* A sudden sense of unease gripped him.

"Jero, you said that there were hardly any survivors, relative to what had once been. But I've seen the Sapholux. I've been here for years and I still see faces I've never seen, let alone met before."

He saw din'Dael's neck tighten and shoulders tense. His mentor's eyes were fixed on the blade he held, his expression blank and detached. "Our people needed to survive, William. I saw to it that they had every opportunity to do so."

Will peered at din'Dael, his pulse quickening. There were parts of the Sapholux he had still never visited; these very halls were proof enough of that. Were there children within the walls? Were there infants?

"Jero, if a child is born and both parents are Lightborne, does it guarantee that the child will be Lightborne as well?"

"History has proven so, yes."

The tone of his words turned Will's unease into cold dread. Will swallowed. His grip tightened upon the cutlass. "And enough Lightborne survived to repopulate the Sapholux that way, right?"

"No."

A great lump settled in Will's stomach. "So, people who were not Lightborne were needed." He let the words hang in the air. *Don't do this, Jero.*

"As I said, William, I brought our people everything they would need to survive."

Will stared at din'Dael, knowing in his bones the answers to the terrible questions he had. "You brought people here, to the Sapholux. You bred them, searching for Lightborne, didn't you?" His voice shook but he forced the words out. When din'Dael did not reply, he pushed on. "Okay, okay. After, then? What did you do with the people after, Jero? You allowed them to return to their homes, right?"

"None came that did not wish to be a part of something greater than themselves, William. All were willing."

Will braced himself against a wall. He couldn't meet the man's eye. *Gods, please let me be wrong.* "You ... you killed them all? After they had served their purpose?"

"Our people needed to be kept safe, William. No one could know of our presence here."

"Jesus, din'Dael," Will burst out incredulously. "You killed your own allies? The parents of your own people?"

Din'Dael raised his eyes to meet Will's. He seemed to deflate before Will's eyes. A horrific realization dawned on Will. "The children, were they all Lightborne at birth?"

Din'Dael was silent.

Will stared, forcing himself to voice the words. "No, of course they weren't. The power, it doesn't manifest for years, right? You . . . you waited, right? Tell me you waited. I mean, and even if not, you trained them, right? My grandfather always said that people could learn. You taught them all?" Will's mind raced as he desperately sought to convince himself. "Wait, why didn't you train the parents then? Why not . . ."

Will trailed off as he took in the haunted visage of Jero din'-

Dael. The man looked old, tired. “You didn’t wait. What did you . . . oh gods.” He knew the answer just looking at din’Dael’s face. “All of them? Children who had spent their entire lives beneath your roof? People born and raised within your protective walls? Oh gods.”

“The gift does not come to all, William.”

Will staggered against the wall, the oppressive weight of so many dead dragging him down. He’d seen din’Dael slaughter the Shale like they were nothing, but this? He shook his head. “You’re a monster.”

Din’Dael closed his eyes. “The world has always had monsters. I did what I had to do to save my people. I live with what I’ve done. We all do.”

“The others, they know?” A numbing glaze covered Will’s thoughts. *Do not invest emotionally,* din’Dael’s lessons said. *Emotion only serves to undermine reason.*

Din’Dael nodded. “They find life more precious now than ever before. That is why we need you, William.”

Will stared at him, not understanding. *Emotion only serves to undermine reason.* He drilled it into his head like a mantra.

“Like you, our people cherish life above all else, now. For nearly a millennium they have struggled to rebuild, to reclaim an existence. But that existence is only within these walls. They will need that same level of compassion from their leaders in the wars to come.”

Not like this. No way. I’ve got to get the hell out of here. “You’re insane.” Will took a tentative step toward the exit. “You want me to *lead* them? No. Never going to happen.”

Din’Dael’s face curled in rage, then the room echoed with maddened laughter. He flung the sword down and closed rapidly on Will, grabbing his wrist. “They have not seen war, death on that scale, in years. Most never have. The force of Radiance has begun to reclaim its numbers, but not its fury in battle. They have grown”—he sneered—“afraid.”

"Good," Will said as he wrenched his wrist from din'Dael's fist. "They at least have a soul, then."

"They *need* you, William. We all need you. Don't you see?"

Will glared back at him. "All I see is a monster."

Din'Dael didn't appear to have heard him. "They are afraid. Of the world. Of their power. Of me. But you, William, you can be the symbol they rally behind. You can help them overcome their fear."

"Jesus, din'Dael. Do you hear yourself? They've never even paid me a second glance. They don't want me here and that's just fine by me." Will couldn't focus. A piece of him was slipping away. The Halls of Legend, the aerilite, the countless dead that led to the reformation of the Lightborne; his head was swimming.

"Don't be foolish. You are a legend to them, William. They fear you. You know a courage that they do not. You stood alone before Dorian and you did not falter. I witnessed this."

Will hesitated. "I think you must have been watching someone else, Jero. *He never gives out praise like this. There's got to be something else going on.* "I was terrified."

Din'Dael's face tightened. "You did not falter," he repeated, forcing the words out through nearly clenched teeth. "In the face of imminent death, you chose life. Just like me."

Murdering innocents is hardly what I'd call choosing life. Will frowned and bit back the words. There was something in the man's demeanor that made him pause, something pleading. He eyed the door, then glanced back at Jero. "I don't understand, Jero. I'm not . . . I don't understand what the hell you're expecting."

"You may think me a monster, William. You may think the ends do not justify the means. But all I have done, I have done for the survival of our people. Make no mistake, war is coming." Din'Dael let the words hang in the air. He clapped his bare fist against the shield in a jarring crash. "Dorian appeared to us himself, in the flesh. I know the man. He would not do such a thing unless he were convinced that he had already won. Which means we are already behind. Whatever his grand plan is, we are trailing. It is already in motion. We must move in force and we must do so quickly. We must regain lost time."

Din'Dael's words were laced with urgency. His breath came in rapid, shallow gasps. He raised a hand—no anger in the movement, this time—and placed it upon Will's shoulder.

"You stood against Valmont. That is more victory than many within these walls can claim. You have earned your place amongst us. And, regardless of whatever you may think of me in this moment, I have faith in you. That, alone, would be enough for our people to follow you against the Necrothanian cult and whatever else Dorian will bring to bear. You do not have to approve of what I have done, but—if you truly do believe in preserving life—you will help protect our people."

Will peered at him, searching for whatever it was he knew he was missing. "There's more to this than you're letting on, Jero. What aren't you telling me?"

"There are elements at play that are crucial to the survival of our people, William." His eyes searched Will's face. "It may be hard for you to believe, but Dorian is hardly the worst of them."

Valmont isn't the worst? Will searched his memory but could come up with no other villain who had ever visited the same horrors upon Aeril in any of the stories he'd heard. He waited for din'Dael to go on, but the man did not elaborate. *There's always something with this man.*

Will gave a defeated sigh. "Training or not, I don't know what you expect me to do against Valmont. I've seen you in action, Jero. I'm not anywhere close to that. My ability pales in comparison to yours and—I don't mean this to sound harsh—you yourself have been unable to defeat him."

Din'Dael relaxed and gave an easy smile. "This is true. But with our powers combined, we shall stand a chance. More than that, you should not give me so much credit. I hold something you do not."

The Lightborne held up his left hand to Will. It glowed emerald. Will heard Dahla's familiar cry, and a split second later, the great bird swooped into the chamber. She sped past him and perched on a nearby suit of armor, wings outstretched at full span. Din'Dael closed his hand into a fist and an inaudible pulse began emanating from it. "What do you know of the Relics of Antiquity, William?"

An unconscious tremble ran through Will's body. His eyes were fixed on the green glow coming from din'Dael's hand. Gone were the previous moments' doubts, the quiet fear that din'Dael's revelations had instilled in him. "Truthfully? Nothing."

Jero din'Dael smiled at the answer. "Not going to regale me with legends and fairy tales?"

Will shook his head, swallowing every question racing through his mind. "Not this time."

"Very well, then." Din'Dael chuckled and dropped his eyes to the green glow of his hand. "Velier of the *Crimson Twilight* saved this world and all worlds. He was a mortal man who touched the gods, who was embraced by the Hesperawn themselves. He saved existence, William, the very thing itself. But in doing so, existence, *reality*, fractured. It is said that the Ways are the final vestiges of the old world, a decaying remnant of the time before Velier's Gift.

"When he was embraced by the Hesperawn, this mortal man was imbued with their power. He used that power to fuel the World Tree, the Tree of Ages, and grant life a second chance. His own life ended in the effort. But the power of the Hesperawn remained, imbued in that which had touched their eternal power. Velier's raiment, as it were, contained small traces of the immortal essence, of the power of creation itself."

Velier's raiment? "You mean the Relics of Antiquity are, what? Clothes?"

Jero din'Dael raised a bemused eyebrow at Will. "Velier and the Thorns of the Rose were not the benevolent warriors that *The Veleriat* makes them out to be, William. They were a band of thieves, rovers who were immortalized in epic because of one good deed." He smiled and motioned with his glowing hand to Dahla. "No one has ever documented what every Relic is. I, personally, am acutely aware of only two. The one I hold is known as the Emerald Eye." A gleam of his old madness shadowed his face. "It was a ring, before. Now it is something more."

Will stared at the glowing hand. *Morella was right.* "And the second one?"

"Patience, young William." Din'Dael's eyes burned white as he stared at the emerald fist. A small pulse in the air quickened. "The Relics are said to each bear a unique trait, known only to the wielder." He smiled and looked over at Dahla. "But what they all share in common is the powers of their amplification. Whatever abilities the user possesses, a Relic of Antiquity will amplify beyond what they could ever imagine. One bearer, one Relic, that is the way of it. Blood will bind a Relic to a man. But an attempt to bind oneself to multiple Relics will result in the combined force of the powers obliterating the host."

Din'Dael lapsed into silence and peered at William. Will waited for him to continue, but he seemed to have reached the end of his lesson. The pulses of power faded away and the glow in din'Dael's flesh ceased. Dahla, suddenly uninterested, flew quietly back up the stairs. Din'Dael followed her after replacing the shield and sword.

"Wait, the second Relic. Jero, you said you knew of two?" Will called to the retreating figure. "You know another?"

Din'Dael turned back to him, a strange, zealous grin on his face. "I said patience, didn't I?"

Will went up the stairs behind din'Dael, uncertain of what to think. The trail of bodies at the man's feet was staggering. Yet Will forced himself to remember that the rules of his own world didn't exist here. Aeril was different. *They'll skin you while you scream,* his brother had said once. *They try to carve out whatever it is that makes you you.* This world fed on power and the powerful fed on the weak. If din'Dael had spoken honestly, then the people who had sacrificed themselves to rebuild the Lightborne had believed in the cause. *Was that enough, though?* Could he excuse the countless deaths at din'Dael's hands, so many innocent lives, simply for that belief? *I just don't know.*

Dahla had returned to her high perch within the chamber, her head flicking back and forth with its predatory gaze. Once Will had cleared the alcove, din'Dael retrieved the glass that served as a key and sent another burst of power through it, returning it to its original form. Setting the cup back on the table, he turned and made for the dark stone door at the end of the room. Standing before the small carving, he gestured to Will.

"Come, try your hand at opening it."

Will did as instructed. Mirroring din'Dael's previous actions, he splayed his fingers within the small rent and channeled his Flare into the door. He was met immediately with a fierce response. It seemed to latch on to the Flare and pull at him with such a force that Will let out a startled cry.

"Do not allow it to drain you completely, William. Find your balance. You control your power."

What began as a surge of outward power suddenly became a struggle to hold it back. Will grit his teeth at the resistance, the sensation somewhat similar to overextending his Shade. *Back when that was possible,* he thought with frustration. The pull hurt, an aching strain. A bead of sweat rolled down his forehead. Finally, he managed to regain control. Just as he found a level, balanced state, the door fractured and split. The stone shot out and up, allowing just enough room for a man to walk through.

"Excellent," din'Dael said casually while he strode through. "Most excellent. Come, come, William. You don't want to be stuck holding doors open all day."

Will removed his hand and shivered. Despite the physical separation from the wall, he could still feel the strange pull on his insides. Every step felt like he was wading through molasses. When he passed beneath the door, his ears rang in a piercing hum. He forced himself to move faster. He entered the chamber beyond and nearly panicked when the tether still remained. Frantically, he sought to sever his connection to the door. He scrambled after din'Dael and the farther he moved from the door, the less binding the connection became. After a few steps, it severed easily.

"Well, that was new," he muttered, flexing his fingers and shaking out his hand. He took a deep breath and relaxed a bit at the faint smell of incense and woodsmoke. For the first time, he surveyed the room they had entered. He had expected a twin chamber to the previous hall, filled with treasures and alcoves. Instead, he found a gigantic cavern filled with countless books.

No, more than books, he realized. Nearby was what appeared to be a smithing anvil and forge, long cold. Past those were piles of ancient leather and wooden mannequins of all shapes and sizes. There were gems and cutting stations and shelves of ingredients and reagents set before glass flasks. It was a production room of such magnitude that Will let out an involuntary gasp.

In the center of the room was an enormous structure that reminded him of an oversized cradle. It sat low on the ground and was filled with lush blankets and cushions, embroidered with such finery that each piece was its own work of art. Whatever was meant to be held within, however, was absent. Din'Dael was striding straight for it, humming again. Will rushed to follow.

"Before you ask," din'Dael said humorlessly when Will approached, "this was the personal chamber of Shigei O'Saq, the Guardian of our Order."

Shigei O'Saq. Will's eyes grew wide. *I'm within the chamber of a dragon. Of a god.*

"It was here that he spent the majority of his time, only

emerging when it was most necessary." Din'Dael's words were hollow and laced with spite. "He was a brilliant strategist and researcher but preferred to remain secluded from his students. Very few ever earned his attentions."

They passed to the far side of the room, Will biting his tongue to fight back the flurry of questions. *What Mad would give to see this.* He grinned as he scanned the room. It had everything his brother could ever dream of and more.

Din'Dael led them to another of the dark doors at the back of the room, this door nearly hidden by a small curtain. The door itself was smaller than the two they had previously come through, and din'Dael bade Will to its far edge.

"Do you recall when we first arrived here, William? The journey through the gates of the Sapholux?"

Will nodded. *Hard to forget.* He shuddered at the memory.

"The process here is much the same as then. Precision timing. Precision force of strength. No room for error, understood? On my count."

Will placed his hands against the door and waited. At the end of din'Dael's countdown, he Flared, sending a surge of lightning into the door while his mentor did the same next to him. The door quavered and shook before opening and sliding into the walls. Will lowered his hands and flexed his fingers. *Three barriers of entry to this one room?* He couldn't stop the foolish grin of anticipation that split his face.

The dim room was quite small compared with the previous chambers. At its center was an altar of carved marble, upon which a lush golden pillow rested. Approaching, Will saw the hilt of a broken sword resting atop the cushion. It was the color of charcoal, the rough, matte darkness a sharp contrast against the brilliant cushion. The snapped remainder of the blade was wide and rough, and the hand guard had rough catches all along it. The quillon was wide and barbed. A piece of fabric had been folded and curved to replace the missing blade, giving the crude hilt an elegant appearance.

Din'Dael clasped his hands behind his back, stiffening slightly. He stood an arm's distance from the altar. "What you see before you is one of the most prized possessions within the Sapholux, William. This blade is known as Flint."

Will chuckled despite himself. "Not the grandest of names."

"The Shard of Night, William. The Dawnbreaker. The Immortal Blade. What you see before you is Velier's own sword."

Will's head spun. "Jero, this . . ."

"Yes, William. This is a Relic of Antiquity."

5

SHADOWBORNE

"Son of a bitch!" Madigan gasped and gingerly removed his mangled arm from the trap. Everything hurt. He'd always thought himself a quick study, but this? *And here I'd thought Grandda's damn lessons were bad enough.* Training like this was something new, something verging on truly abusive. Mad grit his teeth. *Just another goddam day in paradise.*

His other wrist throbbed angrily, but that was nothing new. Months had passed since he'd broken it and still it plagued him. Not for the first time, he missed Will and his damn blood fangs. He just flat out missed Will. That was a pain that never faded. *Dammit, kid. Where the hell are you?*

He cradled his arm, his mind reflecting on those last, horrible moments with his brother so long ago. One second, he and Will were gaping in horror at the appearance of that damn bastard Valmont. The madman had smiled at them, the bored, disinterested smile of a psychopath. The next moment, blackness. Mad's world was darkness and dirt, the earth filling his mouth and nose.

He could still feel the grittiness of it all between his teeth.

Oh yes, Cephora had saved him, had stolen him away through whatever damned means the Earth Warder could. In the same stroke, she'd abandoned his brother to die. Mad didn't care what her reasonings had been, that was the simple truth of it. Cephora had acted and, because of her, Will was . . . gone.

He's alive, I know it.

His gaze fixed on the blood, Madigan felt the familiar tug of loss and anxiety pull at his heartstrings. *Except I don't.*

He shook the thought from his mind and eased some weight back onto his bloody arm. *Not the time or place.* He scanned the surroundings, breathed a sigh of relief, and waited. *At least it doesn't look like she heard me.*

Assessing his damaged limb, he scowled. The infusion of Shadow and glass had burst out in a silent explosion, heading straight for him. Thankfully, he'd managed to shield his face from the rush of energy and shrapnel. When the trap had sucked his hand back into it—the twisting power and rough material encircling his arm and slicing into his flesh—he'd feared he might lose the limb. He'd only just armored the limb in his Shade, barely forcing the foreign material out and away from his body. Had he not . . .

Ileta takes too many goddam liberties with her training.

Grumbling another curse, he continued his slow crawl forward. He clenched his teeth against the pain in his arms and kept his body as low to the ground as possible. His Shade was a misty aura, probing, testing, searching for any additional challenges his instructor may have left. He avoided two more before finally reaching the edge of the wood.

In the center of the foggy clearing sat the object of his search for the day. Even with the overcast cloud cover, the sun briefly reflected upon the dull metal of the ring upon the dead log. Fallen haphazardly to the ground next to it flapped the leather glove.

His noctori.

Mad had not seen them in nearly two years, but he would have recognized them anywhere. He felt a pang of longing at their proximity but forced himself not to rush; he was certainly not out of danger yet. *Slow down, idiot. Don't get excited and screw this up.*

He scanned the clearing and saw no sign of Ileta. He looked up, one of the earliest lessons she had drilled into him—"No one ever thinks to look up until it is too late and they've got a dagger protruding from their neck"—and saw nothing.

He was just about to move when he saw it. A distortion, something slightly off in the grey haze of the sky. He couldn't describe it exactly, but he didn't need to. Ileta'd schooled him enough to know that, when dealing with a Shadowborne, if something looks askew then it probably is. Locking the location into his mind's eye, he cleared the rest of the area. *This is it, then.*

He tentatively probed the area directly in front of him with his Shade. There was nothing. *She knows I'm coming, though. She's here somewhere.*

Eyeing the density of the fog, Madigan manipulated his Shade to match the surrounding air. Draped around him, the Shade would be the perfect camouflage for such a day.

Don't get cocky. She's probably masked in the same pattern.

Edging forward, Madigan crept into the clearing. He glanced at the floating anomaly. It hadn't changed. He moved again, the wrap of his Shade dulling the pain of his arms. Like a soothing balm, the Shadow energy was slowly and delicately reweaving the broken fibers of his skin and flesh, rebuilding what had been damaged. The energy wasn't even close to the capabilities of Will's blood fangs, but it was something, nonetheless.

He paused ten feet from his goal; only a few moments until he could reclaim his grandfather's gift. Blood pounded in his ears. Five feet. Three. Madigan grinned. Bracing his less-damaged arm on the log, he reached out a shaky hand to grasp his prize.

A jade dagger shot upward from the trunk. The blade pierced Madigan's forearm and lodged solidly between the bones.

Mad shrieked in pain and rolled away, all thoughts of stealth abandoned. The log exploded, hard wooden splinters slicing toward him. Madigan's Shade barely deflected them in time. He scrambled backward, shuffling awkwardly, then scrambled to his feet and gripped the blade protruding from his arm. Just then, the surrounding fog shifted and billowed into a single stream.

Madigan let out a low groan, realizing his error. The stream of fog collided into him like a sledgehammer, propelling him backward. He flew through the air and crashed into the underbrush at the edge of the woods. Dazed, he planted his feet and dug his Shade into the ground to brace against the blast. Deflecting the wave with his Shade, he charged against the onslaught, driving a wedge into it.

The resistance broke and the stream of fog faded. Mad stopped running and held his ground. Ileta stood before him, a wry smile on her angular face. When they first met, he'd found the smile unfathomably attractive. Now, all it did was unnerve him.

The morning fog was gone. The strange anomaly that hung in the air was gone as well. Madigan cursed himself for falling for such an obvious deception. *All a goddam distraction, all of it.* Suddenly conscious of the blood loss from his arm, Madigan knew he had to act fast.

He squared off before his instructor. His hackles rose at a subtle shift in the wind. *No, not the wind.* He eyed Ileta. *There it is.*

She was twisting the expanse of her Shade in such a dispersion that it became nearly invisible. Madigan took a tentative step forward, and the gust increased a hundredfold, launching him into the air. Too late, he sought to ground himself with his own Shade. Thrown off balance, he tumbled through the air toward Ileta.

Completely out of control, Madigan hurtled across the clearing. The smiling Shadowborne took a single step toward him. Her arm flashed out and caught him just above the ear with a blow that rocked his vision and his equilibrium. She drove him to the ground and Madigan collapsed at her feet. Her swirling Shade's force immediately calmed. The ground was a cloudy haze. His ears rang, but not so much that he didn't hear her disappointed sigh. She turned her back to him and stepped away.

Madigan struck. In a fury, he tore the dagger from his arm and whirled on Ileta. She spun, sensing the attack. Before he could close the short distance between them, she vanished into a darkness so impossibly black that his mind could hardly register it. In the same instant, the clearing blazed in a blinding, brilliant display of light.

Madigan cried out. The dagger fell from his hands as he desperately sought to shield his vision. His eyes ached at the intense brightness. Then he was airborne again, flying back from a sudden shockwave. He slammed into the ground and the breath was driven from his body.

"Enough." Ileta's voice was harsh and she held up a hand. "At this point you're only going to succeed in injuring yourself further and I don't have time to put you back together."

Madigan coughed. "I've got you on the ropes." The words came out in a wheeze. "But I'll let you off this time."

"Staunch those," she said, raising her eyebrows and looking at his bleeding arms. "It won't do for you to bleed out and make all this for nothing."

Madigan wheezed and forced himself to sit up. He condensed his Shade around his mangled limbs, pressing the broken flesh and sinew together. Cool and soothing relief flooded the limbs. He trusted the Shade to knit them in the strange, surreal fashion that it always did. Nonetheless, his arms wouldn't fully recover for weeks. *Assuming nothing else screws them up more.*

"That was a ridiculous attempt," Ileta went on. "Striking at my back like that? Come now, Madigan. I expect more from you."

"It was a feint," he lied.

She raised an eyebrow at him. "You know better than that. Throw no feints. Do not hesitate. Act. If your opponent reacts before you complete your strike—"

"Change your attack into one that undermines their committed defense," he finished for her. "I know. It . . . it wasn't a feint. It was frustration."

"Obviously."

He clamped his mouth shut and turned his attention to the fallen pieces of his noctori, scattered in the eruption of the downed log. *That goddam log.* How had it not even occurred to him that she was hiding inside it? It seemed so obvious now.

As though she had heard his thoughts, Ileta smirked. "You have a tendency to overcomplicate things. You're looking for the most well-hidden traps and letting what should be obvious just pass you by." She cocked her head to the side and chuckled. "You really need to fix that."

Mad grumbled and didn't meet her eyes. "I'm working on it."

All humor left her face. "Work harder. You've been 'working on it' for a while. At some point, you're going to need to actually succeed."

Madigan said nothing. While her words were harsh and her demeanor left much to be desired, he knew it was all worth it. It had to be. Ileta was skilled. Brutal, but skilled. There was a ferocity about her that pushed him to excel. Where his grandfather had always held back at the last moment, had kept things safe, Ileta struck. She had no problem with punishing him in battle and leaving him with injuries as reminders.

"Go." She bent down and pocketed both pieces of his noctori. "Make food. Clean yourself up first. I don't want your blood dripping into it."

Without a word, Madigan nodded and headed for their camp. He fought back the frustration. *Every goddam time. How does she do it?*

She was still a mystery, his strange instructor. He still didn't know who she really was, where she had come from. Even in their long time together, she had remained more tight-lipped than even Cephora.

Cephora. Madigan scowled. The Seeker had been so much more than she let on, he now knew. Capable of more. *And she left Will to die.* She could have stood and fought. The three of them—four, if that bastard Lightborne had gotten off his ass to help—could have taken Valmont. At the very least, they could have shown him that they were a force to be reckoned with. But no. Cephora had chosen flight and abandonment and yet somehow, *somehow* she had still been surprised when he, in turn, had abandoned her.

Her refusal to go back for Will. Her misdirection in leading him to Greygarde, the den of the Seekers, to suit her own needs. Her stubborn, tight-lipped way of keeping her plans to herself. She'd led him down a series of subtle backstabs and betrayals that pushed him to a near breaking point. Ileta's sudden appearance on a blank expanse of road one day when he was railing and yelling at the Seeker had seemed like divine providence.

Mad glanced back at his instructor. In the two years since, he'd learned little more about her than he had that first day. All that mattered was that she was a far more skilled Shadowborne than he had ever dreamt of being, and she *wanted* to train him. *And all these damn Aerillians are secretive anyway.*

He could deal with that. He didn't need to know the secret of who she was; he needed the secrets of what she could teach. The lessons were brutal and painful, but Ileta was teaching him. She held answers and offered them regularly enough, even if he didn't want to hear them. That was something Cephora had never done.

Madigan grimaced, catching himself clenching his fists. His arms ached fiercely, but the cool Shade was numbing enough that he could put it far from his focus. *How quickly the brain can adjust to pain.* He shook his head. *If only Will got to know more about being Shadowborne.*

He looked down at the dark, cloudy cast of his own Shade over his arms. He was still astonished by the capabilities of the damn thing. *No.* He stopped himself. The Shade wasn't something separate from him, wasn't something transcendent of him. Madigan was still surprised by *his own* capabilities.

And that's all thanks to Ileta. Her and the Umbriferum.

Yet another topic she kept her mouth shut on. Her own formal training was apparent and, from what Mad knew, that meant the Halls of Shadow. But like everything else, she remained tight-lipped and scowled whenever he brought it up. She had known the ranks of the Order to some extent, had been trained by someone, that much was obvious. But who?

That train of thought was the one that unnerved him most, the one that kept him awake at night: who was she serving *now*? She would not tell him; not how she found him on the road, not where she came from, nothing.

Madigan forced himself to suppress his suspicions. *As long as I get what I need out of this whole goddam mess. As long as I get strong enough to find Will. As long as I make sure I know how to pass all this on.*

Assuming Will's alive and has his Shade back.

The Shade was more than Jervin had ever let on, more than Jervin could possibly have understood. No one but a Borne truly could. Madigan returned his attention to it, feeling the power twisting and cooling his injuries. The Shadow energy poured over him in its invisible cascade, amplified by the key he wore. Mad still had no idea how it worked, but hot damn, it was awesome. *Just imagine if I had Will's, too. Doubling down on this would be . . .*

A terrible thought stopped him in his tracks: Did Valmont have his brother's key?

Fury boiled inside him. *Damn Cephora. Damn her.* After everything that had happened, Valmont had been alive. Will was right. Morella, too, for that matter. *And we didn't consider their concerns for one goddam second.* Oh, Madigan entertained it in the depths of the Shale, sure. But as soon as he saw the imprisoned din'Dael, he immediately reverted to his false belief in the mad sorcerer's death.

Mad's eyes stung thinking about Will and those final weeks together. *I let you down, kid.*

Perhaps nothing would have changed if Mad had believed him, but he could not help but think they would have been more prepared. Trod more carefully. *Something.* Instead, they'd been caught unawares, literally sleeping, when the man and his entire goddam army appeared from nowhere. *I got comfortable. Let my guard down.* Even when Mad had been prepared to fight the man, Valmont hadn't looked the slightest bit concerned, as though Mad and Will were utterly insignificant.

No, not insignificant. Otherwise he would not have come after us.

Not for the first time, Madigan spiraled down the question of Valmont. Why had he come? How had he come? And why had he not struck them down immediately—why had he alerted them?

Frustrated, Mad shook his head and pinched his eyes. As ever, there were too many factors he didn't understand. All he knew was that he'd lost Will, his only family, and he hadn't been able to do a damn thing about it since.

So, he took the pain of Ileta's training. He took the risk of trusting her. He trained to improve. Whether it was to rescue his brother or to avenge the deaths of his family, all Mad knew was that he had to train to be more. To become more than Shadowborne. To be *better* than Shadowborne.

To be better than Valmont.

6

FLAMES OF LIGHT

The blazing inferno of Radiance stormed around Will. The flames bit at him, their teeth fiery knives against his skin. He inhaled the ashes of his simple robes. His body was naked, exposed before the Lightborne, his brethren. All watched while their Blades unleashed their fires upon Will. He suppressed the awkward shame that bubbled within him. *We are one people, William,* din'Dael had said. *We are all the same within the heart of the flames.*

The pain was excruciating, but Will's tears evaporated before they could fill his eyes. Again and again, the power built into a burning crescendo. Again and again, he fought the urge to fall to his knees and cry out. *Show no weakness,* din'Dael had told him. *Be their beacon, their blazing justice.* Will did as instructed. He did not flinch. He bore the flames.

Jero din'Dael, Revenant of Light, approached. The Maddened Flame wore thin tan robes and no shoes. The hood of his robe was drawn back and his eyes flickered with white fire. He held a milky dagger in his hand. Something about it seemed immediately familiar to Will. Din'Dael stepped into the torrent of fire and approached him.

There was no release from the surging power of the surrounding Blades when the Revenant approached Will, no lessening of power. The thin robe burned into nothing in a matter of seconds. Din'Dael raised the dagger above Will's head. Will grit his teeth, closed his eyes, and bowed his head.

Jero din'Dael brought the blade down and began his work. Will could feel the hot metal working across his scalp, felt the already-short hair falling only to be burnt away the moment it was separated from his body. *Why now and not before?* All the while, the Flares of the Blades worked their fury against the two men. Will's mind wandered, blocking out the crackling whips of fire and lightning, growing numb. He did not falter.

The surrounding Flares ceased. The dagger left his skin and Will opened his eyes. He knew what came next; din'Dael had told him that much, but still he clenched his jaw against it. He held out both arms, palms raised. The Blades dropped to their knees and placed one hand on the ground while outstretching their other. A low, ritualistic hum emerged from them, echoing through the massive chamber.

"You are the very fires of Radiance," din'Dael said. "You are the Blade of Flaming Light."

That's the cue. Will braced himself and drew out his Flare. Blue and white lightning danced across his skin. Jero din'Dael placed the dagger along his wrists and Will surged his power. In the same instant, din'Dael brought the blade back across them in one quick motion. Din'Dael, swift and precise, placed the dagger in Will's hands and stepped back.

Blood pouring from his opened arteries, Will raised the blade into the air, lightning from his Flare crackling along its edge. His vision wavered. His fingers felt thick and foreign. Only a handful of seconds had passed but he was rapidly weakening. The room narrowed. The roar of the flames muted. Din'Dael's hands clasped either side of his face and Will knew the moment had come.

Both men surged in a cloud of brilliant light. White lightning erupted from the hands of the surrounding Blades as they joined their powers with the two men standing in their center. Will briefly saw din'Dael's hand glow green, then his vision went dark. Only the sound of screams amidst the roaring crackle of lightning remained.

The lightning ceased. Will collapsed, the dagger held limply in his hand. The air smelled of electricity and ash. Dark spots danced across the back of his eyelids from the brilliant lights. *Up, he urged himself. Get up, Will. You're not done yet.*

Weakly, he rose to his knees. Blackened, scorched trails of dried blood covered his arms and the surrounding dais, but his wounds had been mended, cauterized in the way of Radiance. His head pounded. The surge from din'Dael had had the force of colliding freight trains. *I don't know how much more of this I can take.* He forced himself to maintain an impassive expression, praying that he would not pass out.

"Who you once were has been burned away." Din'Dael's booming voice echoed through the room. Will saw two of the man for a moment, then blinked the vision away. "You are a phoenix, strength reborn from the ashes of weakness."

The Sapholux echoed with the words, whispered like a prayer by the surrounding Lightborne. Will took a tentative breath; his lungs were already beginning to feel normal again.

"This man came to us a stranger. An outsider. An unknown," din'Dael continued. His voice hurt Will's ears. "But within him, we found Light."

"We found Light," echoed the Lightborne.

"Light," din'Dael said, turning his attention back to Will, "to drive away darkness. Light to burn away the shadows. Light to purify."

"Light to purify," the Lightborne repeated.

Will met din'Dael's gaze and saw that the man had covered himself with a new robe. The Revenant smiled down at him. "Within these ancient walls, William Davis was burnt to ash." He paused and let out a wry, toothy smile as he approached Will. "And now, within these ancient walls, a new man has risen from the flames."

Will blinked. *A new man?* Din'Dael hadn't said anything about this.

"This man"—he leveled a finger at Will—"blood forged by the fires of Sapholux, this man is now Noctis Thorne, Blade of Light."

"Noctis Thorne, Blade of Light," came the echoing Lightborne.

Din'Dael's smile twisted maniacally at Will's startled expression. "Arise, Noctis."

Will did as he was bid, forcing his legs to remain steady. Din'Dael held his hand extended. Will retrieved the fallen dagger and passed it to the great man. Then one of the Blades—Rienne—approached and tied an ash-colored skirt about his waist. Another Blade—Penth—brought a brown leather pauldron and buckled it over his shoulder. More Blades approached, swarming Will, adorning him in the armor of a Blade. When they had completed their work, they backed away and he stood in their midst, fully armed, fully armored.

"Noctis Thorne," din'Dael boomed. "Welcome home."

"THORNE?" WILL RAISED AN EYEBROW. HIS THROAT WAS STILL SORE from the morning's events and his voice came out as a hoarse croak. "You just had to bring my grandfather into it, didn't you?"

The ceremony had ended some time before. He had been paraded amongst the Blades while the remaining Lightborne looked on. Din'Dael had followed at the rear, carrying the white dagger. Once they exited from the great chamber, Dahla had swept over. She'd quickly clutched the dagger, barely hesitating before taking off in flight with the blade secure in her talons.

The thirty Blades welcomed him into their ranks eagerly before din'Dael called them off and took Will for himself. They walked in silence through the corridors of the Sapholux until they arrived at a large chamber near one of the great gathering halls. Only when they were alone did Will finally break the silence. Now, having done so, he waited.

Jero din'Dael mockingly raised his own eyebrow and leaned in until he was just inches away from Will. He paused there, gave a slow blink, then gave a great, booming laugh.

"It is an apt name for our purposes, young Noctis."

"Will," Will said with a snicker. "My name is Will."

All humor vanished from din'Dael's face. "No, it is not." He leveled a stern gaze at Will. "You are Noctis. Were you not listening in there?"

Will rolled his eyes. "With all the thundering going on, it would have been easy to miss." Din'Dael didn't look amused. A shiver of nerves ran through Will. "I just figured it was a formality. No one is actually going to call me that, right?" Din'Dael's expression didn't change and Will suddenly felt very self-conscious. "Tell me I'm right."

"William Davis is dead." Din'Dael overenunciated every word. "I watched him bleed out and die."

Will suddenly felt very cold. *That wasn't quite what I had in mind when I agreed to this whole Blade thing.*

"Come," din'Dael said, grabbing his shoulder roughly and shoving him in front of a mirror. "Look at the man before you. Is that William Davis?"

Will stared at his reflection and tried to hide his surprise. Din'Dael wasn't entirely wrong. The armored figure that looked back at Will was one he did not recognize. He looked . . . stony. Carved marble. He was lean and wiry. His face was gaunt. There were deep, dark circles under his eyes and the eyes themselves had changed. He couldn't explain how but they looked cruel. Hard. Cold. *The eyes of a killer.*

He tried to shy away from the sight but din'Dael held him close. "Look at yourself, Noctis. Look. William Davis was a child, a boy who played at being an imaginary hero. No"—he gripped Will tight, silencing the protest— "William played. His world was a game. One that he did not survive."

No, that's not . . . The more din'Dael spoke, the more Will tried to fight what he heard, but he couldn't avoid hearing elements of truth in din'Dael's words.

"You are not that. You are a warrior." Din'Dael's voice was hard as iron. "You are an instrument of devastation to our enemies. You are worthy of bearing your grandfather's name. You are Noctis Thorne."

Will stared into his own eyes, foreign and distant. He searched for himself in the face that stared back. He searched for the subtle similarities to his brother, for the easy laugh and casual smirk. All traces seemed to be gone. *What have they done to me?*

"You *burn,* Noctis." Din'Dael's hands loosened on his shoulders. "From the day we met, you have burned. You fight it, I've always seen that, but you cannot deny what you are. You are a walking weapon, an instrument of justice. You are a gift to the Sapholux, to all those who call themselves Lightborne. You will help us bring peace to this flailing, misguided world."

Will was lulled by the cadence in din'Dael's voice. "Peace . . ."

"Peace." Din'Dael smiled. "Once we stand victorious over the bleeding corpses of our enemies, we shall have peace."

Not unlike the Ancient Romans, Will thought as he remembered his grandfather's lessons. *Noctis, that's Latin—of night. A thorn of night.* Something about that resonated with him. What had Madigan always said? A dagger in the dark? Will smiled.

"Noctis, then." *Just play the role. Let the Lightborne call you what they want.*

Jero din'Dael clapped him on the back. "Yes, my friend. Come, it is not every day that the Sapholux welcomes a new Blade."

HOURS LATER AND WITH A SWIMMING HEAD, WILL RETURNED TO his chamber. The celebration had been immense, the great hall filled with liquor and trays of food. All in his honor. *Noctis's honor.* He laughed. Noctis. There was something to it, something to the mad fantasy of a new identity. Was it so mad? Was it such a fantasy? What existed of his world before the Sapholux? *Nothing* —he smiled humorlessly—*nothing that wasn't burnt away.*

Perhaps din'Dael was right, he thought through the haze of liquor. Maybe William Davis really had been only a shell, a cocoon from which this new being had emerged. *An ashen husk to a reborn phoenix.* Maybe that name, William, had been the last vestige of an innocent ideal—that justice was possible through innocence. That peace was possible without bloodshed.

He scoffed at the notion, his grandfather's training too ingrained for one night's revelry to undo. Nothing could take *that* part of him away, right?

Hours ago—*was it really only hours?*—he had believed as much. Since the morning's strange ceremony, he had heard enough to call it into question. Justice and peace would only be possible through the means that din'Dael foretold: over the corpses of their enemies. That, at least, had not changed. Valmont. The Necrothanians. Senraks the Vequian. Jero din'Dael and Noctis Thorne would destroy them all. Din'Dael had told him, professed it before the whole of the Sapholux. Had promised him his vengeance.

You, Noctis, are the instrument of retribution. Din'Dael's voice echoed in Will's mind. *Our retribution and your own.*

He snickered drunkenly and collapsed onto the bed. They had all cheered at din'Dael's words. There had been feasting throughout the Sapholux, a celebration of survival. Of knowledge and overcoming all adversaries. The wonders of this place! The fantastical powers of Radiance! Had he ever wished for anything else? Had he really wanted to find a way to return to being Shadowborne?

"Nope," he said to the empty space. He could hear the slur in his speech. "Nope, nope. That was Will. Not Noctis."

He chuckled. *Talking to yourself? Is that the touch of madness in all Lightborne?* He rolled over. That was foolish, anyway. He hadn't seen had the slightest hint of madness in any Lightborne since he'd first arrived. Jero was just eccentric. And who even said his grandfather was correct about all that? No one else had said anything about it, never warned against it. Hell, since he'd arrived, he'd learned plenty that Jervin Thorne had probably never dreamt possible.

Don't get cocky, kid. Madigan's voice this time. Will wondered where his brother was now, wondered if Mad would even recognize him when they met again. *If we meet again.*

He groaned and covered his face with an arm, bending his legs up onto the bed as he did so. *Too much today. Too many voices. Too many memories.* All those Lightborne. All din'Dael had said. All his brother and grandfather had said or might have said. It all kept playing over and over in his mind. He felt like he had when he'd just arrived in the Sapholux, a maddening slew of silent voices crying out for his attention. *Maybe I am going crazy.*

He'd known all the voices, save one. Twice he'd heard it. The same voice. The same word. *Come,* it told him, once in his dreams, once when he was alone in the desert. *Come* was all it ever said and when she—for somehow, he knew it was a she—beckoned, he had followed. Who was she? The ghost of his mother? Will snorted. *Right, Will. Now you've got ghosts knocking around your brain.*

THINK NOT OF HER.

The roar filled Will's mind like a thunderclap. He scrambled, letting out a startled cry and flailing before falling to the floor.

SHE IS NOTHING.

"What the hell?" Gasping for breath, Will placed a hand on the bed and pulled himself to his knees. "What in the goddam hell?" That was no memory, no way. There was nothing familiar in whatever had spoken those words. The voice had been like a physical presence, a screaming titan with the power of ages booming directly into his brain. Futilely, Will scanned the room. He saw no one, heard nothing.

"Too much today." He shook his head. "Too goddam much." He climbed back onto the bed and put his head between his knees. His battered mind seemed at war with itself, answering whatever random thought it put into his head. *Just need to get some rest, that's all.*

He took a deep breath and paused. There was a peaceful silence in his brain. The scattered memories and phantom voices of inebriation faded into the obscure fog that lingers on the edge of dreams. He embraced it, the exhaustion of the day dragging him toward the abandonment of sleep.

FIND MORELLA.

The roaring words tore him from the brink of sleep. He thrashed against it again, clapping his hands to his ears. Nearly hyperventilating, he pinched his eyes shut and curled into a ball. *What in the goddam hell?*

Silence.

He waited. Nothing. Whatever it had been, it was gone, disappearing just as quickly as it appeared. Will wracked his brain for any trace of familiarity in the voice, but nothing came. *Definitely not hers, whoever the hell she is.* There was nothing gentle in this voice, nothing soothing or comforting. There was no soft urgency to it. No, it nearly shattered his sanity making its desires known.

Find Morella.

Morella. During the first few months in the Sapholux, din'-Dael had done everything in his power to push Morella from Will's mind. *No use lamenting over the dead and lost,* he said. *Focus your energy on vengeance. Destroy those who took your happiness from you.* Part of Will wondered if din'Dael would have said the same if he'd known that Will considered him among those who had separated him from Morella. The other part knew that din'Dael wouldn't have cared in the least bit.

She's dead. You saw her, at the end. You saw the army of the dead. He'd told himself that countless times, but it never stuck. He didn't really believe she was dead. He knew she wasn't. There was no logic to the feeling; he couldn't explain it in the slightest, but still, he knew she was out there, somewhere. And apparently, some strange, raging part of his unconscious self was screaming for him to find her.

A fire of urgency lit inside him. *What if . . .* "Nope," he said thickly. "Don't go there again. Not you, Noctis."

I sound like a damn idiot. After the long, strange day and the flowing wine of the past few hours, he was far beyond logical thought. Morning would see things improved. Morning would bring clarity. Morning would bring a plan. *Tomorrow. I'll figure this all out tomorrow.*

Will stretched out again on the bed. He went to run his fingers through his hair but was caught off guard by the bare skin and bristling velvet of his newly shorn head. *Din'Dael's blade. Blade. I'm a Blade now. A Blade of Light. Whatever the hell that's worth.*

He stopped the thought in its tracks. Where was this sudden flippant doubt coming from? It was reminiscent of his early days with din'Dael, not what he had now become. He had long ago abandoned that part of him. Din'Dael had taught him to forget the past, embrace the path of a true burner. A Lightborne. But something had been rekindled by that damn voice and its order to find Morella. *Why? Why now?*

His question was met by silence. Instead, a small inkling of a forgotten memory sparked, a flash of memory he had thought burned away: Morella's laughter.

Will recoiled from the memory, but the years of training and thought-control within the Sapholux were suddenly of no use. Everything came flooding back with that laugh. Her crooked smile, the warmth of her skin, her—*No*. He forced himself away from it, focusing instead on the other Morella, the one din'Dael had trained him to think of. The sneering face. The cruel demeanor. The killer. Madigan had seen it in her. Cephora had seen it in her. Why hadn't Will?

Because Will was weak. Noctis would not have made that error.

He froze. The thought was not his own.

FIND MORELLA.

The command burst into his weary mind once more. It tore at him, ripping through his defenses like paper. He knew, then, that this was not some part of his own self speaking to him. There truly was something else in his head. *So that your minds may always be your own,* his grandfather had often said. What had he known that he'd never shared?

As the night wore on, Will grappled with sleep and prayed for the absence of dreams. His mind filled with forgotten memories and pain, Will slowly unwound thread by thread, thought by thought, until William Davis and Noctis Thorne were both bare in his mind's eye, surrounded by everyone from his past. When the last breath of wakefulness faded from him and he finally drifted into uneasy sleep, his last image was of everything, everyone, erupting into flames.

7
REVELATIONS

Will awoke to the uncomfortable sensation of being watched. He wiped the sleep from his eyes and rose. He could feel a distinct presence, something both foreign and familiar. Scanning the room, he saw nothing. There was no sign of anyone nor any changes from when he had stumbled into the room the previous night.

His head throbbed. *Definitely too much.* The entirety of the previous day itself, and the night that had followed, felt like a dream. Everything in his memories did. It was as though a thin veil of fog covered his entire life up to this moment. Only one thing, one thought, burned bright and true: It was time to leave the Sapholux.

Will undressed and bathed, the movements mechanical. He felt a stranger in his own body. It was no hangover, at least not one that he had ever experienced before. Yesterday's events, the strange induction ritual and surging power from the Lightborne left him feeling raw. *What the bloody hell happened to me yesterday?*

He dressed and, without even thinking, reached for the trunk at the end of the bed. Opening it, he clasped the belt of blood fangs to his waist. He unwrapped the small cloth at the bottom of the chest and withdrew his grandfather's key, draping it over his neck.

Immediately, his mind cleared. His body relaxed with the cool touch of metal. It had been years since he'd worn the key, and yet the tingling sensation of its constant activity against his skin felt like . . . *like coming home.* The small jolt of electricity. The spiking hum. Its strange pulses surging through his body. *How did din'-Dael ever convince me to take it off?*

Will scanned the small, spartan room. He had his new armor and cloak. He had his blades and the aerilite cutlass from din'-Dael. He had his key. There was nothing else worth taking; he had what he needed. He closed the door and set out in search of the Revenant. *He'll be furious. Taking the honors of the Sapholux and then leaving?* Will braced himself.

It did not take him long to find the man. Din'Dael was in the main war room of the Sapholux looking over a map stretched out on a table. A group of Blades surrounded the table, all listening to a report from one of them. Quennar, Will recalled. He had been absent from yesterday's ceremony.

Din'Dael glanced up when Will entered the room. He met the young man's eye and raised a hand, beckoning him forward without interrupting Quennar. His face was stern and hard, obviously taken by something of great import. Will saw that Kenwal, most senior of the Blades, had a look of deep concern on his face. Rienne was there as well, pinching the bridge of her nose. Whatever he had walked in on, it wasn't good.

Quennar was speaking at a near whisper. When Will drew within hearing range, he could hear a tremor in the man's voice.

"Numbers beyond what we previously estimated." He wiped a bit of sweat from his brow then gestured at the map. "Or so my man says. I trust him, but if what he says is true . . ." Quennar shook his head and saw Will approach. "Then we need allies." He waved vaguely toward Will. "Even given our newly bolstered strength."

"One man is not enough to make a difference, one way or another," din'Dael responded. His voice was grave. "Not even one of your strength, Noctis."

Will glanced at the map on the table then met din'Dael's eye. "Make a difference against what?"

Kenwal answered. "Necrothanians, a large gathering. They have been clustered for some time around this small mountain"—he pointed at a spot on the map—"but a portion of them are on the move. Scouts have been watching for some time now, and there can be little doubt. They move on the Sapholux."

"Or so it appears," din'Dael interjected. "Dorian would never be so foolish as to launch an outright assault on us." He gave a grim smile. "He doesn't even know that we exist."

"He knows that you do," said Kenwal. "That may be enough."

"No." Din'Dael's tone brooked no argument. "That is not his way. There is something else at work here." He paused then looked at Will. "What are your thoughts?"

My thoughts? Will glanced from Kenwal to din'Dael, then to the trembling Quennar, then finally to Rienne. Her face gave nothing away. *Looks like becoming a Blade means I suddenly get to have an opinion.* He glanced at the map and hesitated. "I don't think I have enough information to have any thoughts on the matter," he said softly. "I only just arri—"

"Precisely." Din'Dael's face split into his manic grin. "Noctis's thoughts mirror my own. We simply do not have enough information." Will sensed that he had just given din'Dael the opening he needed. "For too long we've been secreted away within these walls, relying on the reports of outsiders on our payroll. We need to gather our own intelligence."

Quennar looked faint. Rienne let out a soft sigh and closed her eyes, shaking her head. Kenwal's mouth was set in a hard line and he was glaring at their commander.

"Quennar already explained it, Jero," the senior Blade said. "We don't have the forces."

"Nor will we ever now that Dorian has returned." Din'Dael slammed his hands down on the table as he spoke. "The moment will *never* be right. We will *never* have the advantage. We must outthink him. Outmaneuver him. To do that, we need to be outside in the world beyond the Sapholux."

Will watched din'Dael's words sink into those in the room. He, of course, knew that din'Dael was ready for the Lightborne to prove the strength of the Sapholux, to enter into a world absent Shadowborne, without the influence of the Umbriferum. And now the Blades around him knew it too, and they were recoiling from it. *This is what he meant when he said they needed a catalyst for change.*

"Jero," Rienne said quietly. "Your people do not want war."

The room descended into an uncomfortable silence as the Revenant eyed Rienne. She did not waver under his fiery scrutiny.

"*Our* people do not have a choice." Din'Dael was calm. The contrast to the manic, table-slamming man from moments before made his words all the more chilling. "Dorian Valmont has returned, Rienne. You were not here the last time. Nor you, Quennar." His gaze roved until it fell on Kenwal. "But you were, old friend. You remember a world with his presence."

"I remember your rivalry," Kenwal began. "I remember how it destroyed our Guardian."

For a moment, Will thought din'Dael was going to strike the Blade. He did not, however, and only the briefest twitch at the corner of his eyes bore witness to the internal struggle.

"Shigei O'Saq," din'Dael spoke in slow, measured tones, "was not a casualty of my personal relationship with Valmont. Do not suggest such again."

Will saw an opening. "I'll go." All eyes in the room quickly turned to him. "I'll find out what's going on."

"No," din'Dael said with a shake of his head. "I have a different mission for you, young Noctis." He paused and drew back from the table, returning to his full height. "Come, let us adjourn. Tensions are high and we have much to think on. I thank you, all, for your counsel."

The others did not argue. While the small council vacated, Will lingered. Rienne frowned and raised an eyebrow at him. Will smirked and jerked his head toward din'Dael. She gave a small nod, but then her eyes hardened as they fell to the fangs around Will's waist. With a look of disgust, she turned and followed Quennar and Kenwal from the room.

"That one is trouble, Noctis. Step lightly."

Will turned back to din'Dael. The tall man's eyes were fixed squarely on him. Inexplicably, Will felt very small.

"Just a friend, Jero." His thoughts briefly drifted to Morella and hints of the previous night played across his mind. "Nothing more."

"She is right, you know. These people, our people, they do not want war." Din'Dael sighed and shook his head, resting his hands on the table once more and looking at the large map. "No one ever does. And yet war always comes."

"Then you have to protect them," Will said, stepping closer. "However you can."

"Countless days, Noctis. That is how long the Sapholux has stood. Some say that these walls predate even Velier and the Breaking. No one living knows. Shigei O'Saq did not even know." He sighed and turned to Will. "And somehow, Dorian is a threat to them. None of us know how. None of us even know why." His eyes grew momentarily distant. "There is something wrong, Noctis. Something tainted within these walls. You can see it. The fear, like a sickness, creeping through our brethren. It should not be so. Not even against Dorian."

"Jero," Will said, choosing his words carefully, "you have a

Relic of Antiquity. There is another one housed within these walls. Why don't you use them to fight?"

Din'Dael glanced at his hand and Will saw the pale green glow dimly show itself. The key at his chest, so familiar as to have been already forgotten, sputtered and popped, surging to life. Will rolled his shoulders involuntarily and blinked. *That's new.*

"No one can be bound to multiple Relics, Noctis. And one was not enough, when last Dorian and I met upon the battlefield."

"How is that even possible? Does Valmont have one as well?"

"I do not believe so." Din'Dael shook his head. He pulled out a chair and sat, placing his head in his hands. "I do not know what Dorian has done to himself, but he did not die."

A cool shiver crept up Will's spine. "You had the chance to kill him?"

"I did kill him," din'Dael said softly. "It did not stop him." He looked up and met Will's shocked gaze. "Do you understand, young Burner? I watched him die. I bled the life right out of him and saw the light of life leave his eyes. And yet he still fights."

Will said nothing.

"He was not always a monster, Noctis. He was brilliant. He was the greatest mind these lands had seen in longer than anyone could say. Long before the Wars of Dawning, even I admired him. Lightborne, Shadowborne, history shows that peace can exist between us." He gave a humorless smile. "For a time, at least."

"What happened?"

The smile disappeared. "Too much." He shook his head and stood. "A conversation for another day, young Noctis. In the meantime, you and I have something to discuss." He crossed the room to where a small table held glasses and bottles. Grabbing two glasses and a bottle, he beckoned Will over. He filled a glass and handed it over to him. "You're leaving."

How did he know? Then he saw that din'Dael was not insinuating anything, did not know of Will's own plans for departure. Din'Dael had something else planned.

"Well, you did say you had a separate mission planned for me."

"That I did." Din'Dael tipped his own glass back and drained it quickly, then refilled it. "Quennar and Kenwal believe that Dorian marches on the Sapholux. I do not share that belief, but their fears certainly illustrate a point that needs reconciling. The Lightborne are alone in the world."

Will sipped his glass and nodded. "Right, like you and I talked about before."

"Quite right. Regardless of Dorian's plans, it is apparent to me that the Sapholux needs allies. And in a world threatened once again by the Necrothanians"—he chuckled lightly—"an army of Lightborne suddenly seems rather useful, I would imagine."

Where is he going with this? "Yeah, the . . . effectiveness of the Borne is certainly not something to underestimate," Will said carefully.

Din'Dael nodded. "There is only one ally of any worth to us, only one citadel large enough to house the Lightborne and strong enough to withstand an assault from Dorian's minions." He snorted at the last word and shook his head before taking another drink.

Will's breath caught. "You mean the Nordoth."

Din'Dael smiled. "I do."

Mad . . . Whatever had happened to his brother and Cephora, surely they would have regrouped within Undermyre. At the very least, the Crow would have wanted a report on everything that happened. But their venture with Cephora, the terrible day at the Shale, that had been so long ago. Would Mad still be there?

"When do I leave?"

Din'Dael raised an eyebrow. "That's it? No questions from such a usually inquisitive mind? No request for more information as to how this is part of the greater scheme?" Will opened his mouth to respond but couldn't find the words. Din'Dael leaned forward in his seat. "No. You have questions, but they are not for me. You leave at once." He glanced at the blood fangs and cutlass then gave a mirthless smile. "As it seems you had already planned."

Taken aback, Will suddenly *was* filled with questions. If the Lightborne needed him, needed the Nordoth, he would do what he could. But there was so much more. "You hate the Crow. Why reach out to him now?"

Din'Dael smiled. "As I said, Noctis, we need allies."

Will considered for a moment. "What do you want me to say? I don't expect that the Crow will exactly welcome the idea of an army of Borne sitting within his walls."

"You're clever, Noctis. You'll find a way. Of that I have no doubt."

"Fine." He thought for a moment. "I don't know these lands well, Jero, not at all, really. How far is it to the Nordoth from here?"

Din'Dael laughed and sipped at his drink. "Less than half the continent, give or take."

Will groaned. He had no idea how large the continents might be in this world, but if they were even a fraction of the size of those back in Cascania, he was in for a long journey. "And I'm guessing you expect me to make this journey alone?"

"Don't be ridiculous." Din'Dael shook his head and gestured to the rafters. "You'll have a guide, of course."

Will raised his eyes. And there she was: Dahla. The great bird was perched high above and was staring at him, her head cocked to the side, her golden eyes boring into him.

Fantastic. "I'm sure we'll have delightful conversations," he muttered. The thought of so long a journey with only the bird was not a pleasant one. Still, there was something about her that was comforting, familiar. She'd been with him on his last journey through the desert and, other than din'Dael, the only friend he'd had within these walls for quite some time at the start.

"She will take you as far as needed. She will have to break off after and guide Rienne for the rest of her journey."

"Wait, break off?" Will said in surprise. "With Rienne? What do you mean?"

"Now come the questions." Din'Dael sighed and shook his head. "The world does not pause and wait for your comings and goings, Noctis. The amassing Necrothanians must still be dealt with. Rienne will be seeking out other potential allies. For that, she'll need Dahla far more than you shall."

Will cocked an eyebrow at the man. "And they might be . . .?"

"Your other old friends. The Seekers. They are, most likely, far better equipped to handle the Necrothanians."

Will tried not to let his surprise show. Cephora had called herself Prime of the Seekers, so of course that had to have meant there were more like her. *More people who could control the ground?* No, she'd called herself the last Earth Warder, whatever that meant. So, the Seekers, then, they were something else. *Bounty hunters or mercenaries, perhaps?* "Better equipped than Lightborne . . ."

Din'Dael smiled. "They have their methods."

Will was suddenly aware that he still did not know what exactly the Seekers' methods were. What he'd seen of Cephora's powers had been those of an Earth Warder. What were the Seekers capable of? *How the hell do I still know so little about this damn world?*

"So, Rienne then. She goes to treat with the Seekers and I go to the Nordoth. Alliances, right? Pincer move to sweep up the Necrothanians in the middle and cut the legs from underneath Valmont's army? Sounds like quite the tidy plan, Jero."

The tall Lightborne smiled at him. "Tidy, indeed."

"And our paths coincide, for a time? Rienne's and mine?"

"They do."

Din'Dael was offering less and less information. Will knew the signs; he would get no more out of him than that. "Alright, then. Tomorrow?" He raised a questioning eyebrow to his mentor. Din'Dael said nothing. *Helpful, as ever.* "We'll leave tomorrow."

"One final thing, Noctis. The Lightborne will march for the Nordoth in a few weeks' time." Din'Dael leveled his gaze at him, setting his empty glass back on the table. "We will not be long behind you. Our people will have been promised accommodations. Do not let them down."

In other words, failure isn't an option. Not knowing what to say, Will gave a brief nod and dismissed himself. A few weeks to establish a relationship with the Crow and win over the Nordoth. A few weeks to explain that the Lightborne were alive and marching en masse, armed with weapons of aerilite, to the very gates of Undermyre. A few weeks to meet whatever demands the old man and his council would set.

Oh yes, what could possibly go wrong?

8

TRAVELS WITH RIENNE

A strange uneasiness hung in the air when Will awoke the following morning. He had spent so much time within the walls of the Sapholux that the worlds beyond seemed unfamiliar now, no more than an echo of a dream. And yet, the realm of Aeril still seemed more familiar than the one he had called home for so long. *Is it even right to still call it home?* His whole time in Cascania, the world he had known, had been his grandfather's world, the home that he and Mad and Will had made together. That world was gone. Home was gone.

The thought left him disheartened. His mood soured more when he met with Rienne; she didn't even look at him. As they prepared their few belongings, she kept her gaze averted and said nothing. *What the heck did I do wrong?*

He paused and watched her check her supplies, the fastening on her cloak, and then repeat the process. *She's nervous, idiot. Stop thinking everything is about you.*

Nerves made sense. Rienne had never before left the protective walls of the Sapholux and, now that he knew what to look for, Will saw the trepidation plain on her face. Why had din'Dael chosen her, of everyone? Why did he think she would be the best representative to the Seekers if she knew so little of the world? *The inner workings of a madman's mind. I'll never figure him out.*

Will wondered how much time the two of them would spend together on the road. Din'Dael had made it clear that they would be parting ways eventually, but Will hoped they would at least be together long enough for Rienne to find some level of comfort beyond the Sapholux. It was a bitter hope, but a hope nonetheless. She was venturing into a world that had once sought, and very nearly achieved, the destruction of her kind. *Our kind. Stop trying to separate yourself.*

Will put the light armor of a Blade into his pack and donned his new cloak and fresh travel leathers. They were unblemished, not stained with scars and memories like those he was wearing when he first arrived. *Not yet.* He hung the aerilite cutlass from a baldric and settled it beneath the cloak. He fastened his fangs about his waist and touched the key around his neck. *No matter what, I'm never going to take this off again. A reminder of the real me.*

As Will made his way to the gates, the blood fangs brought looks of discomfort and disapproval from the Lightborne. The knives seemed to add to the mystique that had grown around his rapid elevation within the Borne. He heard the whispers in the corridors as he passed, saw the looks of mistrust on the faces of those around. It was jarring. *Here I thought that damn ceremony had moved us past that. Nothing new, I guess.*

Will retreated further into his own mind as they walked. No matter how much he had trained and developed his Flare, he'd always been separate from the other Lightborne. But was that really so strange? He'd been Shadowborne, once. Perhaps their distance was due to an echo of that former power. He snickered to himself. *After all this, I'm still daydreaming about damn Shades.*

He expected grandiose fanfare from Jero at their departure, given what he had come to know of the man, but when Will and Rienne approached the killing gates, din'Dael stood alone.

Perhaps it's another of his strategies, sneaking us out and heralding us as righteous warriors seeking the betterment of the Lightborne. That would be right up his alley. He would compare them to Velier's band, setting off into parts unknown to save the world as they knew it. *All so he can turn it on its head.* Eyeing din'Dael, Will felt a familiar mix of fascination and repulsion for the warrior.

Din'Dael smiled casually, his mind seemingly elsewhere. He passed Rienne a sealed scroll that she placed within a leather case, and whispered advice Will couldn't hear. Whatever it was, it did nothing to alleviate Rienne's nervous expression. He then glanced at Will, glanced at the blood fangs, and laughed. That was all.

"Dahla will find you," Jero said between chuckles. He made a shooing motion at the pair. "Go. Be on your way."

"Do you know when?" Will asked. Jero simply stared at him. "I mean, at least tell us which way we ought to head." Jero raised an eyebrow. *Sure, fine, whatever. We'll go wander then.* Will sighed. "You could point," he said flatly.

Din'Dael snickered and clapped him on the back. "Just venture southwest, my young Burner. I believe that's correct. Southwest or southeast. I can never recall. Put the Sapholux at your back and set out. That's the key."

"Helpful," Will muttered. He turned to Rienne, but she was already striding though the gates. Din'Dael gave Will another shooing motion, turned on his heel, and then off the Revenant went.

Will readjusted his pack and started out after Rienne. *Well, here we go.*

The sun was just cresting over the distant mountains and casting its glow against the Sapholux when he exited the killing gates. The scarred sky became a mix of greens and purples against the orange, an oddity Will had come to accept as normal. Back in Cascania, he'd seen pictures of the Northern Lights, and each rise of the Aerillian sun reminded him of them. The jagged scar itself was a sharp contrast to the vibrant colors, its milk-white glow pulsing faintly. There was something otherworldly about it, something unnatural. Will shivered and shook his head. *Just one more damn casualty from din'Dael.*

Southwest. Or southeast. They settled on heading due south. At first, Will tried to make small talk, but it was apparent that Rienne was too taken with the world beyond the Sapholux to speak. So they stayed silent while the great stronghold of the Lightborne grew ever smaller behind them. Rienne walked upright and direct, her eyes set dead forward, never once looking back at the fortress she called home.

Will's mind wandered as he fell into the walking trance of travel, the sand and craggy rock beneath his feet so reminiscent of his previous travels in Aeril. *There's more to this place, isn't there? More than just sand and desert?* There had to be. The land around Undermyre had been lush and bordered the sea. What was across the sea, he wondered. What was across the desert? *All this time here and I've seen so little, still know so little. All this time since I left home . . .*

Four years was his best guess. Four years since the death of his grandfather. He couldn't say for certain; there were no calendars, no measurement of the passage of time as familiar and reliable as it had been in Cascania. Everything back home had been so straightforward, so simple. There was something about Aeril that didn't quite add up. *Unfinished. It seems like a work in progress.* And for the four years he had spent in this world, what did he really know? He had traded one tunnel for another when he first arrived. He had traded a chamber in a tower for a dorm in a fortress. He'd crossed the vast wildlands, briefly, and a formidable desert. But really, all he had done was trade one desert for another, one confinement for another.

Oppressive self-doubt crashed down upon him. *What have I even accomplished?* He had lost his brother, lost the calming Shadow he had set out to learn more about. In its place, he had discovered something destructive and foreign. He'd grown no closer to uncovering the truth of what din'Dael had done to him. The aggressive force of the Flare was far stronger than the Shade Will had known, but he did not feel like himself. He felt colder, disillusioned.

Maybe I really am Noctis now.

The thought disquieted him. Whatever din'Dael might think, might pronounce to the gods and the Lightborne, he was William Davis. Nothing could change that, could it?

He glanced at Rienne, appearing so cool and collected when her own emotions must be a storm inside her. He wondered how he appeared. *Perhaps I'm better at hiding all this than I think I am.*

"Rienne," he said. His voice was cracked from the dry air and hours of disuse. "How are you holding up?"

"I'm fine." Her response was terse and quick. "It all looks the same as it did when peering from the windows of the Sapholux, so I don't know what you're expecting me to feel."

Her tone caught him off guard. "I just mean . . . I only asked because I know how rapid changes can be strange and . . ." Will trailed off.

She snickered and gave him an eye that made him feel foolish. "Do you think that now you're a Blade, you must take care of me? We are equals, Thorne. What makes you think that you are more equipped to handle the outside world than I?"

"I only meant"—Will paused and considered—"I would understand if this all felt weird or uncomfortable." *Maybe some levity?* He flashed a quick, forced smile. "At least you can admit that it seems like there's more sky out here."

She snickered humorlessly. "Yes, Noctis, there does seem to be more sky."

This isn't going well. Will searched for something to say and came up blank. "It's a beautiful sky though." He peered up. "I mean, even the crack is beautiful, in its own way."

"Yes." Rienne smiled, softening a bit. "It is. Velier's gift is a wonderful thing."

He raised an eyebrow. "Velier's gift? What does endless life have to do with the sky?"

"The sky stretches on and on, limitless. Timeless. As the sky is above, so are those of us below." The edge was gradually leaving her voice as she spoke. "I never lamented my time within the walls of the Sapholux because I always knew that time, like the sky, stretched far beyond the world I knew. There would always be a future, more time to come."

Will held his breath, not daring to speak. *Not when she's finally opening back up.*

"That is the beauty of what he gave us. There is time to explore the world. Time to do it however and whenever I please. Time to discover all things not yet discovered." She shrugged and shifted her pack. "While this is not my expectation of how I would leave those I call family, I cannot say that I am not excited."

"Fair enough," Will said softly. Before he could say anything more, however, a screech pierced the air. He glanced up right as Dahla flew into view. "I hope I don't prove to be too boring company."

"Even if you are, I'm sure the bird will provide some kind of companionship." She chuckled and turned back to him. Then her eyes fell to his knives. The smile left her face. Her expression turned cold once more. She snapped her head back around, mouth set in a thin line. "At the very least it won't pester me with questions about how I'm feeling."

Will had no response for that. He wasn't sure what he had said wrong, but it was apparent their final training session together had soured their previous friendship. That hurt. *But I fixed it. I fixed everything.*

He watched as Rienne quickened her pace and distanced herself from him. Loneliness ached in his chest. *At least, I thought I did.*

For the next few days, there was tense silence between the two of them. Every few hours they would be startled by a cry from Dahla. On some occasions, the great bird would swoop to the ground at blazing speed and soar past them. *Quite the guide you picked for us, din'Dael,* Will mused. But the bird kept them on course, he gathered, whatever that course might be.

Will awoke on the morning of the fifth day with Dahla nowhere in sight. Nor had the bird returned to them the previous evening. Will remarked on it with little commentary from Rienne, but he saw the look of concern in her eyes. *That damn bird built a pattern, got us into a routine. Of course she'd break it as soon as we got comfortable. Definitely din'Dael's pet.*

They broke camp and set out, keeping as much to the same course as they had the previous day. Two hours later, far in the distance, Will made out a flickering shape circling the sky. *There she is.* Unexpected relief flooded him. *Because of a big damn bird.* He shook his head, chiding himself. *No, it's more than that. It means we're traveling in the right direction.*

It also meant that, soon, there would be something to take his mind off his silent companion. Rienne had not spoken, not even glanced in his direction for some time. Perhaps whatever the bird found would lighten the mood.

"Dahla," Will said, pointing to the faraway form. "Looks like we're still on course."

Rienne simply grunted.

They crested a large dune, drawing close enough to the bird for Will to see she was circling a large grouping of rocks. Rienne drew a sharp breath. Will whirled, hands darting to his blades. Rienne's attention was fixed on the rocks; however, her expression was one of reverent awe.

"Is everything alright, Rienne?" Will asked uneasily.

Her eyes briefly snapped back to him, then darted away, her mouth settling back into its grim line. “It’s fine.”

Will studied the rocks. “What are they?”

This time, the look on her face was one of pure incredulity. *You would think I was asking her if water was wet.* She stopped walking for a moment, eyes flicking to Will, then to the rocks, then back again. “You must be joking.”

Finally, an opportunity to chat. He shook his head. “I’m not.”

“Did they teach you nothing, Casc?”

It did not sound like she intended an insult, but it still stung. “I don’t know who you’re referring to. But apparently no, they didn’t teach me anything.”

That brought a smile. At least, the hint of one. “Velier and the Thorns of the Rose spent a year at sea searching for an answer to the end times,” Rienne said. “A year with no port in sight, no lands or isles, nothing.”

Will knew the story. “Right. It was like that until Velier ordered his men to sleep during the day and sail at night so they could follow the stars.”

This time, Rienne’s smile was true. “Not the stars, Noctis. The Moon.”

He shrugged. “Stars, a moon, whichever. They sailed”—he paused at the startled look on her face—“What? What’d I say?”

“Not *a* moon, Noctis, *the* Moon.” Her eyes narrowed at whatever it was she saw on his face. “Wait, Noctis, all this time, you’ve thought that Velier followed just a glowing orb of rock in the sky?”

Will nodded slowly. “I mean, that’s what a moon is. Unless it’s shadowed, of course; then it doesn’t glow. But . . .” He trailed off as her shocked smile spread into a wide grin. She began to laugh. “What?”

“It’s a symbol, Noctis,” she said, shaking her head. “Calling it the moon. It’s an honor, a reminder. A way of paying tribute.”

“To . . .?”

"To *the* Moon. The guide from the heavens that saved Velier and the Thorns. The being that, ultimately, saved our entire plane. You've never heard of the Moon?"

Will checked his memory and came up with a blank. "Not in this kind of context, no."

She closed her eyes and shook her head, then set off walking in the direction of the rocks again. "You have much to learn, Casc."

Will saw the opportunity and grinned sheepishly. "Well, Rienne, I'd love to learn more, and it looks like we'll have plenty of time."

She said nothing, but her face was not as harsh as it had been. They continued toward the rocks, but even after ten minutes, they did not seem to be any closer. *They must be massive. More than massive.*

He wanted to ask more about them, to have Rienne fill the gaps in his grandfather's story. *For all his teachings and tellings of* The Veleriat, *it was just one of Grandda's stories. We didn't know it was a real book.* And, come to think of it, Will never read it. He'd meant to, time and time again when he'd been in the Nordoth, but Madigan had them focused on other aspects of Aeril, historical not literary. *And now they're intersecting. I'll have to give him a hard time about it.*

"She saved them," Rienne said after a moment. "The Moon, I mean. She gave Velier the tools to see in the night, to find the clear path through the darkness. She taught him to embrace it, the darkness."

"I'd heard that but, I don't know, I always just thought it was allegory or something."

"The Moon guided him to a place where the seas dropped into a vast chasm, waterfalls into oblivion. Only a single, magical channel existed to bridge the chasm to the rocky island beyond."

"Right, the island that held the Heart of Eternity. Right?"

"The Moon gave the heart to Velier so he could protect it, and in doing so, protect all things. When he removed the heart, the island imploded."

"And only a tower to the heavens remained of what had once been," Will finished. He stared again at the large rocks. "Wait, Rienne, are you telling me that *that* is the Isle of Eternity?"

She glanced over her shoulder and gave Will a playful wink. "Rumors said it was within a week's journey of the Sapholux, if you knew the right path."

Will didn't fight the nervous rush of awe. *Velier and his companions were here, in this very space, ages ago.* When he'd wandered into Aeril with Madigan, he'd been walking into one of his grandfather's stories. But this? This was walking into ancient myth, the same as if he'd found the Trojan horse or Polyphemus's cave. *Morella was right about* The Veleriat*, too. Why doesn't the rest of the world believe?*

While the gargantuan stones grew closer, the question replayed in Will's mind. The Lightborne took *The Veleriat* as fact, an ancient truth. Morella had, too. But the Seekers—or at least Cephora—had scoffed at the notion, hadn't she? *No, she only said that the Relics themselves were better to have remained lost. This whole world, they* knew *it was real, and yet they shied away from the Relics themselves. Why?*

"Rienne," Will said. "Why does Aeril deny the Relics of Antiquity?"

For a moment, she showed no sign of having heard him. Her footsteps didn't slow. She didn't glance in his direction or speak. But Will saw the way her expression faltered, saw the annoyance that briefly clouded her features. Finally, she spoke.

"Because they are fools."

A historian who is mocked for studying what is recognized as real history and a world of people who accept that history but deny that its traces linger. Now I start to see why Morella expected us to laugh at her when she told us her field. Maybe I didn't give her enough credit.

Rienne's irritation was gone by the time they reached the

stones. Now, she was nearly laughing. She raced ahead into a small crevice between the rocks and trailed her hands along the walls on either side like a child running through fields of tall wheat. Will couldn't help but smile at the sight; she might have grown cold toward him, but no part of him bore her any ill will. Already, he had seen cracks in her frosty exterior and he was hopeful that their friendship could be salvaged.

He followed her into the crevice, brushing his cloak back over his shoulders as he did so. He wanted quick access to his weapons, should the need arise. The gap was wide enough that he never had to squeeze through, but on multiple occasions he had to climb. Rienne was still ahead of him, he could just hear her, but it wasn't like there was anywhere for her to veer off the path.

After a few minutes, he finally caught a glimpse of her. They were deep within the forest of stone and Rienne had reached the end of the path. Or, at least, she had reached the end of the ground path. Will found her climbing a face of sheer rock, the barest hints of a goat path visible. He glanced up at the towering stone, stretching high into the air, higher than he had ever climbed freely before. Dahla appeared briefly, her wings arced as she circled.

So, up then. His fingers twitched nervously. He hadn't scaled anything since coming to Aeril, not since before his grandfather died. That day, the climb had rewarded him with truths and gifts. What might this climb bring?

He removed his gloves and reached for the humming key at his chest, wrapping a hand around it. *How much did you really know, Grandda? What did you intentionally leave out of the stories?*

There was no answer from the dead man, no answer from the strange voices that sometimes called to him or guided him. There was only the screeching bird and the climbing Lightborne who would barely look at him. *Fine then.*

Will began to climb.

9

THE ISLE OF ETERNITY

The climb was long and exhausting. Will, once so nimble and quick, found that his years in the desert fortress had robbed him of much of his previous vigor and dexterity. More than once, he nearly lost his footing or his grip and thought he was sure to fall to his death. Velier's gift, as the Aerillians called it, might extend life but did nothing against a violent end. He had no Shade to protect him this time, none of its restorative invigoration or protective strength. No, if he fell, he would die among the pillars of a myth and be quickly forgotten. The thought frightened him back into focusing.

Time slipped away. When he finally reached the top, shaking and exhausted, the daylight was waning and the air had grown cool. His fingers were bleeding and cramped, his back muscles tight and strained. He very much wanted nothing more than to pass out and sleep for a full day. Instead, he gripped his blood fangs and guided the smallest traces of power to his split hands, knitting the flesh back together and easing the pain.

Will sighed contentedly and flexed his hands. *Good as new.*

Rienne was not far away, sitting against a large boulder with her head resting on her arms. She, too, was the worse for wear. He considered offering her the power of the blood fangs, but remembering her previous reaction, he thought better of it. *She knows I've got them. If she wants it, she'll let me know.* He sheathed the fangs and drew his cloak back over them before calling out to her.

"Hey," he said tentatively as he approached. "You alright?"

She lifted her head and gave a weak smile, then nodded. "It didn't look quite so tall from the bottom."

Will chuckled. "No, it didn't."

"I've never done that before, nothing like that." She was shaking her head now, staring back at the ledge. "I don't know what came over me but I just . . . I didn't even question it. The trail ended, so I went up."

Will slid to the ground next to her, leaving enough space between them that he could stretch his arms out along the stone. "Discovering the myths you grew up on are grounded in reality is enough to make anyone do something crazy." He chuckled. "Trust me, I know."

She glanced over at him. "You've done this before?" She gestured around her. "Not, not *this,* but things like it?"

"I'm Casc, Rienne. I thought this whole damn world was a myth. A fun bedtime story from the overactive imagination of an old man."

She stared at him. "The Casc, they really don't know? Not about any of this?"

Will shook his head. "Not even the slightest. At least, none that I knew of. None that my grandfather ever spoke of. He closed the passage from the Ways and, unless people had gone before him, yeah, there was no one."

"What about the other Waygates?"

Waygates? The question lingered on the air a moment before Will answered. "What do you mean?"

"The other entrances to Cascania from the Ways. Did your grandfather close them all?"

"Other entrances?" Will shook his head. "No, there's only one to Cascania."

She rolled her eyes. "Come on, Noctis. There's never only one."

There's more? Somehow, Will had never considered this possibility. His grandfather always said he closed the Cascanian path; Will had just assumed that was all there was to it. Had he meant he'd closed them all? Had he even known there might have been more? *Of course, Grandda knew all about that stuff. Why else would he have stuck so close to the Tunnels?*

"There was just the one," he said definitively. "Grandda, he even stayed close to keep an eye on it."

"Ah, so the others haven't been found yet."

He opened his mouth to protest again that there was only the one, but stopped. He had no idea if that was true or not. Plus, Rienne was actually speaking to him again and he wasn't about to shut that down. "I suppose that must be it."

He rose to his feet and brushed himself off. Rienne glanced at him again and snickered. "You're looking spry. It's making me feel bad about myself."

"I had a bit of help." From the quick confusion and subsequent darkness that passed over her eyes, he knew that she understood.

"Ah. I see." She rose to her feet and stretched. When she spoke again, her voice was a cautious neutral. "We should go."

Will's spirits dampened. "You're right. We should."

There was another incline beyond where they had rested, but this one, at least, was more of a hike than another climb. Will was glad of that. Blood fangs or no, he was tired. There were strange spires off in the distance, thin and scraggly. When he drew nearer, Will realized they were the petrified remnants of white trees. The path leveled out and he and Rienne found themselves in an almost perfectly conserved forest of ancient wood where even the thinnest branches remained intact.

"It's beautiful," Will said, caressing the white wood.

"Yes." Rienne's voice was quiet. "This is a sacred place, Noctis. Do not harm it."

"I wouldn't ever—" he began to argue, but then paused when he met her eye. "Of course, Rienne. I'll tread carefully."

She led and Will followed, stepping cautiously and avoiding the low branches. Even in the absence of any foliage, the thin, dense covering of branches blocked much of the remaining warmth from the lowering sun. Will tugged his cloak a bit closer and drew his hood, regretting his shorn hair.

The trees stretched taller and taller the deeper they went. Soon, the sun was almost completely hidden. A low, creeping darkness overtook the ancient forest and Will felt himself recoiling. He had grown so used to a world of luminescent stone that the absence of it was abrasive. On and on the forest stretched in shadow. When they had first seen the stones, it had been impossible to gauge their magnitude. But now? The scope of it all boggled Will's mind. *The final pieces of the Isle of Eternity. Velier walked this very forest.*

"Noctis."

Will snapped his focus to Rienne. Her Flare was up; he could see the trickle of lightning along her arms, but she had not drawn her weapon. In a second, he matched her and approached, the crackling warmth of the Flare sending a shiver down his spine. Ahead, the forest thinned and opened into a small clearing. Rienne stood at its edge. Within the clearing slept a massive beast. At first, Will thought it was a bear, a grizzly perhaps, given its size. But that wasn't it; it had the tusks of a boar and its shoulders were too square.

"What the hell is that?" he whispered, his hand reaching for his sword. *Why the hell didn't I pick a longer weapon?*

"A bristen," she replied. "I don't know how, but it has to be."

Will had no idea what the hell a bristen was, but he had no doubts that if the creature got close enough to him, there was little he could do to stop it. Something about the thing looked like it would just brush off an attack, be it blade or flame. "I vote we find a path around the bristen."

Rienne said nothing. Instead, she stepped forward, into the clearing.

"Rienne!" Will hissed. "Dammit, Rienne, don't!"

She ignored him and approached the creature slowly. Terror flowed into Will. He cursed and threw back his cloak, drawing his cutlass and a blood fang. *I don't care what kind of pain she feels from its power, if that damn thing mauls her, I'm not letting her die.* He ran for her, bursting into the clearing and blazing his Flare to a crackling roar.

Neither Rienne nor the bristen reacted in the slightest. Will raised his sword defensively and approached slowly, drawing back his Flare. He got within ten feet of them before he let it fade altogether and sheathed his weapons. His eyes fell from the creature to Rienne's frozen form.

She sat immobile, brimming eyes fixed on the beast. Her hand rested on the dead animal. No decay had come to it, although it surely had to have been as old as the woods through which they had just come. Instead, it, too, had somehow petrified, immune to the ravages of time.

"Even in myth, they were a myth," she whispered with a quivering voice. "Protectors of the Gardens of the Moon. They're not"—she closed her eyes as she searched for the words—"they're not supposed to be here, Noctis. The Hesperawn themselves may as well appear."

Will said nothing, having no idea what words could offer any comfort. *Sometimes, silence is all the comfort one can offer.*

He knelt next to Rienne and admired the beast, beautiful in its own way. Its eyes were closed, massive head resting upon clawed feet the size of Will's chest, like a sleeping dog. *A being from the bedtime stories of my bedtime stories. How far does it all go?* He remembered what Cephora had said of the bogeyman, about Casc legends being truer than he'd thought. *Aeril,* The Veleriat, *now this? Will we find that all stories are rooted in some truth?*

Rienne rose to her feet a short time later, eyes now dry. "We should keep moving. Dahla is still nearby, somewhere."

Wordlessly, Will rose and followed. He felt out of place, a trespasser witnessing things he should not have seen, things that did not belong to him. *This place isn't mine.* And yet, even that felt wrong. It wasn't his, but neither was it Rienne's. Nor was it din'-Dael's nor Cephora's nor the Crow's. This was a place for those who came before them, for those who transcended written history. *Morella would have loved it here.*

They exited the clearing and passed through another small grove of trees. On the far side they found Dahla in the branches of a tree that stretched above a shallow, dried pool. This tree still bore all its leaves. There was no single color but countless, more colors than Will had dreamed possible. Time had frozen them all into glass. With the final hints of sunlight pouring through the branches, the entire area was alight in brilliant, dancing colors.

Dahla ruffled her feathers and spread her wings at the sight of them before cocking her head and tracking their approach. In a reverent silence, Rienne and Will crossed the narrow stone walk that spanned the dry pool. Empty or not, it did not feel right to walk through its stony bed. There was a small hollow at the base of the tree. It looked empty, but as they knelt to peer inside, something caught Will's eye. Carved into the tree's trunk just next to the hollow were the letters V, L, and R.

"Gods," he gasped. "Rienne . . . are you seeing this?"

She nodded. "I see it." Her voice was a whisper.

Will traced the carved letters with his fingers, his face streaked by tears he could barely feel. He tore his eyes from the letters and looked up at Dahla. The bird met his stare, and for the first time, Will felt something there, a connection. Then she was gone, flying into the fading light.

Rienne laid one hand on the tree, her eyes fixed on the hollow. She reached out with her other hand and clasped Will's fingers. Will said nothing, not needing to ask why. He knew it just as well as she did. Dahla had guided them to the former home of the Heart of Eternity.

THEY CAMPED BENEATH THE TREE OF GLASS, CAREFUL NOT TO disturb their surroundings. The morning held a still silence, but not one of malice. Whatever tension had existed between the two had, while not completely faded, at least dimmed. They broke camp, mechanically going through the motions, each of them breathing in the memory of the place. Will wrestled with his thoughts, glancing at Rienne periodically to try and gauge her. He still didn't know how to say what he wanted to, or even if he should.

Before leaving the small pool, they stood once more by the tree with glass leaves. Rienne knelt and whispered a faint "Thank you" that Will barely heard, before kissing her forefingers and pressing them against the carved letters. She rose and the pair looked through the glass canopy, marveling at the beauty.

"I'm sorry, Rienne. I never meant to hurt you."

She stiffened at his side but said nothing.

Will did not look at her. "I followed Jero din'Dael to the Sapholux because I needed his help. My brother, Madigan, and I, we rescued din'Dael from the Shale. I . . . we killed them. All of them. Before that, though, din'Dael did something to me to make me this way." He paused and turned to her. "I was never meant to be this, Rienne. Jero din'Dael twisted what I was, somehow. I don't know what he did. Lightborne . . . I never . . ." He trailed off, searching for the words.

"What, Noctis? Just say it."

"I'm Shadowborne."

He expected her to laugh or to snicker, to disregard it entirely. She did none of them. "Show me."

Something inside him ached. He sighed. "I can't." He saw doubt creep into her eyes so he hurried on. "That's what I meant about following din'Dael. Before I freed him, Madigan and I, both of us were Shadowborne. My Shade . . . I was twelve when I first found out about it, but my grandfather, he already knew. I trained for years to hide it. That was all he could teach me about it, and we came to Aeril to learn more. Everything that happened after that has just been one big stream of cause and effect, and din'Dael, whatever he did, I needed him to undo it. I wanted to go back to what I was."

She considered him a moment then dropped her eyes to his belt. "The blood fangs, they cause you no pain?" He shook his head. "Never?"

"No. Well, not unless we're talking about the blade's toxin. That hurts like a bitch."

Rienne nearly cracked a smile. "And Jero din'Dael, he knows?" Will shook his head. "No one knows?"

"Only my brother. And the Crow. He and the people in his court knew, but they kept quiet. As far as I know, they think I still am, if they think of me at all."

Rienne studied his face. "I want to believe you, Noctis. But no creature is both. Maybe something in forgotten legend, perhaps, but you are human and not something from the ancient world."

"I know," Will said with a sigh. "I know that's the way things are supposed to be, but, Rienne, I'm telling you the truth."

"How?"

Will raised an eyebrow. "What do you mean?"

"If it is true, how did din'Dael change you?"

"I don't know. I broke him out of his containment, he killed a bunch of Shale, and then I made some glib remark."

This time, she did smile. “Of course you did.”

“Then he put his palm on my forehead and gripped my hair in his other hand and just . . . I don’t know what he did but goddam it hurt. It felt like he was carving me from the inside out with a blade of pure fire.”

She chuckled. “Oh, yes, not in the least bit dramatic, are you?”

“I’m serious.” Will felt suddenly embarrassed. He met her eyes, imploring her, but had to turn away. “I mean, I don’t know, Rienne. Look around us. What about this is normal? What about any of this is expected? This carving, that—what did you call it—that bristen? Maybe that damn bird brought us here so we could believe in the impossible for one damn day.”

“You think Dahla brought us here so you could convince me you’re actually Shadowborne?” Rienne was still smiling. “She’s a smart creature, Noctis, but I doubt that was her intention.”

Will felt defeated. He’d finally told someone about being Shadowborne and she’d brushed it aside. He’d never even told Morella. *I could have shown her. She saw me after the change. Dammit, Mad, why didn’t I tell her?* “We should go.”

“The blood fangs truly don’t harm you? Not at all?”

“Not at all,” Will said solemnly.

“Well, maybe there is something to what you’re saying,” Rienne replied with a shrug. There was no levity in her voice, nothing to suggest she was anything but genuine. “I’m not saying I believe you, Noctis, but I suppose I’m not saying I don’t believe you either. Either way, apology accepted.”

Will’s spirits lifted considerably. He smiled at her and stuck out his hand. “Friends, then?”

Rienne returned the smile and grasped his outstretched arm. “Friends.”

10
ANCIENT ARTS

Madigan was finally healing. The past few weeks had been the worst he could remember, worse than anything growing up with Will and Grandda had ever been, by far. Hell, they'd been worse than the final hours of the Shale. Then, at least, he'd had Will nearby with his blood fangs. Every bit of his battered, broken body was able to be put back together just like *that,* no problem. He never imagined that simple training could be worse than the Shale.

He managed to sit up, shivering despite the pile of blankets Ileta had supplied. Much as it pained him to admit it, the shaking had nothing to do with the cold. He hated to acknowledge that simply *sitting up* was such a struggle. *Just need to hold it a few seconds. Just a few.* He grit his teeth.

A noise sounded just outside the tent and his eyes snapped to the entrance. He held his breath. The flaps didn't move. *Just the wind. Good.*

Ileta would give him hell if she came in and found him like this. For all his trainer's severe demeanor, she was actually a remarkably gentle caretaker. That being said, if she caught Mad doing anything beyond lying prone, well . . . *I don't exactly feel like being strapped down.*

Sweat trickled down his brow. He inhaled sharply at the flare of pain in his back. That only set his cracked ribs off even more and he winced, letting the pain wash over him. *No point fighting it. It'll run its course and be done with you long before you're done with it.*

He flexed the fingers of his left hand. *At least they're responding.* They still looked foreign, wrapped so tightly in his quivering Shade. Despite the weeks in this quasi-cocooned state, he still hadn't gotten used to seeing his body through the thin fog of darkness.

Regardless of his fevered thoughts on the matter of its necessity, he appreciated the technique. Ileta had shown him how to manipulate his Shade in such a matter well before the fall, but only for more minor injuries. That the ability seemed to be working at all like this was, well . . . *A goddam miracle.* Hell, the fact that he was even alive spoke to its credit. *She may be a harsh teacher, but her lessons certainly serve their purpose.*

It had been his fault, really. He'd been angry and overzealous, like he was a goddam kid again and Will had gotten the best of him. At least then he'd been able to use his size and strength to his advantage, overpowering his little brother. Now? With a Shade handy? Hell, he'd never thought Ileta would stand a chance against him.

Obviously, he hadn't been thinking rationally.

He wiggled his toes and, thankfully, found them responsive too. That hadn't been the case a week ago. After he'd first regained consciousness he'd been terrified that he might never walk again. Ileta hadn't commented one way or the other, but the look on her face put a panic in his bones he was unlikely to ever forget.

For the first three weeks, it hadn't looked good. Mad still

didn't know which part of his spine had broken, and damned if he had any experience with magically assisted healing (beyond Will's damn knives, of course). He'd never been *that* jealous of the kid's knives before; he always preferred the noctori, by far. But after the fall? *Never around when I need you, kid. Though you'd probably never let me live it down.*

Mad eased back so the pillows again supported all his weight and stared at the ceiling of the tent. Damn but he wished he could have seen the fight. A video camera, man, what that could do for his training. The bout had been a good one, he was sure of that. Ileta was a fantastic swordsman and her skill with her Shade far surpassed his own, but the Master of Blades had not trained her. He had trained Mad, though, and that day? Damn, he'd felt it in every fiber of his body.

Ileta, though, she'd been patient.

He glanced around at the blank walls of his tent and tried to make sense of the time of day. Ileta'd done an amazing job of sealing the place so no cool breezes drafted in, but it also made figuring out the time nearly impossible. *A watch. A watch and a video camera.* His stomach growled. She'd be back soon enough, he was sure of it. With food. Bone broth, more than likely. His stomach growled again. *A watch and a video camera and some goddam tacos.*

His noctori had been a whirlwind against her own. Earning it back, finally, had been fantastic. Mad had felt the thrill of the win and he wanted more. With his noctori in his hands, Ileta had been failing to put up any successful offense. Their Shades collided and darted this way and that, his unconscious mind probing at her defenses, striking at her legs, her eyes, anything he could while maintaining his own defense. The two were at a near stalemate in that regard, but when it came to the noctori, damn, Madigan had the advantage.

He felt the win. He *felt* it. He had seen every possible defense she could throw, every possible maneuver she could make, and he'd *known* that he was going to take her down. And Ileta, she was pressed so hard, was so focused on her defenses that she'd lost track of her surroundings. She hadn't realized that the edge of the cliff was right behind her until it was too late. And when her situation dawned on her, Madigan saw the briefest flicker of an opening while she gauged her counterattack. He seized the moment and struck.

Which, of course, was what Ileta had been planning the whole time.

Madigan raised a shaky hand to the bandage around his head. Shade or no Shade, Ileta insisted that he keep his head wrapped. Apparently, the sight of his split skull was bad enough that she didn't trust only magical properties to fix it. The bandage was still tight, which was good. It meant that he still wasn't moving around in his sleep. The worst of the headaches had faded a few days before he realized he could move his toes, but he was reluctant to mess with the wrap. There was a latent throbbing that stuck around. *Head injuries are nothing to rush,* she'd told him. *There are some important bits of you up there—if you'd ever care to use them.*

Ileta's noctori had taken him just behind his left ear. Well, not fully behind it. When she told him, he'd asked her the stupidest goddam question: *Will it grow back?* Gods, but he'd felt like an idiot. The Shade helped heal things, but it didn't turn him into a goddam lizard who could regrow his own goddam body parts. Still, she'd been patient with him. *I'll just tell the world it's a dueling scar, like one of those people from those old fencing clubs.*

The strike should have ended the match right then and he would have been on his ass for a few days, no doubt, but even as he was losing consciousness, he'd held on. That stupid, idiotic stubbornness and rage had kept him on his feet long enough to whirl in a wild, entirely out-of-form strike. He'd missed by a mile, of course, and as he faded into unconsciousness, felt the earth leave him behind.

There was no part of him that doubted Ileta had done everything in her power to save him. She seemed particularly passionate about that point, promising him that she made every effort to catch him. But his wild strike had put her too far off to reach him in time. She had, however, been kind enough to watch while his unconscious form slammed into the side of the cliff and then bounced and rolled over and over as it smashed into what must have been every goddam rock and root on the way down.

He actually didn't mind that he'd been unconscious for that bit.

She didn't blame herself, of course, which was for the best (not just because it wasn't *really* her fault) but also because Madigan insisted that she didn't. Not that it wouldn't have been nice to have her express a little sympathy, or some regret, or, you know, any sense of ownership of the damn situation. Still, he refused to get worked up about it. He didn't want to deal with the trolling headache that frustration brought with it.

Broken ribs, broken back, broken arms, broken fingers, broken skull. Oh, and of course a goddam severed half an ear. Yeah, waking up to all that had been fun.

At least I did wake up. Ileta seemed pretty certain for a bit there that that may have been out of the cards. She hadn't said as much, but that damn look in her eyes when she told him what happened said enough. And there had been something else about the way she said it, too. She seemed almost relieved when she thought he wasn't going to make it. *One less boneheaded trainee to deal with, I guess.*

Still, she'd been great ever since. She helped him with all the embarrassing things he didn't want to acknowledge. *Don't lie to yourself, Mad. She did all the damn work. You just lay there while she took care of you.* She never commented, though, never made any jokes or disparaging remarks whenever his body had gotten away from him and tears ran down his face. He appreciated that. She was good, his teacher.

Mad glanced down and wiggled his toes again, first one foot, then the other. He smiled. It was silly, he supposed, to be so excited about such a little thing, but each day still felt like the whole damn situation could be hit or miss, despite Ileta's assurances of his full recovery. Maybe, just maybe in a few days he would try to bend his knees on his own, just to see if he could. The thought alone made him dizzy, but he wanted to get better and he wanted it fast. *I need to get back out there. I need to find Will.*

She didn't say so, but he knew Ileta believed him about Will surviving the encounter with Valmont. She was a bit cool when it came to Will—she had been ever since he'd met her—although he had no idea why. *She's got her secrets and I've got mine and we're both fine with that.*

Still, family would be nice right now. No matter how much time he and Ileta spent together, she kept him at arm's length. *Because you're her student, idiot. You're not her blood. It's not like you've got Grandda tending to you.*

He heard her rummaging through their camp and felt a great tension release. Apparently, he was hungrier than he thought. That or . . . or yes, he had to admit that he still feared she would up and leave. Disappear without a trace and let him just lie here until . . . he didn't want to think about that. *She's had no real reason to stick around, but she has. She's not going anywhere.* He told himself that every day, but he never quite convinced himself.

He'd be dead without her, that much was certain. Hell, he would have been dead the day of the accident. *And not one goddam person would have known.* The thought terrified him; no one knew where he was, not Will, not Cephora, not a single person. If he had died on his own, he would have been just another one of the lost; here one day, vanished the next. That scared him almost as much as anything else. He never wanted Will to have to go through anything like that, to never have that uncertainty. *Assuming he doesn't already.*

A familiar anger burned in his gut. He knew, *knew,* that Will had escaped Valmont. But that meant Will was somewhere out there in a situation just like his own, with unfamiliar people doing gods knew what. And the worst part was, Will saw Cephora take him. He'd seen the look on Will's face, had seen the confusion and despair. That look would haunt him for the rest of his life. *And Will doesn't even know I'm okay. He just saw the damn earth swallow me up, that's it.*

That was what drove Mad's anger the most: the abandonment. Cephora had taken the decision from him and removed all autonomy from him in doing so. In a random location, in a random part of the Daurhi Wastes, the damn Seeker had been his only chance of surviving. It hadn't been a choice to stay with her, not a real one. But if Will had been with him, they could have figured something out. *Hell, we wouldn't have needed to. Cephora could have saved both of us. She should have.*

But that was done. Ileta had come along and he'd said goodbye to the damn Seekers and now he was fine. His eyes dropped down to his broken body. *Well, fine enough, all things considered.* He'd heal. He'd get back on his feet. He always did.

The thought of getting back on his feet inevitably led down the rabbit hole of what to do *after* he got back on his feet. It wasn't that his training with Ileta wasn't going well, not by a long shot, but he wanted more. He should be *doing* more, not just be hidden away training in a power that very few people seemed to care about. *All so I can go after a madman that everyone thought was dead.*

His grandfather had planned for Madigan to build alliances between the factions of Aeril, to be a bridge to lasting peace. He'd been groomed for command, groomed for leadership, strange as that still sounded. He wasn't supposed to be the one tucked away in training. *No offense, Will, but you should really be the one lying here.*

That brought a painful chuckle. He could scarcely imagine Will having the patience to lie in bed in a goddam tent for weeks on end without going absolutely insane. Hell, Ileta probably would have left him for dead, and if she hadn't done so initially, the weeks of listening to Will's incessant questions and griping would have driven her away, no doubt. *That, or he'd have avoided the situation entirely.* The damn kid's Shade always had been quicker than Mad could understand. When he'd had a Shade, that is.

The chuckle faded. *Wonder what the hell he's doing right now, anyway?* Had Jero din'Dael returned them to the Nordoth? The Seekers hadn't heard anything in the months following the Shale, but that didn't mean they hadn't returned there since. Just because no one had heard anything from Will or din'Dael didn't mean they hadn't made it away from Valmont. *Of course they made it out. So, Will, what the hell are you doing? Where the hell are you?*

He pictured his brother driving din'Dael insane—well, even more insane—with his constant barrage of questions. Mad could only imagine that after din'Dael attacked Will (or whatever the hell that had been) and destroyed his Shade, Will had clawed everything he could out of the Lightborne as to what he'd done. Knowing Will, din'Dael probably fixed it, undone whatever he'd done, almost immediately, especially if they'd been alone together. So, Will then would do what? *Probably exactly what we talked about.*

The Relics, then. If Will had fixed everything, he was on the trail of the Relics and keeping a low profile about it. *That's why the Seekers hadn't heard anything about them returning together. Will was staying under the radar.* Just like Madigan had told him to.

Force of habit sent Mad's hands reaching to run through his hair and he winced. He slowed down and breathed through the pain. He settled for scratching the beard that had grown during his weeks of inactivity. Apparently, Ileta's attentions to body care and cleanliness did not extend as far as keeping him clean shaven. The growth still itched; he could only imagine how he looked. *Hair too long and a beard and living in a tent? Probably like a damn hippy.*

He looked back down at his toes and wiggled them again. Then he tried rolling his ankles. They rolled without nearly as much pain as he expected. *Already better than yesterday. Far better.* Taking a deep breath, he pushed himself back up so he was nearly sitting. Steeling himself, he tried bending his right knee. The blanket moved. Not much, barely at all, but movement nonetheless. His heart began a rapid percussion and a grin spread across his face. *I'll be back on my feet in no time. No time at all.*

Ileta's shadowy form appeared outside the tent a moment before the flap opened. She entered carrying a steaming bowl filled to the brim and a small pitcher of water. She raised an eyebrow at him and Madigan realized he must still have that stupid grin plastered on his face.

"Sitting up and smiling?" she said as she brought the broth over. "Have you been playing me for a fool this whole time?"

"I wish." Mad's voice still sounded weak and hoarse, but at least speaking didn't hurt the way it had two weeks prior.

Ileta gave a small "hmph" then sat on the stool next to Madigan's cot. She set the bowl on the small table next to it and took in the sight of him with the same scrutinizing gaze that analyzed his every movement in the field. "Another week. Then we return to training."

Yesterday she said it would be at least two. Madigan smiled again. "Another week then."

She took the bowl and a spoon and leaned over him. The broth smelled fantastic, like something his grandfather would have made when Mad was sick as a kid. "Ileta," he said after swallowing the first savory bite, "when we do get back to training, I've got a request."

Ileta sighed and dipped the spoon once more, then raised a questioning eyebrow at him. “Only one? Somehow I doubt that.”

Madigan nodded, a motion he’d only just discovered he could still manage. “One.”

She set the spoon back in the bowl and gave him a patient stare. “What?”

“Day one,” he said with a grin, “I want to go back up that damn cliff. I’ve got a bone to pick with it.”

11

UNDERMYRE

The last time he stood in this very spot, Will had been facing the opposite direction. He'd been with Madigan and Cephora, the Undermyrian gates at his back and the whole of Aeril stretched out before him. There had been excitement and hope, a thrill of adventure, of walking into a storybook. There had been a naive promise in his head, his own heroic journey.

That had been before. Before the Sapholux and Jero din'Dael. Before the Shale. Before Dorian Valmont. Before Morella Darklore.

Well, not entirely before Morella, he mused, remembering their brief first interaction. A drink. A dance. A laugh. A kiss. It was a bittersweet memory now, overshadowed by her screams of fear when the undead Necrothanian horde surrounded her. *One more death to make Valmont pay for.*

The Undermyrian gates had been fortified since his last visit, hard as that was for him to believe. From what he had seen, the city was nigh impregnable with its double walls and peninsular terrain. The citadel of the Nordoth, then, carved into the very mountain around which Undermyre had been built, was an impossibility beyond that. Even in the event of a potential siege, an attacking force would have no way of cutting off supplies from the sea. It was no wonder din'Dael wanted to house the Lightborne there.

All he wants is for them—for us—to survive. Was he doing the man a disservice by believing there was more to it than that? He shook his head slightly. *Things are never so cut and dry here.*

A steady stream of foot traffic came and went through the gates. The soldiers guarding them paid little heed to who passed through. *Seems lax given the step up in defenses.*

Will thumbed the blood fangs, replenished during his last few weeks of solo travel. His training in the Sapholux had prepared him well for hard living and he'd borne it without too much complaint. After all, who could he have complained to? He'd said a fond goodbye to Rienne weeks ago, tipped his nonexistent hat to Dahla, and set out for Undermyre. Now, well, now he needed to figure out how to accomplish the next bit.

Will passed through the gates without issue and found himself surrounded by civilization. He was not ready for it, not after so long. The commotion, the noise, the smell; he reeled from all of them. He stumbled into a nearby woman who batted large, perplexed eyes at him. Will fumbled an apology and turned away, only to walk right into a short man and nearly knock him to the ground. Hand shooting out, he caught the man and steadied him and prepared for a verbal rebuke. But the man just adjusted his billowing scarf and barely even looked in his direction.

I'm like a goddam tourist. He stepped off the main drag and leaned against a building. Even with his suddenly overwhelmed senses, he realized that he had no actual idea how to navigate Undermyre. The month in the city on his first visit had been spent cooped up entirely within the Nordoth, his only outing on the day he and Madigan left with Cephora. Even that had been a straightforward path, venturing straight to the establishment with that phenomenal drink.

Ash something . . . He searched his memory. That was it, the Street of Ash.

It suddenly occurred to him how disheveled he must appear after weeks on the road. If he could find his way to the Street, he could find at least a semi-familiar place to get his bearings, collect his thoughts before going to the Nordoth and the inevitably frustrating meeting with the Crow. *A place to clean up, take a minute.* He nodded to himself. *Good idea.* His heart calmed its frantic pace a bit at the prospect of getting away from the crowds. *Now, it's just a matter of finding the damn place.*

He shied away from the Undermyrian citizens. An echo of an old conversation with Madigan was playing in his brain: *They try to cut out whatever makes you you, and they sew it into their clothes.* He eyed their clothing as he passed, suddenly wary. Yes, there was lots of leather, but surely that was just coincidence? Leather was, after all, exceedingly common for clothes. And Madigan's book hadn't said anything about the general populace, just outliers, right? He glanced about, drew his hood, and walked with his head down.

All the research that Mad had done in the Nordoth, hell, everything Will ever heard from his grandfather, had all been about the Aerillian people's reactions to Shadowborne. *Nothing about Lightborne, not one mention of superstition.* Did that mean the Lightborne were exempt from whatever superstitions this world held? Or was it simply that they were thought extinct? Will didn't have any idea, and he had no intention of finding out. *Just keep a low profile. Keep my head down and fly beneath the radar.*

He wandered the streets for a time, avoiding the main thoroughfares as much as possible. The city seemed more crowded than before. Had the surrounding peoples congregated in the city due to the threat of Valmont? Did they even know that Valmont was back?

He halted, suddenly aware of how little information he had. *Everything Grandda taught me, keeping my head and collecting data, I've neglected it all.* Three years was what he'd estimated he'd spent in the Sapholux, give or take, not that the world of Aeril gave that any thought. Three years of hiding away to train while the rest of Aeril moved on.

Has it, though? He took a deep breath, forcing himself to push down the strange agoraphobia and to pay attention. There was no urgency about the people around him, no apparent stress. But would the threat of attack really change anything for them? Everyone who surrounded him held the same simultaneous aloofness and attentiveness that he remembered. *What do you do with an eternity? How does the mind cope with that?*

He shook his head. *Focus, Will.* He traced his steps back to the main gate. Before, they had stayed the night at the Street of Ash and then left through this very gate, he remembered that much. And he remembered that the Street had been within an easy fifteen minutes' walk. If he could find that same route, he could get back there. *Something will come from it, I'm sure.*

A stairway on a nearby building offered a slightly higher vantage point. Will made for it and climbed. Surveying the nearby rooftops, he saw a lantern in the distance, illuminating a red banner beneath. Something about it triggered a flash of the Street's interior in his mind's eye. *That's gotta be it.*

He raced down the stair, making sure his hood was pulled forward as far as it would go, then made for the vibrant banner. Now that he knew where to look, he saw the fringe of its crimson coloring flapping in the wind above the buildings in stark contrast against the surrounding grey and brown of the decayed city. His heart fluttered as he drew nearer and sounds of music began to emerge. It crescendoed briefly when a couple opened the establishment's door and stumbled into the street, laughing and dancing. Will smiled; he had found it.

Standing before the double doors, a wave of uncertainty took him. *What if Morella is inside?* His mouth dried at the thought, its moisture suddenly appearing in his palms. He wiped the sweat on his pants and berated himself. Of course Morella wasn't inside. Morella was dead, more than likely. And if by some miracle she had managed to escape Valmont, then why the hell would she just happen to be sitting in the Street of Ash? *It's been three years, Will. You think she's just sitting around waiting for you? Get your head out of your ass.*

The momentary excitement was rapidly replaced by longing and nostalgia. Resigning himself to the way the world was, and not what he'd wished it would be, Will pressed open the doors and walked into the Street.

He was immediately beset by the roar of applause and boisterous music. The scent of woodsmoke mixed with light perfume lingered in the air and beneath it all, something he couldn't place, something that only deepened his sense of longing. There were more curtains to pass through than there had been before, and when he at last stepped through the final barrier, he could not help the sad smile that crept to his face.

The Street was alive. Whereas during his previous visit he had only witnessed Morella on the dance floor, this time it was bursting at the seams. The floating lanterns spun and twisted, casting their yellow light amidst the flurry of crimson curtains, making the whole room seem alive in fire. The boisterous joviality, the pure life breathing within the walls as people cheered and clapped and spun sent Will's head spinning. The agoraphobia vanished. Tears crept into his eyes. *This is life,* he realized as he watched, *not a world of war and battle. Not the militant Sapholux. This is what life should be.*

It was too much to take in. After so long with the isolated Lightborne, Will's senses were overwhelmed. Before he knew it, he was stumbling back through the curtains and out into the cool air of the Aerillian sky. His heart was pounding as he sucked in air. He threw back his hood and wiped the unfallen tears from his eyes. He locked his fingers behind his head and stared up at the amber sky. *What the hell is going on with me?*

Stepping away from the entrance, Will closed his eyes and concentrated on his breath. It took longer than he could believe, but eventually his heart rate returned to normal. *An anxiety attack? That's a first. Hopefully the last, too.*

He shook his head to clear it. Suddenly, the stoic Nordoth held more appeal than the vibrant Street. Will set his sights on the towering monolith, its ever-present gaze fixed upon the city below. *To the Crow, then.*

He drew his hood and glanced around, seeing no apparent path. It was there, he knew. He'd find it. Trusting his instincts and faded memories to guide him, Will set off.

Escorted by four guards, Will was led into a familiar dark chamber. If any of his escort had been among those he met on his last visit, none let it show. In any event, none seemed to recognize him. They fell a few steps behind and allowed Will to approach the central dais of the audience chamber. The flames were low at his side, but he noticed how the guards positioned themselves so he would have to pass through the fire should he wish to flee. *Wouldn't that be a sight to see,* he smirked to himself.

Within the shadowed chair that overlooked the room sat a tall, narrow-faced woman. Her robes were identical to those worn by the seneschal that had so cruelly handled Will and Mad. *A new appointee, perhaps?* Will eyed the woman. *Maybe the wounds Mad inflicted upon the bastard were worse than the Crow let on.*

The woman sat patiently, her face impassive and calm. A runner approached and handed her a small sheet of paper while whispering in her ear. The woman's eyes never left Will's. There was something in them that reminded him of the Crow's unnerving gaze, but he refused to waver. He stood silently, in no mood for the political games of the Crow's court. *A world without kings,* din'Dael had told him, *that had been their intent. But rather than rule themselves, the people appointed their strongest warlords to rule them. How was that any different, William?*

Will actually found himself amused by the whole spectacle, the theatricality of it all. He had seen the chamber illuminated, knew of its sprawling grandeur. Despite the seemingly narrow confines of the space he and this new seneschal shared, he knew that the eyes of a hundred guards and retainers were on him, hidden by the shadows. *The shadows that move on command. Is the Crow himself Borne? Is his Shade so expansive that he can fill and control this whole room?*

The thought was disconcerting. It would certainly explain how the man had amassed so much power if Will's own ability—*former* ability—had been deemed impressive. If the Crow was Borne by Shadow, how would he react to Will's unexplainable transition to Radiance?

For the first time, Will considered that here, within the Nordoth, he might finally find some answers.

"You have returned to us, I see," the seneschal spoke at last. Will straightened and returned his full attention to the woman. Her voice was controlled, revealing nothing of her intentions.

"I have," he responded, inclining his head slightly as he did so. "My apologies, I do not recall your face from my previous visit to these halls." The words sounded forced and overly formal, but the seneschal smiled faintly. *Maybe this introduction will be more pleasant than my last.*

"Your own face has changed much, William Davis."

"Thorne," Will said. *Might as well play the hand that Jero dealt me, see where it goes.* "Noctis Thorne."

A calm silence stretched between them. The seneschal cocked her head and raised an eyebrow. A moment later, she nodded her head and gestured to someone unseen. "Very well. Please amend the records to make note of this development." She returned her attention to Will. "Noctis Thorne, then. What brings you to the Nordoth on this occasion?"

Much more polite than her predecessor, Will mused. *How much else has changed?* He brushed the thought away. It didn't matter; more changes were coming. "I have come for an audience with the Crow."

"Yes, I would have expected as much." She steepled her hands, looking very much like the man she represented. "You understand that the Crow is a very busy man, of course. You may trust me to treat with you in this matter. Surely you understand."

Will glanced quickly around at the surrounding shadows before peering into the distant blackness beyond the seneschal's seat. *They're not making this easy, are they?* He sighed. *Well, might as well keep up with my tradition of making an entrance here.*

"Very well"—he paused for effect and stood just a little straighter, rapidly rehearsing the speech he'd prepared—"I come on behalf of Jero din'Dael as representative for the Halls of Light, bearing word from the Revenant of the Sapholux. He seeks an alliance with the Nordoth for the defense of the realm against the forces of Dorian Valmont and the Necrothanian plague that is assaulting the lands of Aeril."

He'd had weeks to think of the words and yet, once they left his lips, they did not seem to effectively communicate what he sought. The seneschal did not appear moved in the slightest.

"If Jero din'Dael seeks an alliance with the Crow, why has he not come himself?" The seneschal raised a questioning brow. "I mean no offense, young Master Thorne, but why do you act as proxy when it would have been just as easy, and more compelling, for the Revenant to act?"

Will smiled. *Time to rock the boat.* "Because Jero din'Dael is preparing the Blades of Light and the armies of Sapholux to march for Undermyre."

A hush fell over those present. To her credit, initially the seneschal showed no reaction. In fact, if anything, she seemed amused. *Either she doesn't believe me or she already knew.* He studied her face. *Or she is just exceptionally good at her job.*

"I trust," she said after a moment, "that should they choose to march upon this city, they do so with more decorum than the last time they set out in force?"

Will smiled and thumbed the bloodstones of a fang. "I believe that all depends on how these negotiations proceed."

Just as it had before, the darkness of the room lifted as though a curtain had been drawn. Blinding light flooded into the hall, but Will did not recoil from the sudden brilliance. Whereas on his previous visit, the room had been filled with people and soldiers, now he could see only the guards who had escorted him in, the seneschal, and just beyond her, the dark stooped figure of the Crow. He leaned forward in his chair, hands steepled, dark features set in grim lines. His eyes bore into Will.

"Master *Thorne*," the dark man spoke. "It appears that we are due for another conversation."

12
A BARGAIN STRUCK

A quiet chuckle, nearly a scoff, rolled out from the Crow. It echoed through the quiet of the empty hall in an unnerving, otherworldly hum. The seneschal stood and moved away wordlessly. The Crow's eyes were fixed on Will, a too-wide smile on his face. Will cracked his neck and waited. The Crow eyed him a moment longer, then rose with difficulty, bracing himself on the chair. He beckoned Will forward—a short, sharp gesture—and turned on his heel. Will smiled and strode toward the back of the room. *So far, so good.*

The darkness of the Crow's private office was a stark contrast to the wash of light from the hall. Will blinked and rubbed his eyes, willing them to adjust. The office had not changed. There were still the walls of books, the neatly organized tables and desks. The measure still stood sentinel against the wall, but something about it caught Will's eye.

He moved closer, feeling his key spring to life against his chest. Intrigued, he watched as the face of the measure swirled, the bright contents within churning upon themselves. The dark smoke had expanded into the face while the lighter smoke had grown more vibrant, nearly sparkling. The two were mixing. Will smiled at the beautiful transformation. *Someday, I want one of these.*

Wordlessly, the Crow made for the ever-present decanter of wine and poured. When he turned back, Will was disappointed to see that the man held only a single glass in his spindly hands. He cursed inwardly. A drink would have been nice. He was thirsty. Truly thirsty. *I should have stayed at the Street. What the hell came over me?*

The Crow slouched into his seat unceremoniously and eyed Will. "You do make an entrance . . . Noctis, is it now?" He let out a scoffing snort. "Indeed, it seems that with you, there is never a lack of—how shall we say it—developments, as it were."

Will turned back to him. "Somehow I doubt my words came as any surprise to you, Crow."

The Crow raised an eyebrow. "Is that so?"

"Jero din'Dael." Will punched his way through the name, forcing every word to stand out. The Crow's expression did not change. "You sent my brother and me on a suicide mission to the Shale to free him. Why?"

The Crow smiled. "A suicide mission, you say?"

"We barely survived."

"So, *not* a suicide mission, then."

Will's blood boiled and he felt a fierce tension in his jaw. He hadn't expected this sudden rush of angry frustration. *This man orchestrated everything that has happened in the past three years.* He folded his arms and eyed the dark man. "I ask again. Why?"

The Crow's smile faded and he set his glass down on the table. "Your penchant for questions has not changed, young man."

"Nor has my intolerance when it comes to people who try to harm me or my brother."

"Your brother, yes." The Crow's humorless smile returned. "And how is Madigan, then? I must say, I am surprised that he is not accompanying you."

Will's stomach twisted. *So, Mad isn't here.* Where was he then? A dark thought crossed Will's mind: Had he been wrong about Cephora getting him out? What if it had been a trick of Valmont's? His heart pounded in his ears. The stretching grin widened on the Crow's face.

"He is otherwise occupied." Will prayed that his voice sounded steadier than he felt.

"Indeed." The Crow cocked his head to the side and leaned forward, peering into Will's eyes. "Let us dispense with the pleasantries, Noctis Thorne—quite the name, I must say. You have embraced your grandfather's line, then." It was not a question. "Yes, quite a name. Reborn, it would seem."

Reborn. The Crow let the word hang in the air as he stared unblinking at Will.

No, he meant it differently. Re-Borne. The word lingered between them. Coolness crawled into Will's spine. *He knows. How does he know? How is that even possible?* Will fought back against the looming chill and forced a smile to his face. *Fine. Two can play at your games, Crow.*

"The fires of the Sapholux strip away what one once was. Blades of Light are forged in the flames. Whomever a Lightborne was before their trials dies."

"So the stories go." The Crow's face gave nothing.

Will caressed his blood fangs and met the Crow's eyes. His Flare sent sputtering lightning dancing across his forearms. He watched the dark man frown slightly. "So the stories go."

A breath passed, not even a moment, but Will sensed the slight crack in the Crow's facade. He took it.

"Dorian Valmont has returned. It would seem he was not as dead as you would have had us believe." The Crow chuckled, the news obviously no surprise to him. *Of course not. Jesus, Will, it's been years. Get your head clear.* "He and his forces are massing in the northwest."

"Indeed they are, young Noctis."

"Jero din'Dael sent me to treat with you." Whatever crack Will thought he'd seen was gone. The Crow suddenly seemed very bored, sighing and shaking his head slightly. "To find a mutually beneficial arrangement."

"As you have already stated."

"The Lightborne will move against Valmont in force when the time comes. But a more strategic—"

"The Nordoth," the Crow interrupted. "Yes, I understand din'-Dael's desires quite well." Will began to speak but was silenced by a gesture from the man. "You are mistaken, Noctis Thorne. Your information is incorrect. The Necrothanians amass in the north-west. Dorian Valmont is not with them."

Will eyed the man. "Is that so?" *He was never this forthcoming. What does he want?*

"Valmont, it seems, entered into the Ways."

The sense of dread returned to Will. "You're certain?"

The Crow shot him a glare. "Three men died for the privilege of that discovery, Noctis Thorne." He spat the words. "Valmont has made for Cascania."

Home. Will paled.

"I will entertain Jero din'Dael's request for an alliance between the Sapholux and Nordoth"—the Crow's smile was unnerving—"so long as you, Noctis Thorne, move against Valmont in Cascania."

Gods, he's trying to get me killed. Will stared. Why was he being so blunt? What was his angle? "The Lightborne will arrive before I return, Crow."

The man waved a dismissive hand. "Messengers were sent to them with terms the moment you entered within the walls of Undermyre. They will wait."

He'd already known? He already had everything planned out before he even spoke to me? "Terms, you say?"

The Crow smiled. "You have been on the road for some time,

Thorne. You shall remain within Undermyre and recover until you are prepared to venture to Cascania."

Will was silent. *It was all arranged before I even set foot in this damn office.* He eyed the Crow, rapidly searching for some new approach. None came. *I have no choice.*

The Crow watched him over the rim of his wine glass before brushing the empty cup aside and rising. "Very well, I'm glad that we have an agreement."

Frustration roiled inside Will. *I haven't even answered him.*

"Recover, young Thorne. Your chambers have been prepared. Inform me when you return from Cascania." He smiled then turned his attention to the papers on his desk. "You are dismissed."

Will said nothing. *Like a fly in a web.* He turned and made for the door.

"William," the Crow called. "One final thing."

Will turned at the mention of his real name. "Yes?"

"We once had a conversation regarding certain, ah, abilities of yours," the Crow said. "Some of your *fiercer* capabilities, you could say. Ones that I recommended you contain."

You mean my Shade. "I recall."

"I must say, I am surprised by the degree to which you managed such a feat."

Will stared. The dark man's thinly veiled probing soured Will's already frustrated mood. *So, he doesn't know how it happened either. So much for answers.* He frowned. "My brother and I always were full of surprises." *Give me something on Madigan, you bastard. Show me you know something about what happened to him.*

"So it would seem." The Crow frowned. "Very well then, on your way."

Will whirled and left without another word. His fingernails dug into his balled fists. He was tired and thirsty and now just plain angry. Again, he berated himself for not resting first at the Street. *At the least, the Crow could have offered me a damn drink.* As the door closed behind him, his thoughts drifted to the Atlantean wine and the memory of its flavor. *That or the Fita'Verxae,* he mused. While he knew that wine wouldn't have done much to quench his thirst, at least it might have helped calm his nerves.

That goddam man. That goddam man and his maneuvering.

He emerged, bristling, into the abandoned audience chamber. The silence grated at his already frayed nerves and he sighed in exasperation. *Today just isn't going as planned. Not one bit.*

"Sir?"

Will was halfway through the hall when the soft, tentative voice called from his left. He stopped and turned. Ynarra, looking just the same as she ever had, stood a short distance from him. She dropped her gaze and gave a small curtsy when his eyes fell upon her.

"Ynarra, it is—"

"Sir, this way, please. Sir." She curtsied again and spun toward a side door, scurrying away from him.

Well, it's nice to see that some things don't change.

Smiling despite himself, Will hurried to catch up with the girl. They walked together in silence for a time, passing through corridors and hallways that were as vacant and silent as Will remembered. *Time works differently here . . . or it just stands still.* He glanced at Ynarra. Something about her seemed different, but he couldn't place it. She seemed as if—

"Sir." Ynarra's voice was soft. She hesitated a moment but then the words, quick and trepidatious, came flooding out. "Sir, I do not know how well you remember me, sir, and please forgive me for saying as much, sir, but it is pleasant to lay eyes on you once more. Sir."

Will was shocked. He couldn't recall if he'd ever heard that many words cumulative from Ynarra, let alone all at once. "Ynarra, of course I remember you. It is good to see you as well."

The girl flushed and clamped her mouth shut. *No, no, I didn't mean to scare you back into silence, dammit.* Her pace quickened and she seemed to be struggling for a breath, then she slowed once more and resumed speaking.

"Yes, sir. That is kind of you to say. Very kind, sir. You and, and your brother, you both. You both were very kind to me. On your last visit. When you stayed here. The last time. Sir."

"Of course, Ynarra," Will said cautiously. "We appreciated you very much."

Will hadn't thought that Ynarra's flush could deepen any more, and when it did he had to stifle a laugh. *I've missed this,* he realized, *positive human interaction. Has it really been so long?* Will glanced out of a nearby window they passed in order to give her a moment of privacy. They were still on the main level of the Nordoth. In fact, he realized that they had rounded to the main courtyard and it was just outside the window.

"Oh, yes. Thank you, sir." Her voice was quiet and clear. "And please, forgive me again for saying so, sir, and I do not mean to overstep, so please tell me if I do, but what I mean to say, sir, is that I hope you have been well. Sir."

That I've been well . . . Not quite how I'd put it. "Thank you, Ynarra. I hope that you have been well, too."

"And, sir," she continued as if not having heard him, "I hope that your brother is well as well. I know that it is not my place to say so, sir, and I do apologize for speaking out of turn, but I"—she took a deep breath—"after the Seeker's report I"—she shook her head—"I apologize, sir. I should not have spoken. Please, this way." She took an abrupt turn and began to climb a nearby stairwell so well hidden in the darkness of the hall that Will nearly missed it.

Wait, the Seeker's report?

"Ynarra, please," Will said as he raced up the stairs after her. "What did you mean by that? A Seeker came, you said? Was it Cephora?" His heart leapt into his throat. "Ynarra, was Madigan with her?"

Ynarra said nothing but continued her quickened pace while

the spiral continued its steep rise. Will struggled to keep up. Taking the steps two at a time, a hint of familiarity sparked within him. *I've been in this stairwell before.* He glanced up. *The last time, with Cephora and Madigan.* Ynarra was leading him to their old room.

"This way, please, sir," she said and took an abrupt turn onto a landing. Her voice was wavering, distant. She was retreating back within herself.

No. Will ran out after her as the girl exited quickly through a side door. "Ynarra, please," he said again. "Please tell me what you heard. I . . . I need your help."

She paused, a ring of keys in her hand. She selected the correct one, unlocked the door, and stepped into the room. Will didn't move. His heart was hammering in his chest at the thought of his brother. *Come on, Mad. Come on.*

"This way, please, sir," Ynarra called from within. "Please."

That final *please*, there was something in the way she said it that shook Will out of his heartache. He entered the room and was hit by another wave of nostalgia. Like everything else, the room was just as he remembered it.

"Ynarra," he said softly. The words caught in his throat. He couldn't even look at her.

"It . . . it has been some time, sir," the girl said. Will's eyes leapt from the floor and found hers. They were bright and earnest and hopeful. "I . . . I overheard, and I do not mean to say that I was eavesdropping, sir, I only mean that I was in the area and the voices were loud. I apologize, sir." Her gaze fell away.

Her eyes flick down to the ground in deference every time she apologizes. What is her story?

"No." Will's voice was both pleading and steady. "No, you have nothing to apologize for, Ynarra. Please, tell me what happened."

"Yes." She nodded again and glanced off to the side. "It . . . it was some time ago, sir. The Seeker, Cephora, she returned to the Nordoth, to the Crow. You were not here, sir, nor was your brother. The Crow had questions for her and he did not like her answers."

"Do you recall what she said?"

Ynarra nodded quickly. "I do, yes. Yes. She . . . There had been a fight, sir. A disagreement, I mean. Between the Seeker and your brother."

They made it. Will's head swam. The relief came with such force that he had to brace himself against a nearby chair, his knees threatening to give way. *Mad's alive.*

"And there was someone else, sir. A Shadowborne."

Will's head snapped back to attention. *What?* "A Shadowborne?" *First the army of Lightborne at Sapholux, now another Shadowborne. Is nothing as dead as this world seems to think?*

Ynarra glanced past Will to the open door and her mouth quavered a bit. *Gods, she's terrified.* He stepped aside. "Ynarra, of course, I am so sorry. You may go if you like. I never meant to make you feel trapped."

"No, no." She shook her head and ran for the door then quickly closed and locked it. "No, sir, I do not feel trapped. I . . . I apologize, sir, but you and your brother, sir. I felt safe. When you were here. It was good when you were here, sir."

Realization dawned on Will and he took a step toward her. "You're still safe, Ynarra. Madigan and I would never harm you."

"I know, sir." She nodded quickly and cast another furtive glance at the closed door. "Your brother, sir, Madigan, he followed the Shadowborne. He left Cephora, sir."

Will nodded slowly. *Jesus, Mad, what the hell are you up to?* "Thank you, Ynarra. When was this? You said it was some time, do you recall how long?"

"It has been a few years, sir." She turned down her eyes as she spoke. "I am sorry, sir."

Dammit. "No, please, no apologies, Ynarra. You've given me more hope today than I've had in a long time."

She looked up, meeting his eyes, and smiled. It was not her

usual smile. It was filled with hope and gratitude, not an ounce of fear or deference. "I am glad to hear that, sir." The smile vanished quickly and she looked at the door. "I am sorry, sir, I must go. I will bring refreshments soon. There are fresh linens on your bed, which is located on the second loft. The curtains may be drawn and the windows will allow fresh air and light, if you wish it. The washroom is between the third and fifth—"

Will held up a hand and smiled. "I remember well, Ynarra. Thank you for your hospitality."

"Sir, I—" She paused and made for the door. "Yes." She turned back to him, a brief hint of a smile upon her face once more. "Thank you, sir." She spun and, in one swift motion, unlocked the door and stepped through, closing it quickly behind her.

She did not lock it.

Will placed his hands on the table and dropped his head. *What a day. What a goddam day.* He scanned the room, memories hitting him like a freight train. In a daze, he walked to the library. It was clean and tidy, but the books were just as they'd left them, even down to the ones that lay open upon the table. Will stumbled out of the room and looked up at the rafters, to the hidden cross-section where he had spent so much time. *Learning to control my Shade. Had I known then what I know now, I might've just burned this whole place to the ground and been done with it.*

Something inside him began to ache. He looked at the table where the wine and food always used to be, but it was empty. It would be some time before Ynarra returned with any kind of refreshments, and he was still thirsty.

He crossed the large room to the window and threw back the curtains. The cold breath of fresh air swarmed over him and, as he had done so long before, he grabbed a nearby rope and leaned out the window. Far below him lay the courtyard. The air was cool, the breeze fresh and salty.

Will breathed deeply and stared out at the vast expanse of Undermyre. If he had fallen, before, maybe he would have survived. He'd had his Shade then. Now . . . *Shades and the Flares, so different.* The Shade guarded Shadowborne. The Flare, though, the Flare's only purpose was destruction.

Maybe it's still there, hidden away inside me somewhere. He climbed onto the windowsill and felt the wave of vertigo wash over him. *Maybe it would come back if I really needed it.* He stretched farther and leaned out over the courtyard, only his grip on the rope stopping him from plummeting to the stony courtyard. *Just a jumpstart to wake my Shade back up.* The rope began to slide in his hand.

His key, cold and tingling against his chest, brought him back to his right mind. He tightened his grip and pulled himself back into the room. *No, that's not how this works, Will.*

He wrapped his cloak tight around his body and huddled into himself as he stared at the world below. Madigan was alive, somewhere out there, that's what mattered. *He's alive.*

Maybe she is too.

There was no cool embrace of his Shade to comfort him. There was no brotherly banter or warm embrace of a lover. There was no wine from Ynarra to drown the flood of memories. Nothing to stifle the fear that the hope she had given him would be dashed any moment. He was back, trapped within the Nordoth, utterly alone with nothing tangible to connect to the life he'd once had.

Trapped within the Nordoth . . . Will turned back to the room's entrance. Ynarra hadn't locked the door. And the Crow, what had he said? *You have been on the road for some time, Thorne. You shall remain within Undermyre and recover until you are prepared to venture to Cascania.*

Undermyre. Not the Nordoth.

Will smiled. He closed the window curtains and raced to the door. *Nostalgia, then.* There was one place where he could still find some connection to it.

The Bottled Embers called him.

❧ 13 ☙
BREATHING ASHES

With a wide grin on his face, Will left the Nordoth uncontested. The guards in the courtyard eyed him warily as he passed but did not interfere. He felt no need to ask permission, no need to seek approval. *Before, the Crow put a gag order around my very existence. Well, not this time.* Freedom within Undermyre. Freedom to explore. The notion put some pep in his step.

The streets passed in a blur. There would be plenty of time to explore in the coming days, should he wish it. At the moment, the only thing on his mind was returning to the Street of Ash. A part of him knew he was being foolish, that at the very least he should have bathed in the Nordoth's luxurious washroom first and removed most of the grime from the road. Ynarra would return with refreshments. There would be wine, perhaps even *Fita'Verxae*. He didn't even have any coin to pay for food or drink at the Street.

Still, something compelled him forward. Like a marionette, he was drawn through the doors, through the vibrant curtains and into the Street. The same intoxicating revelry of his earlier visit bombarded him. The music was more a physical force than anything else, the drums clamoring inside his skull along with the roar of the crowd and cheering hoots from the many dancers. Above all was the rowdy laughter of life echoing to the rafters. He felt no rush of anxiety this time, no fear. All that remained were the fumes of forgetfulness upon the air—the promise of Bottled Embers.

Will's gaze drifted to the dance floor, packed with forgettable faces lost in their enjoyment. He scanned every face he could see, watching for those he might have missed while the crowd parted and spun to the music. His buoyant spirits faded somewhat. There were many dancers, yes, but there was no *her*. No Morella.

Of course not, you idiot. He knew she wouldn't be there. Couldn't be. Morella was dead, he had to accept that. But in the brief time he knew her—*gods, it feels like a lifetime ago*—she was captivating, alive in so many ways. To him, she had been . . . more.

He shook his head to clear it. *Nostalgia, Will. That's all you're here for.*

Scanning the room again, he spotted an empty seat at the end of the bar. Dropping his hood, he maneuvered through the throng of people toward it. There were people standing all around the lone stool and yet no one sat. *As if the gods themselves were saving it for me.* He eased his way in, silent as a shadow, and turned his back to the dancers.

The bartender gave him a wry grin that did not fully meet her eyes and gestured to him, acknowledging that she'd seen him. He peered at her a moment and then realized that he knew her: it was the same woman as before, the one who served him the night he'd first seen Morella. Her hair was now a vibrant, shining violet and far shorter than it had been, but there was no mistaking her. *Gods, what was her name? Something familiar . . .*

The woman made her way across the bar, sliding drinks to patrons and deftly depositing their payments into a hidden trough. Will leaned over the bar and saw the trough was angled so the coins slid down to the end. *Just like a pool table.* He smiled. *Not a bad system.*

The bartender sidled up to him and brushed more coins into the trough, flashing a brilliant smile as she did so.

"Clever, that," Will said with a wink while nodding to the trough. "Reminds me of a game I used to play a long time ago."

The woman's face fell, growing sickly pale. For a split second, she stared at Will with a truly alarming expression of both sadness and horror. Then, in a heartbeat, it was gone and the bright, professional smile had returned. The eyes, however, remained wary.

"I'm sorry," Will said quickly. *What the hell did I say?* "I didn't mean to offend you. I just meant that it seems like a good system, is all."

The woman laughed and shook her head, her eyes relaxing. "No, no worries, friend. For a moment you reminded me of someone else who used to come in." She winked and passed a steaming mug to the person at Will's right. "Used to sit in that exact same seat of yours, most nights. And with how different you look since your last visit, well, I had to do a double take." She grinned and laughed, then shook her head. "Ah, memories."

This woman's good. Will raised an eyebrow. "The last time I was here—you remember me?"

"Why, of course I remember you. I make it a point to know my patrons," she said while she waved to someone else farther down the bar. "Every single one that walks in this door."

"Impressive," Will said. "Especially given the size of the crowds. Seems like business has increased since I was last here."

She shrugged and set to work making a drink. "Business always booms when people need a distraction. These days? Well, there's plenty to be distracted from." A moment later she set the drink on the bar between them. "Bottled Embers, right?"

Will eyed the glowing beverage and smiled, shaking his head slightly. "I can't believe you remember."

"A good memory is a useful thing in my line of work."

Will reached for the glass but stopped, remembering his empty pockets. "I'm sorry, thank you, but I can't. I don't have any—"

She held up a hand. "You've the look of a man who needs a drink. This one's on the house." Her gaze flickered again and the words died in her mouth. "Funny thing, that," she said quietly. She momentarily looked very different than the bright and smiling bartender, like she was a completely different person. Then, someone called to her from a few seats away and the expression was gone. She pushed the drink toward Will and smiled conspiratorially. "Excuse me a moment, no rest for the wicked." She winked again and moved away, her casual laugh easily returning as she moved down the bar.

Will wrapped his hands around the warm mug and inhaled the fumes. The sweet, tangy, spicy aroma set his mouth watering. His head spun. The liquid touched his lips delicately, the echo of an absent lover's kiss. He drank in the memories.

The liquor hit him hard and fast. He swirled the glass and found the music calling his body. It built and intensified, growing to a crescendo. He drank again.

How much life had changed. How his world had grown and evolved, twisted and untwisted. *What of before is even left?* Madigan was gone, Will's anchor to another life, another world. A world before Flares and Jero din'Dael. A world before the Shale. A world of family and games and dreams and the promise of magic. A world of daring adventures and beautiful dancing girls. Will's world. How it had fallen in such a short time.

Will's world, he mused to himself. *I even think of it separately.* Maybe there was more to the rituals of the Sapholux than he'd thought. Maybe din'Dael was right. Maybe William Davis did die in the flames. After all, Will had been Shadowborne. Noctis

Thorne, though, Noctis was Lightborne. Noctis was a Blade of Light. Noctis was a warrior. He chuckled to himself and raised his glass in a toast. *Before and after . . . change. Fine, then. I can do that.* He drank. *Noctis Thorne it is.*

The bartender returned and eyed him. "You alright there, stranger? Your head looks like it's barely screwed on."

"I'm fine, thanks," Noctis said. "Better than I've been in a while, I think."

"Glad to hear it," she said with a nod while skillfully mixing another drink.

Noctis watched her for a moment and then sighed. "I'm sorry, especially given your excellent recollective abilities, but I seem to have forgotten your name."

The woman laughed and shook her head. "You're hardly the first. Call me Clarice."

"Clarice!" Noctis clapped his hands. "That's right. Can't believe I missed that one."

"Well, as we said, friend, it has been a while." She slid the drink down the bar to a waiting hand and swept more coins away before setting to work on a new drink.

"It has. It has, indeed." Noctis traced a finger along the rim of his glass. "Alrighty, exam time: The last time I was in, do you remember who I was with?"

Clarice nodded. "Of course. Anytime Cephora brings someone in, I take special notice."

So, she knows Cephora by name, that's good to know.

Clarice skirted away and made a rapid succession of drinks, distributing them with equal speed. A customer to Noctis's left called out and she returned to his side of the bar, mixing and pouring again.

"That night, I danced with a young woman. Short dark hair. Tattooed wrists."

"I remember her," Clarice said without looking up. She slid

the drink across, swept away the coins, and waved to another patron. "Haven't seen her in a bit of time. Quite a bit, actually."

"No." Noctis shook his head. "I imagine you wouldn't have seen any of them." In his mind's eye he again saw the earth swallowing his brother, heard Morella's cries of terror.

"Well, Cephora stops by plenty as of late, but I can't say I've seen the other gentleman you were here with," Clarice said over her shoulder. "Want me to pass along that you're about when next I see her?"

Noctis froze. Cephora was nearby. *Perhaps Madigan is as well? Somehow?* It was a fool's hope, he knew. Wherever his brother might be, if he'd been within Undermyre or any of the surrounding areas, the Crow would have known. He sighed inwardly and shook his head, then realized that Clarice seemed to be waiting for something. She was watching him intently, concern plain upon her face.

Of course, she asked you a question, idiot. "Please do." His voice sounded hoarse. He took a drink and realized he was gripping the glass so tight his fingers were turning white.

"Do you have a place to stay?" Clarice's look bordered on pity.

Noctis frowned, again realizing his disheveled state. *I must look like a derelict.* He quickly downed the last of the Bottled Embers and stood. "I, I do," he stammered as he went to push the stool in. "Thank you, but I'll be fine. I have a place."

"Sit." Her tone brooked no argument and Noctis nearly laughed. Her hands were busy out of sight beneath the bar while she spoke. "Listen, kid, I don't know your story. I don't need to know your story. But I know that it intertwines with Cephora's story, and that? Well that one has enough going on in it to give me nightmares for years to come." She held up a finger as another patron called from farther down the bar. "So, you plop a squat right there, I fix you another drink, and while you sip at it you let me pull a few strings."

Noctis raised an eyebrow. "Really, that isn't necessary. I'm not lying. I've got a place to stay."

Clarice gave a quick flourish and passed another Bottled Embers over to him. "Most people have a place to stay. That doesn't mean it's safe."

Noctis sighed and accepted the drink. "Safety is a luxury I haven't been able to afford in some time, Clarice. I appreciate the offer but I'll be fine."

She almost hid the frown with an easy laugh and wink. "Drink," she ordered. "Stay and drink for the evening. The night's on me." She held up a hand to stifle his protestations. "No, I don't want to hear it. Whatever you're in, you've got the look of someone who needs a night of freedom." She flashed a bright grin at him. "And that is exactly what I offer here at the Street."

She didn't allow him to answer; she was already turning and making her way down the bar. Noctis watched for a moment. Clarice's laughter and smile while she collected money and mixed drinks was such a contrast to the world he had come to know. He stared into the depths of the Bottled Embers, getting lost in the fiery core. *I should go,* he mused. *I should . . .* His thoughts trailed off as the music's rhythm beat at him again. The Nordoth could wait. Jero din'Dael could wait. *Clarice is right. A night off from the world would be nice.*

Noctis indulged.

Hours passed and the glass before him was never dry. Slowly, ever so slowly, the weight of memory lifted from his shoulders and he found himself relaxing. He lost himself in the music and the burning fire, letting the filth and waste of time slough off his shoulders. *One night where I don't carry the weight of a world I don't even know. One.*

Gradually, the Street began to empty. The music quieted. The dancers left. Soon all who remained were patrons who looked as though they never actually left the bar but simply faded into the woodwork when the alcohol stopped flowing, only reemerging when the taps resumed the following day.

I need to talk to Cephora, Noctis mused while resting his head on his arms and staring into the hypnotic drink. *Everything suddenly seems in flux.*

He lifted his drooping head from his fists and drank. He spun on the stool and stared at the empty dance floor. Clarice, cleaning the tables, glanced up at him. He smiled drunkenly back at her. "I think I'll be off." His voice was slurred and thick.

Clarice raised an eyebrow. "You sure you don't need a place to stay?"

Noctis smiled and waved a dismissive hand in the air. "Appreciated."

He turned and stumbled for the curtains. Clarice called something after him that he could neither hear nor understand, so he twisted back and opened his arms in a wide shrug. A theatrical smile plastered across his face, he dropped into a deep bow and doffed his nonexistent hat. He rose and, with a flourish of his filthy cloak, strode through the curtains and out into Undermyre.

It was as close to nighttime as the city ever seemed to get. Its strange, lingering breath of daylight made him think of what summers in Alaska back home must be like. *Back home*. He shook his head at the thought, unable to fathom the concept of home anymore, of that life before Aeril. It had been a world of prepping for Aeril, nothing more.

No—he shook his head and stumbled into a wall, catching himself with a hand—*that's not all.* Cascania had been real, just as much a part of him as anything. *I knew that world, once. But after all this?* He scanned the silent street, drew his eyes to the luminous sky. *How could I ever go back now, if I wanted to?*

The night was cold, colder than it had any right to be. Almost immediately, Noctis's teeth began to chatter. He huddled deeper into his cloak and pulled the hood, his mouth a grim line against the chill. *Since when is this city cold?* He could see his breath in the air. His throat hurt when he tried to swallow, dry and scratchy, but he brushed it to the back of his mind and set off into the night.

Weaving down the street, Noctis focused entirely on putting one foot in front of the other. The city seemed surprisingly empty; he couldn't remember ever seeing a single part of it so abandoned. *Not that I have a lot to go off on that last point.* He placed a hand against a wall to steady himself again, his legs rubbery. *Maybe one too many tonight. Perhaps I—*

He stopped, nerves suddenly on edge. His key had been tingling since he'd left the Street, but suddenly it was popping and growing wilder by the second. His thoughts were muddled but he struggled to bring himself back to sobriety. *Something's wrong. Something's coming.*

A sound echoed behind him, the shifting tumbling of gravel scraping along cobblestone. Warm static filled the air as electricity danced across Noctis's skin. Lightning split across his clenched fists as his Flare raged to life.

"Will."

The voice was hoarfrost on iron. His knees suddenly felt off-balance and his head swam. The single word was filled with loathing, but the voice was unmistakable. Noctis turned.

She stood barely an arm's reach from him. Her ivory skin reflected the evening light, her black hair still cut short to frame her face. But the playful, crooked smile was gone. Instead, her lips curled down as she stared at him. Her anger-filled eyes, so dark they were nearly black, were fixed firmly on him.

Noctis's throat was suddenly very tight. Something warm ran into his eyes. The crackling electricity dissipated. *A dream. This has to be a dream.*

"Morella?" The word came out as a near cry. His key blazed against numb skin. He took a tentative step toward her. She did not soften. "Is it really you?"

"You look sick," she said, her eyes darting over his face. "The exterior finally matches what's inside."

Noctis's head swam. He felt cold and hot. Something in the back of his throat seemed to be ticking. "Morella, I thought—"

"Don't," she sneered. "Don't you dare."

For a moment her expression nearly resembled Valmont's from the last time they'd been together, surrounded by the sorcerer's undead army. Noctis broke under those hateful eyes. Tears started to run down his cheeks. *She's alive.*

"I thought he killed you," he said, taking another step closer. "I thought he—"

Her slap nearly drove him to the ground.

"Not another word." Her voice trembled. "Not one more word."

Noctis stood, stricken. His head swam from the Bottled Embers. His face stung. He opened his mouth to speak, then closed it and looked away from her hard eyes.

"You left me." Her words were venomous. "You *abandoned* me with that monster. *Look* at me, Will."

His head seemed to wobble when he raised it to meet her eyes. He felt sick beneath her gaze but he did not turn away.

"You, Will. *You.*" Her words were calm, detached. "Everyone I've ever met has beaten me down, Will. Everyone abandoned me. But I never thought that you would be the worst of them." There was a slight tremor in her voice, a small crack in her armor. Her eyes filled with tears, and her next words were barely audible. "Why did you leave me?"

What could he say? The sight of her drove everything from him, all the hardened armor of his training pierced by her words. How could he tell her that he never wanted to leave her behind, how many times he had cursed din'Dael for pulling him away from her? How many nights had her screams for help filled his head? No words came. He tore his gaze away. Self-loathing overwhelmed him.

She threw herself into his arms, nearly knocking him over as she broke down into sobs. Her hands clung at him, cradled his face while she kissed his cheeks and neck. “What happened to you, Will? Where did you go? Why didn’t you come find me?”

Noctis couldn’t speak. He stood, immobile, before eventually enough life returned to his limbs to wrap the woman he loved in his arms. *Because I do love her, don’t I?* He pushed the thought away; it was a question for another time. Right now, what mattered was that she was alive. She was present, tangible, and in his arms. For the first time, he realized that her scrolls and books were nowhere in sight. *She lost everything.*

“I love you, Will.”

Noctis felt himself go rigid. *Spinning. Spinning, just like the night we met.*

“I love you, but I’ll never forgive you.”

She reached up and took his head in her hands and pulled herself up to kiss him. She tasted like tears and misery. When she drew away, her face had hardened once more. “Goodbye, Will.”

14
A TRAITOR'S BLOOD

Noctis stood in silence, the sting of Morella's slap as warm on his face as the breath of her lips from the kiss. She was gone, disappeared. He didn't know when or how it happened; one second she was there, the next she was gone. It took him a moment to realize that he was standing in the middle of the street watching the swirling wind. A single snowflake drifted from the amber sky. He felt empty.

Where had she come from? Where had she gone? Why had she chosen this moment to appear? He had known the girl, once. He knew that if she had approached him now, it was because she had been watching him for some time. Had she been in the bar? Had she been amongst the spinning dancers? The revelry, the intoxicating flavor of the place, maybe he had missed something. He didn't want to believe that he could have missed *her,* of all people, but it was entirely possible. Things had changed. He had changed. He was not who he once was. *No, not at all.*

Noctis gathered his thoughts while another gust of wind set his teeth back to chattering. His mind was still fogged with drink, the brief sobriety from the fear of a potential attack had immediately been overshadowed by the shock of seeing Morella. Any momentary clarity had immediately departed with the slap of her hand and the taste of her lips. Now he existed between two states: one, cold and sober, calculating what he should do next. The other, the foolish part, desperately wishing to scour the streets and find Morella and throw himself on her mercy.

Logic won.

He pulled his hood back up and took a deep breath. He forced himself to stand upright, though the movement made his head spin. He swayed as he took a few steps on the ancient cobblestones. *How many others have walked on this road?* Were these roads older than the Roman roads in Casc, set years before he could even fathom? And yet here they lay, threatening to twist his ankles. The floating lanterns seemed dimmer, like they, too, had turned away from him. Not just the lanterns—the entire city seemed to have turned against him—the dark, the cold, the absence of human life. Whatever momentary peace he had found within the Street of Ash was gone. Now he felt nothing but confusion and a rekindled loss.

At least she's alive.

More snowflakes swept from the sky. He had never seen the weather turn like this, not in the entirety of his visit in this world. He chided himself after a moment, realizing the foolishness of the thought. *Of course not, idiot. You've been holed up in the damn Sapholux.* Desert nights got cold, but not *that* cold.

Perhaps, like time, all aspects of Aerillian life flowed unending and without reason. It had been warm during the day, then at night there was this? *Nothing here is very real by my standards.*

Noctis smirked, despite his mood. *Why should it be? Why do I still hold to the truths of a different world?* He glanced up. Was dawn near? Another brilliant day? *How are you even supposed to tell?* He supposed that once he arrived at his quarters in the tower the sun would already be shining once more, the snow just a memory. He hoped so.

He stumbled through dim streets, the floating lanterns muted by the incoming fog. *Snowy nights in foggy streets. I should find this beautiful.* He did not. His head pounded, his throat was dry, and his heart ached. He felt even more alone than on the day he lost his family and found Jero. *No. That wasn't me. That was a foolish boy.*

Still, he could not explain the walls that pressed in on him and surrounded him in this loneliness. He longed for something familiar. He longed for the warmth of Morella. He longed for his Shade.

Noctis never had a Shade—he shook his head—*that was someone else. The same someone Morella loved. Someone who no longer exists.*

FIND MORELLA.

Noctis reeled, the pounding voice roaring within his skull. Loud and harsh, it repeated its order. There was less fury in it this time, but there was something else to it. It seemed more . . . present. Perhaps his drunkenness was bringing him closer to the void between sleep and dreams? *That's where it lives. The world of ghosts.*

FIND MORELLA.

Noctis winced. *I did find her. Or rather, she found me. Regardless, she wants nothing to do with me.* Not for the first time, Noctis wondered if he was going crazy. *So many voices. So many things. So many people I've let down.*

The gates of the Nordoth grew closer. Noctis threw back his hood and stumbled. The guards eyed him when he approached supporting himself against a wall, but they said nothing. They acknowledged him when he passed and lifted a hand. *They seem to know me already. How does the Crow do it?*

His legs ached as he made the climb to the citadel; the drunken haze could not hide that fact from him. In fact, the drunken evening seemed to be hiding nothing. It was as though the universe had dredged up every could-have-been from the depths of his heart while the night held up a mirror and cast all his disappointments out into the world.

He passed through the inner gate without issue and crossed the courtyard to the hidden stair that led through the Nordoth. He dreaded another climb, but he braced himself against the wall with his shoulder and gripped the handrail. Then, forcing one foot in front of the other, he began to climb.

By the time he rose to the top of the stairs and stumbled through the halls to his room, a thin sheen of sweat covered his forehead. Thankfully, the door to his chamber was still unlocked. He opened it and stumbled into the dimly lit room. As the door closed behind him, he saw that Ynarra had left a tray of bread and wine for him. He smiled. Just what was needed.

He grabbed both the loaf of bread and the wine before setting off for the library. He needed a distraction. Something to take his mind off everything. *The Veleriat,* perhaps? It was well past due. *Maybe see if I can pick up some more things Grandda missed.* He smiled and ripped off a chunk of bread with his teeth.

"Off on an evening stroll?" said a voice from behind him.

Noctis froze midstride and glowered. He chased the bread with a swig of wine before turning to answer. Cephora was dressed in her same mottled green and black garb, but she wore thin plates of armor over it. Her staff and a bow were strapped to her back. She still bore her habitual look of casual boredom. *Nothing's changed, it seems.* And yet, as he studied her, something did appear different; something in her eyes.

"I'm not one for staying in one place these days. Not unless I have to, and I have had to for far too long." He brushed back the hood of his cloak and heard Cephora take a startled sniff. *Yeah, one of us changed,* he mused, taking another drink.

"So it would seem." Cephora crossed the room and poured herself a glass of wine from a second bottle he had not seen. "It has been quite a while, Will. It is good to see you."

Noctis just stared at her. He felt her eyes crawling over him, inspecting. *What is she looking for?*

"Will—"

"It's Noctis, now," he said, removing the cloak entirely. "I was christened that in the fires of Sapholux under the guidance of Jero din'Dael."

"Were you, now?" Cephora's eyes were hard. "Very well, Noctis."

Noctis's head was swimming but he stood his ground. "I don't recall inviting you, Cephora. Nor do I believe that Clarice would have had enough time to pass along my message. Why're you here?"

"Do friends need invitations?"

Noctis laughed, a harsh, biting sound. "Friends, is it?"

Cephora frowned. "My, my. You have most definitely been spending time with Jero din'Dael."

"Meaning?"

"You sound nearly as bitter as he."

Noctis cocked his head and glared at the Seeker. "Perhaps he's been equally disappointed by those he considered friends."

Cephora mirrored his head tilt and raised an eyebrow disdainfully. Noctis sneered at the sight, frustration and disappointment filling him. *Do not be weak,* came din'Dael's voice in his head. When he looked at Cephora, however, he realized that his anger, his words, were petty things. Weak things.

"I'm sorry," he said after a moment. "I've had a rather long evening, filled with unexpected reunions."

"I understand," she said dismissively. "Perhaps the promise of an additional one would help."

His heart leapt in his chest. *Mad?* He forced down his emotions and simply raised an eyebrow. "Madigan?"

The Seeker nodded. "Yes, Madigan."

Noctis's pulse beat rapidly. "I heard there'd been a falling out between the two of you. Was my information incorrect?"

Cephora's mouth became a grim line. She paused, meeting Noctis's eyes. She took a drink from her glass before abandoning it on a nearby table, then relaxed into one of the seats next to it. "Your brother and I had a disagreement, yes."

Noctis smiled. "Knowing Mad, that doesn't surprise me."

She cocked her head to decide and gave it a slight shake. "He believes I mishandled the situation regarding"— she waved a hand dismissively—"the events following the fall of the Shale."

"I wouldn't say he's wrong."

Cephora sighed and looked at him with a bored expression. "Will—I'm sorry, Noctis—I made a decision. I saved who I was able to save. If I had not taken your brother and had chosen you instead, your brother would certainly be dead. Jero din'Dael would not have saved a Shadowborne, and Valmont would have struck him down. The two of you have power, yes, but it is a young power. It was especially so, then."

"I take it his powers have grown since?"

She met his eyes and smiled. There was no warmth in it. "Spoken as someone who has noticed their own powers increase, I take it?"

Noctis was silent. She was baiting him. Long ago he had promised honesty to this woman, he and his brother both, and in all things he had betrayed that promise. *Just like she betrayed me,* he reminded himself. Did he really owe her anything? *Will might have, but I am not Will. I am Noctis.* The thought was a comforting one. He was not confined to the same limitations as Will.

"I've seen some changes." He decided to leave it at that and let her read between the lines.

Cephora reached for her glass and took another drink. "Of that I have no doubt. The question is, what will you do now?"

Noctis smiled. "Well, you did say there was the potential for a reunion soon." He tore off another chunk of bread with his teeth, as if to punctuate the statement. He raised an eyebrow to the Seeker. "What the hell happened between you two, anyway?"

"I took him to Greygarde," Cephora said. "The base of operations for the Seekers. They deserved a report on the changing scope of Aerillian happenings and Undermyrian politics."

Noctis's mind raced at the thought of Mad surrounded by so many other Seekers like Cephora, at the wealth of knowledge that must be contained within their halls. *Mad ran from that?* Madigan had a thirst for knowledge that Noctis could not even begin to match, a mind that could and would soak up every bit of information he could glean from people like the Seekers. And yet he turned away from them? *He really must have been in a bad way.*

"I'm guessing Mad wasn't too keen on that. He tried to convince you to turn back, I presume."

"Every day."

"I did the same to Jero for quite some time. But then I wised up. The expanse of the Wastes and an army of the undead separated us, I figured."

She nodded. "My rift moved us far, but not far enough that we could not still hear the creatures. That, I think, was what was hardest for your brother. He knew that somewhere within those hellish ranks you might be dying." She cocked her head to the side and swirled the wine in her glass. "Obviously, that was not the case. How did you escape?"

"Jero. He got us out."

"Us? The historian has been with you this whole time?"

Noctis's head pounded. "No. Only din'Dael and me."

Cephora was silent for a moment, then she rose and walked over to him, placing a hand on his shoulder. "I am sorry. It is never easy to leave anyone behind."

Noctis briefly considered telling her that he had seen Morella only minutes before, but he dashed the thought away. He owed nothing to this woman who had left him for dead. *She made her choice; she can live with it.* "That day was full of the unexpected," was all the answer he gave. He shrugged his arm away from her grasp and, feeling slightly self-conscious, set the bread and wine on the table. He reached for a glass and poured himself more wine then tore off a small chunk of bread.

"You return to the civilized world slowly but surely, I see."

Noctis shot her a glare. "Why are you here, Cephora? Mad's not with you, and I'm getting the feeling that that's probably for the best."

"Madigan is in trouble."

Noctis froze. *Dammit, Mad.* He watched as Cephora seemed to gauge his reaction. *She's baiting you. She's here, rather than out looking for him.* "If that's the case, why wait for me? Why not go after him yourself?

"He is your brother, Noctis, but to us he is more than that. He has the potential to be more than just a Shadowborne."

Noctis gnawed at the bread. "My question still stands."

"He made it very clear that he wanted neither my involvement nor my help. While I can honor his wishes and have no direct contact with him, I cannot sit aside and do nothing. He will listen to you."

Noctis laughed. "When has Mad ever listened to me? I think you put too much stock in our relationship."

Cephora eyed him. "This is no laughing matter, Noctis. I believe your brother is in mortal danger."

Noctis cursed and clenched his fists. Lightning danced over their surface. Cephora almost seemed to falter for a moment. "Mortal danger?" He shook his head. "Madigan is fine. He can handle whatever comes at him, he always has. Even before he discovered he was Shadowborne. Unless Valmont is the one who took him, my brother is in no danger."

"Noctis," Cephora said in a voice that oozed patronizing patience, "Valmont is dangerous, yes, but there are other forces to consider. I believe that one of them has taken your brother under her influence."

"Her?" Noctis forced himself to relax, allow the tension to leave his body. The static in the air faded. *And I always thought*

Madigan was the one with the hot temper. "So, this time you abandoned Mad. Who to, I wonder?" he said flippantly.

Her eyes narrowed but she did not acknowledge the biting comment. "Another Shadowborne."

"So I've heard."

"A skilled Shadowborne." Cephora continued. "She found us while we were returning to Undermyre."

"And she managed to drag Madigan away from your guidance, is that it?"

Cephora looked unamused. "Something like that."

"A Shadowborne to train a Shadowborne," Noctis said. "Just as I was trained by a Lightborne. I hardly see the danger in that."

"You know the history of the Shadowborne, Noctis, at least enough of it to know they were killed."

"By one of their own. Valmont, along with his Necrothanians."

"Valmont was dead, Noctis." Cephora pinched the bridge of her nose and sighed. "Or at least he had us convinced that he was."

Noctis hesitated, realizing the implication. "Someone else killed them?"

Cephora nodded.

"And that's who has Mad?"

"That, Noctis, is what we need to determine."

Dammit. He peered at Cephora. "Who was it who betrayed the Shadowborne? Who destroyed Umbriferum?"

Cephora met Noctis's eye. "The same Shadowborne who pierced Dorian Valmont's heart and sent him to his death from the peaks of Umbriferum."

The flesh on Noctis's arms rose in goosebumps. "And that is?"

"Aurellaine Valmont. His daughter."

15

FANNING THE FLAME

Noctis raged after Cephora departed. *More Valmonts? More of that damn bloodline?* And now, one of them had his brother under her influence. It was a brilliant move on Valmont's part, absolutely brilliant. Cleave Madigan and this Aurellaine, the bastard's own daughter, together and then corrupt Madigan to his will. Gods, it was something directly out of one of his grandfather's stories, something that, of course, Valmont would have done. *And no one saw fit to ever tell us he had more family. Thanks, Grandda.*

He worried his key between his fingers. *Come on, give me something.* No response came, none of the strange prescient thought. *Fan-freakin-tastic.*

He dropped the key and raised his wine glass instead, draining it before pouring another glass from the fresh decanter. Ynarra had come right as Cephora left and, seeing the state Noctis was in, had been kind enough to supply two decanters of red. *Liquid happiness or liquid forgetfulness,* he scoffed to himself. *Right now I'll take the latter.*

His years of training with Jero din'Dael had taught him much about the Aerillian people's expectations. But, still, he could not understand why his grandfather would have omitted something as important as Valmont having a daughter. Where was the logic in that? *Nowhere, there was no logic whatsoever. Just one more of his damn secrets.*

Something inside him hardened, a piece of him he couldn't quite place. *Not my grandfather. Will's grandfather. Noctis has no grandfather.*

Which meant Noctis had no brother. Madigan Davis had no place in din'Dael's plans, other than as a potential adversary. The world would be better off with him hidden away. *He is Will's brother, not mine.*

Noctis shook his head, part of him still clinging to the idea that he could be both. Those words, those sentiments, they were din'Dael's. Madigan. Cephora. The Crow. Morella. He'd hardly returned to Undermyre and already his plans were in disarray. *Whatever excuse for plans they'd actually been.* One conversation with Cephora and, suddenly, din'Dael's mission of righteousness seemed less dire. The look of disappointment on her face when he'd spoken of the purging of Will and forging of Noctis had made his transformation feel hollow.

He stumbled up to the loft and slumped onto the bed. *Because it is hollow, idiot.* Even having only just decided to embrace being Noctis, to embrace the path that din'Dael set out for him, he was already feeling torn. He was who he was, wasn't he? Morella's touch, her voice, her warmth, that was as real to him as it had ever been, and that was Will. She'd called him Will and he hadn't fought it. Because he was both, both Noctis and Will.

So, I should be able to do both.

A lopsided smile crept to his face. He could do both. He could find his brother, could rescue him from Aurellaine Valmont. They'd be reunited and then they could return to Undermyre together and treat with the Crow in din'Dael's name. A Shadow-borne and a Lightborne together could surely convince the man to join forces with the armies of Sapholux. They shared a common enemy, a common goal. They shared the belief that this world could be better.

Noctis drained the glass and set it on the bedside table then fell back onto the soft bed. He *would* do both. If he was to figure out where Mad went, he needed more information from Cephora. But he needed more than to just find his brother; he needed to know what he was going to be up against. That meant Aurellaine Valmont. He needed to research the hell out of her, needed everything he could get on who she was and how she worked.

He sat up, his eyes drifting to the small library tucked in the alcove below. He and Madigan had pored through those books the last time they'd been here and had found no mention of Valmont having a daughter. Sure, they might have missed something, but he doubted it. That meant he needed different information. More books. More records. More history.

He needed Morella.

The thought of her brought back the all-too-recent pain of their earlier encounter. Her palm's sting against his face still felt fresh, although he knew that it was just the shadow of a memory. *Find Morella,* the harsh voice had hammered in his head. Was this why? Was she the key piece to defeating Aurellaine Valmont? And if so, what was compelling him toward her? *What are these goddam voices in my head?*

He rose again and steadied himself with the handrail while he made his way back to the lower level. Moving to the window, he drew back the curtains to reveal the whole of Undermyre in its perpetual dusky state. Somewhere out there was Morella, alone and without her life's work, lost thanks to Will's decision to bring her into his world. Now he needed to find her again and bring her back into the fold. *To save my brother. To save the world.*

Could he do that to her again? Ask her to follow him once more in a venture that had nothing to do with her? *I have to.*

Find Morella, the voice says. Very well, I'll do just that.

When he woke, nursing a cruel hangover, Noctis set about finding the historian. He didn't know the city, didn't know the surrounding area, but he knew Morella. All he had was instinct, but he trusted it. He bathed then grabbed his cloak and fresh clothes. He scribbled a quick note to Ynarra, wrote *For your eyes only* on the cover of the folded paper, and set it between the empty decanters. He left his cutlass but took his blood fangs, just in case. Then Noctis departed the Nordoth via the hidden stair.

Convincing himself that it was the best course of action, he made his way to the Street of Ash. Short of finding a murdered caravan and trail of bodies on the road, every time he had encountered Morella had been in the proximity of that tavern. Clarice had mentioned lodgings, had offered him a place to stay. That meant the Street of Ash had rooms available, and he intended to buy one for as long as needed.

On the dime of the Crow, of course. He chuckled at the thought. *Such a gracious host.*

His key trembled and stuttered when he first saw the floating lanterns dancing above the entrance to the Street. Noctis smiled. *That's gotta mean something, right?* He pushed his way through the curtains and into the empty bar, realizing that it must not be open for business yet, although he found Clarice arranging chairs and wiping down tables. The easy, fluid movement that came with mastery of one's craft showed even in these simple acts, and Noctis stood watching, impressed. *People like this are who Grandda wanted to save.*

"And he returns," she called in her usual chipper voice. She didn't even glance up from her tasks as she bustled about. "Welcome back." She finished the table she was working on before turning to appraise him. "My, my, but don't you look the worse for wear this morning? Cleaner round the edges, sure, but a bit puffier around the eyes." She grinned and made her way over to him. "Haven't finished setting up shop yet, but what do you say? Need to nip back what nipped you last?"

He hadn't known many bartenders—any, really—but had always heard that the best could make you feel right at home. Clarice, then, deserved a place right at the top with the very best.

"Thank you, but—" He paused and considered. "Actually, that would be lovely. Thank you."

She winked. "Coming right up." She moved behind the bar and Noctis followed, leaning against the counter. "I've gotta say, though, you haven't got the look of a fella who came in strictly for drinking purposes." She raised an eyebrow at him as she set to work gathering bottles and pouring. "What can I do for you?"

"You offered a room. I'd like to take you up on that."

"Sure." She nodded without looking up. "Sure. A beat with Cephora is collateral enough for me. Room's on the house."

"No, I insist," Noctis said. "Whatever the cost of the room, and for food and drink, forward them on to the Nordoth."

Clarice whistled but did not pause in her work. "Is that so?"

"It is."

She poured the drink into two glasses. "A room of your choosing, then. Any particular requests?" She placed the glasses on the counter, one in front of each of them.

"One that overlooks the dance floor."

She smiled and raised her glass to him. "Very well. Got a name on you?"

Noctis raised his own glass in return and tapped it against her own. "Noctis Thorne."

Clarice smiled. "Thorne, is it? Very well, then. Welcome to the Street of Ash, Master Thorne."

They drank.

TIME FADED, AS IT DOES WHEN ONE REMAINS IN A SINGLE SPOT FOR long enough. Noctis settled into a routine of battling between self-doubt and conviction as the days slipped away in the flowing river of alcohol and revelry of the Street. He existed in a foggy haze of smoke and vapor and booze, the cacophony of the Street pushing all thought and concern from his mind. Somewhere, distantly, he knew that din'Dael had probably continued his march with the Lightborne, ignoring the Crow's dispatch. They would be arriving soon. But those were afterthoughts, vanishing into the fog of the present as quickly as they came.

He rarely descended from the balcony of his room where it overlooked the dance floor. He had a direct line of sight to Clarice behind the bar who, despite being the sole employee and forever rushing amidst the bustling business, somehow managed to make him feel like he had her full attention. He knew she must seem like that to every one of her patrons; that was what made this place so vibrant. Not the music, not the seemingly endless flow from the taps, no, the Street was the embodiment of Clarice's spirit. *A place worth saving.*

For hours each day, Noctis leaned against the railing of his perch and followed the movements of the bar's patrons. Some days were busier than others, some days the bar was nearly empty, but the energy within its walls remained lively regardless. With every passing day he found himself slowly fading into the woodwork of the place, a lost soul feeding off the joy and happiness of those who surrounded him. *Time truly stands still here,* he mused as he swirled the liquid in his glass. *The Street exists outside of time and thought.*

He'd had two Bottled Embers and was well into his third on the day Morella returned. Somehow, he missed seeing her enter the bar, but it was impossible not to recognize her once his eyes caught sight. His body tensed, but he stayed where he was. Morella looked at no one, spoke to no one, made no move for the bar but instead fixed her eyes on the empty dance floor. While Noctis looked on, Morella began to dance.

Her movements were as fluid as he remembered, her hands and tattooed wrists swaying as her body spun and twirled, just as before. Her raven hair caught the air as she dipped and twirled. There was no break in the music and no break in her dancing. His insides twisted at the sight of her pale skin in the dim light, at the memory of her lips against his own. *Back when I was someone else. Someone she loved.*

With effort, Noctis tore his eyes away from her dancing and caught Clarice's attention. He raised his drink and nodded toward Morella. Clarice set to work and Noctis returned his attention to Morella, the sole figure on the dance floor watched by the dazzled eyes of the surrounding patrons. Spinning, her ceaseless spinning—he found himself leaning far over the railing, drawn to her. He tightened his grip and pulled back. *Calm down. Just take it slow.*

Without breaking from her motion, Morella accepted the drink from Clarice, who winked at her and gestured toward the balcony upon which Noctis leaned. When she spun away from the bartender, Morella's eyes flickered up to Noctis. Even through the haze of alcohol, he caught the briefest hint of a smile on her face. She paused, stepping for the briefest moment out of her dance to raise the glass to him before downing it in a single draught. She set the empty glass on a nearby table, then looked away from him and resumed dancing.

Conflicted, Noctis waited. He made to move for the bar, but Clarice appeared bearing another drink. He stayed put. Morella, too, had another. His head was swimming, the motion of Morella's body as intoxicating as the ever-flowing Embers. The room seemed to dim even more, the darkness drawing in until all the illumination was solely upon Morella, like she was ringed in a spotlight. Noctis began to sway to the music from his perch. He closed his eyes for a brief moment, savoring the warmth of the drink and the music. When he opened them, Morella was gone.

Heart racing, Noctis scanned the room. She was nowhere to be seen. A hand pulled on his shoulder and spun him around. *How did she get up here so quickly?* Morella pushed him against the wall and pressed her mouth against his, wrapping her arms around him and continuing to sway in time with the music.

She kissed him hard, with a new ferocity. She pushed him backward, against the curtains, never ceasing to move. Her hands traced the bare skin of his body—he had no memory of his shirt coming off. The red lanterned lights from the ballroom swam around them as Morella pushed him to the ground and straddled him.

The world disappeared as their skin met. Noctis felt the fires raging in his body flare to life in a blazing fury. Static filled the air. White hot lightning danced across his skin and covered Morella's naked body. It crackled and sparked along her skin, mirroring his own, and she screamed in delight. The tempo of the rhythmic music increased in time with the motion of their own bodies. Noctis's world erupted in fire as Morella's nails tore red rivets across his chest.

They lay together, bare and blatant for any who had cause to look up. The world below was an afterthought. She was his world.

"Never leave me again, Will." Her head lay against his marred chest. When she raised it, her cheek was smeared with his blood and her tears. "Never leave me again."

The demand, the grotesque sight, they unnerved him more than he knew how to say. A sudden flash of uncertainty echoed deep in his mind. Still, he found himself nodding.

Morella lay her head back against his shoulder and traced the bloody tracks on his chest with her fingers. Noctis stiffened, suddenly very conscious of the fact that they were still on the balcony. The curtains afforded them some privacy, but not much.

He ran his fingers along her bare back and kissed the top of her head.

"We should move, Morella. We need to talk."

Her body tensed and she drew back from him, eyes suspicious and mouth curled down. "Will . . ."

He took her hands in his. "Nothing bad, Morella."

Still wary, she nodded and rose to her feet. Naked before the entire room, she raised her arms above her head and stretched. Looking down at him, she smiled at the surprised shock on his face before feigning demurity and covering her breasts. Abandoning her scattered clothes, she stepped away from him and into his room, beckoning for him to follow.

Heart racing, he did.

NOCTIS TALKED WHILE MORELLA LISTENED. HE TOLD HER OF din'Dael and the Sapholux. He told her of the pain of losing her and Madigan. He told her of how, at the end of everything, din'-Dael had seen to the purging of Will and the new guise of Noctis. He told her of the journey through the desert, of the Isle of Eternity, but he kept his conversation with Rienne to himself. He told her of the Crow and Cephora and the previous weeks in Undermyre. And he told her of the coming of Jero din'Dael at the head of an army of Lightborne. When he finished his telling, she sat in silence.

"That sounds like quite an adventure, Will."

"Not quite the way I'd planned it to go." He'd held back in some areas without really knowing why. He'd told her nothing of the hoard of aerilite weapons beneath the Sapholux, nor of the Relic housed within its depths. Those things didn't feel like they were his to tell. *Better to wait until the time is right.*

"No," she said softly. "I would imagine not."

She seemed suddenly distant, withdrawn. *I can't lose her again.* "Morella, when din'Dael took me, back at the Shale. I heard you. I heard you screaming. How did you escape? How did Val—"

"Stop." She closed her eyes and held up a hand to him. "If we are to find something resembling what we once had, you must promise that you will never ask me what happened there."

He closed his mouth and looked at the ground. "I'm sorry. I only meant—"

"He let me go." Her voice quivered. "He . . . it is nothing I'd care to describe again. He showed an ounce of mercy. Perhaps for everything I had on the Relics. Everything I'd ever worked for."

"That madman just let you walk away?"

Her eyes became hateful and her mouth twisted. "Hardly."

Noctis didn't press further. "I'm glad you're here," he said instead. "You're the only person I could imagine who might know how to help my brother. Cephora, she thinks he was taken by someone I didn't even know existed. Valmont's daughter, Aurellaine."

Morella's body tensed and her expression grew even darker. Her eyes turned hard and she glared at Noctis. "Oh?"

"Cephora believes Aurellaine took Mad under the pretense of training him in the ways of a Shadowborne."

"The woman was Shadowborne?" Morella's voice was a whisper laced with malice. Noctis nodded. "And Cephora is sure that it is Aurellaine Valmont?"

"To be honest, I don't know. Our meeting wasn't entirely pleasant."

"I can't imagine why," Morella said wryly.

"I don't know anything about Aurellaine Valmont. I'd never heard the name up until a few weeks ago," Noctis said. "I don't know what danger Mad could be in, but I know for certain that he knows even less about her than I do. I need to find him. I was hoping you could help."

"And how would I do that?"

"Come with me. Teach me what you know of Valmont's daughter."

She barked a laugh. "You think I'm an expert on her, do you?"

"I think that if you know more than her name, you know more about her than I do."

She looked at him quizzically for a moment then smiled and bent down to kiss him. "You're right, lover."

"You'll come with me?"

"The Relics, Valmont, a Lightborne, and a Shadowborne? Oh, I wouldn't miss this for anything."

"And us, then?" Noctis said softly. "Should I be reading into the past hour's activities as much as I am?"

Her mouth tightened a bit, but she winked at him nonetheless. "Will. Noctis. Whatever you're called, you're mine. I'm not going to let that change."

Noctis didn't say anything and she nuzzled back against him. His chest itched where she had scratched it, but it wasn't that that had him distracted. *Hers,* he thought. *Why does it seem like there's something else behind her words?* He didn't have time to linger on the thought because she began to trace her fingers along his chest.

"It has been far too long," she said. When she climbed atop him once more, whatever lingering thoughts and doubts were dashed from Noctis's mind.

He was hers.

16
THOSE WORTH SAVING

Noctis returned to the Nordoth the following day while Morella opted to remain in his rooms at the Street. He didn't ask where she had been staying previously. She had made it very apparent that whatever had happened before their reunion was hers and hers alone. Much as it ate at him to suppress his questions, he bit his tongue and didn't ask.

Ynarra was leaving his chamber in the Nordoth when he arrived. Her face split into a wide grin when she saw him, but then she immediately flushed and, before he could speak to her, turned and scurried off in the opposite direction. Noctis chuckled to himself. *That girl is something else. I see why Mad liked her.*

He retrieved the fresh decanter of wine and made for the library. Morella had agreed to help, but she didn't imply that she was the wealth of knowledge about Aurellaine Valmont he'd hoped she'd be. Regardless, perhaps there was some mention of the woman somewhere within the tomes. He set the decanter of wine on the table and poured himself a glass, drank in the flavor with a smile, and set to work.

Nothing.

Hours dragged by. Many books he was able to discard completely, histories predating the Wars of Dawning, simple biographies, and firsthand accounts of political maneuvering between Undermyre and the surrounding territories. Anything pertaining to Valmont and the fall of the Shadowborne, or really anything from the past few hundred years, was scarce. There was nothing he hadn't seen before. He frowned. There simply *had* to be more than this.

When the second decanter was empty, hours later, Noctis pushed himself to his feet and stumbled to the window and drew the curtains. It was impossible to tell the time of day, but he knew it had grown late simply by the drag of his body. He thumbed the fangs' bloodstones and considered using a bit of their power, just to keep going.

There, staring out at the glowing city and thumbing his daggers, a pang of confusion rose in his mind. It was small, a minor inconsistency that he nearly discarded, but it nagged at him. Rienne had said that the fangs' power shouldn't have worked for anyone wielding the power of Radiance, something about opposites contradicting one another.

And yet, when he'd first known Morella, he'd used them frequently enough. Morella knew what the weapons were and, as a historian who specialized in such things, surely she knew what Rienne had known. But when he revealed himself to her as Lightborne, she'd said nothing about the daggers. *She probably just forgot,* he thought. They'd been distracted by other endeavors, after all. *But still, something to put a pin in and ask her about. Maybe she's heard something about people realigning themselves, willingly or not.*

His eyes fell to the part of the city that housed the Street of Ash where his lover was undoubtedly dancing. She had more answers than she let on, maybe more than she even knew. *In some ways she's just as guarded as she was the first day we met.* He had to find a way to get her to open up to him.

Closing the curtains, he considered his bed in the loft. Large and soft, yes, but lonely. In all their time together, he and Morella had only spent the night together on hard ground under thin blankets. And last night, well, there had been little sleep for either of them last night. He smiled. Wine or no wine, the Street wasn't *that* far of a walk.

He grabbed his cloak and stumbled out the door.

DURING THE NEXT FEW DAYS, THEY FELL INTO A PLEASANT, IF distracting, routine. Filled with liquor, dancing, and the warmth of skin, Noctis and Morella lost themselves in one another. In his rare moments of sobriety, Noctis considered that Madigan would surely have groaned at the life he was living, but he pushed the thought from his mind. Growing up with Jervin, then spending the majority of the time since either on the road or cooped up in a training facility, there had been little to no time for Noctis to simply enjoy life. *Hedonism, the philosophers called it. I see the appeal. And, honestly, it's about time.*

After nearly a week, however, Noctis started feeling antsy. *Mad is in trouble, don't forget that. Get your head clear and go help.*

He looked down to where Morella lay curled up in his arms. He kissed her softly on the head. "Morella, we really need to get a few things figured out."

She nuzzled her head against his chest. "Is that so?"

Noctis wrestled with himself. Gently, he eased her away and sat up. "If Mad is in trouble, I can't just . . ." He trailed off.

"Why don't we go up to the Nordoth?" She kissed the fresh cuts her nails had made in his back. She draped her arms around his chest and nuzzled the back of his neck. "At least for a brief time. We can talk there."

Noctis craned his head around and smiled. "Yeah?"

"Absolutely. Plus, I'd like to get the layout of the place in case you disappear on me again and I need to find you."

"You think I plan on disappearing on you?" He chuckled lightly.

"Not if you know what's good for you," she said and playfully bit his ear. "But still, you've got your responsibilities there, eventually. This way, if you're gone for too long and not able to make it back to me here, I can come hunt you down."

He rolled his shoulders and pulled her around to face him. "I'd like that very much, I think." She grinned wide. He kissed her gently and they fell to pleasant distraction once more.

Later, Noctis guided Morella along the now-familiar back roads that formed the quickest path between the Nordoth and the Street. The guards at the various checkpoints didn't even glance his way anymore, even when he was accompanied by a stranger on his arm. He showed her the hidden door within the courtyard and the winding stair within and, laughing drunkenly, they climbed the stairs.

"I never knew this passage existed," Morella whispered excitedly. "It'll make coming and going without notice *much* easier. Are there more like this?"

"I wouldn't know." Noctis grinned and squeezed her hand. "I only ever venture out to make my way to your bed."

"*Our* bed." She squeezed his hand back.

Noctis felt like a child again, sneaking out at night and breaking the rules. Then something Morella said triggered in his mind and he paused, turning back to her. "Wait, you didn't know about *this* passage. So, you've been in the Nordoth before?"

She chortled and rolled her eyes before nodding. "Briefly. I attended one of the council's open-proclamation sessions once. It was very dull." She smiled conspiratorially. "I may have snuck off and explored a bit."

Noctis feigned shock. “My, aren’t you just the scandalous rebel?”

She wrinkled her nose at him and smiled. “Oh yes, best stay on your toes around me.”

They reached the top of the stair and Noctis led her into his chamber. It had been days since he was last there, but nonetheless, there were refreshments and a jug of wine waiting. He poured a large portion into the single glass and offered it to Morella. She gave him a flirtatious ‘ooh’ as she accepted it and took a sip.

“We can share,” she said with a wink.

Without another word, she downed the contents of the glass in a single breath and grabbed the bottle. Rather than refilling the glass, however, she took Noctis’s hand and, after a quick scan of the room, made for the stairs that led to the loft.

“Morella, we really should—” He was cut off as she whirled and pressed her lips against his. Drawing away, she gave him her coy, crooked grin and continued leading him to the steps. *Oh, I suppose Mad can wait,* Noctis mused.

Morella set the bottle on the bedside table and pressed Noctis down onto the lush blankets. His eyes fell to the vacant bed at the other end of the loft and his thoughts became distracted by his brother once more. No, it couldn’t wait. *Now’s not the time.* He rose to his feet. “Really though, this whole Aurellaine thing—”

Morella shoved him hard enough to knock him back but lightly enough to still be playful, and he fell back onto the bed. Pushing up onto his elbows, his thoughts became focused solely on her once more. She disrobed and climbed onto the bed, kissing his chest and his neck. *Just relax. He can wait.*

No, he can’t. “Morella, really I think that—”

This time he was cut off by something below them on the landing: the sound of the door opening. Noctis quickly glanced to the side and saw Ynarra enter, carrying a small tray of food and beaming.

Morella, too, had noticed the newcomer. She frowned. She pushed herself up off Noctis and strode to the top of the stairs.

Ynarra, who had been glancing around the room looking for Noctis, suddenly saw the naked woman standing with arms crossed. Her eyes widening, Ynarra opened her mouth to speak but quickly thought better of it. Her face blushed a vibrant red. She dropped her eyes and hurried into the room with the tray, following the routine so familiar to Noctis from his first stay.

Morella, still scowling, reached down and wrapped a nearby shawl around her waist. While Ynarra busied herself, Morella strode down to the lower level, eyeing the girl. Noctis, scrambling to adjust his clothing, quickly followed.

"Apologies, sir," Ynarra said quickly, keeping her eyes down. "I did not know that there was a guest. Beyond you, sir. You are our guest. I meant your own guest. Sir."

"It's fine, Ynarra," Noctis said, raising a friendly hand and smiling. "You have no need to apologize. I should have—"

"Another glass," Morella snapped at the girl with an authoritative tone that brooked no argument. "Another bottle, while you're at it. Quickly."

Ynarra glanced from Noctis to Morella before quite abruptly dropping her eyes to the ground. She curtsied limply. "Yes, mistress. I am sorry, mistress."

"Quickly, I said."

Ynarra's lips trembled as she curtsied once more. Then she spun and raced from the room.

Noctis looked at Morella in disbelief. "What the hell was that?"

Morella eyed him. "Excuse me?"

"What the hell was that?" Noctis said again. "Why did you treat her like that?"

"I don't understand what you're asking, Noctis," she said, making no effort to mask her impatience.

"You had no right to treat her that way. She's just a shy, innocent girl who is just doing her damn job!"

Morella, who had been staring at him with an expression of distaste, suddenly burst into raucous laughter. "Oh, my sweet, ignorant Casc. That *shy, innocent girl* is one of the Unborn, or was once. She would just as soon skin you alive as serve you wine."

This time, it was Noctis who burst out laughing. "Ynarra?" he said incredulously. "You think Ynarra is violent?"

"Of course she is," Morella snapped at him. "Do you know nothing of the Unborn?"

Noctis felt his jaw tense, the familiar palpations of frustration in his stomach. "No, Morella, I do not know anything of the Unborn."

She sighed and shook her head, then reached for his hand and pulled him in the direction of the loft. "Come on, lover. Let's be done with this."

Listen to her, let it go.

"No." The quiet stillness in his voice surprised even him. "She has been nothing but kind to me and if there is something more to her, I want to know what it is."

Morella rolled her eyes and crossed her arms. "Fine." She spat the word. "First off, you can tell simply by her physical appearance where she comes from. However, if you were blind to that, the tattoo beneath her eye? It's the marking of a captured Unborn. In the lands beyond the Daurhi Wastes, where slavery is still common, that is the mark placed upon such." She shook her head and lowered it at Noctis. "Anyone with any amount of education could easily see that."

She'd know better than I would. He searched Morella's eyes, hoping to see something in there that . . . what? Hinted at a lie? Why would she lie about something like this? No, she wasn't lying. And yet, even if it was true that he knew nothing about Ynarra or her past, it didn't change his stance.

Noctis chose his next words carefully. "She is simply a serving girl within these walls. Whatever she was before she came to the Nordoth, whatever she was before I met her, is not my concern. After our grandfather's death, she was the first person to extend any true kindness to my brother and me. I will not see her treated so harshly by someone. *Especially* someone I brought into her world."

He expected another outburst, another twisted face and cruel eyes, but Morella simply scoffed. "However you'd like it, lover." She turned toward the loft, holding out a hand and looking back at him over her shoulder as the shawl fell to the floor. "Shall we go make up?"

Her naked body was as intoxicating as ever, but Noctis shook his head. "I'd rather not." His voice came out flat. "There are more important matters to deal with."

Now came the outburst. The depths of her temper, which he had come so close to forgetting, flared and returned in force. She said nothing but the look on her face spoke volumes. Morella turned and stormed up to the loft, retrieving her clothes. She pulled them on unceremoniously and made for the door, giving Noctis a wide berth.

"I'm going to the Street." Her voice was flustered, angry, impatient. "Maybe, once you get over your own goddam arrogance long enough to stop pushing away the *one* good thing you've got going for you, we can pick up where we left off." With that, she turned and stomped from the room.

Noctis was left alone, confused and frustrated. A moment later, the door handle turned and he felt his heart race, but it was Ynarra returning with the fresh bottle of wine and two glasses. She looked momentarily terrified as she entered the room. Seeing only Noctis, she glanced around furtively and moved quickly, keeping her head down.

"It's fine, Ynarra. She's gone. I'm sorry about that. You've got nothing to worry about."

"Worry, sir?" Ynarra said quietly while setting down the tray. She did not raise her head to meet his gaze.

"I spoke to her about . . . about the manner in which she addressed you. She'll . . . I'm sure she'll be more courteous in the future. But still, I apologize." He smiled, feeling something between tension and defeat. "You're still safe here, Ynarra."

"Oh, sir, thank you, sir, but it is not necessary," she said, curtsying and ducking her head awkwardly. "I mean, please, sir, do as you will, of course. Sir."

"Ynarra." Noctis held up a hand. "You don't need to act like this. It's okay, I mean it. You're safe here."

She kept her eyes on the floor and nodded. "Yes, of course, sir. We are all quite safe here, sir. If you are concerned about safety, sir, I will see that there are more guards in this wing. If you desire it, sir."

"Ynarra, please," he replied. "You don't need to call me sir. Call me Will."

He noticed his error as soon as he said it, but before he could correct himself, she finally raised her eyes. They were brimming with tears.

"Ye . . . yes," she stammered. "Thank you, Will." Then she dropped her eyes quickly.

"What I meant before, Ynarra," he said slowly, "is that *you* are safe *here*. In this room. With me and with Madigan, whenever he returns. Don't think of this room as part of the Nordoth, please. It's separate, apart from the world beyond these walls. Think of it as somewhere that *you* are safe."

She looked up at him again and this time the tears were running freely down her cheeks. "I . . . I understand, Will. Thank you, Will."

Before he could say anything else, she turned and fled.

He plopped down onto the loft's stairs and rubbed his eyes. They were dry and puffy. In fact, every part of him felt thick and slow. *What the hell am I doing?*

I don't like the effect she has on you, Mad said, once upon a time.

He's not wrong. Morella was like a drug to him; the past few weeks had proven as much, a world of distraction and intoxication. But more than that, there was something about her, something dangerous and fascinating. *I keep coming back. There's still so much I don't know about her. About any of this.*

He sighed and glanced at the wine longingly, then shied away from it. *No, I need to clear my head.*

Morella knew of Aurellaine Valmont. If he was to have any hope of rescuing his brother, he needed to know what Morella knew. *That, and figure out wherever the hell Mad ran off to with Aurellaine.*

Cephora had made it very clear that Madigan took the lead when the unknown Shadowborne approached them. Mad had determined a place to go—and that meant it was probably one that Noctis knew about.

Much as Noctis tried, however, nothing came. His thoughts were sluggish and muddled. *Cephora probably backtracked everywhere we went looking for him, and she's a hell of a lot better at this than I am.*

An idea sparked somewhere at the back of his mind. He got up and moved to where he had tucked away the few belongings he brought from the Sapholux. He withdrew the cutlass from the sack and fastened the baldric across his chest. He tucked a hand around his key and raised it to eye level while letting the other hand rest on the familiarity of the bloodstone. The key's colors were as hypnotic as ever. *Why can my eyes never keep up with it?* The pulsing of strange electricity raced across his skin when he released the key to settle against his chest. *What* is *this thing?*

Now's not the time to get lost in that. He brushed the thought away and made his way to the window where he drew the curtains wide, letting the cold air of the high altitude blow into the room. He grasped a cord and breathed deep the fresh salt air. He hung out the window and thought back to his first night in the Nordoth. It had all been so new, and when the danger had seemingly passed, he'd felt the thrill of Aeril and Undermyre. The thrill of adventure, of a new world. He had hung out of this very window, had discovered *The Veleriat* in the library, had climbed the rafters and discovered the place where he finally tapped into his Shade.

Noctis's insides twisted with a sudden sense of loss. He'd tried for so long to ignore his Shade, to suppress it or move past it. But whatever the powers of Radiance, they could never completely fill the piece of him that had been lost. *Do I really remember it though? Or am I just grasping at the memory of a memory, searching for something I never really knew?*

He pulled himself back inside the window and, forgetting himself, poured a glass of wine that he drained quickly. Glancing up, Noctis smiled and ran to the far wall with the hanging ropes. He climbed to the cross section of the rafters where he had spent long hours meditating in search of answers. Perhaps now, as then, he might find some degree of direction.

Lying prone at the top, he peered down at the room. He had last looked down from this perch when he and Madigan had stopped the men assaulting Ynarra—the "test" staged by the Crow to prove to Cephora that the brothers were useful. The high space dredged up memories that din'Dael's fiery rhetoric had tried to burn away, memories of a happier life. A life *before.*

For that was truly the case, he realized. His life had broken in two, with a before and an after. The break wasn't at the death of his grandfather or the discovery of the passage to Aeril; it came in the Shale when din'Dael first laid his hands upon him, changed him. Noctis stared at the distant ground and let his mind wander. *I set out to know what he did to me and didn't even realize I gave up, somewhere. I became the tool that din'Dael needed me to be.*

Training in the Sapholux had been so all-consuming, so different than training with his grandfather. Jervin had been tough and strict, but it came from a place of love. He trained Will to be a better version of himself, not a foreign version of himself. Not someone forged from other people's beliefs. *So that your minds may be your own,* Noctis remembered. *Grandda was always adamant. I've lost that.*

He had lost so much since Jervin gave the keys to his grandsons, since Senraks murdered him. Noctis's eyes widened. *Senraks. I haven't thought of that creature in months.* How much else had he missed? What else of his home had he forgotten? What else could—

His breath caught in his throat. Trembling swept through his limbs and he set a hand against a beam to steady himself. That was it.

He knew exactly where to find Madigan.

17

WINTER WINDS

Madigan shivered. Winter had come in strong this year, the river wind's biting chill more forceful than he could remember it. It always managed to find the smallest creases and crevices in the tent he called home and dig at him with icy claws.

He often wondered if it might not have been better, perhaps, to put themselves back on the grid. At the very least get an old RV or small trailer. *Something that at least had some actual goddam doors.* Ileta had scoffed at the idea when he first mentioned it and had done so ever since. Her disdain for his world and its technological luxuries was glaringly apparent. So, Madigan had just sighed and braced for the uncertain weather patterns of the Pacific Northwest.

They'd been fortunate, at least. Ileta did a damn good job of keeping the camp tight and, after her initial survey of the area, had actually put together a pretty clean site that stood up damn well to the weather, whatever the season. They'd done a good job of shoring up the surrounding areas and building relatively solid environmental defenses. His grandfather would have been proud, had he been alive to see it. Those winter nights camping up on Mt. Hood certainly paid off.

Still, the wind is a bitch.

It was dark when he woke, not that that was too much of a surprise. He tossed and turned for a time, debating on returning to sleep as Ileta now didn't seem too terribly concerned with early morning wakeups. Ultimately, he opted to venture out into the cold and see what the day had in store. Breathing hard to get his heart racing and bracing himself for the November chill, he unzipped the tent.

He stepped out into the white stillness of snow. His bare skin immediately prickled, making the numerous scars even more apparent. His Shade, a constant part of his presence now, drew near to his body as he pulled at what warmth there was in the air. It didn't help.

Madigan sighed. The cold still bothered him despite Ileta's frequent protestations that he should have adjusted to it. "One of these days, you're just going to have to figure this out," she had said two days ago when he collapsed in the snow. It was a common phrase of hers.

His failure, to the best of his understanding, was to fully use his Shade to draw heat from the particles of light that cascaded through the air, then use the heat to thermoregulate his own body. Apparently, the opposite could be done in cases of extreme heat. He hadn't gotten the hang of that either.

Maybe I'll just go invest in a goddam space heater.

He sat cross-legged on the snow, pulled his Shade back, and let the chill cascade about him. There was something familiar about it, something about being in his home on frosty mornings. While the house was long since destroyed, this place was still home. He knew the trees, the smells, the sounds. All that was missing was an annoying little brother. That, and their grandfather's laughter. But that was something he'd never hear again.

Will, though, with Will there might still be a chance.

Mad looked around, scratching at his beard. When he'd finally recovered from his fall, he'd had every intention of ridding himself of the damn thing. But when he'd seen his reflection, he hadn't actually hated the look. The whiskers had been wild and in need of a trim, but after he attacked them with scissors, yes, it worked.

Not to mention it makes the cold a lot more bearable.

Madigan glanced at Ileta's tent. She hadn't stirred yet. That was a rarity but one he'd gladly take. The morning was peaceful, and he wasn't sure how ready he was for her sharp tongue to break the calm. He had a tentative, reserved affection for her that still bordered on fear, but they'd definitely found their stride. Ever since the fall, though, she'd been different. In the weeks since his recovery, she'd insisted that they return to Aeril, return to a hidden place she knew. Mad had refused. After that, a strange, weary disappointment suffused her.

Wherever her hidden destination was, it would no doubt further her secret agenda. And Madigan, well, he wanted to keep as much control of the situation as he could. *Which still isn't much.* Some semblance of control meant someplace he knew and knew well. Aeril didn't have that to offer. Cephora—his mouth twisted downward at the thought of her—had not even pretended to understand. Ileta, while frustrated by his choice, had at least acknowledged his desire to train in secret, safe from Valmont and whatever Necrothanian forces were being mustered against him. *Assuming it's even me that he's after.*

Mad breathed in the cold and thought back to those first days together. Although annoyed, Ileta led him to the Ways. They traveled closer to Undermyre than Mad cared for, but given that he and Will had exited the Ways and entered the Nordoth in a single day, he supposed that wasn't too terribly surprising. They'd had to dodge multiple patrols, all bearing the tall pauldrons that marked them as agents of the Crow. Ileta had seemed just as determined to avoid their attentions as Mad was.

At least we saw eye to eye on that one.

Navigating the Ways had taken only a few hours. Ileta was extremely familiar with them, though he wasn't sure why that surprised him. The pair ventured toward the Cascanian path that his grandfather had sealed so well, once upon a time. Mad told Will, once, that there would be plenty of time for exploring the Ways together at a later date. He still hoped to be proven right.

They'd crossed through the cavernous chamber with the bridge where he and Will finally saw the proof of their grandfather's tales. They'd passed through the ancient door barring the Cascanian entrance and into the world beyond. When they'd crossed the chamber with the decayed corpse of the creature Will killed to save their lives, a strange sense of separation had come over Mad. A dissonance. *Will will find me, if he survived,* he told himself. *He'll figure it out.*

That had been nearly three years ago, by Cascanian standards, and there was still no sign of his brother. *He survived,* Mad thought as the chill of the snow set him shivering. *He has to have survived.*

Ileta got them through the roof of the chamber easily, but the manner in which she did so left Mad in shock. She *floated.* They both had. The memory, the feeling of it, still stuck with him. The sensation had been nearly as cold as the ground upon which he now sat, but his adrenaline had spiked, excitement racing through him like he was a kid on a carnival ride. She had encircled them both in her Shade and then used it to change the room. The strange light from the pool had grown and intensified, spreading to the walls but, rather than diminishing, the darkness had compressed around them. Compressed and pushed them up, into the air.

He couldn't wait to learn that trick.

After that, navigating through the tunnels had been surprisingly easy, something he never would have guessed from his first adventure into them. Ileta took them along a different route than the one he and Will used. She stepped easily through the trap-laden paths, showing Madigan how to use his Shade to probe and balance, then moved through the dark underground with barely a second's rest. They'd surfaced, finally, after Ileta destroyed a cement wall in the path that led them into a dusty, web-ridden basement on the east side of the river.

And just like that, Madigan was back in Portland.

The first few weeks had been more about establishing a base to operate from rather than any real training. He'd been convinced when they'd approached his home that the city would have reclaimed it, that they'd find a new housing development just like those he'd seen popping up everywhere along the way. But for whatever reason, the land was untouched. Overgrown and in poor condition, yes, but still there.

He'd avoided the wreckage of the house and the memories of the terrible battle that was waged there. He hadn't been ready for that. Instead, they'd set up camp a short distance away, near the old gardening and storage sheds. The bikes and wagons were still in there, so he and Ileta were able to travel quickly to the family's storage unit where he and Will had outfitted themselves. It, too, was untouched, and the wreckage of Will's bunk brought the memories of that time flooding back.

It took some time to move what they needed but in the end they'd been able to set up a pretty respectable base.

Up until then Ileta had been a relatively silent companion. She'd accepted Madigan's lead, seeming to default to him on "Casc matters," as she put it. But once their training site was set up, her demeanor changed completely. Throughout the beginning of their training, there had been a constant mutual frustration; she was disappointed by his lack of skill with Shadow, and he was disappointed by her lack of compassion and her secretive nature. When he pressed her for more information on who she was and where she'd come from, finally, she'd smirked and shaken her head.

"I serve one who bears great interest in you, Madigan Davis, one who would see you trained to your full potential. Trust me, it will all work out for the best."

"That's quite a leap of faith you're asking."

"It will all be worth it," she said with a sly grin. "In the end."

That had hardly created unyielding trust. Arguing had achieved nothing; she'd established herself as the dominant party almost immediately. So, Mad begrudgingly learned to follow. But, goddam was she talented, incredibly well versed when it came to the capabilities of Shadowborne. Beyond the simple manipulation of a Shade that Mad had grown accustomed to and seen Will use, Ileta demonstrated abilities he'd never even imagined.

When they sparred, her skills with her noctori were dazzling. She could reform blades faster than his eye could catch. Whereas Madigan trained constantly with a bastard sword, she used every manner of weapon that came to her mind, switching between them in an instant. It kept him off balance. He had grown accustomed to fighting Will and his Shade, but Ileta was something different entirely. She changed weapons both on offense and on defense faster than Madigan could adjust.

He loved it.

Ileta also had knowledge of things that both the Crow and Cephora had scoffed at. She'd told him how at no point had she ever believed that Valmont was dead and that she'd always considered the man to be simply biding his time. When he told her of din'Dael's release from the Shale and the man's destructive madness, she'd rolled her eyes and asked him what he'd expected.

Although he had no proof, Mad assumed her knowledge came directly from whomever it was she served. But all she would ever allow him regarding the hidden master's interest in him was that it was more than just his ability as a Shadowborne. That it stemmed from the fact that somehow Madigan had lured Valmont from whatever hole he had been hiding in and survived to tell of it. She would not, however, say how her master came by the information.

At first, Ileta questioned him at length. His account of the brief confrontation with the sorcerer hadn't stirred her in the slightest, although she commended him for standing his ground against 'the one known as Bloodborne.' Whether it was bravery or foolishness (she seemed to believe the latter), she found the sheer impudence (Mad now thought it to be more ineptitude) impressive. She lauded that he struck a blow, even though the strike failed.

That conversation had led him to a deeper understanding of the power of Shadow, this time regarding the noctori. In his brief introductory lesson from his grandfather, all Mad knew of the weapon was that it was Shadow magic and could change shape. Ileta laughed so hard when he told her that, Mad's face had turned beet red. Eventually, she explained the noctori's strength. More than being a blade formed from Shadow, it could be empowered by Shadow—by his Shade. He could lend it strength, pouring the darkness into it. Valmont had simply done the opposite when Mad struck, sucking all energy from the blade.

The knowledge that he could have empowered his blade against Valmont hit Mad like a ton of bricks. What if he had known that before? Sure, there was no guarantee that the blade would have had the strength to counteract Valmont entirely, but what if it had been? What if he'd been able to strike the man down, then and there? That question of 'what if' had never left him, had plagued his mind and led to countless sleepless nights. He'd hounded Ileta with questions, wondering at the number and size of the gaps in his learning. She, in turn, had humored him with her knowledge.

Madigan traced his fingers in the snow. Yes, Ileta was knowledgeable, very much so. She was also more dangerous than she let on. She was cool and controlled and powerful. In the same fashion that their Shades poured from their bodies in a cloud, she seemed to be surrounded by an aura of captivating danger. Even to this day, it was difficult to meet her eye and not feel pierced. Ileta gave him pause.

He still didn't know what to make of that. He did know that he was progressing, whatever that meant. He knew that his skill had quickly surpassed whatever his brother's had ever been, but it was still nowhere near Ileta's. *Three years here, and I still struggle to keep up.*

He needed more. He needed to achieve her level of mastery. If there was a subtly hidden aspect of the Shade, he needed to discover every bit of it.

I need to be the best. I need to come at this from every angle.

His thoughts turned to Will and all the years he'd spent hiding who he was. Never being able to fully explore something so intrinsic and personal? That sounded like absolute hell. Mad's Shade was as much a part of him as a limb. Knowing that it existed within him but being unable to access it would have been like being forced to use crutches when both legs worked fine. He would constantly be wanting to just lower the leg and use it, never fully understanding why the world told him he couldn't.

He frowned and ran cool, wet hands through his hair. He had been complicit in Will's suppression. He had forced his brother to diminish himself, something that Madigan couldn't imagine doing to himself, now. That Will had complied and had continued to comply for so long, despite whatever circumstances arose, was a testament to the kid's strength.

Then it was ripped away from him.

Jero din-goddam-Dael. Damn that Lightborne. Who knows what that bastard did to Will?

In the silence of the cold morning, a depressing hopelessness clawed at him. He tried to keep an open mind, to stay optimistic. But Madigan mourned for his brother. Whatever he told himself, he truly did not know if Will was still alive. He hoped he was alive, wanted him to be alive, but he did not know. It gnawed at him that despite memories of years of happy times with Will, the most vivid one was the terrified look on his brother's face when Cephora tore them apart. He desperately wanted Will to be alive, wanted new memories to push aside that look of surprise and fear, but . . . *It doesn't look good*. The only thing he had to go on, to fight the depression, was hope itself.

That's not a whole goddam lot to go on.

Madigan hated the plague of questions and uncertainty. Did Will get away from Valmont? Did he undo din'Dael's actions? A part of Mad knew he might never know what happened that day, what happened to his brother. His heart wrenched at the thought.

The sky was just lightening when a sound from Ileta's tent pulled him from his melancholic thoughts. He exhaled slowly and rose to his feet, the chill from the morning filling the hollowness inside him. The flap of the tent opened and Ileta stepped out. She raised an eyebrow at him and snickered, shaking her head.

"You should have been sleeping. You need your rest."

Madigan cracked his neck and stretched before shaking his legs to loosen his knees. "I've rested long enough."

Ileta smiled at him. "We shall see about that."

She took off running and Madigan followed, navigating Jervin's old trail along the levee without thinking. He glanced over at the scorched patch of earth well beyond their camp where his home once stood. A comforting determination settled in his breast.

Yes, I've rested long enough. It's time to get back into the world. Time to get answers.

18
AURELLAINE

"You want to take me where, exactly?" Morella eyed Noctis sidelong, her expression somewhere between amusement and irritation.

The Street was busier than he had seen it in some time. Clarice handed him two drinks the moment she saw him and gestured up to the balcony. Morella's pale skin caught the lamplight and he steeled himself. He climbed the stairs, expecting a chilly reception, but he hardly set foot in their room before she threw herself at him. The greeting had been far better than he'd anticipated, capped off by two additional Bottled Embers that Clarice set outside their door. All in all, not a bad morning.

"Home," he answered. "Portland. Well, Cascania," he followed up quickly, "but Portland specifically."

"Portland?" Morella raised an eyebrow. "What, is it on the sea?"

A smile tugged at Noctis's mouth. "A river," he said. "Two, actually. But they lead to a larger body of water, yes."

She sipped at her drink and walked to the balcony. She still hadn't bothered dressing, but Noctis was growing accustomed to it. Plus, the majority of the patrons never thought to look up. "And you think your brother is there with Aurellaine Valmont?"

Noctis hesitated before nodding. "I believe he is there with a Shadowborne." He took a drink, letting the rejuvenating warmth flow down his throat. "Others believe it is Aurellaine. I have no idea who Aurellaine is."

She snickered. "That is an easy enough education if you wish to hear it."

He raised an eyebrow at her. "I thought you said you didn't know much about her."

"I don't. But I suppose I know more than the average person." She gave him a sultry gaze and pressed her body against his, tilting her head so their lips were nearly touching. "And I *definitely* know more than a foolish Casc."

Noctis smiled and leaned down to kiss her, but she pulled back and wagged a playful finger at him. "Tut tut, Mr. Thorne. Here I thought you were in the mood for a history lesson."

"I'm in the mood for many things, Ms. Darklore."

She laughed and kissed him, then drew back and drank. "Well, one thing at a time. Aurellaine Valmont, then. You want to know what I know?"

"I do." He reached for her hand. "I need to know what I'm going up against."

"What *we* are going up against." She gave a wry smile and squeezed his hand. Despite the early hour, she turned and waved to Clarice for another round of Bottled Embers. She sipped at the glass in her hand and then stared up at the floating lanterns, her face a mask.

After Noctis intercepted Clarice and returned bearing the drinks, he found Morella wrapped in a shawl on one of the lounging chairs on the balcony. She did not meet his eye.

"I don't have my notes anymore," she said, "but I never bothered to write much about Valmont's daughter. My research was focused on the Relics."

Noctis felt a pang of regret. He still had not shared the entirety of his experiences in the Sapholux, the education he received under din'Dael. *We both have things we're keeping from each other,* he thought as he took a sip and eyed Morella. "I know," he said. "Just, anything you have."

"Aurellaine Valmont." She sighed deeply. "Rumors say she was brought into this world wrapped in her Shade. Just rumors, surely, but they underscore her power. She was Borne since she was born, apparently, something that is almost unheard of. She was Valmont's blood but was born after he'd been captured, during the Sundering, supposedly. As a child, she never met the man."

Noctis watched and waited as Morella paused. Already, he had questions he forced himself to hold back. *Just let her do this her way.* He sipped at his drink and sat patiently.

"The timelines are messy, though. Supposedly she was raised in Umbriferum, guided by Maruq T'Aroth, but that goes against the birth during the Sundering." She shook her head and drank. "Whatever story you hear, one thing was constant. She was as skilled a Shadowborne as any who ever lived. So they say. Her father's daughter. Secretive and duplicitous. A master of disguise. The Umbriferum supposedly used her skills for their more"—Morella gazed around the room—"uncouth operations. Again, no one really knows."

"She was an assassin?"

The hint of a smile tugged at Morella's mouth. "Something like that. Infiltration, assassinations. For every great act of Umbriferum there are countless horrors kept hidden." She drank again. "Aurellaine, though, she never knew anything else. A trained weapon, guided by Shadow. Supposedly, she didn't even know that she was Valmont's daughter. Everyone else in the Order did, but not her."

"Is that why she betrayed them?" Noctis burst out. Morella shot him an impatient glare and he clamped his mouth shut.

"Sorry, go on."

"The Umbriferum used her. The entire Order was complicit. Like I said, they have their own dark history. Everyone does." She took another drink and tugged at the shawl around her, seeming to retreat deeper into the chair. "Of course, she'd heard the stories of Valmont, how could she not? It was only a matter of time until she found out her own truth.

"When she did, well, no one really knows what happened next. A confrontation, most likely. One that resulted in her being excommunicated from all she'd ever known, I suppose. Except that someone like that out in the world, uncontrolled? Umbriferum couldn't have it. So, they tried to kill her."

She was staring at the lanterns now, seemingly no longer aware of Noctis. He watched as her face became a blank mask, the dancing lights casting swirls of red along the canvas.

"She fought back, of course. Won. That was around the time rumors of Valmont began to swirl again. Stories say that she sought him out, feigned joining his ranks, and tried to kill him. Blood fangs to the heart and a nice fall into oblivion. Everyone thought she succeeded. Probably did it to try and get back into the good graces of the Umbriferum. It didn't work. She snapped. Killed them all."

Morella's eyes regained their focus and fell into the swirling colors of her drink. "After that, no one knows. Lost to the winds, it would seem."

Despite what he had heard, Noctis felt a pang of sympathy for Aurellaine. *Why is everything a tragedy here? Are there no happy endings?* There had to be. His grandfather had known the goodness of this world, had seen something in it that made him want his boys to come here. *Or was he just like me? Did he just* want *there to be goodness here and thought we could help?*

Morella was staring at him, her face searching his with an intensity that made him uncomfortable. He realized that he had not yet spoken.

"If she tried to kill her father, why did she then turn and become an agent of his? Doing his work after she thought him dead?"

Morella considered a moment before answering. "No one except for her could know for sure, but people have their opinions."

"Why, do you think?"

She laughed, bawdy and lovely, and the tension in his chest released at the sound. "I'm a historian. I try to stay objective."

"Surely, though, you've got some idea?"

She paused a moment, staring at him. "I think she did it to save him," she said finally. "I know that sounds absurd, but think about it. Valmont was being hunted by every power that Aeril could throw at him. The Hesperawn themselves sought him. What better way to escape than to be dead?"

"You're saying it was staged?"

She shrugged. "I'm saying that Valmont spent years trying to prove that he was equal to the Hesperawn, that anyone could be. A public display of his supposed death and subsequent survival would definitely challenge the notion of simple mortality. So, do I think it was staged? No. I think Aurellaine stabbed her father through the heart and threw him from the mountain. I just don't think that the blade or the fall could have killed him."

"The landing is what would have killed him," Noctis said with a wink. When Morella frowned in confusion, he explained. "The fall isn't what would have killed him. The landing at the end of the fall would have." She continued to stare at him without responding. "It's a joke."

"I see," she said flatly.

"Sorry, I didn't mean to make light of it. Please, go on."

"Aurellaine wouldn't have wanted her father dead one way or another. She'd lost the Umbriferum and the Borne and herself. Then she'd discovered some long-dead trace of her family still existed. She wanted *something* good in her life, and everyone wants to believe their family is good, wants to see goodness in them. So, my thoughts? Whatever she did, she did it under his direction."

Noctis paused before speaking hesitantly. "Morella, what about *your* family? Where did you come from?"

She didn't meet his eye. "Like I said, lover, everyone wants to believe their family is good, regardless if all evidence points to the contrary."

It was obviously a sensitive subject, so he steered away from it as quickly as possible. "So, Valmont orchestrated the whole thing then?" Noctis shook his head. "He put it all in motion to prove that he could cheat death."

"More or less, yes," Morella said, nodding. "That is my belief, at least."

"That's a lot to take in," Noctis said. After a moment's pause, he shook his head again. "Actually, it really isn't. Valmont was clever—*is* clever—and if he used Aurellaine to ensure that his work would continue whether he survived or not, no one could ever be fully sure that he died."

"Which he didn't." Morella smiled.

"Which he didn't. So, what then? We can assume that Aurellaine did his work for him while he was away, right? Away doing whatever it was he was doing?" Morella nodded. "Then why did he choose to come back now? What was it about the timing? It couldn't just be Madigan and me that drew him out."

"No?" Morella was silent a moment as she peered at him. "Two powerful Cascs, one Shadowborne and one Lightborne, who free his greatest adversary and level an impenetrable fortress that had stood since time immemorial? You don't think that might cause someone to come out of hiding?"

Noctis dropped his gaze to his hands. "I hadn't thought of it that way."

"Not to mention that they are the descendants of the Blademaster. *And* they managed to get the last surviving Earth Warder into the mix," Morella went on. "I don't think you're giving yourself enough credit. You've caused quite a stir."

"I suppose so," Noctis said mildly. *And here we thought we'd been moving so quietly.*

"Then there is also the fact that you reopened the Ways."

Noctis eyed her. "How, exactly, did we reopen them? Or, rather, how were they closed? It was just a simple door that we pulled open."

Morella laughed. "Oh, lover, you really do have so much to learn still, don't you?" Noctis was silent, although he was feeling rather defensive. Morella smiled and went on. "You entered the Sapholux with din'Dael, didn't you?" He nodded. "Then you're familiar with the etched doors, yes?"

Noctis thought back. He remembered how similar the final barrier had been to the door within the Ways. "Yes, I remember the doors."

"The carved intricacies, the filigree, things of that nature within them, yes?"

"Yes."

"And do you remember what it took to open it?"

"Power," he answered. "Our combined powers of Radiance."

"Correct." She smiled at him. "Only Lightborne are capable of opening the passages to the Sapholux, just like only Shadowborne had the powers to open Umbriferum."

This was news to Noctis. *And if the Sapholux were hiding an army of Lightborne within its walls, is there an army of Shadowborne hiding within Umbriferum?* If no one was able to enter, how would anyone ever know? *Nothing stays dead . . .*

"Jervin Thorne wasn't Borne," Morella continued, seeming unaware that Noctis was lost in his own thoughts, "and, as such, had no method for sealing such a door." At a questioning glance from Noctis, she rolled her eyes. "The Ways weren't sealed. The doors were unbound. Jervin Thorne discovered a way to lock the Ways without the use of any surviving magics."

Noctis's mouth went dry as his thoughts drifted to the key draped around his neck. *Just your minds, boys, your minds and your spirits,* his grandfather had said when Will asked what the keys unlocked.

"Somehow"—Morella's eyes followed his hand that moved to rest on the key—"you and your brother managed to open something that had proved impossible for anyone else. The pair of you possess something that no one in all of Aeril has—at least no one known."

Keep them secret, Jervin's voice echoed in Noctis's head. His throat was dry as he spoke to her. "Do you have any idea what that possession might be?"

She reached out and caressed his face, tracing his jawline with her fingers and trailing them down his throat. She rested her fingers against his chest. "I have an idea," she said softly, "that I know where the key lies."

Noctis's fingers twitched as he met her gaze, unwavering. His heart was hammering. "Is that so?"

She kept her hand against his chest and pulled herself to straddle him. "The key is in your blood."

He was taken aback but did not break eye contact as he struggled to maintain his composure, hoping that he managed to hide the relief flooding his body. He actually managed a laugh and shook his head. "I thought you were going to say . . ." He gestured to his chest.

She looked skeptical. "What, that little trinket?" She rolled her eyes. "Magic seals require more than *simple* keys, lover."

Simple, right. He scoffed to himself. Nevertheless, he exhaled to release the tension he felt.

"Blood, though . . ." she went on and draped her legs over him.

"Right, blood." Noctis's heart fluttered as Morella wrapped her arms around his neck. "That would be quite the key."

"You and your brother were both battered by the time you reached the door. It makes sense, then, that your bloodline was the key to opening it." She pressed her lips against his and pulled her body even closer.

Noctis leaned back, away from her kiss. "How could he have—"

"Sanguinar," she said, drawing him closer. "Ancient magic, predating the Borne." She kissed him again. When he tried to draw back, she kissed him harder, sucking on his lower lip. He pulled away once more and she bit down, sinking her teeth into his flesh. He cried out and shoved her off his lap.

"Gods, Morella!" He rose to his feet and clapped a hand across his split lip. His fingers came away bloody. "What the hell?"

"Just a bit of fun." She winked at him and licked the red blood from her stained lips. "I thought you would enjoy it."

"Well you thought wrong. I mean, this isn't exactly the right sort of talk for *that*."

"You asked," Morella said casually. "What, would you rather I just keep on talking about theoretical ideas? The musings and notions of a historian? Wouldn't you rather have something *tangible* to hold on to in this moment, lover?"

She was enticing, yes, but Noctis was resolute. "At this moment, what I would like is a plan," he said while he tongued at his cut lip. "What I would like is for this whole thing to be over and done with and put behind me."

Morella stared at him hard. "And what then, Noctis? What is your grand plan once we find your brother?"

"I don't know," he said after a moment. "I thought I knew. I did know. But that was before I *knew* Madigan was alive. Before I knew you were alive. It was easier to think about the long term when anything worth losing was already lost."

Her gaze hardened, then softened, and she dropped her eyes to the floor. "You think I'm worth losing?"

He stared back at her, incredulous. "Of course I do."

She sighed for a moment before meeting his eyes again. She looked as though she was on the verge of tears, sad tears, and he had no idea what he had said wrong. "You make things so much harder than they ought to be, sometimes," she said.

He opened his mouth to ask what she meant but she cut him off by shaking her head. *What the hell does that mean?* Just when he thought he was finally beginning to understand her, something else came along and swept his legs out from beneath him.

"Yes, I believe your grandfather sealed the door with blood magic," she said quietly. "No, I don't know how. Yes, I believe that Aurellaine was in league with her father." She paused and, after a moment, shook her head. "No, I don't know what either of their goals were. Yes, I believe your brother is in danger"—she reached out and let her hand fall on the empty seat next to her—"No, I don't think we will be able to save him. I do not think he will survive."

Noctis's stomach lurched. "Why not?" His voice was flat, toneless, dead to his own ears.

Morella looked up and met his eyes. He was surprised at the darkness he saw there, the deep sadness.

"Because no one who has stood before them ever has."

19
DEPARTURE

Home.

Noctis stared at himself in the mirrored wall of the washroom. Preparing to return to Cascania was proving . . . difficult. He'd thought that outfitting himself would be the most complicated issue; even in Portland people would take notice of bladed weapons and flowing cloaks. But the real struggle was not the perception of others. The notion of Cascania, of Portland, of *home* felt small, diminished somehow. His memories felt hollow, faded.

So much has changed. He took in the face that stared back at him. The shorn hair. The hollow eyes and gaunt cheeks. It was a hard figure. *I'm not who I once was. How quickly a life can change.*

That was true on more levels than he cared to admit. If he was right about Madigan's return to their home—and he was certain that he was—then he would once again be reunited with his brother in a matter of days. But how many days had passed since they had been so forcefully separated?

"A lifetime." The words rolled off his tongue unbidden. For it was actually a lifetime—the lifetime of Noctis. How would

Madigan see him? Would they still know each other as they once had? Or would din'Dael's prophecy ring true, that their opposite Borne forces would overcome any sense of blood ties and one of them would end up dead.

No. Noctis shook his head, feeling foolish. He understood his brother. He understood Shadowborne. He had *been* Shadowborne. Some fading piece of his memory still felt that connection. Or, rather, felt its absence. Madigan had said it right before they'd parted: Will was something different. Something Borne of both.

But that was Will, he thought to himself.

WILL IS DEAD.

He froze. Since he'd found Morella, the voice had been silent. Noctis stared at his reflection, focusing on his eyes and his breath. He cupped his hands in the basin, lifting cool water to his lips and sipping it. The liquid rolled on his tongue a moment, then he swallowed.

It didn't help.

"No." Memories of the horrible thirst clawed to the forefront of his mind. "No, not again."

He cupped his hands again and brought another drink of water to his lips, gulping it down greedily. This time, the dry tickle was gone. To be certain, he took one more drink and splashed water across his face, feeling the hard edges of the bone beneath the rough growth of beard.

He felt fine. *Thank the gods.* The maddening pain of the cracking thirst was nothing he ever wished to experience again.

Noctis dried his hands and face and exited the washroom. Ynarra would return soon, hopefully with the requested items. *And more wine,* he thought absently. It occurred to him that between the endless supply of wine from the Nordoth and the Bottled Embers from the Street of Ash, he and Morella enjoyed a pleasant buzz more often than not.

And back in Cascania, I can't even drink legally yet. He smiled. *Or at least, I couldn't before.*

The smile faded. How long had he really been gone? He'd kept a rough estimate, but how long really? How many birthdays had come and gone, back in the world he had once known? In Aeril, no one seemed to pay any attention to such things; the passage of time was a strange, ephemeral thing. Within Undermyre, where the shift between day and night was nearly nonexistent, how would one even begin to speculate on something as abstract as time?

His thoughts were interrupted by the chamber door opening. Wrapping a long towel around his waist, he stepped into plain sight just as Ynarra latched the door behind her. She glanced up and met his eye quickly, then dropped her gaze to the floor. Noctis saw her tense, and her eyes darted back up. Her mouth opened to speak, then broke into a smile, then tightened into an uncertain grimace. The whole scene played on repeat until Noctis smiled and inclined his head in a slight bow.

"It is good to see you, Ynarra."

Her face split into a wide, relaxed smile. "Yes, Will." She beamed. "It is good to see you as well, thank you."

He approached slowly, in case he startled her back to uncertainty by crossing the room at a speed she deemed unsuitable. She carried a bag that had been sewn together to look roughly similar to the pack he had first carried to Aeril. On top of it were a bundle of clothes and a jug of wine with two glasses. Deftly, she slid the glasses and wine onto the empty table near the door.

She met his eyes with a timid, shining glance and then approached him. He held out his hands and she placed the pack and clothing into them. He glanced at them and nodded appreciatively.

The items were not exact, by any means, but they were near enough that the Casc people would not notice unless they looked too closely. *I don't even think of them as my own people anymore,* he thought wryly.

He inclined his head to Ynarra in gratitude and she beamed once more. "These will do wonderfully, thank you."

"Yes, of course, Will." She nodded in return. She began to wring her hands in front of her, thought better of it, and clasped them behind her back. She bit her lip and returned to fold her hands in front. She gave a small, nervous laugh. "I did the best I could with what I knew of from what you and your brother had worn. When you first came. Here, I mean. To the Nordoth."

Noctis ran his fingers along the items and smiled. "Ynarra, you did this yourself?" She glanced away and nodded quickly. "They're perfect. They're absolutely perfect."

She grinned and gave a small, nervous laugh. She looked almost startled at the sound and, not for the first time, Noctis wondered just what, exactly, her story was.

"Ynarra," he said cautiously, "would you like to stay for a glass of wine?" Her eyes grew wide and her mouth tightened. "So I can express my gratitude to you for this"—he raised the bundle—"this and everything."

She bit her lip and, after a moment, nodded. "Yes, Will, yes. I would like that very much."

He made his way over to the table and poured wine into the two glasses, then turned and raised one to her with a smile. She returned the smile but did not approach. Instead, she glanced around the room, searching.

Noctis waited a moment, hand extended, while she scanned the room. *What is she looking for?* She stopped searching and looked back to him, concern apparent on her face.

"What is it?" he asked.

"I do not see the lady Morella," she said quietly.

"No," Noctis responded cautiously. "She is not here, at the moment."

Ynarra stared at the glass in his outstretched hand and then to the one still on the table. After a moment, realization dawned on Noctis.

"Ynarra," he said, "this glass of wine is for you."

The look of shock on her face would certainly have sent him into roaring laughter had it not been simultaneously heartbreaking. "O—oh," she stuttered. "Oh. Yes, thank you, Will. Yes."

She began to approach and he flashed his friendliest grin. When he held the glass out to her, however, she paused, curtsied, and walked straight past him to the door. When Noctis turned, she opened the door, gave him one last, fleeting glance, then dropped her eyes and curtsied once more before leaving.

Noctis was left alone, glass of wine still outstretched, completely dumbfounded.

"THIS IS CASC ATTIRE? INTERESTING."

Morella stood in front of the mirror, twisting back and forth as she moved this way and that in the clothes. From a distance, they looked even better than Noctis had hoped. She wore black boots and blue denim jeans, or at least a spun material close enough to denim that it would pass. A dark grey hooded shirt completed the look while a cut, black leather jacket accented her curves delightfully well.

"Close enough to it," he said and smiled. "You'll look right at home."

He was wearing nearly the exact same thing. He was pleasantly surprised at the mobility the clothing offered, how the jeans actually had some stretch to them and the jacket allowed him a full range of motion. *That girl certainly is talented,* he thought as he imagined Ynarra working away, building the clothes simply from memory. Standing, he crossed to Morella and stood next to her in the mirror.

"You look taller," she said as he adjusted the jacket slightly.

"It's the fit of the clothes," he said. "I'm the same height."

She turned from the mirror and stared at him as though he had just said something profoundly stupid. "I know that. I said you *look* taller, not that you are taller."

He chuckled. "Sorry, still trying to wrap my head around going back. I'm a bit distracted."

She smiled and nudged him playfully. "I can understand that."

Morella walked away from the mirror and began to remove the clothing, tossing it to the floor while moving to the bed. She sat and kicked off the boots, taking a long drink of the Bottled Embers. "When do you plan to leave?"

"Soon." Noctis removed the jacket and shirt. Ynarra had done quite well. Beneath the clothes he was able to tuck away his blood fangs quite easily. He draped it all across the arm of a nearby chair. "Once the Crow's man arrives to guide us to the Ways."

Morella gave a languid stretch then stood and reached out to his jeans, undoing the top button. "Then we have some time."

TWO HOURS LATER, OR AS NEAR TO IT AS NOCTIS COULD GUESS from the buzz of Bottled Embers he finished, they were leaving the Street of Ash. They were wearing their usual clothes, their Casc items tucked in the pack to keep them in good repair. Snapshots of the Shanghai Tunnels raced through his brain. He could recall only bits; everything had blended together in the hours of twisting darkness, but he remembered the dank, slimy mud of the underground corridors. He thought it better that they kept their new clothes fresh until such time as they mattered.

Clarice had waved him away when he left, giving him a small metal bottle to travel with. "Just a nip of a reminder," she said with a wink. "I'll settle up with your patron. Not a worry, love."

"Thank you." Noctis smiled and swirled the bottle appreciatively. "A little of this will go a long way, where we're going."

"You just come back soon. You're good for business."

I don't doubt that. Noctis smiled and turned on his heel, then brushed through the curtains. *Come back soon. That's the plan.*

Their guide was an older man, nearer Jervin's age than any of the Crow's other soldiers. He offered to carry the pack but Noctis turned him down. Without further comment or ceremony, the man turned and strode off. Morella squeezed Noctis's hand, winked, and followed.

Exiting from Undermyre, they followed the coastline for roughly an hour. Despite his time within the city itself, Noctis had never ventured so close to the sea that bordered it. The water was a deep, crystalline glass that stretched off to the horizon. He wondered what lay beyond. Did the Crow's reach extend that far? Or was it like the stories he could recall from Cascania, where the ancient peoples believed that the sea stretched forever. He imagined sailing those waters and smiled at the prospect. *Someday,* he mused.

Someday, a beautiful voice filled his mind.

Noctis stopped in his tracks. He spun and, seeing no one, looked up at the sky. His heart raced. *It's her.*

"Coming?" Morella called back to him a moment later. "Or are you too taken in by the sights?"

He chuckled and caught up, feeling both foolish and elated. Of course there would be no one; there never was. The voices existed only in his mind: one beautiful, one harsh. He longed for an answer to them, for somewhere to associate blame or understand a diagnosis. But if there was one thing that he'd learned in this strange world, it was that answers seldom came.

Just what I have to live with. Two sides of me wrestling for control.

He put the thought from his mind and focused on what was to come next. The road swerved, taking a hard path away from the sea. In the distance Noctis saw a wall surrounding what appeared to be a barrow. Carved statues, their features long since eroded by the salty sea wind, guarded the passage. The group passed through a gap in the walls and, ahead of them, the path angled downward into a cave.

"There's no one on guard?" Noctis said as he scanned the area.

Morella eyed him sidelong. "Why would the entrance to the Ways be guarded? The gardens belong to the world and its inhabitants."

"When I first came, I heard that being in the Ways was forbidden. Is that why we need an escort?"

"The gardens are for everyone," Morella repeated. "It's the passes beyond them that are forbidden."

Noctis conceded the point. They entered a large crack in the ground by a long, deep stair hewn from the rock. He felt a pang of sympathy for the soldiers who had carried him and Madigan, unconscious, from its depths. The sentiment quickly vanished, however, when he recalled his mistreatment at their hands. *I hope it was as miserable for them as it was for us.*

The guide did not pause in his stride but took the stone steps with the graceful ease of an expert. Morella, steadying herself against the wall, followed. Noctis paused before beginning his descent, turning once more to look at the land of Aeril and wonder how long it would be before he returned.

He chastised himself for not having sent word to the Sapholux, to din'Dael, then brushed the thought aside. Jero din'-Dael had waited for centuries to move on Valmont; he could wait a bit longer.

Turning back, Noctis followed Morella into darkness. Before long, however, the darkness faded. The surrounding rock face was the same, brilliantly shining stone that permeated Aerillian lands. When the sky faded to a pinprick above them, the walls swelled outward and trees appeared, rising from the stone. The damp air was warm and he could smell fresh water. When the stair leveled out, he saw a series of pools on either side. Green vines hung from the walls, strung amongst the trees. Between the trees and the vines, it was more greenery than he had seen since he'd first come to these lands.

He wondered if at some time in history the Cascanian entrance to the Ways had been as beautiful as the Aerillian entrance. Perhaps a time before the river had risen, or before buildings and concrete had taken over. If, before the passage became a tool of industry, it had held a hint of the splendor that now surrounded him.

Another hour of walking through the tall, winding tunnel and he was once again distracted by memories of being in this passage. Or, rather, his lack of memories. To have been unconscious for so long couldn't have been healthy. What exactly had Shifter drugged them with? The dagger had to have been laced with something.

Unless it works like my blood fangs, he considered as his hand fell to brush the bloodstones. He had not used them since healing his chest after rekindling his romance with Morella. The energy within the bloodstones themselves was low; he could only just sense the faint flows of their power. They would be harder to replenish back in Cascania, where there was less game. But if all went well, they wouldn't need to worry about the supply. It could all go easily enough; no one was even certain that it was Aurellaine Valmont who had disappeared with his brother.

I need more information, as always.

He saw signs of the door that barred the entrance to the Ways well before he saw the door itself. A series of arches and statues marked the way. Each was a ruin. The arches were broken and crumbled, though the debris had been cleaned up. Some statues were shattered, others were missing limbs or heads. For some, only remnants of the base remained, while others looked as though they had been melted into volcanic glass. The surrounding walls and path were all a darkened black, evidence of a blast pattern.

"What happened here?"

"Valmont." Morella looked at him with a gaze as solemn as her voice. "Haven't you heard the stories?"

Realization dawned on him. Of course he had heard the stories. Valmont's final capture, the death of his followers while the sorcerer was forced to watch. Witnessing the death of his wife, her body and soul ripped in eternal torment within Theros. Valmont's retribution, impossibly, as he eluded death. The resulting blast had nearly destroyed both Radiance and Shadow's Orders and had murdered Shadow's Guardian, Maruq T'Aroth. Noctis's own grandfather had only just survived the destruction. Yes, Noctis had heard the stories. He just never imagined he would see ground zero.

The bright and glorious future of Aeril, obliterated right here, right where I now travel.

They approached the door that barred entrance to the Ways. The ancient wood was blackened and cracked, the hinges as rusted as those he had seen at the Cascanian entrance. And yet, it stood solid. He heard Morella give a sharp intake of breath and he took her hand. She twisted, a wry smile upon her face.

"I've never passed through this door before," she said, caressing its surface with her free hand.

"You? My amorous, adventurous historian, has never set foot within the Ways?"

"I never said that." Her voice had adopted a playful, holier-than-thou tone. "I just haven't been *here* before."

Noctis gripped her hand tighter when she went to pull away. "Wait, there are more entrances?"

Morella's loud, boisterous laugh echoed through the blackened tomb. "Oh, Will, of course there are." His mouth tightened and she dipped her head apologetically. "Noctis, yes," she said with mock gravity. "Of course, mighty Noctis."

He felt suddenly foolish. *Is it really so important to leave your old self behind?* "How many entrances?"

She laughed again but it was the old soldier, their guide, who answered. "How many stars, Burner? How many nightless days and dayless nights? How many worlds within worlds?" The old man rested a hand on the handle of the great door. "I do not think that even the Hesperawn know the answer," he said solemnly.

"A blasphemer," Morella said with a smile. "A poetic blasphemer. Perhaps I'll mark you in the dedication of my chronicle."

The air suddenly seemed too heavy. "How exactly did Jervin seal the Ways, then?" A cold bite came from his key. *Something is wrong.*

"The same way you opened them, lover." Morella's tone was whimsy-laced severity. "With blood."

Before Noctis could stop him, the old man pushed the great door open. Noctis dove to the side, shoving Morella to the ground as a flurry of spears thrust through the open space. The ragged weapons shredded the old soldier as they propelled him, gasping, into the air. A single strike from an unfathomably large blade clove their guide in two. A shambling hulk of rotten flesh and bone ripped the two halves apart and stepped into the passage, roaring.

Necrothanians.

20

THE WAYS

"Reaper!" Morella shrieked. "Reaper!"

Noctis and Morella scrambled backward, the Necrothanian monster upon them. The creature lurched, dragging its feet through the viscera of the dead man. It opened its mouth and roared, thin and raspy, more a death rattle than a battle cry. Nevertheless, the sound sent a chill down Noctis's spine.

"Out," Morella cried, grabbing at his arm while they pushed to their feet. "Out, out! We have to get out!"

"Stay back." His voice was cool and calm despite the fear in his breast. *All that training, well done, din'Dael.* The air surrounding them crackled with electricity. White charges of lightning danced across Noctis's skin. He took his eyes off the creature for one breath, enough to face Morella. "Whatever happens, stay safe."

Her face paled. Noctis turned back to the oncoming mass of bone and dead flesh. Its milky eyes stared unseeing. The strength with which it hefted its massive blade had nothing to do with the decayed muscle that clung in tatters to its bones. There was something else at work here, something dark and twisted.

Sanguinar. Noctis took a deep breath and braced himself. His mouth was dry and his heart hammered in his chest. *So, this is what Valmont found.*

The creature roared again and Noctis stepped forward, key singing against his skin. His trembling hands glowed white and he clapped them together, launching a bolt of blue-white lightning into the creature's center. The bolt landed in its unarmored chest, searing and charring the dead flesh. The force of the blast knocked it back but did not drive it to the ground. It raised its massive blade and charged.

Noctis paled. He risked a glance back at Morella, saw her staring at him, shock upon her face. *I've got to keep that thing the hell away from her.*

Steeling himself, Noctis ran straight for it. The two collided, the blade cleaving a path through empty space where Noctis's head had been only a second before. Hands balled into fists, Noctis pummeled the undead body. Each strike he charged with fiery lightning, his burning fists pounding into its torso.

The creature recovered and lashed out, slamming into Noctis and driving him backward. The wind was knocked out of him; he fought for gasping breaths and drove his heels into the ground. Tumbling to the ground, he barely managed to roll out of the way as a giant, bony leg smashed down where he had just been. Panting, he scrambled away and reached for his cutlass.

Noctis's hand closed around the hilt of his cutlass, but before he could draw it he was thrown through the air again. He landed hard and grimaced as his ribs screamed in pain. Glancing up, he saw that the monster had turned its attention to Morella.

Loosing a guttural cry, Noctis's Flare surged around him in white lightning. He ran at the creature and slammed a charged elbow into its spine. The flesh hissed and sizzled where the strike connected. Coughing at the rising smoke, Noctis kicked at the back of the thing's bony knee, driving it to the ground.

The scent of smoking, putrid flesh nearly overwhelmed him,

but Jero's training had been thorough and Noctis shut off his sense of smell from his conscious mind. The creature struggled to rise and Noctis thrust blazing fists down. He grabbed the creature's exposed spine and, with a roar of his own, drove his fire into the bone. He pushed with the lightning and pulled with the force of his own rage. The spine cracked and split in two. Still roaring, Noctis yanked and tore the two pieces free from the flesh.

He discarded the bones and kicked at the creature's outstretched arm. Hefting the rough weapon it had been reaching for, Noctis charged it with fire until it was blazing hot. In an instant, he thrust it into the base of the monster's skull.

The impaled creature continued to struggle.

Impossible. It doesn't have a spine. It should be immobilized.

Noctis stepped beyond the creature's reach and held out both his hands. A blaze of fire engulfed the creature. Noctis did not stop the flow of power that surged from him, pushing the flames harder and harder. The orange blaze turned white. He saw the great blade glow and begin to fold in on itself, melting into a pool of metal. The creature itself continued to struggle even as its limbs turned to ash.

Nothing remained but scattered debris and a pool of hardening metal when he finally dropped his hands. He turned back to Morella, a short distance down the path. The dagger in her hand was steady when he approached, her eyes never breaking away from his own.

"I thought you would have run farther," he said through heaving gasps.

Her eyes took him in, looked him up and down, appraising him. "Just what did they do to you in the Sapholux, Will?"

"They killed Will," Noctis said softly. "I guess this is what they forged from his remains."

Her eyes darted away, in the direction of the entrance to the Ways. They grew wide and her jaw dropped. Before she could speak, Noctis whirled. Blazing his Flare to a brilliant roar, he filled the corridor with a stream of white-hot fire. Dancing blue lightning swam within the blaze. He heard people scream and he recoiled, but he did not relent. *Real people, not that shambling horror. Real people.*

He did not release the furious blast until there were no more screams.

The cavern smoldered. The ruined statues bore evidence of new injuries. Noctis passed them all, numbly walking toward the Ways. He stepped into the passages without hesitation. Within were five charred corpses. Had the fire not sealed their fate, their weapons, acting as lightning rods, would have. The black, waxy features that remained were twisted in fear and agony.

Valmont's cultists.

He withdrew his blood fangs and set to work. The flames had consumed much of the bodies, but he took what remained. Finished, he stood. Morella had followed him into the passage, stepping carefully over the smoldering bodies.

"A reaper, you called it?" Noctis's voice sounded distant and hoarse even to his own ears.

"Yes." Morella had her arms wrapped around her waist. She was staring at him, studying him.

"It looks like Valmont might be expecting us," he said quietly. The adrenaline was fading and his head was beginning to spin.

"We need to return to the Nordoth." Morella's voice was a cautious whisper. "We need to warn them."

"No." Noctis returned the blood fangs to their sheaths. "We move on. We've got to find Madigan."

"But—"

"The Crow suspected Valmont was in Cascania. He should have expected that he'd be doing . . . whatever this was. He'll send another patrol soon enough." Even he was surprised by the lack of emotion in his voice. "Especially once our guide fails to report back."

Morella peered at him and kicked a fallen sword from her path. "They really did kill Will, didn't they?" Noctis didn't answer. She reached out and caressed his cheek, standing on her toes to kiss him. "Perhaps you'll survive longer than I expected, lover."

THEY FOUND THE BODIES OF THE CROW'S PATROL A SHORT WHILE later. They had been dead for some time, Noctis noted, and wondered if he had been correct about the Crow sending another group soon. It didn't matter. He was committed to finding his brother. He was committed to saving him from Valmont, whichever Valmont came first.

"That thing, the reaper," Noctis said while he eyed the tattered corpses, "it did this?"

"The cultists probably helped. I imagine they let it do the majority of the work though."

"What was it, exactly?"

Morella chuckled but there was no humor in it. "That thing was Valmont's answer to his followers. That was how he helps them achieve eternal life."

"They want *that*?" Noctis asked incredulously. "To be turned into walking corpses?"

She shook her head. "He somehow binds their spirit to their body. Or *a* body, at least. No one knows how, exactly. As long as the body stays alive, everything is fine, people live on forever as they always have."

Noctis stared at her. "But they already have that. That's the whole point of Velier's gift, right? How is this any different? Any . . . better?"

She shrugged. "It isn't, really. But Valmont's power allows a continuation of the consciousness to remain even after the host's death. As long as there is a form to exist within, the spirit lives on. They become a true Necrothanian. It's Velier's gift in life as well as in death."

Noctis considered for a moment. "So, part of it was as conscious as you and me?"

"In theory. Seeing one firsthand, I don't know if I'd believe it. It looked rather mindless." She snickered quietly and shrugged once more. "But that's the theory. He claimed to have discovered the secrets of true immortality, promised his followers that they would never fear death if they embraced his vision."

"People will do just about anything to prolong the inevitable."

Morella was quiet before she nodded. "Yes. They will."

They pressed on. Neither Noctis nor Morella spoke much while they walked, but she held his hand, intertwining her fingers with his own. The part of the Ways through which they trekked was as scarred as the Aerillian entrance. He remembered that the burst of power from Valmont had not happened on his return to Aeril, but on his passage into Theros. The blast had surged throughout the Ways, obliterating all in its path.

"Morella, where is the entrance to Theros?"

She went rigid. "Noctis—"

"Did Valmont destroy that portion of the Ways as well? Is there still access to it?"

"We do not go there." She shook her head and sped up. "No one goes there."

He halted. "But is it still open?"

She shifted uncomfortably before nodding. "It is. But it's . . . broken."

"Broken how?"

"Just broken." She shook her head and gripped his hand, pulling him along as she resumed walking.

"I need to see it."

She whirled on him, fury clear on her face and in her eyes. "No. You do not." She spat against the blackened stone. "You Cascanian outlander, you think you know us? You think you know our history? You know nothing about us, what happened to us."

Noctis was taken aback by her sudden rage. "Morella, I only meant—"

"Damn what you meant, Lightborne. Damn your presumptions. Damn you."

Lightborne? She had never called him that before, not with malice, at least. He held up his hands, softening his expression. "I'm sorry."

"Damn your apologies." She turned away from him and hugged her arms around herself.

"Damn them or don't, they're there." He risked putting a hand on her shoulder. She tensed but did not pull away. "You're right. I don't know. Help me understand."

She gave a derisive snort of laughter. "You won't."

"Help me try."

Morella turned back to him, her eyes dark and distant. She held her dagger and placed the tip at the soft spot just below his sternum. She stared at him hard, unblinking. The blade did not pierce the clothes, did not reach his skin, but he knew she could skewer him faster than he could react if she chose to do so.

"You'll understand eventually." Her voice was just above a whisper.

Then she dropped the blade to the ground and threw herself into his arms, kissing him hard. He stood in shock, arms frozen, brow furrowed, before kissing her back. *What the hell is going on?* She stepped away from him and placed a hand over his heart.

"Do not make me show you the way to Theros, Noctis." She met his eyes and implored him. "Do not ask that of me."

He nodded cautiously. Her face softened into a crooked smile and she drew herself into him again, kissing him once more. When she pulled back, she retrieved her dagger and returned it to its hidden place within the folds of her clothing, then set off down the corridor. Noctis rubbed his scruffy jaw and pinched the bridge of his nose, shook his head, and followed.

After an hour, signs of Valmont's blast faded. They had passed multiple twists and turns that could have led to Theros, but Noctis said nothing. Morella walked with confidence, seeming to know the correct path through the Ways, and his own intuition was pointing him in the same direction. It was strange, almost as if, within the Ways, Cascania was the magnetic north to his internal compass.

Morella eventually slipped her hand back into his, but conversation did not follow. Noctis waited, trying to push away the thoughts of her rage and focus on what he would do once he found Madigan. How would any of them know if it really was Aurellaine Valmont who had taken him under her wing? It wasn't as if there were wanted posters with her likeness posted around Undermyre. He wanted to ask Morella more about her but was certain that, if he wasn't careful, he would make things worse by opening his mouth too soon. Fortunately, she broke the uncomfortable silence a short time later.

"What should I be expecting?"

Her question pulled Noctis from his train of thought and he gave a slight start. "From Madigan?"

She rolled her eyes. "From Cascania."

"Right, of course." He searched his scattered memory banks, trying to pick items of importance out of the jumble of information that seemed to exist just below the surface, out of reach. "First, no one calls it Cascania. The city we are going to, it's called Portland—"

"Yes, I remember that much," she interrupted. "What else?"

"Portland is in Oregon, which is part of the United States. The United States are a part of . . ." He trailed off, realizing how deep that line of geographical context could go, and a hint of his old curiosity brightened. "Morella, when you look at the sky at night, the stars, what do you see?"

She rolled her eyes again. "Stars."

Noctis shook his head. "I mean, what are the stars, to you? All the people in Aeril, what do they think the stars are?"

"Every culture has their own interpretation of the heavens," she said. "Some say the Hesperawn placed them in the sky as a marker for all the lives lost during the flood that remade the world. Some say that they are the ever-watching eyes of the Hesperawn themselves, hence why they flicker and flutter as they dart to different parts of the land. Some think that they are just drops of ever-burning fire scattered through the night sky to brighten the night, a gift from the Hesperawn to act as guides."

Noctis smiled at that last one, an accurate mythological interpretation of what his world knew to be scientific fact.

"What else?" Morella pressed. "Tell me more about your home. How dangerous is it? Are the people armed?"

Noctis considered for a moment. "Anywhere can be dangerous, but it's different than Aeril. There are more people, more laws to govern them. As for armed, there are many regulations in place. Some people may be armed, but most aren't." She snickered and he thought of that hidden dagger. "You're a historian, Morella, use that as your lens."

"Fair enough. Big, lots of people, most unarmed. Should be easy enough to manage."

"There's more." Noctis struggled to come up with words. "There isn't magic there, not anymore. There are no Borne. Velier's gift touched only Aeril, not Cascania. People's lives are short, by Aerillian standards. Shorter still, given the violence they inflict upon each other." He shook his head and sighed. "Sometimes it seems that violence is the one thing that stretches to all corners of reality."

Morella snickered and squeezed his hand. "Why, Noctis, have you been studying history?"

"Once upon a time, maybe. Now, I need only look at the worlds around me."

The passage bent and opened into a wide, high-ceilinged chamber. Many different paths shot off from the one central room. A flicker of memory came—Noctis knew this place. He had been there with his brother when they first found the Ways. They were minutes away from returning. He stopped.

"No magic." Morella glossed over his last comment. "No Borne. Violent, short lives. Still manageable."

"There is technology, though. Different technology than Aeril. Advanced. Many of the things that come from the Aerillian magics, Cascania has found ways to do through other means."

This piqued her interest and she squeezed his hand. "Care to elaborate?"

"Imagine that this cavern was dark. Pitch black. How would you find your way?"

She gave him a look that said that was the most ridiculous question she had ever heard. "A torch, most likely. Flint and steel. Fire." She gestured back the way they had come. "Or I'd bring rocks to light the way, if we're going over the top."

Noctis held up a hand and let the small blue trickles of lightning dance across his fist. "Imagine if you could harness this power. Put it in a small box, if you will. Then use that power to shoot a beam of light outward, using this as a source of power."

She cocked her head. "Perpetual energy as a projection?"

"The more you use the beam, however, the more it drains the current." Noctis shook his head, feeling like an idiot. "I'm sorry, I've never had to explain this before."

Morella shrugged. "Your people harness energy and get it to work for you. The energy drains out eventually and, what, needs to be recharged? Sounds similar to those." She gestured at his blood fangs.

And those Borne by Radiance. Noctis smiled and nodded. "That's actually pretty accurate. That's the basic idea though, harnessing the energy and using it for other purposes. You can use it as a source of fuel to power machines that have been designed to create things on a larger, faster scale than a person could do on their own. The more you create, the more streamlined the process becomes and the more advanced the creations become. You can build massive structures, travel across land and water, even fly through the air."

Morella laughed aloud and shook her head. "Your people have become inventors, then? Creators? Fascinating."

Encouraged, Noctis went on. "People began to study the world, trying to understand it on a better level. They discovered medicinal properties in some things and figured out how to extract the properties to create more potent healing medicines. Some devote their entire lives to the study of medicine, finding new and better ways to help people live longer, happier lives . . ." He trailed off and there was a moment of pause as Morella smirked at him.

"So, in your world as well, people spend their entire lives trying to push away their death?"

He gave a tentative nod. "It's different though. People do it to help."

Morella shrugged. "That's what his cultists said about Valmont."

"It is different though." He sighed. "I'm just doing a terrible job of explaining it. You'll see."

"I'm sure I will."

Noctis didn't like the turn of the conversation. Either his explanations felt inadequate or Valmont's coercive reasoning was rooted in just enough truth to inspire hope. *That's what it is. The best lies always contain a kernel of truth.*

They set off once more. "We're close, I take it?" Morella said.

"We are." Noctis moved with long, determined strides as he saw the bridge approaching. "Madigan and I came through this passage."

She gave a start and hugged the wall when the passage

narrowed and the wide chasm opened up to the side. "Gods, you could have warned me."

"Sorry," Noctis said as he reached for his canteen. There was a nervous tickle in the back of his throat. "I'd honestly forgotten it." He took a swig of water and swallowed, forcing himself to ignore the trepidation he felt.

"How could you forget something like that?"

He cleared his throat again. "The Sapholux played with my brain. It's still a mess."

Morella watched him. "Played with your brain, did it? Well, that's not a surprise. The longer you spend in the Sapholux with Jero din'Dael the more time there is to screw up someone's brain."

Noctis didn't answer. *The longer you spend in the Sapholux . . .*

There was an entire army of Lightborne within the Sapholux, just charging their batteries, and who knows how long they'd been inside? *Long enough to not want to risk everything. Long enough to fear the end.*

He considered the implications of unleashing a horde of Lightborne upon the world. Would they all be as powerful as din'Dael had been when he was freed? Besides the Revenant, Noctis had only seen his own power beyond the Sapholux. *And I'm the new guy, despite din'Dael's fancy words.*

Yet the passivity of those who dwelt within the Sapholux made Noctis believe that din'Dael's radiant wave would not sweep across Aeril. Their people wanted to live, had no interest in risking death by fighting the Necrothanians. They had lived too long in a place too isolated. There was no more raging fire, not unless din'Dael managed to stoke it. *And he's attempting that with threats of death.* That wasn't the way to inspire people. That was the path to turning them away from you, the path to driving them to seek new guidance. *One who wants the same thing they do.*

A chill coursed down Noctis's spine. If he was right and din'-Dael really did drive the Lightborne away, what if they found a new leader who believed the same thing they did? What if they chose to fight in the name of life and the promise of it never ending? What if the army raised by din'Dael to destroy Valmont joined his Necrothanians instead?

It was a terrifying prospect, one that Noctis didn't want to think about. Unfortunately, it lingered. *They wouldn't . . . would they?* He couldn't discount it entirely.

"Cascania is through there?" Morella interrupted his thoughts. The heavy door was ahead, closed and secure.

Maybe we stopped the Necrothanians before they were able to enter.

Noctis nodded. "That, at least, is the path that takes you to Cascania. We'll come out underground in a cavern with a large pool. Following the path above will put us in the network of tunnels that runs underneath the city."

"How many days travel to reach your brother, then?"

Noctis shook his head. "Not days. Hours. Assuming that he is, in fact, where I think he is."

"There's only one way to find out."

Whatever protective binding his grandfather had placed upon the door was gone. Morella grasped the handle and the large, heavy door opened easily at her touch. Unceremoniously, Morella ducked her head and pulled herself through into the darkness beyond. Noctis adjusted his pack, took one last glance back through the Ways, and approached the door.

The silence of the passage was shattered as Morella's scream ripped through the air. Lightning rippling across his body, Noctis burst through the door.

21
PULLING SHADOW

"You're slowing down," Ileta said, crossing her arms. "This shouldn't be taking so long."

Not the least bit like a broken record. Madigan doubled down and refocused his efforts. They were in his grandfather's old cellar. The musty, damp earth smell wafted into Mad's nostrils but offered no familiar comfort. Nothing could be comfortable, right now. Nothing ever would be again.

"I'm"—he suppressed a wince and dropped his voice to a whisper—"I'm working on it."

"Work faster."

The cellar was pitch black. Ileta had locked the trapdoors behind them and had used an old black tarp and some duct tape to block any light coming through the entrance. Once she was certain that no stray bits of daylight were peeking through any cracks, she took a small stool and stood on it just underneath the hanging incandescent bulb. Wordlessly, she unscrewed the bulb, freeing it from its socket, and the room was plunged into darkness.

Madigan had long since learned the value of silence under

Ileta's tutelage. He waited, not speaking, in the center of the room while she moved off to the side of the cellar. After a moment, the unmistakable sound of soft, thin glass crunching against the stone floor broke the silence.

"It is dark," she said simply. "Change that."

Change it? He fumbled in his pockets to see if he had any keys or anything that could make a spark but Ileta halted him.

"Do not use a tool."

Madigan nodded, though she couldn't see it. He scanned his memory for anything in the cellar that might help. *Grandda had to keep spare lightbulbs down here somewhere.* Closing his eyes, trying to remember the space, he made to move. He was halted once more.

"Do not move. Do not leave the center of the room."

No tools and no movement, great.

He allowed his Shade to flow forth into the darkness, thinking that it would be best to—

"Do not use your Shade."

Madigan's eyes shot open out of sheer habit and he scowled. "You have got to be joking."

Ileta was silent.

"I can't move and I can't use my Shade? What the hell am I supposed to do?"

"Be Shadowborne."

Helpful, very helpful.

That had been two hours ago. Ileta had offered no more help other than one hour ago when she said, "Pull," and that was it. Madigan was going stir crazy. His mind was playing tricks on him in the pitch black. Being underground and so far from the city meant there was almost utter silence. Were it not for the chill in the room and the occasional sound of Ileta's breathing, he would have sworn he was in a deprivation chamber. *Except those are supposed to be relaxing.*

There was nothing relaxing about this. He was cold. He was

stiff. He was frustrated. He was "pulling," whatever the hell that meant. The closest he had come was to think of how he pushed outward with his Shade, so he was trying to do the opposite. Nothing. He kept trying and the only fluctuation he felt was a pinching between his eyes like he had been crossing them too hard for too long.

He wasn't going to give up though. Nor was he going to give Ileta the satisfaction of asking for help. She may be a maddeningly difficult teacher, but she was an effective one. She knew when to help, and if she hadn't offered any yet, then she wouldn't supply any if he asked. Madigan fought back his frustration and pulled.

Another hour passed. The headache worsened. Madigan's left leg was going numb, for some reason. *You've been locking it, idiot. Loosen up.*

There was an audible sigh from Ileta. "What are you doing?"

"I'm pulling." Their voices sounded absurdly loud after so much time in the silent darkness.

"No, you're not."

"Well I'm trying, dammit."

"Stop. Relax a moment."

Madigan did. He dropped to the floor and put his head between his knees as he rubbed at his leg. He was seeing stars. *Funny how you can still see light in the dark.*

"What do you know of light?"

Madigan chuckled at the symmetry of their thoughts. "Radiance? Nothing much, really. I heard a few stories as a kid but—"

"Forget Radiance for a moment. Just light in general."

"It's . . ." Madigan paused. Science had never been his strongest subject, but he remembered one key thing. "Alright, so, light is a thing. An actual thing, not just a nonentity, right? There's this whole joke about how if you are ever having a bad day, think about the sun. It's this huge, roaring ball of fire and power, right? And it projects all of this amazing light in rays and stuff. And these rays, they're racing across the solar system. They're heading for the planet, they're passing through clouds and planes and buildings and trees, everything in their pursuit of just getting a chance to touch the Earth. And you, whoever you are, stop them at the last second and block them, and that's what your shadow is: proof of your power over the sun."

There was silence, then.

"That's absurd."

"Well, I mean yeah, it's not meant to be anything other than fun."

"I can work with it though," she said abruptly. Madigan was surprised at the levity in her voice. She went on without waiting for comment from him. "In your absolutely pointless theory, you do what? Block the light. Your shadow is the absence of light, correct?"

Madigan mulled it over. "Yeah, pretty much."

"And to let the light return?"

"You move."

"Correct. You move the darkness away and allow the light to fill the space."

Her tone said that this, apparently, was the big secret. He still didn't get it. "So, I should move my Shade elsewhere?"

Ileta gave an exasperated sigh. "Madigan, I already told you this has nothing to do with your Shade. You are Shadowborne. Just move the darkness and light will fill the void."

"You want me to just pull at the darkness?"

She gave an exasperated sigh. "Pull the darkness into you and the vacuum should be what?"

Madigan muttered under his breath, feeling like an idiot at her patronizing tone. "Light."

"Now pull the damn darkness. This is getting boring."

Just imagine how it is for me then. He grumbled and closed his eyes once more. If there wasn't darkness, there had to be light, is that what it was? He'd never really given much thought to it. He supposed it made sense; there wasn't an in-between, there was no quantum state of light and dark where things existed in-between, not that he knew of.

He didn't know if he believed in whatever it was Ileta was having him do, but she was the expert. She was the one who had come to him, seeking him out for training. *Though she'd still never explained how she found me. How the hell do people keep finding Will and me?* For all their intention of a secret mission, it certainly hadn't panned out that way. First Cephora, although he supposed the Crow had sent for her. Then the repeated encounters with Morella. Then Valmont's sudden and seemingly random appearance. Then Ileta, appearing from nowhere on the road. Some secret.

Come to think of it, Ileta's appearance was almost as sudden as Valmont's.

Was that just some special part of being Shadowborne he'd never heard of before? Not for the first time, he wondered if Valmont and Ileta were connected. After all, she refused to tell him anything about her past, refused to tell him who she worked for. Everything seemed a little too neat and tidy, though, a little too obvious. From the stories he'd heard, that wasn't Valmont's way. Valmont was subtle, whereas Ileta was anything but.

"Dammit, are you even trying, Madigan? What the hell is taking so long?"

He sighed. *Alright, pull the darkness. Right.* He thought back to his shadow analogy, but stepping to the side was out of the question; there was no light to move away from. He thought about it not having anything to do with his Shade and concentrated on that. *I always use my Shade to push out, so to pull I would need to . . .* to what? Find somewhere to move the darkness to, that was the logical step. But how to move it? And where to move it to?

I always think of releasing my Shade outward. What if I tried pulling it farther in?

He pushed outward with his Shade, exploring the feeling in his body and—

"Put your goddam Shade away, Madigan."

"Just give me one damn minute, I'm working through some shit, alright?"

He loved their little conversations.

He felt the sensation of his Shade around him and then, rather than releasing it, he drew it back. It began to pool into itself. He pulled harder, imagining the Shade condensing at his center, the size of a pinprick. He thought of black holes, of something so dense that light couldn't possibly escape, and pulled the Shade deeper into itself, growing smaller and smaller.

The edges of his vision began to flutter. He sensed rather than saw Ileta nodding. He pulled harder and could swear that he could almost make out the outline of her pixie-cut hair against the cellar wall. The room was definitely brightening. Emboldened, Madigan pulled with every bit of strength he had, pouring his frustration in as an added bonus. For a brief second he was able to make out Ileta's features. Then it all came crashing down.

His head erupted into immense, splitting pain as his Shade contracted even further. He doubled over and collapsed, gasping. He felt like he was being kicked in the gut over and over and over. He clutched his head. He curled into the fetal position, coughing violently.

Don't overextend. Cephora's words echoed distantly in his head. This was so much worse than that, infinitely worse.

"Shit," Ileta said. She was there in a second, hoisting him onto his hands and knees. He leaned his head against the cold floor, which did not help his raging headache at all. The light behind his eyelids was still too bright. He wanted to bore his eyes out.

Ileta moved in front of him then gripped him by the hair and pulled his head up and back. If he'd been able to see, he would have been staring straight at her. "Sorry for this," she said. With a head-rattling crack, she brought her open palm flat against his face with enough force to drive him back to the ground. At the sound and strength of the impact, he thought his head would burst open, blood and brains spilling across the darkness.

He caught himself before he fully connected to the ground. The overall pain had actually lessened. His cheek stung and he had no doubt that he bore a bright red handprint across his jaw, but that paled in comparison to the previous pain.

"Ow."

"You're bullheaded and overzealous. I said pull."

"I was pulling." He rubbed his jaw and winced.

"You were pushing."

"How the hell was I—"

She flicked his forehead. "You pushed your Shade into itself, correct?" He didn't answer. "That's what I thought. Then, when you finally did start to pull at the darkness, you pushed it deeper into your Shade. *That won't work.*"

"No shit," he fumed. "So, what the hell am I supposed to do, then?"

"Exactly what you did in that middle step when you did it correctly. Pull the darkness. You're Shadowborne. You control the darkness, not just some small bit of Shade. Leave your Shade the hell out of it."

He bit back a comment and grit his teeth. *Fine. I control the darkness*. Mad closed his eyes and focused, ignoring the pain in his head. *So, I just need to ignore my Shade. Peachy*. There had been that sensation of the world fluttering around him when he'd pulled. He turned his attention there, focused on that feeling. The flutter was the key, he knew it. But it was like peeling back a film you just couldn't get ahold of. Every time he grabbed at the darkness, he grabbed at nothing.

No, that was wrong. He had felt it. He could feel the darkness on his face the same way that a claustrophobe could feel the walls closing in on him. There was something tangible there. Without moving his hands, he brushed at it with his consciousness—he could have sworn he felt something. He brushed again and, yes, there was definitely something there. It was thin and wispy, spider's silk blowing in the wind. But it was there. He grasped the thread and pulled.

Countless more threads appeared. Something was unraveling around him. He grabbed each and every one and drew it back, peeling it toward him. More and more came and every time, he held the darkness, pushing it somewhere deep inside him. He opened his eyes.

The room had brightened.

With a calm fury, Madigan pulled at the seemingly infinite web of darkness. The more strands he controlled, the more the light appeared. It was not the same light as the incandescent bulb, though. It reminded him more of the deep glowing light that permeated the Ways. It was not simply light that shone, it was the utter absence of darkness.

"You'd think I was asking you to move a damn mountain or something. Next time, try to speed it up a bit."

He held the threads and looked at Ileta. She was smiling, despite her words.

"You're such a patient instructor."

"I do what I can." She shrugged lightly. "Now, move around. Walk. Get used to the sensation."

Madigan did as instructed, but not without difficulty. He was strangely off balance and his mind, though clear, felt like he was in a dream state when he tried to move.

"Find your balance. Think of it like any form of exercise, small, controlled movements and then work your way up from there."

"Taking three steps isn't exactly what I would call a difficult movement."

"It was when you were an infant. Slow down. Move carefully. Don't screw up again."

Such gentle words of encouragement.

Madigan moved slowly, adjusting to the extra weight (for he could think of no better word) of the darkness in his mind. His head began to ache again. He was fatigued. That wasn't normal; he shouldn't be so tired from so little.

"Now, release just a little bit, but do so with control. Keep the light around us but let the entrance return to darkness."

Madigan turned his attention to the invisible threads coming from the trapdoor. Easing his grip on them, he saw the fluttering again. His head ached. No, it was more than that. Madigan's head felt filled to bursting, and every time he blinked, he wanted to vomit. *People get used to this?*

Gradually, the darkness returned to the entrance, but Ileta remained illuminated. Her arms were folded but she was smiling freely now. His nose began to run. He sniffed it back and tasted iron in the back of his throat.

"Alright, let go," Ileta said, moving toward the door. "I'm not in the mood to clean you up if you pass out and bleed all over yourself."

Madigan let go, releasing the strands from where he had balled them up tightly in front of him. They snapped back into place like a released bow string. Ileta pulled down the tarp and opened the cellar door, allowing the afternoon light to fill the space.

Madigan pinched the bridge of his nose and wiped off the blood that trickled down. His eyes fell to his shadow. *Blocked at the last second before reaching the Earth.*

"You need water." Ileta's form was silhouetted in the doorframe above. "At least, I do."

"Water sounds great." Madigan took a few tentative steps and swayed. *I've been standing still way too long.*

Outside the cellar, Ileta stuck her face beneath the ground spigot and drank deep. Madigan followed suit, washing the blood from his beard. The cool water snapped his senses back into place. He let it run down his face before drinking. It was cold and fresh, that homey, earthy flavor he and Will had enjoyed so much as kids after a long day's training. His headache started to fade.

"You did well," Ileta said while Madigan splashed water through his hair. "Once you finally stopped fumbling around like an idiot long enough to focus."

"Yeah, well, not all of us are inherently brilliant like you."

Ileta playfully smacked him on the back of the head, momentarily plunging his face back into the water. He snorted and sputtered, unprepared for the sudden splash and inhaling in his surprise. She snickered and they both laughed.

"Questions?" She eyed him up and down. "Or do you think that next time you'll be able to do it without another lesson?"

"No, I've got it."

"Good. Next time, we'll move the other direction."

Madigan raised an eyebrow. "Other direction?"

"You pulled the darkness into you and brought light. The reverse is the same."

Mad grinned openly. "So, I can move the light and make it dark?"

Ileta pinched the bridge of her nose. "Yes. That would be the reverse of making it light. Just remember, baby steps. There's a reason we went into the cellar. It's small. There isn't a lot of space to work with. Makes it easier."

"Couldn't we have started with a closet or something?" Madigan stretched his neck, which popped.

"Could have, yes." She shrugged. "But we didn't. As you improve, the smaller spaces will come easier. Larger rooms are more difficult. Anything bigger is damn near impossible."

Madigan's mind darted back to his first meeting with the Crow in the large antechamber of the Nordoth. Before, with the seneschal, the space had seemed dark and cramped, but when the Crow appeared it had been revealed to be one cavernous audience chamber. The thought of trying to pull so much darkness, to control a space so enormous, seemed absurdly difficult. *Was it the Crow? Did he move so much?*

He had never questioned whether the Crow was Shadowborne or not. He thought it unlikely and dismissed the thought almost immediately, but surely he must employ someone Shadowborne. *Except Cephora said no one had seen shadow magic performed in years. If not that, then what?*

"It's more than just controlling the level of visibility in a room, you know." Ileta's words interrupted his train of thought and he glanced at her, raising an eyebrow. She nodded. "You felt it. That energy? That power? You can harness it. Manipulate it the same way you do your Shade." She tottered her head from side to side. "Well, not quite the same. But you can use it. You'll see."

However the hell I'm supposed to manage that. "I'll have to try that next time."

"Baby steps."

"Right, baby steps." *She's not just throwing me to the wolves then. Good.* "So, listen, I'm really appreciative of everything, Ileta, but I've gotta ask—"

She gave a deep sigh and shook her head. "You never learn, do you?"

He smirked. "I need to know. Who is it that—"

She held up her hand to cover his face. "Quiet."

"No, really. I want to—"

"I said quiet!"

Madigan stared at her, eyes wide. She had never been so vehement when he asked her questions. "Ileta—"

This time she lunged at him and drew him close, clapping her hand over his mouth. The move caught him completely unawares and he stood still in shock. She wasn't looking at him, but at something off in the distance.

"Someone is coming."

"You can hear that?" he whispered, pulling her hand away from his face. "Who the hell would be coming out here?"

Her face turned down in a frown. "No one good. Get to the trees. Now."

Mad knew better than to argue. The two of them made straight for the trees atop the levee. A car rumbled in the distance, growing closer and kicking up dust as it made its way down the long drive that led to the lot that used to be his home. *No one official should be coming by. Grandda had this place all paid off.* The accounts were still good for years to come; it was the first thing he checked when he and Ileta arrived.

The car came into view and he recognized the yellow and black of a taxicab. *Who the hell would be coming out here?* It paused next to the double trailer, idling for a moment before slowly creeping forward. It stopped at the end of the drive, a short distance from the old fire pit. After a moment, the rear doors opened.

A man he did not recognize exited the cab. Mad couldn't see his face. His hair was buzzed close and he wore blue jeans and a black jacket with a hood. He handed the driver a wad of bills and Mad heard Ileta curse.

"More than one. This could be a problem."

Madigan barely listened. The second person had emerged from the taxi, a woman. She was dressed in the same style of clothes as the man. Her hair was dark and cut to frame her face. Even from this distance he could see how pale her skin was. As the cab reversed out and she reached for the man's hand, Madigan saw what he already knew would be on her wrists: tattoos. Morella Darklore.

Madigan's mouth went dry as a small fire of hope flared to life in his chest. The man turned and looked straight toward the trees and Madigan could finally see his face. Thin, gaunt, and rough, but a face he knew.

His brother had come home.

22

THE BROTHERS OF DARKNESS

"That was amazing." Morella's grin stretched wide as she watched the car speed away. "Oh, that gives me so many ideas!"

Noctis nodded and gave her a halfhearted smile as he took her outstretched hand. "They're helpful, yeah. At least you're not screaming this time."

Morella pouted playfully. "I was crossing into a new realm! I was excited."

"Yeah well, thanks for toning it down a bit." He surveyed his old home, a sudden wave of suppressed memories flooding him. Someone had cleared the wreckage, but the evidence was still apparent. The stone foundation of the former house had a deep fissure that ran the length of it. The ground from the uprooted cedar tree had been cleared, but the base of the trunk remained. It was old and weathered, just a fallen log, now. If Madigan had been there, he had been busy.

"There's so much green." Morella shook her head. "There are parts of Aeril that have green like this, but nowhere near as much. You grew up here?"

Noctis nodded. "It's home."

His ears caught a faint sound and he whirled around. A tall, bearded man with long hair was sprinting from the levee as though chased by a swarm of bees. He ran with the fearless abandon of a child. He ran with an air of desperation. He ran straight for Noctis.

"Noctis . . ."

Noctis tensed. "I see him."

"Will!" the man cried out, growing closer in his frantic run. "Will!"

Noctis stared, not daring himself to believe it. Then, the next thing he knew, he was running with the same wild joy. They collided with a force that sent them spinning. Noctis threw his arms around his brother and held him fiercely. Madigan gave a half-choked sob, arms gripping his brother tight.

"Holy shit, Will. It's you? Holy shit, it's really you."

"I'm here, Mad." Noctis felt the warm streams of tears running down his cheeks. "I'm here."

"I thought you were dead." Madigan pulled him even closer. "I couldn't . . . I didn't want to believe it. Jesus, Will, I'm so sorry I left you."

"I'm alright, Mad, I'm alright."

"How the hell did you—no, no that can wait. Dammit, kid, I was so scared."

"I know." Noctis couldn't help himself. "You always were a big baby."

"You goddam bastard." Madigan laughed and pulled back to get a proper look at his brother. "Look at you, man. You've changed."

"You're one to talk." Noctis waved his hand around his hair and face then gestured to his brother and shrugged.

Madigan laughed and embraced his brother again. Noctis noticed that a second figure had appeared from the trees, watching them with arms crossed. She was lean and muscular and had angular features. Her hair was short, shorter even than Morella's, and cut into wayward, pixie-like spikes. She didn't approach.

So that's the Shadowborne. The supposed daughter of Dorian Valmont.

"How did you get here?" Madigan asked, rubbing Noctis's buzzed hair.

"A cab." Noctis jerked his head back toward the drive and smiled. "Didn't you see?"

"You bastard." Madigan pulled him into another hug. "You know what I meant. How the hell did you pay for that cab, anyway?"

Noctis grinned. "I used to be a pickpocket, remember?"

"Old habits, right?" Madigan smiled and clapped him on the back.

Noctis returned the smile. It was so good to see his brother, to feel the old banter return. He wanted nothing more than to fall into their casual camaraderie, but the stakes were too high. He forced himself to focus, to remember why he was there, finally. "Really, though, it was Cephora. I found her in Undermyre."

Madigan drew back and frowned. "And she filled you in?"

"As much as she could. You didn't leave her much to go on. I just got lucky with the rest."

Madigan eyed him and some of the joviality left him. "Will, are you okay? You seem—"

"Of course he is. He's better than ever, actually."

Both brothers turned to look at Morella. She stood, arms crossed in much the same fashion as the Shadowborne on the levee. Her face was turned down in a half frown, but she smiled when they turned. Noctis noted that it didn't fully reach her eyes.

"Morella." Madigan's smile matched hers. "Good to see you."

"Likewise." She approached and intertwined her fingers with Noctis's. Something in Madigan deflated. Morella inclined her head toward the distant figure. "Who's your friend?"

Noctis glanced back over his shoulder. The Shadowborne had not drawn any closer. *She's not happy we're here,* he mused. *I wonder if she knows that we suspect.*

"I'll let her do the introductions." Madigan held up a hand and waved for her to approach. When she made no move to do so, he dropped his hand and turned back, shrugging. Whatever his reservations about Morella, they were quickly overcome as he took in Noctis again. "Shit, kid, look at you. You look like a total badass. How the hell have you been?"

Noctis smirked and shook his head. "That's a hell of a question, Mad." He glanced at Morella and squeezed her hand. "Mind giving us a minute?"

"Not at all." She squeezed his hand back then leaned up to kiss his cheek. When she drew back, she shot a quick wink at Madigan then turned and strode away, looking as cool and calm as if she owned the place.

"What's going on?" Madigan's enthusiasm was dimming visibly. "Will, how have—"

"Just . . . give me a second, Mad." He looked around, scanning the foundation, looking at the charred tree trunk. "It's a lot to take in."

Madigan nodded. "I know. It was hard. Coming back was . . . everything was a mess still. Overgrown, yeah, but still a mess. Clearing it took some time."

Noctis was silent for a moment. When he spoke, his voice was hoarse, nearly breaking. "Did you find him?"

Silence.

"No. I didn't find him."

Silence.

"How long have you been back?"

"I don't know, really." Madigan ran a hand through his hair. "I got out of the habit of keeping track of time the way we used to. Ever since I left Cephora. A few years. Three-ish, probably, given the weather changes."

Noctis closed his eyes and nodded. "I saw the date on the way in. Somehow . . . it feels both longer and not at the same time."

"Me too. I didn't know we'd been gone for so long." Madigan smiled. It was distant and sad. "Some people go spend four years in college. We just spent that time getting a different education." The silence lingered again.

"Alright, go ahead," Noctis said.

"Jesus, finally." Madigan whirled him around. "Look at you, man. You look like you've been through hell. What happened? What happened with Valmont? What the hell is happening in Aeril? Where the hell have you been?"

Noctis chuckled despite himself. "First, a lot happened. Second, din'Dael got us out. It was bad." He shook his head, pushing the memory down with the rest of the baggage he didn't like to think about. "Third, I genuinely don't know. And fourth," he sighed, "I've been in the Sapholux."

Madigan raised an eyebrow. "The Sapholux?" Realization dawned on his face. "Jesus, Will. Were you there with din'Dael? What did he do to you?"

"He trained me." Noctis avoided any mention of the other surviving Lightborne. *Not until I know he's still the same Mad.* His eyes darted to the Shadowborne in the distance. *Not until he can be fully trusted.*

"Trained you?" Madigan looked him up and down. "Trained you how? Did you find out what the hell he did to your Shade?"

"The Shade is gone."

"Bullshit."

"Mad, it's gone. You were right. I'm something else." He held up a hand. Blue and white lightning crackled across its surface. He shrugged, as if the whole matter was inconsequential. "Lightborne."

"Will—"

"It's Noctis now."

Madigan stared at him. "Noctis?" The word dripped with sarcasm. "What the hell do you mean *Noctis*?"

"The fires of the Sapholux burn away weakness." Noctis spoke with grave determination, as if reciting an ancient oath, a code. "What emerges from its fires is born anew. The old, weak shell is burnt to ash, charred away until it is nothing. All successful Lightborne are reborn and renamed." Saying it to his brother made the whole thing seem like the most ridiculous load of crap he'd ever heard. He cracked a smile and winked. "Hence, I am Noctis."

Madigan eyed him and laughed. "Seriously, kid, you really had me going there. Did they really tell you to say that shit?"

"Jero was very dedicated to tradition." Noctis ran a hand along the velvet fuzz of his head. "Not gonna lie, I bought it. I absolutely bought it."

Madigan clapped him on the back. "Of course you did, kid. You've always been a sucker for that type of noise."

"Yeah, well, they knew all the right words." Noctis shook his head. *Gods, did I really let myself get so caught up in it?* "I don't know. It felt right. But maybe . . . maybe I need to regain some sense of self."

"Don't go getting all culty on me."

Noctis chuckled dryly. "I'm working on it."

"Grandda worked damn hard to drill all that 'no one's tool' shit into us."

"Heh, he sure did."

Madigan smiled and pulled him close again. "I'm glad you're here, Will. Or *Noctis*. Whatever you want me to call you, you'll still be a pain in the ass."

"Whatever you want, man. I'm not gonna lie, though. Noctis sounds pretty cool."

"Ha! That it does. Latin, right?" Noctis nodded and Madigan chuckled, shaking his head. "Jeez, did you pick it out yourself?"

"Surprisingly, no. That was a din'Dael thing. He thought it

was poetic. That you were the Shadowborne but I was the one who operated from the shadows."

Madigan chewed his lip and scratched his beard. "So, you didn't tell him about your Shade, then?" Noctis shook his head. "There's a chance then, right? There's a chance you could still get it back."

Noctis sighed. "Sure, there's a chance. But the people I've talked to about it don't give me much hope. The truth is, Mad, I'm okay without it. I didn't spend my days in the Sapholux lamenting my Shade."

"Oh yeah? You'll have to tell me about that sometime."

"We'll see." Noctis rolled his eyes and threw his hands to the sky in mock exasperation. "Ancient secrets of the Order and all that."

"You're an idiot," Madigan said and the pair laughed. "Come on, kid, let me introduce you to Ileta."

Ileta, not Aurellaine. Noctis followed his brother automatically. *Maybe it isn't her. Maybe this whole Aurellaine thing is just one big damn mistake.*

The Shadowborne did not move to meet them when they drew near. Noctis could feel her eyes upon him, drilling into him, inspecting him. She was beautiful in a severe way. She kept her emotions guarded, the cool smile on her face more of a sneer than anything resembling a welcome. He could sense her power and saw her Shade billowing around her feet. He had to fight back the sudden urge to Flare, to send electricity through the air and demonstrate his own power.

So, this is what din'Dael meant. Opposites.

She was dangerous, he could feel it. Some people hide their intentions, their instincts behind masks of coy civility or demurring behavior. Ileta was not one of those people. She wore her ferocity like armor. She exuded power and control in a magnetic, almost hypnotic way. *Like Valmont.*

Noctis realized he was clenching his fists and forced himself to relax. There was no way she knew that he knew. *If what I think I know is accurate.*

Morella was striding casually. She seemed calmer and more at ease than he had ever seen her, although her crooked smirk was betrayed by her intentional eyes. *She must be as on edge as me,* he mused. *She's just hiding it better.*

"Ileta," Madigan said when they approached, "this is Will, my brother. Or Noctis. He goes by that too."

She didn't move, only snickered. "Lightborne."

Noctis felt his brother tense. "Nice to meet you, Ileta."

"And . . . and this is Morella Darklore."

Morella and Ileta peered at each other, neither speaking for a moment. There was something dangerous in their interaction, something Noctis couldn't place. The moment of tension stretched a half second too long before Morella's loud, boisterous laugh snapped it like a twig.

"Ileta." She beamed and clapped her hands together. "It's a pleasure. I never imagined I'd meet another Shadowborne after Madigan."

"Is that so?" Ileta's words were pointed, harsh.

"It is." Morella smiled a little too broadly.

"Ileta's been great," Madigan said, a little too forcefully. "She's a fantastic teacher. Different than Grandda, that's for sure. But she's got a lot of knowledge and is relentless in drilling it into my thick skull."

He was the only one who laughed.

Noctis's skin was crawling. There was definitely something in the air. He felt defensive and aggressive at the same time. He peered at the Shadowborne. His key began to crackle and pop against his skin. He focused harder on Ileta, wondering what she was planning. But she too seemed to have noticed something. Her gaze had drifted away from them and back in the direction they had come from.

"Alright, well, this is just damn awkward." Madigan ran his

hands through his hair. "Don't everyone be too cordial now."

Noctis could feel the anger rising in him. *It's got to be her. Look at her, she even looks like Valmont.*

"Come on, guys." Noctis heard the nervous trepidation in his brother's voice. "Will, lighten up a bit, kid. Help me out here."

"Madigan," Noctis began, "I think that—"

"Quiet," Ileta snapped.

"Excuse me?" Morella glared. "What do you—"

"I said quiet!"

Morella's face twisted in rage. Ileta stepped toward them, drawing her hands together. Noctis groaned and reached for his knives. He hadn't thought to look before, but Ileta was wearing a noctori. Lightning crackled across the hilt of the blood fangs as he closed his fists around them. He prepared to strike.

But Ileta was still looking past them, had not even noticed that he'd armed himself. Noctis turned, following her gaze to the road in the distance. The key was vibrating, popping, twitching. "Something's coming," he said.

"Yes," Ileta responded. "Something big."

Madigan cursed. Noctis couldn't help but smile at the sound. *Just like old times.* His brother's Shade misted around them, then, similar to Ileta's but very different in color. Mad's was more earthen colored, dark browns and blacks, whereas hers was based in dark greens that flowed and twisted. Seeing the two colliding, intermingling, clouding, sent a pang of nostalgia through him. *That was supposed to be us. The Brothers of Darkness.*

"Perhaps this might be a good time to mention that Morella and I had a bit of a run-in in the Ways."

Ileta didn't look at him. "A run-in with what?"

"Necrothanians."

Madigan cursed again. Morella stepped back into the trees and out of sight. Ileta, however, seemed to relax. *No, not relax exactly, but something.* She seemed less tense, more casual. *That isn't a good sign.* Noctis looked for Morella but she was gone. That was good; she could take care of herself.

Lead the attack. Choose the ground. Decide. Jero din'Dael's words in his head, Noctis strode away from Madigan and Ileta. His brother called out to him, went to grab him, but he shrugged it off and ignored him. Noctis walked down the levee and directly to the end of the drive. Madigan and Morella were both at his back in the distance, which was good. If Ileta tried to attack him, they would be able to protect him. That meant he could focus entirely on the threat at his front.

A figure appeared in the distance, but it was not big by any means. It moved like a man but walked with a strange gait, as though the legs were too long for the body. At first, Noctis couldn't make out the features, could only feel the waves of power pouring off it. But as it drew closer, Noctis recoiled.

There were no features to make out. The face was a near-blank mask of stark white flesh. No nose, no eyes, no hair. Only a mouth broke the single plane of tight skin. The mouth stretched nearly halfway around its skull and twisted up in a terrifying, permanent grin of teeth, too long and too many. It stopped a short distance away from him and, though it had no eyes, Noctis felt the grotesque creature's gaze upon him, boring into him.

"Child of Thornnnnne."

Noctis paled. Images of death and destruction surged back to his mind's eye. The profound sense of loss that he kept buried deep inside began to claw its way to the surface. He clenched his fists and fought down the waves of panic. "Senraks."

The moment lingered between the two, Senraks with its fanning grin of razored teeth, Noctis steeling himself.

The crackling, roaring bolt of lightning took Senraks full in the chest and sent the creature reeling backward. Noctis followed it up with blast after blast as he brought the air to life, awash with blazing fire. Senraks recovered with a hissing roar and surrounded itself in its Shade.

Noctis drew the blood fangs and launched at the creature, the blades glowing from the surging power he coursed through them. Then, he was flying through the air, battered by the Shade. He landed hard on his side and rolled away while the storm of his lightning raged and crashed into the creature. Senraks was transforming, growing.

A figure raced past him. Noctis caught sight of a bastard sword held high, of a Shade whirling. Madigan met the creature full on as its tentacles lashed out toward him. His brother's Shade solidified into an impassable wall that stopped the battering tentacles short. Madigan severed one tentacle with his noctori and propelled himself back with his Shade as Senraks swatted at him with solidified darkness.

Noctis rushed back in, mindful of his blasts now that his brother had joined in the attack. He spaced himself far enough from Madigan that his brother was out of range, then he unleashed a wall of white-hot fire and lightning around him in a whirlwind. Throwing caution to the wind, he ran for Senraks.

Jervin had been a master of blades, but he had not been Borne. As the two brothers engaged the creature, Senraks roared in fury and pain. Under their combined onslaught, coordinated through years of training, the creature gave ground. *We're winning,* the thought raced through Noctis's mind. *We're finally going to kill the bastard.*

He was knocked away suddenly by the creature's Shade. Senraks beat at him repeatedly in a full assault. The wall of fire disappeared and Noctis rolled away a second before the blood beast crashed its full weight onto him.

The creature was gone from his reach, then, retreating. Madigan was a storm of viciousness as he battered at the blood beast. Then, Noctis saw another Shade winding through the chaos. Ileta joined the fray, fighting alongside his brother. Suddenly, Senraks gave ground before turning into full flight. The blood beast ran.

Noctis glared at Ileta. *She waited to join until the bastard was already retreating.* Madigan was yelling for him, urging him to his feet.

"We've got to get after it, Will!"

The blood beast was moving away far faster than they would be able to keep up. Noctis rose to his feet, still glaring at Ileta. "Tell me you've got a car, Mad. Something."

Madigan nodded. He whirled, running full speed back toward the trailer. Noctis locked eyes with Ileta. She had not released her Shade. "Where the hell were you?"

Her eyes narrowed. "You need to check yourself, Lightborne."

Noctis couldn't contain his boiling fury. "I know who you are, Ileta. Who you really are."

She smirked and shook her head. "I doubt that."

The sound of spinning tires on gravel interrupted them. Noctis was thrown completely off as Madigan screeched to a halt driving an old, beat-up minivan. The windows were down and his brother shouted through.

"Move your ass, Will!"

Noctis threw open the passenger door and jumped inside. Ileta followed a moment later. Noctis threw his head out the window, scanning for Morella, but she was still hidden in the trees. Madigan pressed the pedal to the floor and the van lurched forward.

Today's the day, Grandda. Senraks dies.

23

VOID

"Where the hell did you even find this thing?" Noctis was clutching the door and had his feet firmly planted on the ground. He drew a sharp breath as Madigan barreled around a corner and pushed the van to move faster.

"Cheapest thing I could find on the lot that ran," Madigan said, not taking his eyes off the road. Noctis turned and glanced at the backseat. Ileta was eyeing him with . . . wariness? Suspicion? He couldn't read her face.

"There it is," Mad shouted. Noctis whipped his head back around and sure enough, the blood beast was in front of them, off in the distance. They were gaining on it.

"We should turn back." Ileta gripped the driver's seat and pulled herself forward. "This isn't right."

"No way in hell are we turning back," Noctis snapped.

"Madigan, turn the van back. Now."

Noctis watched the flurry of emotions that crossed his brother's face. The van started to slow. "What the hell, Mad? That thing murdered Grandda! It's right there!"

"Stop the car, Madigan. Turn it back."

"Will you two just let up for one goddam minute?" Madigan snapped. He kept the van moving but the urgency of the pursuit was gone. "Ileta, what's wrong?"

"What's wrong is that she doesn't want us to kill that bastard," Noctis urged. "Now catch that damn thing."

"Don't do it, Madigan. Your brother isn't thinking clearly." Noctis whirled and glared at her. She met his eye with a wry smile. "Perhaps it's the taint of Radiance clouding his mind."

Noctis snapped. Flaring, he reached out and seized his brother's thigh with charged fingers. Madigan shrieked as Noctis sent electric impulses coursing through his brother's leg. The limb went rigid, shooting his foot down onto the accelerator. The van screamed forward, the force shoving them back against their seats. Ileta was thrown back and rolled over the middle seat into the back.

"What the hell, Will?" Madigan shrieked again. "What in the goddam hell?"

That thing isn't getting away this time. Noctis kept the leg pinned as they closed on the figure of Senraks. *We must have got it good; the bastard is moving slow.*

His brother was shouting at him, cursing at him while the van sped forward. Noctis ignored him. Din'Dael had been right after all: Madigan didn't have the strength to follow through. Will hadn't had the strength. Noctis did.

The blood beast stopped in its tracks and whirled on them. Neither Noctis nor Madigan had a moment to react. Somehow, through the haze of fury and bloodlust, a small part of Noctis's brain recoiled at the sight of the creature. At the last second, just before impact, it seemed to be smiling.

The van crashed into Senraks. The force of the impact sent Ileta flying forward from the rear of the van. She smashed into the windshield and collapsed limp on the dash. Madigan was thrown forward and slammed against the steering wheel before slumping over it. Ileta's still form slid from the dash and crumpled against him.

Noctis stared at her unconscious body. *Good riddance.* He threw open the passenger door, fighting back waves of dizziness and disorientation. He stumbled out of the van. Senraks was still. There was no sign of the beast's Shade, no activity from any of his limbs. Noctis approached the center of the body. He drew his blood fangs and kicked the still creature. "I may not know how to kill you, bastard, but I can drain you dry." He prepared to strike. *For Grandda.*

"I see that Jero finally let you out of his sight."

Noctis froze. *No*. He turned.

Beyond the wreckage stood Dorian Valmont. His hair waved in the light breeze as he took a step forward, cocking his head to the side. "Tell me, William Davis, why are you here?"

Fear coursed through Noctis's body, absolute terror as the dark man said his name. *My name . . .* A million thoughts raced through his brain. He wanted to obliterate the sorcerer. He wanted to scream for his brother. The sudden futility of everything crashed down on him. *Oh gods, Mad. What have I done?*

He stared at the wreckage of the van, to the still form of his brother—his only family. What had he done in his mad pursuit of the blood beast? *What the hell did din'Dael do to me?* Noctis Thorne, what a ridiculous notion. *Mad needs me. Gods, he needs his brother, not some goddam tool of din'Dael's.*

Will gripped the fangs tight and raised them as Valmont closed the distance between them. The sorcerer's Shade trailed along the ground behind him, oily and thick, a toxic sludge upon the ground. Valmont was holding something in his spindly hands, an orb of swirling, pale amber. Will's throat was dry but he forced the words out. "Dorian Valmont." They sounded weak.

Valmont inclined his head. "A pleasure to make your acquaintance, young one. For too long, our introduction has been postponed." The man's fingers danced upon the orb's surface.

"The pleasure is all mine, I'm sure." *Jesus, Will, what the hell are you doing?* His eyes flitted back to the van. Madigan still hadn't stirred.

"I'd heard you were the reasonable one." Valmont smiled casually. His gaze followed Will's to the van. "Pity, that. I do hope they survive."

Will's mind jumped to Ileta and he scowled. "I'm sure you do."

"There is no need for such hostility between us." Valmont's voice was musical, hypnotic. He toyed with the orb while staring directly into Will's eyes. "I have come only for words to be shared between us. Again, I ask, why are you here, William?"

Will's eyes darted back to the van, then to Valmont, then to the orb. There was something sinister about it, something terrifyingly simple. "I'm . . ." *Gods, he's going to kill us all.* Something snapped in his mind and he grinned wide. "I'm just here to meet up with my brother."

Will slammed the blood fangs down into the still form of Senraks. The blood beast shrieked and roared, lashing out. *Not dead, then. Not yet.*

Valmont stepped back awkwardly to avoid the flailing blood beast. The look of pure surprise on his face was enough to make up for Will's sudden pain from being dashed to the ground by a flailing tentacle. The strange orb rolled precariously in Valmont's hand before tipping and plummeting. Will scrambled to his feet, fear tying his stomach in knots. Faster than he thought possible, he saw Valmont's hand dart out and barely catch the orb with his fingertips. He looked up and met Will's eye. Cocking his head to the side, Valmont smiled.

He dropped the orb.

Without waiting, Will turned and raced for the van. He glanced back just as the orb shattered on the ground. The pale, amber void within sent a pulse through the air like a shockwave. It knocked him off his stride and he fell to his knees. Will whirled to look back. The ground at Valmont's feet withered and died into a brown shadow of decay. The point of origin bubbled and then the decay began to fizzle and stretch. Will scrambled backward. The corruption spread outward from the point of impact with a terrifying rapidity.

Senraks was caught by the escaping force and screeched with fear and pain as the amber liquid scorched ground and creature alike. Will looked on in horror as the creature's flesh began to fall away in sheets, the rapidly decaying tentacles sizzling and steaming. Will yelled for his brother.

There was movement in the driver's seat. *Thank the gods.* Madigan stuck his bleeding head from the window, confusion and anger plain upon his face. But when he looked past Will, the pure terror that came over him was enough to send Will running even harder. The engine began to sputter and turn over as Madigan flooded it with gas, the old, beat-up van blazing to life.

"Go!" Will threw himself into the still-open passenger door. Ileta was gone. He had no idea when or how, but right now it didn't matter. He slammed the door shut while the van sent dirt and rubble spitting out behind them.

"God dammit, Will," Madigan shouted and punched him in the arm. "God dammit! What did you do?"

"Just get us the hell out of here, scream at me later." Will pushed energy from the blood fangs toward his brother, healing whatever damage had been done. Madigan looked simultaneously relieved and furious as he slammed a fist against Will's arm.

"What in the goddam hell, Will? What. The. Goddam. Hell?"

"It was a trap, alright?" Will was gripping the seat while the van roared precariously down the gravel road. "I didn't know, Mad. How the hell could I have known?"

"Ileta tried to warn us, you ass." Madigan punched him again. "You could have listened instead of going on a goddam suicide mission and burning the hell out of my goddam leg."

"I thought that"—he glanced in the rearview mirror—"oh shit. Oh shit, Mad. Faster!"

The corruption was spreading. Trees were consumed in decay as the deadly radius of the orb expanded outward farther and farther. Madigan swerved the van and raced ahead. They weren't far from their home. If they could make it there, they could, what? They could what? Turn and fight? Will spun his head around. *We may not need to. Maybe Valmont got caught up in all that death.* He doubted it.

Something large was crashing amongst the decaying trees. Something was chasing them. When it came into sight, Will's stomach dropped.

Senraks. Or, rather, what was left of Senraks. The tentacles were gone, only putrid remnants of decayed flesh left clinging to the strange amalgamation of bone that made up its body. It looked strangely human, but giant, the size of a house. It dragged itself after them, propelled by the two massive forelimbs. Only the forelimbs were nothing but bones, splitting and cracking, dark with decay. How they were not crumbling to dust under the strain of movement was beyond Will.

"Holy shit," Madigan swore, having seen the figure in his mirrors. "What the hell—is that the blood beast?"

Will nodded. "Get us out of here, Mad. I've got this." His brother met his eye for a moment before setting his jaw and focusing on the road. Will moved between the seats and into the back of the van. He heard Madigan curse when Will used a blood fang to knock out the rear window. The shattered glass flew into the road. Senraks was almost upon them.

Will Flared and unleashed a bolt of lightning. He missed. Madigan swerved the van as Senraks took a horrible swipe at the car, sending Will crashing around the back. The remnants of the broken window dug into the flesh of his arm. Will gasped in pain and blood began to stream down his skin. He forced himself back into position and launched another wave of attacks at Senraks, forcing the creature back.

The corruption had slowed its spread, Will saw. *Whatever that damn thing is, it has limited range, thank the gods.* He couldn't believe the scope of the damage when he looked to the distance behind Senraks. It was a wasteland. The trees themselves had withered, their bark pruning and softening with rot. Against that backdrop, the gargantuan decay of the creature that pursued looked all the more horrific.

"You really screwed up, Will." Madigan shook his head, yelling over the groan of the van's tired engine. "Jesus, you've been home five goddam minutes. What the hell did you do back there?"

"Valmont was there," Will fired back. "He had something, some kind of device. It . . . it destroyed everything." They were nearly home. *If we can just hold out till we get there, then . . .* then what? There was nothing there.

"Valmont? How the hell did—"

A roaring bolt of black lightning crashed into the side of the van, caving the metal. Suddenly blinded by the light and flung into the air, Will was whipped and thrown. He slammed into the seats and roof while the van rolled and tumbled. Finally, it skidded to a halt.

What was that? Will coughed, tasting blood. *I should be dead. How am I not dead?* Then he saw the darkness that cloaked him within the cabin. Madigan.

Madigan groaned. "What the hell did that?"

Will didn't know. Before he could react, the car was spinning again, knocked with such force that Will was thrown from the shattered back window. He tucked his arms and rolled, squinting his eyes closed while dirt and gravel tore at his clothes and skin. When he came to a stop, he saw the bones of Senraks slamming against the van again and again. *How is that bastard still functioning?*

Sanguinar. Of course. *Just like that damn reaper Morella and I—* Will froze. *Morella.* Will's heart raced. They had made it back to their property, but where was she?

He didn't have time to worry. The living corpse of Senraks

was shredding the van, peeling back sheets of metal. Madigan forced himself from the crumbling driver's side window, his Shade forming a barrier between him and the whaling limbs. Senraks smashed the van completely before abandoning it and turning its focus to Madigan's retreating form.

Will struggled to his feet, dripping blood from a hundred different cuts. *Gods, this thing is unstoppable.* He broke into a limping run, sapping additional resources from the bloodstones to keep him on his feet. How much power had he absorbed from Senraks before the eruption? He didn't know.

He struck out, blasting lightning against the abomination. Senraks roared and hurled the smashed van at him, sending it spinning through the air like a discus. Will ducked and it collided with the distant trailer, reducing them both to wreckage. He summoned his strength and closed the distance between himself and the creature. It focused just enough attention upon him to allow Madigan to regain his feet.

Will watched, awestruck, while his brother attacked. The noctori blazed to life, but it wasn't the bastard sword Will had always known. Instead, it was a massive warhammer. His Shade encircled and immobilized one of the bony limbs and, while it squeezed, Madigan brought the warhammer down with such force that the cracked bone shattered beneath the impact.

Senraks lashed out, swatting at his brother. Will darted forward. Closing the distance, he saw that the dead flesh clinging to Senraks's bones was brightening, the color returning. *A golem, of sorts,* the Crow had said. Realization dawned on Will. Senraks was rejuvenating.

He cursed and launched another assault. He had to think of something fast. *It's weak. It has to have a limit.*

Yet the creature seemed unstoppable. Even with the combined strength of Will and his brother, they barely seemed to be making any impact upon it. *How do you destroy something that can't be destroyed?* Darkness flooded the area; the creature's Shade had returned. Senraks struck out against Madigan and sent him flying.

It's regaining some sense of itself, not just reacting instinctively anymore. Soon, its cruel, taunting cunning would return, Will was certain. *And then we're done for.*

An impossible idea broke through the fear. It was insanity. It was the work of a madman. *But maybe . . .*

He turned and raced for the stone foundation that had once been his home. *A binding of Blood and Shadow, forged into a creature.* He remembered the Crow's words. And what had his grandfather said in those final, horrible moments? *The blood of my line shall be your undoing.* Senraks was bound by blood—and by blood he could be undone.

The creature ignored his flight and continued to battle Madigan. His brother was holding his own amazingly well, but they couldn't have much time. Flesh was already returning to the golem's form.

Will reached the foundation stone and planted himself on its edge. He was farthest from the trees on all sides here. He gauged the distance. Senraks was closer than the Shale had been, but he couldn't afford to wait. *Assuming this even works.*

Blood and Shadow had created Senraks. Will withdrew his blood fangs and stared at their stones. *A binding of Blood and Shadow and something more ancient.* They were tapped, he could feel it now. They needed energy. The stupidity of his idea threatened to make its way into his conscious mind, but he shut the thoughts out. *This has to work.*

He dropped to his knees in the earth next to the stone and plunged a fang into his leg. He shrieked. Blood gushed. Struggling to remain conscious, he forced the replenishing bloodstones to restore the wound. *One to draw life, the other to restore it.* His key roared and sent shockwaves through his body. He held the restorative fang in his left hand, guiding the flows over him in waves. Still clutching it, he thrust the knife into the hard ground.

Images of the Shale raced through his mind. Will was crying, blood pouring from his leg as he was simultaneously ravaged and renewed, over and over. He raised his right hand to the sky and the air surrounding him began to hum. His head swam from the coursing energy. He closed his eyes and drew the power in.

A torrent of lightning erupted in a deafening clash. The bolts rained down and collided into Will. The pain was unbearable. The power rent his flesh, the fresh burns cracking his skin and peeling it away only to be instantly restored by the constantly renewing flow from the blood fangs. He opened his eyes, seeing only white. He roared for his brother with a voice like thunder.

He couldn't see Madigan, couldn't know if he was clear. There was no time. Will drew upon the force of the lightning, the strength of the key, and the powers of Blood and Shadow that surrounded him from the blood fangs. The wave of power surged in black lightning at Senraks. In his fevered madness, Will could see something within the lightning: a Shade, deep red and black, winding and twisting within the unnatural fire. He channeled the force directly into Senraks.

The creature screamed.

A whirlwind storm of the red Shade thundered to life around the golem. Black and blue lightning split the cloud and collided into the creature again and again. Like countless razor blades slicing away at its flesh, Senraks's body was stripped. The flesh swept into the winds and was incinerated by the blaze. Will felt something inside himself tearing as the beast that had taken his grandfather from him was sliced and burned.

Senraks loosed a cry that sounded almost human. It was lifted off the ground. The surviving tentacles and limbs were wrenched and twisted, a grotesque marionette upon tangled strings. Limbs burst. Flesh bubbled. Again and again, the horrors played across Will's vision. Between his own pain and that of the creature, his was a world of screams. This was not justice, this was vengeance. Punishment. He channeled his pain and anger, his fury and devastation, into the swirling forces of chaos and pressed them upon Senraks.

The thing at the heart of the storm burst out in a smattering of gore. Will did not stop until every bit of bone and skin and muscle was reduced to ash. Nothing would remain of the blood beast that had murdered his grandfather.

Finally, he released the torrent of lightning from the sky. Sobbing, he withdrew the fang from his leg. He tried to heal the wound, but the power of the stones was diminished. *Something is always lost in transference.* Where did it go? he wondered.

Will collapsed. The fury of the dragon fire in his veins subsided. His skin felt too tight. Thirst was clawing at his throat, but he was too weak, too exhausted. *It's dead.*

Something was grabbing at him. There were muted sounds. He couldn't respond; speaking was impossible. He opened his eyes but they wouldn't focus. The world seemed much too bright, much too warm. Darkness was better.

I always preferred the darkness.

He let it take him.

24
A RUMBLE OF THUNDER

The fires raged. Everywhere Madigan looked, flames were rising and roaring, their heat forcing him to use his Shade as a shield. It did little to help. He coughed and sputtered as he stumbled about in the smoke. The Shade could only do so much and, apparently, acting as a filter was beyond its capabilities. That was the least of his concerns, though; the world around him was an inferno. *Jesus, Will, what have you done?*

His body screamed in pain. He was almost certain that his left wrist was broken again and that was on top of the cascade of burns that covered his back and the bruises from the rolling van. His head was pounding and his vision was blurry. He prayed that it was a result of the smoke and not from a damn concussion. Every goddam part of him hurt. Battling Senraks, he'd been going on pure adrenaline and reactive instinct. That was gone now. He was spent. Exhausted.

But he had to find Will.

He didn't have time to revel in the blood beast's death. He didn't have time to wonder about Ileta or worry about the blast of lightning that disabled the van and sent it tumbling. He couldn't afford to worry that Valmont was probably watching his every move and waiting for the opportunity to strike. No, he had one goal right now: save his little brother. *Wherever the hell he is in this goddam mess.*

Whatever Will had become, whether he was some crazed Lightborne fanatic who called himself Noctis or whether it was all just some damn act, none of it mattered. He was in trouble. Madigan didn't know what he'd seen, what it was that Will had done, but he knew he'd never seen him do anything like it before. That whirlwind of fire and lightning had been more than he'd ever imagined. There had been something else in it, too, something dark and twisted. And he had watched it rip Senraks apart, bit by bit.

Madigan himself had only barely gotten clear; the power obviously hadn't discriminated. He was only alive because he guarded himself while he ran and pushed himself to run harder than he could ever remember. He'd gotten clear, but that had only been the start.

Like Senraks, obliterated by the torrential flames, so too had gone everything in the area. The trailer was mangled and melted, its contents alight. The surrounding earth was scorched and barren. And every tree within sight was a blazing fire. He skirted away when he heard a terrifying crack and saw a large, scorched fir fall. *Dammit, Will. Where the hell are you?*

Madigan had never seen an actual forest fire. He'd seen pictures, of course, and the occasional video, but they didn't do the reality justice. The heat was a physical force bearing down on him. The air was too thin, too hot, too dry. With every attempt to inhale he felt scorching air singeing his lungs. He held his Shade so tight around him it was almost a second skin, an armor against the heat, but even its cooling serenity was tested.

And Will is somewhere in this. Exposed.

Mad threw himself to the ground when a sudden cloud of hot

smoke rolled toward him. He landed hard on the injured wrist and cried out in a flurry of curses. The ground was too warm, but it was better than whatever that decay had been. *What the hell did Valmont do?* His thoughts drifted to Ileta, lost somewhere between Valmont's decay and Will's fire. He struggled to his feet and glanced back the way they had come. *She made it out. She has to have made it out.*

She wasn't the only one in the area, though. Morella had at least been in the opposite direction of Valmont. Mad glanced up to the trees atop the levee where they had left her. Like everything else, they were ablaze. But she would have had more room at her back to run.

He shook his head to clear it, wincing at the throbbing pain. It didn't matter. No, what mattered was Will. He was somewhere in this hell. Madigan had seen him go down before the smoke billowed and obstructed his sight. *Somewhere in this direction.* Fighting back the pain and heat and smoke, he ran for his brother.

He found the limp body at the base of the old house.

Madigan cried out and collapsed at Will's side, unable to fathom the amount of dried, caked blood that surrounded the pale figure. With delicate, trembling hands he reached out to touch the form, as if fearing that it would crumble into dust at the slightest bit of pressure. Will was solid though. Solid and warm. Head bowed, hot tears streaming down his face, Madigan sat amongst the swirling smoke and flame.

Wait . . . was that . . .? Madigan felt it again. He scrambled closer to the body and—*yes!*—it wasn't a trick of his mind. Will's chest was rising and falling in slow, stuttered breaths. *He's alive. Damn the gods, the bastard is still alive.* Mad shouted at Will, looking for any kind of response. None came. But the kid was alive. *For now. We need to get out of here.*

Pushing through his exhaustion and pain, Madigan wrapped his arms around his brother and lifted. His wrist screamed at the weight and his head swam. But he refused to allow it to stop him. "I've got you, kid." His voice was dry and scratchy, burnt by the air.

Will felt light in his arms, lighter than he had any right to be. His clothes were ripped and torn. There was a steady trickle of blood coming from his right thigh. The jeans there were slashed wide open and his entire leg was dark with stained blood. *What the hell did you do to yourself?*

Everything cracked and burned around them. Mad squinted against the smoke and scanned the area. There was no easy way out and no way to tell how far the fire had spread. The gravel drive that led to the road was the lone gap in a blazing corridor. The fire would take them before they got anywhere near the road if he took that path. His eyes darted to the levee. It was curled with flames as well, but he knew how deep those flames went; the trees were only so thick.

"Come on, kid. We can do this."

He could feel his skin blistering as he grew nearer to the steep incline. He kept his back to it, keeping his Shade in as much of a protective cone as he could to drive the heat from his back. The smoke and vapor that made it through was still agonizing. His wrist gave out and both he and Will tumbled to the ground. His brother didn't stir. Grimacing, Madigan stood. He dragged Will. Still the temperature increased. The smoke became too dense to breathe and, even if he could, the air was too hot to inhale. Wrapping his Shade about them as densely as he could, Madigan turned his back to the trees and pulled Will into the flames.

All sense of direction vanished. Eyes closed, Mad stumbled over scorched earth and smoldering foliage. The trees tore at him with fiery, brittle branches. His lungs ached and burned from the short, frantic bursts of air he forced himself to take. He backpedaled foot after foot, unable to lift his head from facing the ground. For one terrifying moment, he feared that he might be walking in a circle or only deeper into the trees. He began to falter.

The ground declined slightly. Relief washed through him. He twisted, turning his brother from the path they had come and toward the levee's slope. At the base of it was the momentary safety he sought. Coughing violently, he sidestepped and stumbled down the levee and into the small slough just beyond.

The water's first swirl around his ankles sent a chill through him. They weren't safe yet, but there was at least some reprieve from the heat. Something to cool them. The air was still thick with smoke but less than moments before. Madigan dropped into the cold water and bit back the sharp inhale of shock; his lungs hurt too bad and he couldn't afford the fit of coughing it was sure to bring.

He turned back to his brother. Will was mostly submerged just off the bank, his body in the creek but face just out of it. Madigan fumbled his way back to him and assessed the damage. *Jesus, Will.* If the burns and blood loss didn't kill him, with all those wounds the potential for infection from the slough was staggering.

He shook his head and cupped his brother's face. Will's body temperature was still high, but the water was helping. He was still breathing, though the breaths were shallow. Madigan forced himself to think. He covered Will in his Shade to help cool him. *But gods, you're a damn mess, kid.* Will needed help and he needed it fast.

Mad's stomach twisted. He only had one idea on how to fix it. One idea that he disliked very much.

"I love you, but you're a damn bastard, kid."

He reached for Will's blood fangs. He gripped the longer of the two blades in his hand. It was a good weight, heavy in a strong, solid way. He had never held them before, he realized, had never even thought to ask. *Just like I never offered for Will to try the noctori.* He shook his head against the thoughts and focused.

There was no time to waste wondering about what ifs or could have beens.

"This had better work." Drawing a deep breath to try to control his racing heart, Madigan wedged the blade between his legs. He placed his good hand against the edge of the knife and drew down.

He doubled over and fell sideways into the shallows of the water. His body recoiled against the maddening fury of flames that coursed through his veins. A distant part of his mind knew that it was only the toxins of the fang, but that did nothing to calm the raging fear and pain that gripped him. It took every ounce of control not to loosen his hand.

Will needs help. He clung to that thought like a man clings to a life raft. His world spun and swam and burned, but still he forced himself to hold on, to allow the fang to drain the life from him.

He held the blade for hours, it seemed, although he knew it couldn't have been more than a few seconds. He forced himself to focus, to control the pain and use it to fuel him. He drew his Shade close and felt its strange, restorative cool enwrap him. It barely even dimmed the pain. Finally, he could take it no longer and forced the blade from his marred hand.

He couldn't release it easily, the immobile fingers of his hand wrapped tightly around the blade like Will had shot his electricity through them. When he finally managed to slide the knife away from his blood-soaked palm, he lay, his body in spasms. His hands were curled in front of him, the left useless from the broken wrist, the right trembling from the brutal gash. He forced himself up onto his elbows, pushing himself back toward his brother. He scanned Will's face, frantic with worry. *Come on, kid. This magic shit can't only work when you're conscious.*

"Mad?" Will's voice was weak, but he was awake.

"Don't talk." Speaking made Mad realize how dry his throat had become. *Those fangs are damn potent.* "Use your knives, heal yourself."

There was a moment of silence before Will started to rise. He looked less pale, less ashen than only moments before. His eyes fell to Madigan's bloody hand and they widened. "Did you . . . ?"

Madigan nodded. "No time to think about it now, kid, thank me later. We've gotta move."

"But your hand—"

"Up, Will. We're getting out of here." The heat was beginning to bear down on him again, and from the look on Will's face, he was feeling it too. He shook the discomfort away and crouched down to offer his brother a shoulder to hold on to. Will felt light, frail even. *Goddam, Will, what did you do to yourself?*

They edged along the water, keeping as much distance between them and the surrounding blaze as they could. Madigan did everything he could to block some of the heat with his Shade, but he was exhausted. Battling Senraks, Will zapping his goddam leg, and now the damn blood fangs, everything was taking its toll. "Not quite the reunion I envisioned," he muttered.

"Maybe we shouldn't have come." Will coughed dryly. "Morella even—" He froze, eyes widening. He clutched at Madigan's shoulder frantically. "Jesus, Mad, where is she? Have you seen her?"

"She got clear of the blaze, I saw her," he lied. "Maybe she and Ileta are together." *And if not, I've got an idea of where to find Ileta, at least.*

If anything, it appeared as though his attempt to reassure Will did the opposite. His brother's face twisted in anger and he set off with renewed vigor. "We've got to find her. She isn't safe."

"Neither are we."

They struggled through the boggy shallows, fighting the heat and the mud. Madigan had to shield his eyes when he looked at the blaze. *It's spreading. Goddam, it's spreading.* There was nothing either of them could do to stop it, nothing to contain the inferno. *This whole area is going to go up.*

They made it to a small grouping of trees that were not yet ablaze. They raced up the embankment. On the other side of the levee was a wide flood plain. Madigan looked back the way they had come, looked at the clouds of billowing black smoke. He thought of the surrounding area, the distant neighbors and nearby groves of trees.

"The authorities are going to be out." He shook his head. "They're gonna think some damn kids were playing with fire and destroyed everything."

"They'd be right." Will's voice was hard and foreign. "We'll be gone before they get anywhere near us though."

"Home, though, it's really gone this time."

"Home was gone a long time ago, Mad." Will's voice was dark, filled with anger and sadness. "This world hasn't ever been the home we wanted."

Madigan glanced at his brother, concerned by what he saw. Despite being weakened, Will had his blades out and was scanning the area. His clothes were bloody and wet and shredded. His close-cropped hair and the stubble on his face gave him a harsh edge. His thin face and sunken eyes only added to the grim visage. He looked savage, feral even.

"Will—"

"Quiet," his brother snapped. "Valmont is still out there somewhere."

Madigan set his jaw and tried to flex his right hand. His breath caught at the pain. "How the hell did he get here? How did he know where and when to find us?"

"How, indeed." Will didn't meet his eye and Madigan suddenly felt very cautious. *He knows something. Or, at least, he thinks he knows something.*

There was a flash of movement at the corner of his eye. Both brothers whirled. The lightning that crackled in the air around Will dissipated almost instantly and his harsh demeanor visibly softened. Morella was racing toward them, apparently unhurt although her clothes were singed. Without a word, Will ran to meet her and threw his arms around her.

"Let's get out of here," Will shouted back at Madigan. He grabbed Morella's hand and the pair took off running without so much as a glance at him.

Madigan furrowed his brow. *What happened to being on edge about Valmont?*

He followed, surprised at how quickly Will was able to move despite his injuries. His own body was aching. He wrapped his Shade around his slashed hand and swelling wrist, letting it soothe and calm the pain. He winced as it tightened around the injuries, but it would help. He glanced back over his shoulder at the towers of smoke. *Just gotta get through this. There'll be time to deal with everything later. This isn't like the Shale. This time, we stick together.*

Thinking of the Shale, he turned back to Will and Morella. *How things have changed.* His brother was practically a stranger to him. And on top of that, it seemed like Morella's influence over Will had only grown. From what he'd seen, she appeared to be almost a compulsion for Will. A need.

Whatever had happened to Will, Mad didn't like it.

So that our minds may always be our own. What happened to yours, Will?

25
BAITING THE TRAP

Will was on edge, racing with hackles raised. Valmont was still nowhere to be seen. Neither was the traitorous Ileta. *Not a traitor. She can't betray what I always knew she was.* He held Morella's hand tight. His brother trailed a short distance behind them, cradling his hands in front of him. Keeping watch, Will expected; that was always his way.

They had to veer off the main drag when emergency services began to arrive. The flashing lights, the noise and commotion, seemed so unnecessary. *Just let the place burn. Let this whole damn world burn.*

Burn it all.

He shook the thought out of his head. *What am I saying?*

Morella squeezed his hand and they slowed their pace.

"I just need a quick breather," she said. "What happened? Why isn't that Vequian following us?"

She looked exhausted, covered in soot and grime, and Will realized that she didn't know about Valmont. *She only knows that Senraks was there, nothing beyond that.* A flash of cold nerves pinched his shoulder blades.

"Senraks is dead," Madigan said with a scowl. He was shaking, Will could see. He looked weak. "Will killed it."

She whirled to stare at Madigan. A look of sheer confusion and panic flickered across her face. "You're certain?"

"What the hell do you think started this whole fiery mess?"

Morella turned back to Will and her eyes narrowed. "Then what are we running from?"

"Valmont," he said softly, delicately, as though merely speaking the name aloud would summon the man.

Morella's face didn't move through the emotions that Will expected. She stared at him hard, her mouth twisted in that dark smirk he knew so well and understood so little. "So, he did move to this realm. We were right." She turned and glared at Madigan. "He's hunting you, Shadowborne."

Madigan didn't react to her venomous tone. "Is he now?" He spread his tattered, Shade-wrapped arms wide and shouted at the sky. "I'm right here, you goddam bastard!"

"Mad!" Will darted forward and grabbed his brother's shirt and yanked at him. "What the hell are you doing?"

"She's wrong," he said flatly. "He isn't hunting me. He's waiting for something. Planning something. He won't make his move anytime soon."

Will released his brother. "Your brain is cracked, you know that?"

Madigan sneered. "You really don't see it, do you?"

The two brothers glared at each other. "See what?" Will finally said.

"He's maneuvering us. Herding us. Driving us to do what he wants, where he wants."

"You're insane," Morella muttered, glaring at him. "To even think that you could understand his plan—"

"Plan?" Madigan snapped. "Right, plan. What's our plan, Will? You taking us back to Aeril? Abandoning this world?" Madigan approached, towering over his brother. "Three years, Will.

Almost three years that Valmont must have known where I was. How else could he have just appeared today?"

Will felt cold at the words, but he tried to dismiss it. "Shut up, Mad."

"Three years he waited. And for what?" Madigan looked Will up and down. "Until my little brother shows up."

"I said shut up."

"Why, am I starting to make sense?" Madigan's voice was calm and level. It infuriated Will. "He waited until we were both together again and then he destroys everything we have here. He, what? He presents some big, scary weapon that corrupts everything it touches? Drives us to run again but doesn't pursue?" Madigan shook his head. "No. He knows we'll hide back in Aeril. He's manipulating this whole thing."

"Shut. Up." Will's body tensed. Static rose in the air. He felt the power surging through him. *Burn him,* a distant part of his brain called to him, *cleanse the taint of Shadow from his soul.* He tried to shove the voice down, to ignore it and the part of him that screamed for destruction.

Madigan looked at him imploringly. "We're being played, Will."

The flare of lightning that engulfed Will's hand was the embodiment of the frustration and rage that coursed through his body. He lashed out, his fist striking his brother across the jaw. There was an audible sound of his stunned brother's teeth jarring together as his head whipped back, sending him whirling.

Madigan's Shade was alive in a heartbeat, surrounding him protectively. He spun back to face Will, his eyes solid black, like the pupils had spread to the very reaches of his sockets. He loomed over Will, the darkness billowing around him. Despite himself, Will recoiled. He hadn't even realized that he'd drawn the blood fangs until they were raised in front of him defensively, popping with blue lightning.

"What the hell has happened to you?" Madigan spat out the

words, but his voice was filled with disappointment, not rage. He stared for a moment, then dropped his arms to his side and bowed his head. "Will, it's *me*."

"Morella." Lightning crackled about Will. He never took his eyes from his brother. *I can't believe I was so blind. He's as bad as the rest of them.* "We're leaving. This was a mistake."

"No," she said harshly. "No, you two need to be together. You're stronger together."

Will kept his eyes fixed firmly on Madigan. He shook his head slowly. "No. We don't need him. We're going back. Let him stay with Valmont's pawn."

Mad stared at him agape. "What?"

"You should ask Ileta about it sometime," Will said darkly. "I hear they're quite close." He reached a hand back for Morella. "Let's go. I'm done with this world."

"Will." Madigan stepped toward his brother. "Please. Don't do this."

"If you go," Morella said softly, "I'm staying."

Her words cut through Will's fury. He spun to face her. Her eyes were hard. Her mouth was set in a thin line. And yet . . . *she's bluffing.* He could see it. She was trying to get him to stay, threatening him with something he wouldn't expect. *You're not as good a liar as you think you are, Morella. I'm starting to see that.*

"Then stay. I'm leaving."

Morella's face twisted. "Will, you've fought long and hard to get back to your brother. Don't screw it up now."

"No." This time it was Madigan who spoke. His voice was strained. "No, Morella. I think Will may be right on this point."

Will felt the anger rush out of him as confusion took over. *Manipulating me, eh, Mad?* His eyes hardened and leveled upon his brother. "Good, we finally agree on something." He strode past his brother without a word. Madigan reached out and winced as he caught him with a Shade-wrapped hand. Will tensed and forced down the immediate urge to lash out with his Flare. *He's still trying to control you.*

"Just . . . be careful, Will."

Will wrenched his arm out of his brother's grasp. Madigan flinched. Will's eyes dropped to the slashed hand that had brought him back from the edge of death. Something inside him deflated. He glanced up quickly and met his brother's eyes. There was no chastisement there, no reproach. He looked concerned. *What the hell is going on with me?*

"Yeah. You too."

He walked away. The sky above them was filled with clouds of smoke, but he pushed it from his concern. *I'm going back to Aeril. I'm done with this world.*

He made it fifty yards before Morella caught up to him, cursing under her breath. Will could feel her seething. *I didn't know she cared so much about keeping Mad and me together.*

"You can be a real ass sometimes, you know that?"

"He'll come around once he realizes Valmont is still out there hunting him. He'll come back."

She eyed him, her mouth set in a thin line. "And you're planning what, exactly?"

Will flicked his eyes over to her. He could feel a throb of discomfort lodged in his throat. It was a struggle, but he was determined to keep his voice level and steady. "Valmont is in this world. This world is bridged to Aeril through the Ways."

She raised an eyebrow. "Your point?"

"Don't you see, Morella? We have him trapped. To return to Aeril, he needs to pass through the Cascanian Waygate."

Realization dawned on her face. She grabbed his arm and when she spoke, her voice was filled with incredulity. "You think you're going to, what, trap him in the Ways? Ambush him? You think he doesn't expect something like that every time he passes through a Waygate?"

He yanked his arm away. "I think that it's the only guarantee of his passage, regardless of how long it takes. Eventually, he'll pass through again. We need to be prepared for it."

"And you don't think that sharing that tidbit with your brother is a good idea?"

Will's mouth tightened and he kept walking. "I think that Madigan is distracted. He's too set in his ways. His stubborn insistence and blind trust of Ileta?" Will spat. "This is how I can best protect him."

Something Will said had piqued Morella's interest. "You still don't trust the Shadowborne?" she asked.

"She shows up, throws Madigan's whole world into chaos, and then conveniently disappears right when we engage Valmont? No. No, I don't trust her."

"Mad would probably say the same thing about me."

Will stopped and turned to Morella. "What?"

"He's never fully trusted me. He could make the same argument as you. Senraks shows up and I disappear. Valmont shows up and I'm gone. Once they're both out of the picture, I come back." She shook her head. "Every time bad things happen . . . it doesn't look good, Will. Just like it doesn't with Ileta."

Will took her hands and raised them to his lips, planting a soft kiss on her knuckles. "No, Morella, don't even think that. You've got nothing to worry about. I know you. I trust you."

"I know that, lover." Her words were quiet against the distant roar of flames. "I just meant that I could see your brother seeing it that way. I didn't do anything to help."

Will shook his head. "No, that's totally different. Ileta is Shadowborne. You're not. Of course you were hiding." He felt something old inside him stir. Something painful. "I've seen what happens when people go up against Borne and their assassins when all they have are their wits and their blades. Staying out of sight was the absolute best thing you could have done."

Morella's sweet, crooked smile was light and playful. She

reached up and kissed him. "You know all the right things to say to a girl."

"You left him behind, then?" The Crow's disapproval was plain.

The journey back through the Waygate had been strained but uneventful. Will had expected far more guards patrolling, given the Necrothanian invasion of the Ways, but he was surprised to find only a handful. He'd sent them back with orders for more and then he waited, guarding the passage against Valmont's return until they arrived. Morella had kissed him and promised to wait for him at the Street, then she scurried off after the patrol.

Valmont never appeared. Neither did Madigan. *He'll come around.*

The reinforcements arrived and Will set out for Undermyre, expecting to see the encampment of Lightborne that din'Dael had promised. He'd seen nothing. He'd asked one of the soldiers and the woman had stared at him like he was mad.

Jero din'Dael was not one to shy from his plan simply because of a request from the Crow. Clearly, something had happened. That did not sit well with Will. He made straight for the Nordoth, the clear and present threat of Valmont far overtaking his desire for the warmth of the Street. There had been no charade with the seneschal this visit; the Crow and his retainers had seen him directly. And the dark man's disappointment in Will was obvious.

Will narrowed his eyes at the Crow. "I am not my brother's caretaker. Nor does he require one. He makes his own choices."

"Yes, I'm sure he does."

Will clasped his hands behind his back and stepped forward. The room was ringed in guards and they all tensed, preparing their weapons. "What would you rather I have done, Crow?

Parade an unwilling Shadowborne before you? Would you prefer to infuriate the one person in whom you seem to place hope for Aeril's future?"

The Crow raised a hand. The guards relaxed but did not drop their gaze from Will. The man's voice was patronizing. "William Davis—oh, apologies, I mean Noctis Thorne—ambassador from the Sapholux. This hall appreciates the efforts you have undergone on behalf of Undermyre. Indeed, the information you bring regarding Valmont's whereabouts presents an opportunity that we shall not miss." He leaned forward in his chair and smiled at Will. "That being said, you will understand why I must deny your previous request from the Sapholux."

Will started. *What?* He eyed the Crow. *You goddam bastard. You played me again*. "I see."

"Undermyre would gladly accept the support of the Lightborne from Sapholux in battles to come, but no garrison shall be stationed within the Undermyrian walls."

Will said nothing. The Crow tilted his head in amusement and Will felt his cheeks flush. *Stay calm, he's just trying to get under your skin.* "Beyond the walls, then? Would you allow a long-term encampment nearby?"

"Certainly," the Crow nodded, "as long as Jero din'Dael swears fealty to the Nordoth."

There was a hushed, nervous stirring from the guards. With effort, Will managed to keep his face blank. *There's no way Jero will go for that and the Crow knows it.* He considered the man before him. He was planning something bigger than he let on, Will knew that much, but what? *He wouldn't turn on Jero, not after the efforts he went through to release him. So, what then?*

"I shall return to the Sapholux and relay your terms, Crow."

The Crow raised an eyebrow, the gesture as close to one of surprise that Will had ever seen him make. "Very good. Your quarters within the Nordoth shall remain yours. Ynarra will see that they are properly maintained. Commander Shifter"—the

Crow raised a hand and beckoned, never breaking eye contact with Will—"dispatch the Thirteen to the Waygate, should our young Lightborne here prove correct. But first, have your men escort our guest to his chambers to prepare for his journey."

Armed guards? That was new. Whatever the Crow was playing at, his trust in Will had clearly diminished greatly. Will didn't think his movements within the Nordoth would be as free as they had been. *No more venturing out to the Street of Ash, then, assuming I make it back here at all.* He fought down an urge to protest when the guards stepped forward. *I'd better tell Morella to stay away as well; they'll be more attentive now.*

Will turned and strode off without a word, forcing Shifter and his men to scramble after him. He led the guards to his quarters and was pleasantly surprised to find Ynarra standing outside the door, as if she had been waiting for him. Her eyes lit up when he entered the hall but quickly grew subdued and downcast when Shifter and his guards followed close behind. Will approached and, wordlessly, Ynarra unlocked the door and opened it.

He entered with Ynarra following after him. Thankfully, Shifter and the rest remained outside. It was apparent that Ynarra wanted to speak to him, but the proximity of the guards must have made her hold her tongue. *Whatever this place does to put so much fear in her, I don't like it.*

He wandered the room for a moment and collected a few belongings, but for the life of him he could not think of anything he needed to take. In truth, he was far more concerned about *who* he was leaving behind rather than what.

"Ynarra, thank you."

"I've done nothing, sir." Her voice was trembling.

"Yes, you have. You've done more than you know." He sighed. "I'm going away again. I don't know when I'll be back. Hell, I don't even know *if* I'll be back." He sighed and rubbed at his scruffy jaw. "The Crow said he'll keep this room for me but . . . I don't know if I'll be the one using it." He looked at the girl, taking in her fear, her sadness. "Madigan's alive, Ynarra."

Her eyes shot up and met his own. The unadulterated hope and happiness within them nearly brought a smile to his face. Nearly.

"You saw him, yes? Was he well?"

Will was hesitant in responding. *He was bleeding and broken.* "He was well."

"Does he—I'm sorry, sir, I know I shouldn't pry—but does he plan to . . . I'm sorry."

"Go ahead, please."

Her hands were shaking. "Does he plan to return, sir? Return to the Nordoth, I mean."

Will felt an ache deep inside him. "I hope so. I don't know when, but I hope so. If he does"—he paused and looked into the girl's eyes—"will you keep an eye on him? I'm worried about him."

Ynarra nodded vigorously. "It is my duty to see to the needs of the people here, sir. If he returns, I mean."

This time the smile came easily enough. "He is finishing up some business, Ynarra, business that no one is sure how long will take. But I sincerely believe that he plans to return. There's something here for him to return to."

A hopeful smile flitted across her face and she took a hesitant step toward Will. Whatever she was planning, Will never got a chance to find out. Instead, Ynarra's nature overtook the brief bout of confidence. She bowed quickly then scurried from the room without another word.

"That was sweet."

Will whirled. Morella was leaning against the railing of his loft.

"Morella? What are you doing here?" He made no effort to hide his shock.

"I got bored of waiting at the Street." She gave a casual shrug as if she couldn't be bothered to explain further.

"But why the hell are you in *here,* I mean?"

She raised an eyebrow and then gave a half turn and coyly hid behind her shoulder. "Why, William, can't you see for yourself?"

Will looked on as she dropped the shoulder of her wrap, exposing bare skin. His skin flushed.

"Morella, there's no time. There's a squad right outside the door waiting for me. I've got to get out of here. *You* have to get out of here. If they see you, there'll be too many questions. I'm on thin ice here and I don't exactly know why."

She gave a playful pout, but Will could see the dark frustration poorly hidden beneath. "Fine," she said, "I'll leave right after you."

Will was ready to drop it, but then something snagged in his mind. "Morella, how did you get in?"

"The same way you used. You showed it to me enough times."

"Yeah, but it's locked. Plus, this place is swarming with more guards than usual."

She rolled her eyes. "When has that ever stopped either of us, Will?"

"And the guards below in the yard?"

She smiled. "I can be quiet enough when the mood strikes me. So, what now?"

Will walked to the closed curtains and opened them, displaying all of Undermyre and the lands beyond. "Now it looks like I've got to figure out what the hell happened to din'Dael and why he's so damn late."

Morella's smile disappeared. "You're returning to the Sapholux?"

"So it would seem." He raised an eyebrow at her. "I don't suppose you feel like joining me?"

"Let's see, hours upon hours of endless ease at the Street—all courtesy of the Nordoth, no less—or grimy travel through the desert for gods know how long to see a man who left me for dead? Hard choice."

"A few weeks under the stars, just like old times." Will smiled. "Come on."

She sighed. "The nights get cold out there in the desert, Will."

Will raised a hand and fire flickered across it. "I'll keep you warm."

Her eyes fell to his hand and a knowing smirk crossed her face. Will saw an unnerving darkness behind her eyes, poorly masked by a quick, bawdy laugh. She took his hand and kissed it. "You'd better."

26
BURNING BRIGHT

The guards followed Will all the way to the Street. They watched him enter before finally dispersing. Shifter, however, lingered. The commander approached Will just before he passed through the curtains into the bar beyond.

"Lightborne," the hawk-faced man said. "A moment."

That's new. Shifter had never expressed any interest in Will's movements before. "Yes, Commander?"

"You are certain that you faced Dorian Valmont in Cascania?"

Will gave him a disdainful look. "Trust me, it was him." The commander's expression darkened, though Will's manner did not seem to be what caused it. His interest piqued, Will took a step away from the curtains. "Why?"

"Scouts' reports conflict with that location."

"Wait, you've had eyes on him in Aeril? Since I returned?"

The commander met his eye and his expression was grave. "Understand this, Lightborne. My loyalty is to Aeril. The people. The very land itself."

"And that means . . .?" Will peered at the commander, but the man did not elaborate. *Gods, why is no one straightforward around here?* "Look, I *don't* understand. What are you saying?"

Shifter grimaced and stepped back. "Go. Treat with your kind. Undermyre will not fall to Valmont in your absence." Saying no more, the commander whirled and strode away.

"That's it?" Will called after him. "Seriously? Alluding to something and then, what? Just leaving it in the air like that? Come on. Give me something to work with."

Shifter did not even pause. Will was left in frustration. *What the hell was that about? Why can't things ever just be clear?*

He stepped through the curtains. The Street was rather subdued, but that was fine with him. He caught Clarice's eye and the proprietor smiled then gestured to the balcony of his room. He glanced up and did a double take. Morella was standing there. She had somehow managed to beat him back despite leaving the Nordoth after him. *That hidden staircase certainly does save some time.*

Something was wrong, though. She looked upset or . . . *annoyed*? Her face was not pleased, at any rate. He made his way to the staircase, keeping his eyes on her while they adjusted to the darkness of the Street. Right before he passed from her sight, Will suddenly realized the cause of Morella's irritation: she was not alone on the balcony. *Who the hell would be up there with her? No one knows about—*

Immediately, Will's stomach dropped. Cephora.

What is she doing here? Every damn time she came around, she brought bad news. Oh, sure, she'd mask it by a potential of hope, but then she'd quickly sweep the rug out from under him. Her unannounced presence coinciding with the absence of the Lightborne and din'Dael couldn't be chance. Something was wrong.

He raced up the stairs to his rooms. The Seeker lounged casually inside while Morella remained on the balcony, her arms crossed and a scowl on her face.

"Ah, Noctis Thorne," Cephora said with a sardonic smile. "So nice of you to join us." She gestured to Morella. "I'm pleased to find that you've reconnected with Madam Darklore."

The expression on her face showed her thoughts were the exact opposite of her words. *They never did get along particularly well.* "Cephora," Will said with as much politeness as he could muster. "What's happened?"

"That's it? No idle chatter?" The Seeker spread her arms wide and shrugged. "Must something happen for friends to wish for company?"

Will frowned. The fact that the Seeker was casually smiling was enough to prove to him that something was indeed wrong. "When it comes to our meetings, yes. What are you doing here?"

"Ah, right to it, then?" Cephora's plastered smile fell away. "Very well. How was your journey beyond Undermyre?"

Fishing for news on Madigan. "Productive."

"Returned home, did you?"

"My home was destroyed, Cephora. There's nothing there to return to." *Not a full answer, but enough to make her think.*

Cephora sighed and shook her head. "The same stubbornness as your grandfather. Must it be this way, Thorne?"

Morella laughed and Will allowed a smile to cross his face. "What would you prefer?"

"Let us be frank with one another."

"Fair enough." Will shrugged and gestured to her. "By all means, go right ahead."

The Earth Warder stared at him. Finally, she sighed and shook her head. "Very well. Undoubtedly, you found your brother. Your subsequent return without him gives me cause for concern. Need I be concerned?" Will said nothing, only raised an eyebrow at her. "I bear your family no ill will, Thorne. I only want the best for Aeril. For all these lands."

"At the cost of whatever and whomever it takes, right?"

Will saw that his words stung the Seeker. A hint of remorse washed through him. *She keeps saying that she did what she had to after the Shale.* He sighed and muttered under his breath. *Fine.* "Madigan will return in his own time, assuming Dorian Valmont doesn't strike him down before then."

Cephora's eyebrows raised and she leaned forward in her seat. Will snickered and went on. "Yes, we happened to have another encounter with the man."

"Noctis—"

Will held up a hand to stifle the interruption. "As you can see, we survived. We all did. Valmont, he had something—a device—it destroyed the land, corrupted it." Cephora paled but Will didn't stop. "The Shadowborne Mad's with—Ileta, she calls herself—she seems to be in league with Valmont. Almost as soon as we got there, Senraks appeared." Cephora cursed and Will nodded. "Yeah, that was my reaction too."

"How did you manage to elude the blood beast?"

Will smiled. "We didn't. I killed it." He felt no need to elaborate on the strange power that had coursed through him. His leg ached at the memory.

Cephora stared at him. A bit of color returned to her face. An amused smile unlike any that Will had ever seen from her appeared. "Killed him, did you? Impressive."

Will frowned. *I expected more of a reaction than that.* "Valmont and Ileta both disappeared after that. Morella and I chose to return here. Madigan, being the stubborn ass that he is, chose to remain."

Cephora cursed again and shook her head. "Why?"

"He didn't think Valmont would strike unless the two of them were together," Morella chimed in from behind. "He was convinced of it for whatever reason."

"Something like that," Will muttered.

Cephora pursed her lips and glanced at Morella. "Interesting. Very well, then. Madigan lives. Senraks is"—she smiled and looked at Will—"dead. And Valmont has vanished yet again."

"Trapped in Cascania. Not entirely vanished." Will smiled.

Cephora, however, turned her attention back to Morella. "You don't sound terribly convinced of Madigan's position on the matter, Madam Darklore."

Morella bristled a bit and stared at Cephora. "I'm not, but not for any reason you seem to be insinuating." She interlaced her fingers with Will's and tightened her grip on his hand. "I'm not sure where *you've* been or what you've been after, but I saw the repercussions of your decision that day on the hill. I have lived with Noctis, *been* with him, and I've seen the effect on him of the separation." Her eyes flitted over and met Will's and, while they appeared sincere and heartfelt, there was a strange vacancy there as well. "They need each other. Together, anything is possible. So, yes, I disagree with Madigan's position. He should have come back. He should have stayed with us."

"My, my, my," Cephora said while shaking her head. "I don't think I've seen you this passionate about anything since you 'accidentally' mentioned the Relics in one of our early encounters, Morella." The hand gripping Will's tightened in a brief spasm, then released. She pulled away from him and crossed her arms, glaring at Cephora. "Oh, yes, my memory is long, Morella Darklore. But, surely, as a historian you understand such things."

"Indeed."

"Indeed." Cephora tilted her head and kept her gaze fixed on Morella. "Have you ever visited Greygarde, by chance?"

Will knew that there was—as it always seemed when these two women had a conversation—some piece of the puzzle that he was absolutely missing. "The home of the Seekers, right?"

Neither answered him.

"No," Morella said coolly. "I have not."

"You really should. For someone with your interests, you would find it of great use. Particularly our historical records. They're very, very detailed."

Will could almost feel the anger pouring out of Morella,

though why, he had no idea. All he knew was that Cephora was prodding at her, goading her.

"Alright, that's enough," he said sharply. Neither of them looked in his direction. "Cephora, I think you've outstayed your welcome. Unless you have something of actual use to us, you can get the hell out."

She broke her gaze from Morella and looked over at him. "Jero din'Dael needs you."

"So he continues to say."

"No, Noctis." She shook her head and closed her eyes. "I mean he *needs* you. Now."

That caught him off guard. "What's happened?"

Cephora's smile held no humor. "Necrothanians."

Will cursed and Morella shifted uncomfortably. "Where?" he asked.

"Oh?" Cephora raised a mocking eyebrow. "But I assumed that with your wide network of spies throughout Aeril, you were already quite informed." She scoffed and stood. "Regardless, as requested, I'll be on my way."

"No, dammit. Don't." Will sighed and shook his head. *Every goddam time she comes around.* "How bad? What's happened?"

Casually, Cephora returned to her seat. "You were on a journey recently, yes? With another Lightborne? What was her name . . ." She raised an eyebrow to Will.

"Rienne," he said as levelly as possible. Morella stiffened at his side and Will glanced at her out of the corner of his eye. "Her name is Rienne and she was heading to Greygarde."

"Rienne, yes." Cephora smiled and steepled her hands, looking all too much like the Crow for Will's taste. "She did not make it to Greygarde."

Will's throat tightened but he kept his face neutral. *Dammit.* "What happened?"

She waved a dismissive hand. "Oh, nothing sinister, don't worry." Will could have throttled her then and there but he held himself back. "When she arrived at the Middle Reach, not long after you parted ways, she found something rather unusual. A Necrothanian camp. Digging."

"At the Middle Reach?" Morella chimed in, her voice hinting at unamused disbelief. "There's nothing at the Middle Reach. Why would they be entrenched there?"

"Why indeed?" Cephora didn't even spare a glance for Morella, didn't shift her eyes away from Will for the briefest moment. Will returned her gaze and saw something in it, something dangerous. His stomach dropped.

It can't be . . .

"They've found one, haven't they?" Will couldn't hide the tremor of fear that laced the words. "One of the Relics of Antiquity. The bastards found one."

"What? No." Morella shook her head. "At the Middle Reach? There is *nothing* at the Middle Reach. There's no way they found a Relic. Will, if she tries to tell you there's anything there, don't listen to her." She frowned and stared at Cephora. "As always, this damn Seeker is up to something—probably stringing you along at the Crow's whims again."

"Believe what you will." Cephora shrugged. "The Lightborne woman was unable to discover what they found." The disdainful way that Cephora said the word *Lightborne* irked Will. "But she deemed the situation of great enough importance to return to din'Dael at the Sapholux. Their march for Undermyre took a different direction and by now, surely, the Middle Reach is filled with all manner of madness." She gave Will an appraising look. "You failed to mention just quite how many Lightborne survived within the Sapholux, young Noctis. I'm impressed."

"I didn't keep track of the numbers," he said absently. *And I damn well wouldn't have told you even if I had.* "How did *you* manage to gather all this information, Cephora?"

"Dahla."

Will blinked. *Dahla?* He laughed and shook his head. "The bird told you?"

Morella gave a start at his side and grabbed his hand. "Wait, Dahla?"

"No, of course not." Will chuckled. "Jero tied a note to her talon, is that it? A glorified messenger pigeon?"

"Cephora, did you just say Dahla? As in *the* Dahla? The Bird of Peace?" Cephora only smiled. Morella ripped her hand from Will's and rounded on him. The fury of her words nearly drove him backward. "You said *nothing* about Dahla's involvement!"

He stared at her aghast. "Jero has a bird. I don't see how that seems like pertinent information. What, is she something special or is this just another one of those—"

Morella's slap caught him completely off guard and he stepped back a pace, the angry roar of defiance hot within his chest. He stared at her incredulously. "What the hell?"

"You goddam Casc. You know nothing!"

"Din'Dael and the creature have, apparently, come to some kind of arrangement," Cephora said flatly. Her expression was smug but Will saw hints of concern in the Seeker's eyes. *Oh good, she didn't like me being slapped any more than I did.*

"She's not just a bird then," Will said, rubbing his cheek. He eyed Morella warily. *What the hell was that about?* "Of course she isn't. Nothing in this damn place can ever be simple."

Cephora stood and folded her arms. "On the contrary, it is quite simple. Jero din'Dael has called for your aid, Noctis Thorne. I've passed on the request to Greygarde, since that was your friend's initial mission, it would seem. Given the gravity of the situation, I shall accompany you to the Middle Reach and assess the gathering."

"So you can leave us at the most inopportune moment?" Will muttered before working his jaw back and forth. "Sounds just like old times."

The Seeker frowned. "So I can determine what steps need be taken in dealing with the Necrothanian menace."

"Yeah, well, welcome back to the group." Will looked at Morella who refused to meet his eye. "We're as warm as ever." Cephora laughed aloud. Morella finally met his gaze with a cruel glare. *What the hell has gotten into her?* Then, a thought occurred to him. "Cephora, you said din'Dael sent for me?"

"He did."

"Why?" His thoughts raced back to the Shale, to the ceaseless slaughter at his mentor's hands, to the buffets of lightning and destruction of the ancient prison. "He has his entire force with him. Why does he need *me*?"

She clapped her hands on her legs and rose to her feet while shaking her head. She crossed her arms and smiled. "Come now, Noctis. This is Jero din'Dael we are speaking of."

"The bastard . . ." Morella muttered.

Will pretended he didn't hear. "In other words, you don't know." Will nodded. "Fine."

Cephora gave him a bored shrug. "I do know this, Lightborne. The Necrothanians have not been idle. These cultists in recent years, the brief uprisings, they are not true Necrothanians. Those who follow Valmont would never have left themselves so exposed, let their intentions be known."

"Meaning that for them to show their hand now, we may already be too late." Will nodded. "Sounds lovely. Undead monsters and magic-wielding cultists led by an immortal psychopath. I can't wait."

Even Morella snickered at that. "This could be the end of everything," she whispered a moment later. "Dorian Valmont may lead an army of the dead, but he's not the only madman taking the field. If he and din'Dael fight?" She shook her head. "You saw the Shale, Will."

"Which is why I suggest we leave as soon as possible," Cephora said. "For better or worse, Jero din'Dael has taken an interest in you, Noctis. That places a terrible weight upon your shoulders. If he takes your counsel to heart, you may be all that stands between that man and wanton slaughter."

"I don't see how you made that jump."

"Your voice may give him pause. His hatred of Valmont is absolute, but if what you've told me is true, din'Dael chose to save you rather than strike at his mortal enemy. If din'Dael unleashes the full force of his might in an attempt to kill Valmont, you may have the power to stop him."

Will raised an eyebrow. "Stop him from killing Valmont? You're not making sense."

Cephora pinched her brow and shook her head. "From killing *everyone,* Noctis. If the two of them meet unchecked without regard for those nearby, catastrophe will surely follow. Death, Noctis. Death of the Necrothanians, yes, but what if that also meant the death of all the Lightborne? What if it meant the death of all those within the Middle Reach? The territories beyond? You know the blood lust that fuels Jero din'Dael. You've heard of the destructive forces of Valmont. You could help din'Dael see reason. You could save countless lives."

"I doubt that," Will said, thinking of the many times din'Dael had ignored him over the years.

"But there is a chance," Morella said softly. Her eyes were pleading as she looked up and took Will's hand. "If anyone could get din'Dael to stop, to hold back . . . you can do it, Will."

Will pursed his lips. *I* really *doubt that.* But if both Cephora and Morella believed it, then he couldn't ignore it. "Alright, fine. When do we leave?"

"As soon as you are prepared, Noctis. I've already mapped out the rifts to save time."

Oh fantastic. Will's eyes fell to Morella. She looked paler than usual. Her eyes, when they met his, held a deep yearning for something he couldn't place. *Not me, that's for certain. Something else.* "Tonight, then."

"Tonight." Cephora strode for the door.

"Cephora, one last thing before we leave."

She paused and turned back, raising an eyebrow to him. "Yes, Noctis?"

He smiled, never letting his gaze fall from Morella's. "Call me Will."

27

HOMECOMING

Aeril felt colder than Portland, despite the visible difference in climate. While Madigan's home had been in the depth of winter, the lands around Undermyre remained in their perpetual state of early autumn. And yet despite the warmth in the air, there was an unsettling chill, something that crept into his bones.

Ileta felt it too, he mused to himself as he walked with the Crow's guard. *That's why she didn't want to enter the city. She knew something was out of place.*

That had to be it, of course, because the alternative was something he didn't—couldn't—believe; that Will had been right about her.

She had returned to him, bleeding and furious, not long after Will and Morella left. She'd looked in disgust at his battered arms before immediately snapping defensive orders at him. While the world around them whirled in smoke and flame, the pair prepared for another assault from Valmont.

None had come.

They fell back to their auxiliary camp, a small, sad thing in the trees at the top of the cliff where his grandfather had given him the key and noctori. They'd battled flames and smoke, and more than once Madigan suggested that they simply abandon it altogether.

Ileta refused. She barked commands and protected them against the flames with her Shade. She'd nearly seemed a stranger to him, then, a feral warrior battling nature itself. But there was something about her demeanor that made him truly believe that if Valmont came, she would fight the man until her last breath.

Madigan believed her. He believed *in* her. And that meant he refused to believe he could have been fooled by her for so long. Whatever the hell it was that Will thought he knew about her, he was wrong. There was something more at stake here, something Ileta still hadn't shared with him.

They'd no sooner regrouped at the camp than she'd ordered them to move out, abandoning his home and the corrupted land beyond, still awash in flames and decay. When he'd told her of Will and Morella's return to Aeril, she'd scoffed and nodded. She had even *agreed* with Mad (something he still couldn't believe) about Valmont having waited for them to be together.

That being said, she'd still insisted that they also return. And, given that everything he'd known had been destroyed (again) by that goddam beast Senraks (again), Mad didn't feel much like arguing.

At least Will killed the goddam bastard.

And so, here they were. It was a strange feeling, being back in Undermyre after so long. The last time he'd been in this city, he'd come as a prisoner and left as quickly and quietly as possible on a damned foolish mission for the Crow. This time the Crow seemed to have thrown open the city gates for him. He didn't trust it. *What's that goddam crafty bastard got up his sleeves this time?*

Crowds dispersed before him while he walked with the retainer sent by the Crow. The people knew what he was, now—his injured hand and wrist were still bound in his Shade. He trekked the cobblestone streets of Undermyre, Shade flowing about him like a cloak made of shadows. He could hear the whispers from those he passed and couldn't help but smile. Despite the books he'd read in the Nordoth, the horrible stories of the Unborn, he felt no need to hide, no fear of displaying his power. He was Shadowborne, and he and Ileta were going to save Undermyre from that insane bastard Valmont.

Assuming Will doesn't screw it up somehow. And assuming Ileta comes back.

They had hardly passed through the Aerillian Waygate when she'd abandoned him. He'd long since learned not to ask after her comings and goings, but that had been back in Cascania. Will's words of treachery and deception had again pricked at his consciousness, but he'd pushed them down. Mad had always known that Ileta served someone greater than herself; he'd just never worried about it before. Now, with Valmont trapped back in Cascania, it seemed like a foolish time to stop believing in her.

"Wait for me. Don't do anything stupid," was all she said before taking off deep into the Ways faster than Mad could follow even if he tried. He hadn't tried, though. He went his own way and before long had found soldiers guarding the passages. They were far less surprised to see him than he'd anticipated —*probably thanks to Will for that*—and they'd immediately surrounded him. Explaining their purpose of taking him to Undermyre had been strange, but stranger still had been their formation. Like some kind of damn honor guard. *Ileta would have laughed her ass off if she'd seen it.*

She hadn't, though. She hadn't been there any more than she had been waiting for him when the wide doors of the Nordoth broke open.

Taking a deep breath, he entered the Crow's audience chamber. The room was awash in brilliant light that dazzled from crystalline lights and burst upon prisms floating in the air. The chamber was lined with guards at attention, forming a wide path that led toward the back of the room and the Crow's seat. Madigan hesitated only briefly, the memory of his last visit a stark contrast to the sight before his eyes, then he held his chin high and strode into the room.

The chamber was more crowded than he realized. His eyes, shocked by the transition from dim to light, had missed the scores of people standing along the walls and in the balcony that overlooked the chamber. He suddenly grew very self-conscious. *What the hell is this?*

Then, realization dawned on him: Ileta, of course. A smile broke across his face as he approached the Crow's seat. The hidden master, the hidden agenda, the brutal training, it had all been a convoluted plot from the Crow's ever-twisting mind. Of course she'd run off. Their plan, whatever it had been, had finally come to fruition. That's why the soldiers had been prepared for him; she'd alerted them, somehow. *She knows the Ways better than I do. She knew a shortcut.*

And all this time, Will was convinced that she was some goddam traitor.

The Crow slumped in his seat, smiling humorlessly down at Mad while he approached. Ileta though, was nowhere to be seen. Mad didn't know why that bothered him, but it did.

"Ah, Madigan Davis. I see you have returned to our hospitality."

"That depends, Crow." Madigan inclined his head in a small acknowledgment. "If this greeting acts as any indication of a change in attitude toward outsiders since my last visit, I could very much be interested in your hospitality."

The harsh barking laughter that Madigan remembered from his last audience with the man returned and echoed through the hall. Snickers emerged from the many watching figures, but Madigan kept his attention fixed firmly on the Crow. The dark, hunched man bobbed his head. "Cavalier. To be expected, yes."

Madigan's Shade billowed silently along the ground. He

strode toward the stairs that led to the Crow's seat. "It has been some time, Crow, certainly longer than the thirteen months we agreed upon."

The Crow's mouth fell into a thin line. "Indeed, it has."

"And while I feel ever so much more comfortable now than I did during our last meeting," Madigan said while he spun in a slow circle, gesturing to the crowd, "I do not believe I would be remiss in ensuring my safety within these walls. Under the eyes of all those here and the Hesperawn who see beyond all things."

He had no idea if that was something believed about the Aerillian gods, but he figured it better to project a casual confidence.

"Cavalier, indeed." The Crow leaned back and steepled his hands. "Much has changed since your last visit, *Shadowborne*"—he nearly hissed the word—"but your etiquette and diplomacy remain ever the same, it seems."

The man's tone suddenly seemed far less inviting. *Dammit, he couldn't have sent Ileta. He didn't know I was Shadowborne.* Madigan scanned the room quickly. He saw no familiar faces. *Alright, think fast, idiot.* "Well, we have to maintain some consistency, Crow." *Gotta keep control on my side.* "Otherwise the whole world would spin in reverse, no doubt."

A low chuckle spanned the crowd but was quickly silenced. The Crow did not look amused in the slightest. *I wonder . . .* Madigan forced a smile. *Fine then, Crow, we'll do this the fun way.*

Madigan's Shade swarmed beneath his feet in a pool of blackness. He held the Crow's eyes and never let his sardonic smile waver. Madigan pulled and the countless threads appeared. The room was far, far larger than the cellar and he was met with immediate resistance. Quickly splitting his focus and mentally reaching at the cool key that hung against his chest, he pulled harder. Peaceful floodgates of power opened. The infinite webs of darkness wavered and spun in his mind's eye.

It goes both directions, Ileta said. Madigan focused on spreading the shadows, on pulling the light. He gave one quick, sharp tug and the room immediately descended into darkness. Frantic murmurs began to race through the crowd. Soldiers grew lively. In a flash, only the lights of a few torches gave off any hint of light.

Now, time to add some finesse.

He focused on the torches and pulled even harder than he had in the cellar. The key's focusing power filled him with seemingly unending strength. He drew the torches' light into him, replacing the space with cold darkness. The strain was overwhelming, nothing he had ever experienced in his training with Ileta, but he did not allow himself to falter. He gritted his teeth and grimaced. *Just have to last long enough to make an impression.*

"Enough!" The Crow barked through the utter darkness. Madigan released the tension—the whole ordeal couldn't have lasted more than a few seconds—but the sight that greeted him nearly sent him into the same shock that seemed to have overtaken every other person in the room.

The ground was layered in a thin crystalline frost. The light that returned to the windows fractured along spiderweb circles of ice on the glass. As for the torches, their flames did not return. Instead, dark blue crystalline towers of ice took their place, the flickers frozen.

I can't believe that worked. Madigan exhaled and saw his breath cloud before him. His hand no longer hurt. He tentatively rolled his broken wrist and felt no pain, no restriction. *Fascinating.*

He turned his attention back to the Crow. The man had hardly moved, but the way his fingers gripped the armrests of his chair spoke volumes. Mad had made an impression. He smiled. "You were saying?"

The Crow released his grip on the chair and leaned forward. "Impressive."

He gestured absently to the guard at his side. The man stepped forward and Mad thought he recognized him. *The commander that captured us, of course.* The Crow whispered something that Mad couldn't hear and then the commander—*Changer? Something like that*—beckoned to the soldiers. Those surrounding Mad visibly relaxed, or at least returned to their formal guard stance. The commander himself spun and passed from sight quickly.

"Madigan Davis," the Crow said, snapping Madigan's attention back to him. "The terms of our previous arrangement are still valid in the eyes of the Hesperawn." The hunched man smiled and cocked his head to the side. "Although I do think that you and I shall have some words to, ah, negotiate that agreement further. To our mutual benefit, of course."

Mad nodded. "Of course."

"You understand, of course, that additional steps of protection must be guaranteed within these walls. The same for any Borne who chooses to reside within Undermyre under the protection of the Nordoth."

Mad smiled. "Of course. One can never be too cautious."

"No, one cannot."

Something at the corner of his eye caught Mad's eye. He glanced over and something foreign and long forgotten lurched within his chest. *Ynarra.*

Her pale face was half hidden, covered by her hands. Her eyes were wide and seemed to be brimming with tears, but they were fixed firmly on him. Mad tore his eyes away from her and back to the Crow, but for the life of him he could not remember what he'd been about to say.

"Yes," he began, rapidly searching his mind for whatever it was they'd been talking about. "Naturally it would"—it came to him and he snapped back into focus—"it would be only natural to take additional precautions." The Crow's smile held a sinister note and Mad's eyes nervously flicked back to Ynarra. "What would be required?"

"Fealty," the Crow said without hesitation. "Your unwavering fealty pledged to the Thirteen for the protection of Undermyre and the Nordoth."

The Thirteen? Who in the goddam hell are they? He risked a glance back at Ynarra and saw the commander standing behind her, his hands resting on her shoulders. Whatever had lurched inside him knotted into fear as Madigan realized the implications of what might happen should he refuse. *No. No, no, no.* "Fealty."

The crowd was silent when the Crow spoke. "It is not too much to ask, I would think, of one who claims to oppose Dorian Valmont and the Necrothanians. Our paths are in alignment and the Nordoth makes for a powerful ally." He peered down at Madigan. "Particularly for the Borne."

Mad's gaze returned to Ynarra. He could have sworn that he saw her shake her head slightly, but he couldn't be sure. *Dammit.*

Madigan slowly lowered to a knee. He barely registered the act. He clapped his hands together and formed his signature bastard sword from the noctori. Placing the tip of the shadow-blade on the ground, he lowered his head and touched the pommel. He had no idea if what he was doing was correct or proper within this world. He was simply going from what he'd seen in movies growing up back home. *It better be goddam good enough for this bastard.*

"To Undermyre. To the Nordoth. To the Thirteen."

Mad felt the nauseating wave of pleasure, of *victory*, pouring from the Crow. When he raised his eyes, the dark man was smiling down at him with the first look of genuine satisfaction that Mad could ever remember seeing from him. *You goddam bastard.*

"Well then, Madigan Davis." The Crow leaned back in his chair and steepled his hands, smiling eerily. "Welcome home."

28
THE SEEKERS

Will's head spun. Rift hopping, it seemed, did not get any easier. Cephora estimated that they'd saved at least two weeks of travel, crossing the great expanse to the Middle Reach in only a matter of days. But as far as Will was concerned, he'd take the slow roads any day. *If I never have to follow Cephora into another one of those horrible things, it'll be just fine with me.*

He huddled his arms against himself and blew warm air onto his chilled hands. Between so much time in the warm halls of the Sapholux and the temperate climate of Undermyre, the brief trip into a Portland winter had been the most exposure to cold he'd had in some time. This, though, this cold dwarfed Portland's. He shuffled his feet in the snow and muttered under his breath. He Flared briefly, hoping that the influx of warmth would help. It didn't.

The snow fell in a delicate, steady stream, resting lightly upon the nearly invisible camp of Lightborne. No fires illuminated the grey flurries, no smoke or flame that might accidentally signal the enemy. There had been no alert when his small group approached the camp. The Lightborne were within their tents, crowded together and kept warm by their body heat and Flares. *A cozy night in. Wouldn't that be nice?*

Cephora looked unfazed, as usual. Morella was shivering but seemed determined to ignore it. For Will, though, it wasn't the snow that was doing him in. It was the damn wind with its frigid biting. *How did I ever enjoy going to the mountains with Mad and Grandda?*

"Is this everyone?" Morella whispered, barely audible over the wind. There was a chilled tremor in her voice that made Will aware of his own chattering teeth. "I'd expected more."

"I'm guessing they're camped tight for warmth." Will fought to control the quiver in his own voice. He glanced back at the camp. Whether they were huddled together or not, Morella was right: there were far too few Lightborne. "And no sentries?" Will shook his head in disbelief. "No one standing watch? That hardly seems right."

Cephora gave him a sidelong glance and a quiet, disappointed sigh. "They've been watching us for the past hour, Will."

"What?" Will spun and looked around again. Seeing nothing, he chastised himself. *Right, Will. Spinning like an idiot is going to suddenly bring them into focus.*

"Them and the Seekers." Morella shook her head and laughed quietly. "The Master of Blades trained you for how long, again?"

Opening his mouth to speak, Will almost missed the suddenly severe inspection that Cephora was giving Morella. He clamped his mouth shut. *Morella surprised her, that's all.* He gave Morella a half-hearted smile. She giggled and squeezed his hand.

"I was just testing you," he offered limply. "Congratulations. You passed."

"Oh yes, you certainly are the chosen one of the Sapholux. Blinded by your lights, as usual."

"Indeed," Cephora agreed. But the manner in which she said it seemed off. *Something's got her on edge.* "The fact that they haven't made a move means they know we're no threat. Come, we should find Jero din'Dael."

"They wouldn't have made a move on me, Cephora," Will said. "My people know me."

Cephora's face was full of amusement and condescension. "Mine don't."

"Fair point." *A whole group of people like Cephora, everyone from the Sapholux, and the Necrothanians?* Will's shiver had nothing to do with the cold.

"Will," Morella interrupted his aimless thoughts. "Someone's coming."

Sure enough, a tall figure was emerging from the swirling cloud of snow—a figure that Will would have recognized anywhere. Jero din'Dael wore an unsecured tight vest of what appeared to be sheep hide. A massive sword was strapped to his back, its harness draped across his chest. His scarred arms were bare, despite the cold, and he wore fingerless gloves on each hand. Will half expected to find the man's legs bare, but he was wearing heavy travel pants and boots that laced up to his knees.

Will felt Morella stiffen. His key sprang to life, sending its strange dance of shocks and pulses throughout his body. Ignoring both the key and Morella's obvious trepidation, Will couldn't help but smile. For all his faults, Jero din'Dael brought Will some strange measure of comfort. Morella's lack of it was understandable. As for the key, Will still had to figure out why it behaved the way it did half the time. He inclined his head to his mentor. "Jero din'Dael."

"Noctis Thorne." Din'Dael's hard, chiseled face split into a wide grin. "Where in the blazes have you been?"

"There was a slight detour." Will shrugged and gestured to his entourage. "I'm sure you understand."

Din'Dael threw back his head and laughed far more than the comment deserved. "Of course," he said, wiping a tear from his eye when his laughter subsided. Without warning, din'Dael's face fell and he turned stony eyes toward Will. The severity and rapidity of the change was unnerving. Will's mouth went dry. "Oh, my young burner. Of course I understand." The tall man spat on the ground, approached Will, and made as if to backhand him across the face.

"Jero—" Will recoiled. There was no further motion from din'Dael, but Will's cheek erupted in fiery pain. The warmth of it made the sudden shock of cold that followed all the more biting. Jero's hand remained in the air, his face twisted in disappointment.

"Enough, Thorne. We shall discuss your transgressions against the Sapholux at a later date."

My transgressions? What the hell? He stared at din'Dael in bewilderment. Something had gone wrong—very wrong. For din'Dael to be behaving in such a fashion? *Someone made a big goddam mistake.*

Din'Dael turned his attention to Morella and scoffed, the only acknowledgment she received. He then glanced past her and saw Cephora. "Cephora." His face split into a wild, manic grin. "It has been too long! How lovely to see you."

Will stared at din'Dael while he lavished compliment after compliment upon the Seeker. *What the hell is going on?*

"Enough, din'Dael," Cephora interrupted him. "What is the situation?"

"Come, let us discuss these matters out of this dreadful weather." Din'Dael spun and strode back toward the camp. He paused after a few steps and glanced back at Will.

"Thorne, dispose of *that*"—he waved absently at Morella and Will felt her fume—"first. Really, I can't believe you brought a pet."

"A pet?" Morella raged. She lunged toward din'Dael and Will was forced to hold her back. "You goddam bastard. You foolish, idiotic Lightborne. Do you have any idea who you're talking to?"

Din'Dael cocked his head to the side and appraised her. "No."

He strode away.

"Gods be damned, Will," Cephora whispered under her breath. "You said that his mind was intact."

"A pet? A *pet*?" Morella stepped away from them, shouting after Din'Dael.

"It was," Will said quickly while trying to catch Morella's eye. "He's been fine for . . . for years now."

"I'll show you a goddam pet, you bastard!" Morella screamed.

Cephora frowned and turned her gaze back to the silent camp. "Something has happened, then." She scanned their surroundings, giving nearly imperceptible nods to unseen figures. "This location, it is hardly along the path between Greygarde and the Sapholux."

Will's tore his eyes from the still-muttering Morella back to the camp. He pulled his cloak closer around him. "I don't like this. There are too few of the Lightborne. There should be more."

The Seeker nodded gravely. "The same for my people as well." Her eyes trailed after the nearly vanished figure of din'Dael. "Our information is dated. We need to know what has changed."

Morella returned to them, her normally pale face flushed. "Will, if you think for one moment that you're leaving me behind . . ."

He held up a placating hand. "No. Gods, no." Her expression didn't change. Will reached down and wrapped his hands around her balled fists, giving her the most sincere smile he could manage. "I promised, didn't I? I'm not leaving you."

The tension lingered between them. Then, finally, her face softened slightly. She very nearly smiled. But the anger in her eyes was constant, a blazing fury she couldn't mask. "Good." She followed Cephora's gaze in the direction din'Dael had gone. "Because that bastard owes me an apology."

The weary trio made their way into the Lightborne camp. This time, Will was able to feel the eyes that watched his every move. It wasn't a pleasant feeling. Even though the unseen lookouts must have known him as one of their own, there was an air of hostility—a sense of seclusion and secrecy. He didn't like it.

Din'Dael made for a tent at the far end of the camp while Cephora and Morella followed. Will stayed a few paces behind, scrutinizing the camp. At first glance it seemed neat and orderly. But, much as in Undermyre, upon closer inspection it seemed ragged. Everywhere he looked, it was like the lines weren't clean, the edges were frayed. *Something is definitely off.*

Shaking his head, Will entered the tent. He was surprised to find Lightborne other than din'Dael inside. Rienne was there, and Quennar, but neither looked up at Will's entrance. The familiar faces were comforting, but one was missing. Kenwal, whom Will had grown accustomed to seeing whenever the lieutenants met, was nowhere to be seen. Both of the Lightborne looked haggard. There was a fatigue about them, a tiredness in the whites of their eyes. There was something else there, too, a sense of . . . *Detachment?*

The hairs on the back of Will's neck prickled. "What happened?"

Rienne glanced up. It seemed to take her a moment to recognize him, but after a moment she smiled. "Noctis. You've returned to us." Her voice was light and passive.

Dissociated . . . Will shuddered.

Quennar's eyes were fixed on his hands. His fingers were trembling slightly. Thin, faint cracks of light periodically snapped across his skin. He had not acknowledged their entrance nor reacted when din'Dael bumped him as he crouched down. Will stared at Quennar a moment, realizing that the man's lips were moving rapidly but the words were silent.

"Sit." Din'Dael pointed toward empty spaces on the floor. The man's smile was cruel, but there was a sadness in his eyes that gave Will pause. "Go, Thorne."

What, will we devolve to grunts next?

Nonetheless, he did as he was bid although Cephora made no

effort to do so. As for Morella, Will had never seen her so guarded—not even in the depths of the Shale. Her eyes flashed to each of the seated Lightborne as though they were predators and she their cornered prey. Finally, she dropped to her knees next to Will. Despite this, she kept her body angled toward the door. Will leaned over and gave her hand a reassuring squeeze, but she ripped it away from him and clenched her fists, nearly snarling as she did so.

Will sighed and shook his head. He looked at din'Dael. "Jero, what happened here? Where is everyone?"

The Revenant cocked his head to the side and burst into laughter. Rienne shrank away but Quennar seemed to not even register the sound.

"What happened, Thorne? What happened?" Din'Dael wiped a tear from his eye. Then his face dropped and a black rage replaced the humor. Spittle flew from his mouth when he spoke. "Sheep, Noctis. I'm a shepherd of sheep."

Cephora scoffed then gave a quiet "hmph" from behind Will. Will glanced at her, but she was focused intently on din'Dael and shaking her head. Not understanding, Will pressed on.

"Right, the shepherd tends to his flock and you guided them here, and then?" *I'm missing something.* "You've spent years guiding them, Jero, I get that. I'm asking what happened? Where is everyone?"

"Gone." Rienne's voice was a distant whisper. The edge of her mouth twitched in a broken facsimile of a smile. "They—"

"They're pathetic *sheep*," din'Dael sneered, cutting her off. "All this time, all my life surrounded by warriors, by wolves and beasts. Time stripped them of their claws." He glared at Quennar and spat. "They're failures. All of them."

Rienne winced and looked to the ground.

"Well, well, the mighty Jero din'Dael failed." Morella's voice was filled with malice. "It's no more than you deserve, you murdering bastard."

Din'Dael eyed her as if she had suddenly sprouted wings. He shook his head and turned his attention back to Will, gesturing at Morella as he did so. "What is that?"

"Dammit, din'Dael, quit with the damn dismissals!" Will snapped. "This is Morella Darklore; we've spoken of her many times."

"Who?" Din'Dael looked genuinely puzzled.

"Just focus for one minute." Will pinched his brow and shook his head. *His goddam mind is twisted again.* "Just answer me. What happened? What happened after I left the Sapholux?"

Din'Dael turned the same bewildered stare he had given Morella over to Will. "We prepared for the march to Undermyre. Come now, Noctis. Have your recent journeys scattered your brain so much that you've forgotten what you set out to prepare for?"

This is not the same man I trained with, good god. "I remember."

"Jero din'Dael." Cephora's voice was resonant and commanding. All eyes—save Quennar's—turned to her. "You dispatched Dahla to bring aid, to bring Noctis Thorne. We have come. What was your purpose in sending for us?"

"He didn't send for you," came a gruff voice at their backs. "I did."

Will spun and crouched, his Flare blazing to life. Morella moved in unison with him, her daggers flashing in the dim light of the tent. No one else reacted in the slightest except for Cephora. She chuckled and shook her head. Din'Dael sighed and crossed his hands behind his head before leaning straight back onto the ground.

Will's fingers twitched on their blades and he scowled at din'Dael. *Typical, danger approaches and din'Dael takes a nap.* He took a step closer to Morella and eyed the intruder.

The burly man was tall, though not as tall as din'Dael, and thick with muscle. His black hair was cropped close to his head and a thick black beard was cut square across his face. He was dressed for the weather, in shaggy, though fitted, clothes. He radiated an aura of power, of danger, but Will saw no weapons.

The large man turned his attention to Cephora. "Earth Warder, I'm glad you have come."

What happened next nearly sent Will reeling backward: Cephora *laughed.*

"It is good to see you, Shyldd," she said. "How fares Greygarde?"

The man—Shyldd—shrugged. "You've returned to our halls since I, old friend."

Cephora chuckled. "You heard about that, did you."

"News travels fast." Shyldd's voice was a deep rumble. "Where is the Shadowborne now?"

"Elsewhere." Cephora's smile drooped. "But, from the reports I've gathered, he seems to be passably safe." She scoffed and muttered under her breath, "Or at least he seems to *think* he is."

"Ah yes, the Borne are full of bravado." Shyldd jerked his head toward the inhabitants of the tent. "Particularly *this* lot."

Cephora stepped next to Shyldd and the pair of them eyed the occupants. "Yes, it would seem that the Lightborne have been keeping things rather close to the chest for some time now."

Will rose from his crouch, uncomfortable with the way Shyldd and Cephora were peering at them. From the corner of his eye he saw Morella tense. "Pardon me for asking, Cephora," he said as neutrally as possible, "but would you mind filling in some gaps for the uneducated in the room?"

Shyldd gave a hearty laugh that reverberated against the tent walls. "Ah, and you must be the brother, yes? The Lightborne I've heard so much about. Noctis Thorne, is it?"

Will glanced over at din'Dael before answering. *Sure, we'll go back to that name for now.* "I've worn multiple names in my life thus far, and that is one I've been known by."

The man's grin remained and he nodded to himself. "Aye, Thorne. I am Shyldd of the Seekers." His eyes dropped down to

Will's hands and he raised his eyebrows conspiratorially. "Are you still planning to attack?"

Flare still burning, Will met the Seeker's knowing grin with one of his own. "You never know what might happen," he said nonchalantly. "Best to stay prepared."

"Apparently," Morella muttered while she looked at the flames wisping about his fists. Her blades disappeared into the folds of her cloak. She rose and brushed her hands on her legs. "Morella Darklore, Shyldd." Her voice was both whimsical and condescending. "Pleasure to meet you. Now, what the hell is going on?"

"Fiery one, eh?" Shyldd grinned wide and nudged Cephora. "I like her." Cephora snorted while Shyldd puffed up his chest.

Morella appraised the Seeker. "Oh, you have *no* idea." She smiled flirtatiously at the large man and Will felt a warmth rush through him that had nothing do to with flames. The Seeker himself rumbled with chuckles and nodded while Cephora's smile fell away.

For his part, Will kept his mouth shut but felt embarrassed at the jealousy. *Jesus, Will, because she smiled at someone?* He shook his head, exasperated at himself. *Lighten the hell up.*

"Aye, well, now that introductions are taken care of"—Shyldd nodded his head toward Morella—"if she's traveling with you, I'm assuming she gets to listen?"

Cephora sniffed. "Oh, you couldn't keep information from this one if you tried, Shyldd."

He smiled. "Very well then. Here's the lay of it. That one there"—he gestured to Rienne—"was en route to the Garde, it seems. Another one of din'Dael's masterstrokes toward world domination, no doubt. She came across a Necrothanian camp, a big one."

"Shyldd, I received your message." Cephora chuckled. "Move it along."

"So that's how it's to be, is it?" Shyldd raised an eyebrow and smiled. Despite the brief bout of jealousy, Will couldn't help liking him. "Aye, well. The Sapholux was already on the march, it would seem, so they diverted to the camp. Dahla found me and mine. We were in the area but a few days off. Let me tell you, I wasn't prepared for the sight of that man again"—he tilted his head toward din'Dael—"let alone at the head of a damned army of Lightborne bedecked in the splendor of aerilite." He didn't take his eyes off the prone figure. "Brought back all the wrong kinds of memories."

"I'm familiar with the sentiment," Cephora said.

"Well, wherever the hell he'd been hiding him and his, it had done wonders for his mind, if you catch what I'm saying. Nothing like the man I recalled from the Plains of Desolation. Here, he was convincing. Eloquent, even. But, my own personal thoughts aside, we shared a common enemy then, as ever. We decided that a . . . temporary alliance would be in order." Shyldd rolled his shoulders back and crossed his arms. "I'd be lying if I said I didn't do it to try to and keep him in check should his old character present itself."

Will's eyes followed Shyldd's. The Revenant had begun humming to himself, the same way he had on the night Will and Madigan first rescued him. *Looks like that old character is back, alright.*

"They had a larger force, so we broke off. Moved ahead faster to scout the area. What we found . . ." He trailed off and shook his head. "Well, it wasn't quite the force we'd anticipated but it was enough. Certainly more than our own. No matter what angle we approached it from, we couldn't see how we'd be able to take the camp. There was a bottleneck, a cave entrance that them was filing through. If we could make it past their initial resistance, surprise them, push them back into the cave, their numbers wouldn't matter. An initial push, then a straightforward matter of containment." He looked pointedly at din'Dael. "I should have remembered that things are rarely so simple when dealing with the Borne."

"It's been some time since any Necrothanians were amassed in force," Cephora said, placing a hand on his arm. "We have all grown soft in the peace."

"Aye, well. Din'Dael wouldn't hear anything I said. Oh, at first he listened, gave council. But then that other one, Kenwal? He stepped forward and started to strategize. His plan was . . . conservative, but potentially effective. No glory to be had but little risk. Now, I don't know the current state of the Sapholux—gods, but a few days ago I didn't even know that such words could still be uttered—but din'Dael?" Shyldd sighed and shook his head. "He wouldn't hear it. There was a tension there between those two, obvious to all of us. Words were exchanged—half of it I couldn't even follow— but, in essence, din'Dael dressed the man down in front of everyone. In one gesture he brushed aside Kenwal's plan and abandoned my own. He opted for a show of force."

Will groaned. "God dammit, Jero."

Shyldd held up a hand. "To be fair, he didn't seem himself, Noctis. It was as if . . . as if he was battling with something, something inside him. Two sides of him vying for control. I can't explain it any better than that. He was trailing his words, irritated and distracted. If it had been a small gathering, we could've contained it until the spell passed. But as I said, this was right in the middle of camp. And those damn Lightborne, they love that man. They believed in him to a fault."

Morella snickered and Will glanced over at her. She looked amused. *Gods, she really does hate din'Dael.*

"Din'Dael gave the orders and the Lightborne spread out, moving to circle the Necrothanian camp. They were overextended and spread thin. Exposed. The terrain made it that much harder. Kenwal, again he spoke against din'Dael. You could see the effect the discord was having on the Lightborne. The old Blades, they'd seen battle. The rest though, those who'd been reared in the safety of the Sapholux and never in the world beyond it? They didn't hesitate. Din'Dael pointed and they followed."

"It was different, Noctis," Rienne spoke suddenly. She stared at the ground, her expression vacant. "The Necrothanians, they weren't . . . it wasn't like training. They're not human. They're not even alive. They're . . ." she trailed off.

"The faction split, Noctis," Shyldd said solemnly.

Cephora cursed and glared at din'Dael's immobile form. Will felt a sense of hopeless dread creep into his body.

"Kenwal and the Blades refused to follow din'Dael. Them two"—he nodded to Rienne and Quennar—"were the only of 'em stuck around. I'd say a good quarter of the remaining Borne abandoned the battle before it even started. Din'Dael may as well've said good riddance to them."

"Dammit." Will closed his eyes and shook his head. "Dammit, dammit, dammit."

"At this point, me and the Seekers tried to stop him. Tried to convince him to back down, regroup. When their brethren abandoned them, well, you could see the fear that set into the rest of the Lightborne. That man, though, he wouldn't hear it. Accused us of growing complacent, weak. 'I'll remind you of what strength is,' he said."

"Shyldd . . ." Cephora's face looked ashen in the dim light.

He held up a steady hand to her. "I called for the Seekers to stand down an' they did. But din'Dael still ordered the attack."

Morella snickered again. The cruel smile on her face was made all the more sinister by the fiendish look in her eyes.

"I'll not lie about it, the Lightborne could've had it. They nearly did at first. It's not only us that've not seen a true battle in some time, the Necrothanians suffer the same affliction. We didn't even see a damn commander amongst their ranks. Their lookouts were inept and disposed of without a single alarm. Din'-Dael gave the signal and the Lightborne unleashed hell."

Shyldd's voice quieted a bit. When he spoke, his voice was

thin. "Ages pass and so many things in this world stay the same. You forget. You don't realize what you forget, because it's forgotten. Somehow I'd forgotten what a wave of Lightborne looks like in a coordinated attack. The brilliant glare of fire. The clap of thunder. You couldn't even hear the screams through the roar of it all." His face grew pinched. "The smell, though. The memory of the smell never fades. Crackling sulfur and ozone and burnt flesh . . ." he trailed off. A moment later, he remembered himself and the words came again. The emotion was gone. What remained was a report. "For a minute, it looked like din'Dael's plan was going to succeed. Then, the first counterattack happened."

Will glanced at Rienne. She was silent but he could tell that she was listening. Quennar, though, Quennar's gaze was utterly vacant.

"I still don't know what twisted magic Valmont discovered that allowed him to create such creatures, and I don't know if I'll ever be able to accept it as reality. What emerged from the chaos was like a cloud of bone, spears or the like, propelled with such force that it took the Lightborne clear off their feet when they struck. One wave, one counter, that was it."

Shyldd turned his attention to Will. "Sheltered like that in the Sapholux, Noctis, how many times had death come to them? How many friends had they seen die at their feet?" He didn't wait for Will to answer. "The screams of agony, the blood." Shyldd shook his head. "I don't know who it was who broke first, but the fear cascaded through the ranks. The assault ended almost as quickly as it had begun. Then the true Necrothanians—those damn reapers—were upon them, ripping and tearing. The Lightborne tried to run but . . . it was a slaughter."

"But din'Dael"—Will shook his head—"I've seen him fight. In the Shale, he leveled the entire army and barely batted an eye. He destroyed the whole damn prison! How did—" He stopped, remembering what din'Dael had told him of their power. *Like a battery, it drains and needs time to recover.*

"Oh, he fought hard, make no mistake on that. He took down many of the bastards. Eventually, though, when he saw his own people dead and dying around him, he sounded the retreat. A few Necrothanians pursued, but the majority stayed in the camp. Whatever they're guarding, they weren't going to abandon it."

"How many? How many were lost?"

Shyldd frowned. "You saw the tents, Noctis. There are not many and they are not full."

God dammit, Jero. Will closed his eyes and fought back the anger. "Why this place, then? Why camp here?"

"Because from here, William, we can enter the cave system that the Necrothanian camp guards." Cephora said matter-of-factly. "That is why you called for me, Shyldd, yes?"

"It is indeed."

"What about the Lightborne?" Will asked. "What about everyone else?"

Rienne's eyes were hazy when she met his gaze. "Redemption, Noctis. We shall avenge the fallen and bring glory to their sacrifice."

Will stared, agape. They were the words of Jero din'Dael. His rhetoric. His fanaticism. "Rienne, no. You all need to get back to the Sapholux."

"We attack at first light." Din'Dael sprang to his feet. He was smiling, arms extended. "Our people wish it, Noctis Thorne. They know that, together, you and I shall not lead them astray. Together, we can accomplish great things."

Before Will could speak, din'Dael dropped to a knee and retrieved something bundled at his feet. He raised it and allowed the cloth wrapping to fall away, grinning with wild eyes the whole time. He held the contents extended and beckoned for Will. "Come, Noctis Thorne. Together, let us destroy the Necrothanians."

He was holding Velier's broken blade. Flint—the Shard of Night, a Relic of Antiquity.

29
THORN OF NIGHT

"Is that . . ." Morella's eyes were wide. Cephora cursed and spun away, her agitation in stark contrast to her casual demeanor moments before. Morella placed a trembling hand on Will's arm. "Will, tell me that that . . ."

"You know this blade, Burner." Din'Dael smiled at Will and stepped toward him. "You know what it is and where it came from. *This* is the way."

Flint. Will's heart pounded in his chest. *Gods, he's giving me a Relic of Antiquity.* He swallowed and tore his eyes from the sword to meet din'Dael's. "What's your plan, Jero?"

"My goal today is the same as it has ever been, friend." Din'-Dael held the broken blade out, hilt extended toward Will. "The destruction of our enemies. Peace. You know this."

"William." Cephora's voice cut through the silence of the tent as she whirled back to face them. "*Noctis!* Do not do this thing." She took a step toward din'Dael and the blade, her hands balled into fists. "The Relics are dangerous. Do *not* take that weapon."

Will kept his eyes fixed on din'Dael. His mentor was smiling gently. Nodding to him. Encouraging him. "Take it, Noctis Thorne. It is why I chose you, why I *named* you."

Thorn of night, wielding the Shard of Night. Of course. Will pulled out of Morella's grasp. He felt her fingers dig into his skin, but he brushed them aside. Flint seemed to call to him. He approached din'Dael and the blade.

"Will, don't you dare." Morella seethed, taking a step after him. "You don't know what it will do to you. Give it to me. Let me study it first. We need to know what can happen."

But Will was already tuning her out. The blade captivated him; its history, its power, it called to him, inviting him. He reached out to grasp the hilt.

"One last thing," din'Dael said quickly. "I do hope your fangs still function."

Will didn't have time to respond. His fingers closed upon the Relic. His key sprang to vibrant, terrible life. He screamed, the brutal power of the sword coursing into his body. At the same time, the key gripped him in a searing surge of electricity. His body shook in spasms of agony. Through the pain came a memory of the night his grandfather died. The night of the visions of the tunnel and the creature beneath. The night of roaring pain and agony when magic consumed him.

He barely registered the dagger in din'Dael's hand.

The Revenant lunged and slashed at Will. The dagger cut into the wrist of the hand holding the Relic, scoring a deep gash that ran nearly to his elbow. Will's fingers, spasming around the blade's hilt, couldn't release it. He was dimly aware of Cephora and Morella shouting, but he was too consumed by pain and surprise to react. Din'Dael kicked his legs out from under him and Will slammed to the ground. The room spun. His mentor knelt over him, predatory, and held his left hand to Will's skull. The hand glowed an emerald green.

"Cth'al naq faren. Hoq'narro q'en fel."

A rush of blazing fury emanated from din'Dael and poured

into Will. He instinctively Flared, mounting a near-unconscious defense as the maddening storm of pain coursed through every inch of his body. Absently, he sought the flow of his blood fangs. He gasped as another surge of furious power erupted. Will scrambled for the flows and drew them toward him. His key was a cold storm of blazing fire. The blade in his hand, a lightning rod. Will cried out in defiance as the blood fangs' power sought to staunch his blood.

The tent erupted into flames. Will heard Morella's angry shouts, heard scuffling, heard Cephora cursing. Of Rienne, Shyldd, and Quennar, he knew nothing. His whole being was consumed with the internal battle of din'Dael's power tearing apart his body.

Din'Dael's eyes were bleeding, but the manic smile never left his face. He fought to bring his face closer to Will's and pulled him to his feet. Will struggled, but there was no use. Din'Dael breathed the words into his ear.

"This, young friend, is where your life begins."

The combination of powers within Will erupted. Din'Dael was flung into the air like a child's toy, tumbling before slamming into the snow. Will dropped to his knees, trembling, and collapsed to the ground. Steam rose from his body. The power rushing through him waned.

Will gasped for air in the cold frost of the night. Each breath was a struggle. He went to lift his head and found his insides to be a furious twist of agony. Finally, he was able to turn his head enough to look at his arm. All traces of the wound were gone.

Will coughed and sputtered, each movement sending new tremors of pain shooting through his body. His ears rang. He tried to swallow, but his throat didn't seem to work.

Then, Morella was there, her face a mask of pure rage as she scanned his eyes for signs of life. She placed her head to his chest and ran her fingers along his arm and down to the hand that gripped Flint. She tried to pry the blade from his fingers. "Dammit, let go," she snarled.

"I'm . . . fine," he wheezed. Shock overtook Morella's enraged face before rapidly changing to worry. She abandoned the sword and ran her hands over his face, pulling at him, raising his head. He winced and tried to draw back, but she wouldn't let go.

"You damn Casc," she whispered as she kissed his forehead. "What the hell have you done?"

"Something . . . painful."

Painful didn't begin to cover it. This was neither physical nor mental pain; this was pain of his very being, of his soul. He grimaced as Morella cradled his head in her hands.

"You're alive." Her voice was hollow and her eyes were vacant. "That's what matters, Will. You're alive."

"A surprise, to say the least." Cephora and Shyldd approached. Cephora shook her head at Will. "That was foolish, Will. Exceedingly foolish." Her eyes drifted, scanning the horizon. "Now, where is that other fool?"

The throbbing of his body began to gradually ease. Will tapped the final vestiges of the blood fangs and let the magic do its work. It helped; he felt better. Not good, by any means, but better. He pushed himself up onto his elbows and raised his head.

The tent was gone and many others had been knocked down by the blast. The Lightborne who were housed within, fewer than Will had imagined even on his worst guess, stood huddled, staring at the scene. Rienne was there, a hand on vacant-eyed Quennar's shoulder. Jero din'Dael were nowhere to be seen. Those who looked on all bore the same distracted emptiness of Quennar and Rienne. Whatever this new intrigue, it did not seem to break them from their despair.

"Aye, well. This changes things." Shyldd appraised Will. "No offense, boy, but I didn't think you had it in you."

"Had what in me?" Will managed to raise his left hand and rub his eyes. His right still gripped the sword. "The stupidity to trust a madman who's as likely to kill you as he is to greet you?"

"He wasn't trying to kill you, Will." Morella shook her head. "He was fighting to save you."

Will craned his neck and felt it crack, releasing some of the tension. "Morella, I think you must have been looking in a different tent."

"She's not wrong, William," Cephora said. "Bindings are . . . dangerous affairs."

"Bindings?" Will tried to open his right hand. Again, the fingers did not respond. A sense of panic came over him and he tried again, willing with all his might to move the fingers. After a moment, they began to open in a scream of pain. He gasped.

"Not physical, William. Soul binding." Cephora shook her head. "Din'Dael is a fool."

Soul binding? He dropped Flint to the ground and flexed his stiff fingers. "What, din'Dael and I are connected now?"

Cephora snickered but it was Shyldd who responded. "No, Noctis. You and the blade are connected."

"He's not dead, then?" came a weary voice. Everyone looked up as the crowd parted. A very bruised, very battered din'Dael approached. "That's a pleasant surprise."

Morella spat on the ground at his approach. Cephora sniffed. "You could have killed him, Jero. You didn't even give him a choice."

Din'Dael waved a dismissive hand and limped toward Will. "He knew what he was doing."

"No, I didn't."

Din'Dael didn't seem to hear him. "And now, Noctis Thorne, we have a far better chance against our enemies." The tall man smiled pleasantly while Morella groaned and rolled her eyes.

"None of you are in any shape to fight *anyone*," she growled at him. "A child could best you in your current state." She turned back to Will. "Will, my love, listen to me. We need to leave right now. We need to get as far from here as we can. This is suicide. We have to go." She leaned down and kissed him. "You need to recover and there is no way that this venture can succeed. Let's go. Promise me, let's go."

Will struggled to sit up. She was right, of course. She was protecting him. But when he saw the faces of those around him, the weary, beaten faces of those whom he had eaten with, trained with, bled with, he knew he couldn't leave them. He briefly considered consulting Cephora, to ask the ancient Seeker what her thoughts were, but he stopped.

The crowd of Lightborne trickled away. *This is my decision. It's like din'Dael always said.* Will scanned the backs of the retreating, then raised weary eyes to Morella. "My people need me."

Her beautiful face distorted, her lips curling in a snarl. "Again. Again you don't listen." She shot out a hand and pointed at din'-Dael. "Do you remember what happened the last time you ignored my warnings? Do you remember what you unleashed on the world?"

"Morella, please." Will held up a hand. "This time will be different. I swear."

She gave a spiteful laugh and shook her head. "Oh yes, I'm certain of that."

"It will be." Will looked at her, then at din'Dael, Cephora, and Shyldd, before finally resting his eyes on Rienne. "This time, we control the outcome." He glanced back to din'Dael. "Not a wildcard."

Shyldd chuckled. "Such confidence from one so young."

"He may surprise you yet," Cephora muttered.

Will hurt. He didn't want to show it, didn't want to admit it, but something inside him felt torn out. *Every time din'Dael lays his damn hands on me . . .* He looked up at the man and saw something of the old din'Dael in there. The strange need, the yearning for Will to understand something.

How the hell do I help? His thoughts drifted to the surviving

Lightborne, to the Seekers, to Morella. *How do I save them?* He found himself wishing for Madigan, someone to bounce idiotic ideas off until something solid came from them. *But that's not going to happen.* He was here, now. The people here needed him. Now.

"We can do this," he said with as much confidence as he could muster. "I've got a plan."

All eyes fell to him.

"What?" Morella snapped.

Will's fingers were stiff from where they'd gripped Flint. He flexed them and looked down. "I said I've got a plan."

"Gods, Will. You can't be serious." Morella stood tense and rigid. Will could see her fuming. "*You've* got a plan?"

"Surprise, surprise," Shyldd said, shaking his head. "Cephora, where *do* you find these people?"

Cephora didn't acknowledge Shyldd but kept her gaze fixed firmly on Will. He felt naked beneath her eyes as she scrutinized him, no doubt trying to determine what his plan might be. *Yeah, if she figures it out, maybe she'll be kind enough to fill me in on it as well.*

Din'Dael, however, clapped his hands and laughed. "Ever the inquisitive mind surprises. Ever the youthful delight. *This* is Noctis Thorne!"

Everyone turned to stare at him. Even Will, who appreciated the brief distraction from their attentions, was taken aback. "Yeah, well. Give me some time to get everything straight, alright?"

"Light's fall, Will," Morella muttered, crossing her arms and leaning away from him. "You really are a fool."

Will shot her a look. He wasn't going to take any of her attitude right now, not while he was still reeling from yet another of din'Dael's damn *enhancements*. "Not everyone just turns tail and runs when others need our help."

The look of pure shock that crossed Morella's face was nearly comical. Stealing the humor, however, was the look of spite and malice that replaced it. She glared at him then allowed her harsh gaze to drift to all those present. A sudden silence descended. Will braced himself for a slap. It never came. Wordlessly, she turned and walked away. She paused momentarily in front of din'Dael and Rienne, eyed them both, then spat before continuing. Will made no effort to follow.

"You'll hear about that one soon enough," Cephora said when Morella was well out of earshot. Will thought he could trace a hint of amusement in her voice.

"Only if we don't all get slaughtered in the next few hours." Will pushed himself to his feet. Shyldd stepped forward and stretched out a hand to help him, but Will waved him away. "Thanks, but I can manage." He flicked his eyes at din'Dael. "I've been through worse."

Din'Dael burst into laughter. "Ah, Noctis. I knew you'd understand. You *see* it, don't you?"

"Jero. A word alone, if I may?" Will kept his voice neutral despite the frustration building inside his chest.

"Certainly." The Revenant grinned and cocked his head to the side. "Out. Everyone."

"Out of what, exactly?" Cephora said sardonically. "The cold, perhaps? You destroyed your tent, din'Dael."

Jero glanced around, apparently only now realizing that they were exposed to the elements. He snickered.

"We'll walk," Will said quickly. His body was aching and his head still pounded. "I need to stretch my legs and get some blood moving."

"Oh, young burner, there shall be enough blood spilled to last till the heavens burn, before long." Din'Dael threw back his head and roared with laughter.

"A bit much sometimes, aren't you?" Cephora looked with disdain at din'Dael. She turned and whispered something to

Shyldd. The burly Seeker nodded and the two departed without further comment. The last of the Lightborne set to work righting their tents and returning to their resting stupor. Will watched as Rienne helped Quennar to his feet. The man gave no hint of noticing, nor did he protest when Rienne led him away. *She's had one hell of a time since we left the Sapholux, sounds like. I should talk to her.*

Din'Dael finally broke from his private revelry. He turned a humorless smile to Will and stroked at a nonexistent beard. Without a word, he turned and strode away from the wreckage of the tent. Will bit back the choice words he wanted to throw after the retreating figure. *Bide your time. Keep a level head.*

He grabbed Flint and followed. The Revenant led them away from the camp and up the mountainside a short distance. Despite the steep angle and deep snowpack, din'Dael moved at an impossible pace, nearly gliding across the terrain. Will's own footsteps were dogged and before long he was puffing with exertion and more than a bit annoyed. Neither of them spoke until they were well out of earshot of the camp.

"There," din'Dael said when the lines of the tents were no longer visible. "Privacy, at last."

Will sniffed disdainfully. "Oh? Able to detect the movements of the Seekers as well, are you?"

Din'Dael gave him a rueful, patronizing look. "Shyldd pulled them back before we even made it out of camp, Noctis." He crossed his bare, scarred arms and gave Will an appraising glance before dropping his eyes down to Flint. "A simple touch of the legends and you return to the demeanor of a petulant youth. I'd thought you past such things, Thorne."

"And I'd thought you beyond your own damn ego!" Will shouted back at him. "Jesus, Jero, they're dead. You got them all killed. And for what? Kenwal? Your goddam pride? To take out a camp of Necrothanians and make a goddam statement?"

Din'Dael sniffed. "Ah, yes. Petulant."

"Damn you, Jero. I should have listened to Morella. You should be rotting in the Shale."

The Lightborne laughed, full and loud, before taking a step closer to Will. "Truly, Noctis?" He raised an eyebrow, a wide, stupid grin still plastered to his face. "Tell me then, Burner, what have I done to offend?"

Will's stared in incredulity. "You . . . you don't even get it, do you? All those lives wasted. All those people you preached about saving. Jesus, all the goddam lives you ruined or ended to find even a single goddam Borne, and you just pissed them all away for *nothing.*"

"Oh, Noctis," din'Dael said, shaking his head slowly. "You truly are lost. You have no—"

"My name is William Davis." He nearly spat the words. "I am not the weapon you tried to make me. I am not a mindless follower who believes your idiotic lies." The air between them crackled with static. "You *broke* something in me once, Jero. *That* is why I followed you." He gripped Flint tight, felt the strange, vibrant energy of the blade coursing through him. "*That* is why you've never succeeded with me. I'm not yours."

"Not mine? No, William. You are not mine." He didn't even pause when he passed over the name Noctis, not one trace of hesitation. "Not now, not ever. That is not my way."

"No games, Jero." Will shook his head. *What the hell is he trying to trap me in this time.* "I've had enough of them."

"You still don't see?" Din'Dael's temper flared and lightning rippled across his skin. The very snow in the air surrounding him evaporated and steam rose. "You're *his,* William. You all are." His snarl was nearly feral. His eyes were frantic, darting madly as they scanned Will's face.

"Valmont has no—"

"Damn Dorian Valmont," din'Dael spat contemptuously. "That fool has ever been too blind to know the true threat to these lands."

Will paused, sudden confusion overtaking him. *If not Valmont then . . .?* He stared at din'Dael. The man was agitated, frustrated and angry, but strangely coherent. "What are you talking about?"

Din'Dael's eyes grew distant, looking somewhere into the space beyond Will. "You've heard him, William. I know you have. You've heard them both. The pull, William . . . the *need*."

"Jero, snap back to me." Will wove his head back and forth, trying to meet din'Dael's eye. "Who are you talking about?"

"It wasn't me, William. Surely you must know that." He spun slowly, vacant eyes circling back to face the unseen camp. "I would never, could never hurt them. *Sacrifice* them. But he could. He did. He knew that I would fight . . . that I would try to stop it." He grimaced and held up his glowing fist containing the unseen Relic. "Even with this, I couldn't." He turned back and met Will's eyes. Tears were flowing freely down his face, steaming in the cool mountain air. "I failed them, William. He slaughtered them to weaken me. *That* is why I needed you. Don't you see?"

Will eyed the man warily. This was new. Sure, din'Dael had had previous bouts of rapid change, but not like this. Will didn't like it. "No, Jero. I don't."

The sudden defeated sag of the large man's shoulders caught Will by complete surprise. His entire face slackened for a moment and the look of despairing hopelessness unnerved Will.

"You've heard him, William." Din'Dael stepped closer, his movements dreamlike. "He is the speaker of lies, the father of madness." Lightning-rippled hands reached out and gripped Will's shoulders painfully. Will struggled, but the grip was iron. "He tears away at your mind until you are broken. Don't you see?"

I wish I could, Will thought sadly. It pained him to see the man brought so low by his own madness. "I see the threat, Jero." It was not a lie, but it still tasted like one. *The Necrothanians are the threat. Valmont is the threat. But I cannot find one in the imagined ghosts in a madman's mind.* "And I know that it needs to be countered."

Din'Dael's trembling fingers dug deeper into Will's shoulders. "Yes, William. *Yes.*" His grin flashed wide and white, jubilant. The stream of tears never ceased. "More than you know. Together, *this*"—he removed his hand and balled it into an emerald glowing fist in front of Will's face—"and *that*"—he gestured toward Flint —"and you and I together, William. Together! We can change the face of reality itself."

He was growing ever more manic. Will finally wrenched himself away and stumbled a few steps back through the drift. *He's completely lost it. I've got to steer him back on track.*

Will held up Flint and made a show of inspecting the broken blade. He looked from it to the Lightborne camp and the lands beyond, then lowered the sword and met din'Dael's eyes. He spoke low and controlled, imploring whatever remained of din'-Dael's right mind to hear his words. "Whatever you think you know, Jero, whatever the threat might be, first we need to stop whatever Valmont's people are doing here. Alright? First, we stop this. Then"—he studied the large man's face—"then we'll talk more. But first we need to save our people."

"As it has always been, William Thorne." His emerald fist looked ghastly against the snow. "We do what we must to save our people." Din'Dael's eyes darkened as he gazed at the camp. "Whatever the cost."

30
A WORLD BEYOND

Will's night existed within a sleepless dream. He returned to the camp not knowing what to expect but finding it in worse shape than he'd dared fear. Morella was sulking somewhere out of sight. Forcing himself not to dwell on her mood, he instead busied himself outfitting the Borne and meeting the Seekers.

There were few enough of each, but nonetheless he made efforts to encourage those who needed it and present a face of strength. He had no idea if they bought it; he sure didn't. They'd believed him when he said he had a plan. They trusted him to save them. But he kept coming up empty-handed. He spent hours trying to come up with something, *anything,* that he could give them. Always, he drew a blank.

What would Mad do? He asked himself the question over and over. His brother was the one who planned, who strategized. More often than not, Will had relied on his Shade and his luck and his damn key to give him a leg up. Everything he'd been focusing on the last few years had been so centered on training himself, not any kind of large group. Everyone in the Sapholux had been trained that way.

I've got a whole group of fighters who only know how to protect themselves.

What had din'Dael been thinking when he'd trained them? Not for the first time, Will wondered how things might have been different had Madigan been guiding them, rather than Will and a damned madman. *He shook his head, chastising himself. What the hell came over me back home? Why the hell did I push him away?*

Will paced a short distance away from the camp. Mad always found a way. He would have used every tool to his advantage. He would have seen the invisible threads holding everything together and then pulled them like strings on a marionette. When Will was in the Sapholux, he'd hoped to discover how to lead. But he still had no idea.

More the puppet than the damn puppeteer. He frowned. *Maybe if the puppet was stationary, held in a firm grip, and I had a damn magnifying glass, I could find the strings. But normally? Not a damn chance.*

Will's breath caught in his throat.

That's it.

It was a bad plan. Reckless, really. Foolish, terrible. But it was all he had . . . and it could work. Maybe.

He rushed back to the camp and began his search. When he saw the reaction of every person he sought out, he felt his momentary confidence slipping. Every single person stared at him like he was insane when he outlined their part to play. Morella barely looked at him, but when she did, her opinion of the plan, of him, was clear. Only Jero din'Dael approved, which did nothing for Will's confidence. In the end, though, everyone agreed. Will could feel himself trembling as the assembled parties moved to prepare.

Cephora took his arm. "You know that very few will walk away from this, don't you?" she said quietly.

Will's stomach twisted. "But some might."

"Hmph." She assessed him. "Some. I will gather what you require."

She let him go. He busied himself by helping any who needed it. Well before dawn, he prepared his empty fangs, took Flint, and walked a short distance. The air was calming and cool. He traced the snow with each step until he found a more solid snowpack still within sight of the tents. *Won't be long now.*

"You promised," an angry voice called out to him. Will turned to see Morella following him a short distance away. "You promised, Will."

"We'll see each other before long." He took a tentative step toward her and took her hand when she reached him. "I just need someone I trust watching din'Dael."

Her eyes searched his face. "Meaning?"

"Meaning if this goes sideways and he snaps again, I want you to get everyone out. Jero won't. He'll sacrifice them all for nothing."

She relaxed visibly and shook her head. "What makes you think that I won't just abandon them too? Save my own skin."

"No," Will said, drawing her hands up to his lips. He kissed her fingers and looked into her eyes. "You're good, Morella. I'm sorry about before. You're a good person."

Her mouth quivered slightly. Her expression was strange, almost sad. She tilted her face up and kissed him. The wave of electricity that coursed through his body had nothing to do with his key or his Flare.

"I'll see you at the end, lover."

Her words were barely a whisper. She turned and left without another word and never looked back. Will was alone. He stretched, knowing that even brief sleep would not come. He held Flint and familiarized himself with the blade. *If only it was complete.* Still, the broken edge and guard were enough that he could use it as a weapon.

He drew his cutlass and moved through various cuts and guards and progressions, calming his mind with the peace of practice. It took a few minor adjustments to get used to having Flint in his left hand, but he found his stride soon enough. Still, he was unnerved by it. What little he knew about Relics of Antiquity was that they were never as they seemed and always far more than one expected. But with two of them, Flint and the Emerald Eye, surely he and his people stood a chance against the Necrothanians. *Hell, if even half the things I've heard are true, then a single Relic should have been enough.*

Should have been. It hadn't.

Will returned his cutlass to the baldric and maneuvered Flint into a loop at his belt. It felt awkward at first, imbalanced against the blood fang on his left hip, but after some brief fiddling he made it work. That the fangs themselves were empty gave him pause. *But that will change before long,* he thought wryly. He exhaled deeply and tried to push the dark thoughts of the coming slaughter from his head. His key hummed mildly at his chest, having calmed immensely since the ordeal of the binding. He had everything he needed. All that was left to do was act.

Will left the camp's sightline. He considered going back one last time to make sure everything was progressing correctly. To make sure din'Dael was following through. To see Morella one last time. But instead, he slipped away into the final breath of night to meet his guides. No one saw him leave, but he had to trust them to do what they had to. Trust them to believe they had a chance.

He found Rienne exactly where expected. That was good. When he'd told her his plan and her part in it, he hadn't been sure that he'd broken through her near-catatonic fear. Now, though, some life seemed to have returned to the Lightborne. She looked far more like the friend he'd trained with and sparred against for so long. She rose from her crouch and hefted the small bundle that had lain hidden in her lap. She tossed it to Will who snatched it out of the air, then crossed her arms at his approach.

"With regards from Cephora." A smile tugged at the corner of her mouth. "You know this is a bad plan."

"Yes," Will said with as much nonchalance as he could muster. "But it's better than no plan."

"I'm not so sure that I agree with you there."

Will paused and caught Rienne's shoulder with a touch as she moved past him. "What do you mean?"

She half turned back to him. "Do we really need a plan?" The corner of her mouth twitched a bit, though whether from sadness or humor, Will couldn't tell.

"It's better than running in without a second thought."

"We could always just go home." She raised her eyes to the sky and held them there. "There or somewhere else."

The comment hung in the air. "Rienne, Valmont is evil. He needs to be stopped."

"Someone will always need to be stopped. There's always a fight somewhere."

"Are you saying we should just stop?"

"I liked home."

"Rienne . . ."

"And now that I've seen a bit of the world, I think I'd like to see more of it." She turned and looked at him with a calm face. "I want to live, Noctis. Everyone that died . . . I don't want that. I want life."

She turned away again and kept walking. Will was at a loss for words. *Of course we want to live. But Valmont wants to destroy that, to take that away from us . . .* But she knew that as well as he did. Sheep, din'Dael called them. They'd only known peace. They wanted to keep that.

And is that so wrong?

For the next hour, they spoke little as they walked. A thick fog settled over the landscape, meeting the snow and giving the surreal impression that they were walking within a dark storm cloud. Whatever her personal misgivings, Rienne pressed on, guiding him to their destination despite the absence of clear sight. *Just like when we first left the Sapholux. She's good. She does what's needed when it needs to be done.*

Rienne's steps slowed. She dropped to a crouch then took measured, cautious steps for another five minutes before halting. "This is it."

Will couldn't see any change, but he nodded nonetheless. "You're good to get back?"

"I am."

"Right, then." Will adjusted Flint and loosened his fangs. He focused on his key and felt the comforting vibration humming against his skin. "Thank you, Rienne. For everything."

She watched him prepare, her eyes never leaving his face. "Noctis, don't throw your life away in there."

Will gave her a hollow smile. "I don't plan to. I want to live too."

She reached out and gave his arm a light squeeze. "I'll see you on the other side."

Then she was gone, retreating into the cloud of snow and fog. Will watched it swirl, lost in thought while the world descended into a blank grey canvas. *What if she's right? What if we did just leave, let the world continue their fight without us?*

It was tempting. What did he know of Aeril beyond the small piece he'd seen? Beyond the Sapholux and Undermyre and the lands between? There was so much he didn't know, had never had the opportunity to discover. They could go, leave din'Dael to his crazy schemes. Go and explore the world, two sets of virgin eyes beholding unimaginable sights.

But he knew he wouldn't. To abandon everyone like that would be . . . *Would be what? Not me. Not what Grandda made us.*

Pushing the thought from his mind, Will crept forward in a low crouch, moving as silently as possible atop the light crunch of snow. A short time later, the grey haze of night began to lift. He glanced up, gauging the light against the time since he'd left camp. *Everyone should be well on the move. Time to do my part.*

He heard the sounds of the encampment well before he saw it, the sounds of labor and industry not fully muffled by the snow. The air smelled of woodsmoke and iron, and above it all lingered the earthen smell of dredged rock. Will quickened his pace. As the noise grew louder, an amorphous form appeared in the fog. Will froze. The figure shifted slightly. A man wrapped in a cloak and blankets. A sentry standing idle. Will withdrew the blood fangs. *A dagger in the dark*. He swallowed hard.

With or without his Shade, Will had always known how to move quietly in the darkness. He was on the unsuspecting lookout in an instant. Will grabbed the man from behind and cupped a hand over his mouth. In the same moment, he sliced the blood fang's edge across the lookout's yielding throat. Holding the terrified, dying man firm in his grip, Will backpedaled quickly. Again and again he plunged the fang into the man's chest as the sentry scrambled for footing, clawing at Will's face. The man struggled wildly in his death throes, but Will did not allow him to make a sound. When he finally grew still, silence remained. No alarm had been raised.

Even after the attack, their sentries are useless.

Power surged back into the fangs. Will fought against the nausea, against the smell of blood. He quickly buried the still figure in snow, never looking at the blood-soaked face. He forced himself to take measured breaths in and out, stilling his rapid heart. Then he moved on.

He killed two more lookouts in the same fashion, each time feeling himself sinking farther away from a conscious mental state. He existed in a calm detachment, a world of necessity. This was no battle. Doubtless, they would have done the same to him, had the roles been reversed. Doubtless, they would have raised the alarm and tried to kill him on sight if they'd seen him. Doubtless, they would have tortured him if he'd been captured. Yet knowing that didn't make the cruel job any easier.

When he'd disposed of the third body, Will paused. His hands were shaking. *From the cold. Just the cold.* It felt like hours had passed, but the whole ordeal took no more than a quarter of one. Still, from the Seeker's intel, he knew he'd created enough of a gap in the enemy's line to approach the camp unseen. The thought didn't bring him any comfort; Shyldd's story of the Lightborne's defeat was fresh in his mind. Will approached the lip of the ridge and, steeling himself, peered over.

He'd expected a formal camp, something to be found within a military manual, but what he saw was more akin to a mining operation than anything else. *A large mining operation,* he thought, eyes darting about. Scaffolding stretched up the mountainside. There were signs of massive excavation and construction but no evidence that the Lightborne had ever launched their suicidal assault. All signs of the battle had been cleared.

The rickety walkways and hanging scaffolding made it look like the Necrothanians were carving the mountain itself into a work of art. There were people swarming everywhere, bearing tools and stone as they entered and exited a single cave within the carved rock. *That's it. That's the shaft.*

Amongst the cultists he spied the true Necrothanians, the terrifying amalgamations of dead flesh and bone he'd faced within the Ways. *Reapers.* Dozens of them.

Every instinct told him to run, to turn tail and rush back to Morella's arms and the forgetful bliss of Burning Embers. Death was coming. *But not for me and mine,* he thought blindly. *We'll make it. We've got to.*

Gods I hope this works.

31
SHOCK AND AWE

Will rose and pulled himself over the ledge. He crouched low and scanned the camp, picking his targets. Having decided, he began making his way along the inner lip of the ridge, watchful for the slightest hint that he had been spotted. He moved slowly toward a nearby path through the camp, disturbing as little snow as possible. The wind died but the fog lingered, though that wouldn't last long. His pulse quickened. The brightening sky threatened to give him away at any moment. Time was running short.

No point in waiting. He held his breath and closed the distance to the first row of structures that ran parallel to the main path. It looked ready to collapse, barely held together. Closer inspection revealed the remnants of blackening on the support beams, carefully carved away. The Lightborne's flames had caught, but they hadn't caught long enough.

Creeping between structures, Will maneuvered through the outskirts of the camp, heading in the direction of the shaft. Very few Necrothanians came close to seeing him; they were all concentrated on the main path. *Trusting their sentries, no doubt. You'd think they'd have learned after the last time.*

Still, he knew they'd miss them soon enough. He needed to move faster.

He approached a large, central rampart and veered inside, drawing his hood back and scanning the spartan structure. Roughly hewed timber was held together with fibrous cordage that supported the mass above. The snowy ground had been covered by thick planks. Will crouched and placed a bare hand against the cordage. It was dry. He smiled.

Will reached into the small satchel that Cephora had supplied and withdrew the largest of the small balls. He eyed Cephora's handiwork and smiled appreciatively—the Seeker had come through fantastically, especially given such short notice. He pried at the center of the ball, his mouth turning down in frustration as the tinder and pitch stuck to his fingers. He carved out a small cradle and, after looking at the cords binding the wood, made a small depression in the bottom of the ball. Carefully wedging the hollow bundle into the thick of the cords, he smiled again. *This is going to work.*

Working quickly, he took the discarded bits of ball and rolled them in his palms, trying to capture as much of the pitch and debris as he could. He compressed it into a small, dense cylinder with a narrow tip. He tested it within the hollow, making sure it left enough room for air to circulate. Satisfied, he removed it and, holding it upside down by the narrow tip, Flared. Biting his lip, he concentrated on the tip. A small coal appeared and then flames began climbing up the cylinder. Deftly, Will righted the small tinder and placed it back within the hollow. Wisps of smoke began to move lazily upward.

Glancing about to make sure no one had seen, Will moved to the opposite support beam of the rampart. He repeated the procedure while constantly glancing back at the first tinderbox. It was burning slow, but it was burning. He fit the second ball onto the cordage and lit it. Glancing between the two, he nodded to himself. *They'll catch.*

It was nearly daylight when he exited from the rampart. The lingering fog would hide the smoke, but only for a time. He had enough of Cephora's incendiaries to deal with three total structures. One more was on this side of the main path and, if he had gauged his distance well, it was close.

Will walked cautiously, keeping to the shadows as much as possible and avoiding the glow of firelight. He took one wrong turn, costing him precious seconds, but otherwise found the structure without incident. It, too, was empty. Will placed the devices more quickly this time and moved on as soon as they were lit.

Not long until the flames show. He pulled the bundle closer to his body and shrugged deeper within his cloak. *This is taking too long.*

He approached the main throughway of the camp and scanned for activity. The majority of the cultists were still concentrated on the tunnel's entrance. The rest must be sleeping or deep within the mountain. That told him two things: his fires had not yet been spotted, and time was still on his side.

Steeling himself, he walked with as much casual ease as he could across the main path. *Do nothing that attracts attention. Walk neither fast nor slow. Do not think. Move and act.* No one even glanced in his direction.

This is almost too easy, he mused, ducking into the next structure after a quick glance over his shoulder. Before he could bring his head back around, he walked straight into a small, robed man.

"Watch where you're going, you blithering fool," the man snarled as he shoved Will. "I ought to"—he broke off as he took in Will's startled face—"You're not—"

Will didn't give him a chance to finish. Quick as lightning, he lashed out with a fang. The blade took the man across the throat, silencing him instantly. The startled man scrambled backward, hands clawing at his neck. Will darted forward and threw his arms around the man, the left holding him tight and pulling him to the ground while the right plunged the fang again and again into the man's back. Within moments, the man's struggles stopped, the wet, gasping gurgles falling away.

Will stumbled back from the body, not trusting himself near it. *Jinxed it,* he thought numbly. He stood and looked at the body. *Goddam jinxed it.* His hands were shaking, a tremor that had nothing to do with the chill in the air. *I lost time,* he thought as he quickly began to set Cephora's nests around the structure. *Not much, but seconds count.*

The pack now emptied, Will threw it to the ground—one less thing to carry. He lit the fuses within the nests and watched them catch fire much faster than the previous nests had. He smiled unsteadily. Cephora certainly had a way with making things happen. The smile faded. *That means I've only got about five minutes until the first building is in full flame.*

Glancing one final time at the bloody body on the floor, Will took a deep breath and exited. He pulled himself up onto a raised ledge outside and looked back toward the first building. Smoke, nearly hidden in the morning's misty dawn, was visibly rising from it now. The same for the second building. *Which means this one isn't far behind.* He leapt down and, abandoning stealth, ran for the fourth and final structure.

He heard the first shouts of alarm just as he drew up to it. Pulling his scarf up over his mouth, Will stepped inside and glanced about. Far from being empty storage, as the previous ramparts had been, this structure was filled with stacked crates. They were all overflowing with some kind of mineral, dark and grey. *Mining residue?* Will didn't know a damn thing about mining operations. Scooping a handful of the stuff into his gloved hand, he held it up for closer inspection. He paled.

It's impossible. Will had never seen gunpowder magazines in anything but movies, but he was nearly certain that the cache before him was filled with the stuff. His grandfather had never said anything about gunpowder. Hell, in all the time he'd spent in Aeril, nothing he'd seen had ever suggested that they knew anything about it. But judging from what lay before his eyes, Valmont, at the very least, had figured it out.

Loud cries could be heard from outside. *If they know what this place is, they're going to be here any second.* He grabbed the smallest of the crates and began pouring the powder on the ground while backpedaling out of the building. His feet crunched into the snow of the camp and Will froze. Was gunpowder affected by snow? He cursed himself for his lack of knowledge. *Those old pirate flicks, they always worried about wet powder . . .* He glanced at the snow, then at the crate in his hands. *Not going to risk it.*

Will dropped the crate, turned on his heel, and ran. Flames were licking at the sky in the distance from the three structures he had sabotaged and the camp was in full alarm. *They'll be here any second.* A crack of thunder echoed across the sky and he heard an alarm. *It's begun.*

He whirled, not having any idea how far away he'd need to be from the blast but knowing that he was still too close. Gritting his teeth, Will Flared. White, fiery lightning erupted from his outstretched hand toward the powder-filled crate. Not even looking to see if the bolt connected, Will spun again and sprinted as hard as he could.

Ten seconds later, a deafening boom filled the sky. Spinning debris collided into Will's back, knocking the wind out of him and sending him flying through the air. He crashed into a snowbank, debris raining around him. His ears rang. The air was filled with ash and dust and snow. Gasping for breath, he struggled to orient himself. Pushing himself to hands and knees, his right hamstring screamed out in pain.

Will fell back to the ground and rolled onto his back. He reached a hand down and felt the large wooden shrapnel that protruded from his leg. The slightest pressure on it sent his head swimming and stomach lurching. He lay there for a moment, face buried in the folds of his cloak, adrenaline sweat covering his body.

There's no goddam time. They need you.

Will felt like he was watching himself from a great distance. He saw himself reach back. Saw his fingers wrap around the splintered wood. Felt the sickening agony even through the numb detachment of shock. *No time.*

Will yanked. It was only after he finished retching onto the ground that he realized he had actually pulled the shrapnel from his leg. Suddenly feeling very cold, he guided the power of the fangs over himself, staunching the known wound and any others he was unaware of. The restorative balm quickly brought some piece of him back to himself. *Got to keep moving.*

He tested the leg. Pain free. He checked the fangs. Nearly empty. Four whole lives to heal a leg and restore his vigor; it hardly seemed fair. Something was always lost in the exchange, he knew. *And how much of that is my humanity?*

Will shook his head. He rose to his feet and surveyed the chaotic scene. The blast had knocked out both of the nearby towers and much of the surrounding area, while the other two structures were hopelessly lost to the flames. The fire had spread and was slowly engulfing the camp. *If din'Dael has any sense at all, he's on the move. Which means I need to be in position.*

Trusting his leg to support him, Will raced back toward the main path and the mine shaft beyond. He passed cultist after cultist, ducking his head anytime he neared a reaper. He could hardly believe the effectiveness of the blaze. He cringed when he saw people flinging themselves onto the lesser blazes and smothering them with their bodies. A seemingly endless stream of cultists was pouring from the cave's mouth. Everyone was too distracted to notice him. *Gods, this is going to work.*

Someone off to his left started shouting. Will's breath caught in his throat. *Don't turn, it might not be directed at you.*

He kept moving. The shouting intensified. Over the roar of commotion, he heard hurried footsteps crunching in the snow behind him. The shaft entrance was growing nearer. *Just a little farther.*

A rough hand dropped onto his shoulder and yanked Will backward.

Dammit.

Will whirled, drawing the blood fangs as he did so. He slashed and caught the startled cultist across the chest, the blood fang slicing easily through fabric and flesh. Blending the strikes, Will immediately followed with a rising cut. The fang opened the man from stomach to sternum. Gore splashed Will, the warmth of it on his face shocking him into inaction.

There was the briefest pause within the camp as the stream of surrounding cultists stared in shock. Will recovered and kicked, sending the dying man sprawling. Lightning covered Will's skin and his Flare roared to life. Power coursed back into his fangs. His key sprang to life with a fiery fury.

Steeling himself, Will unleashed hell.

Lightning spun outward from him, spiraling and catching the cultists immobilized in surprise. Their screams leapt into the morning sky and carried on the still air.

Shock and awe. Keep them off balance.

The camp's brief hesitation faded almost instantly. A horn sounded nearby. Guttural roars overtook the roaring fire as focus turned to the invader. Will was painfully aware of the absence of his Shade, of the casual defense he had once relied on so heavily. *Nothing for it now.*

The Necrothanians came at him.

Will turned and ran.

Dammit, din'Dael, where the hell are you? His muscles tensed and seemed to pulse in time with his key. He darted amongst the tents, setting them alight while he ran for the shaft. He lashed out at anything that moved, trying to keep distance between himself and the horde bearing down at his back. *Keep them off balance. Keep them focused on me.*

He hurled himself into a burning tent and threw himself to the ground. He wriggled beneath a flap and rolled out into snow-soaked mud. There were boots on the ground next to him. Will lashed out with a fang and parried an incoming strike. He Flared and a crackling blast of white fire seared the flesh from the cultist's face. Will rose and ran, the horrible croaking cries of the cultist filling his ears.

Deal with the horror later.

Will scrambled for another structure, setting the base alight and beginning to climb. The tunnel was so close. Gauging his distance, Will sprinted and leapt for the neighboring building. A line of them seemed close enough to each other that he could use them to reach the mountain. Gritting his teeth, Will ran for the next one. Launching himself into the air, Will realized his error. He slammed hard into a beam and tumbled to the ground.

A reaper appeared before him. Will scrambled away from it while the creature roared its terrifying, guttural battle cry. The shaft's entrance was just beyond the monster. The reaper and fifty cultists stood between him and his goal.

Only one thing left. Will sheathed the blood fangs and reached for his cutlass. With his free hand, Will drew Flint. Raising the broken blade before him, he reached for the flows of energy emanating from it.

Instantly, a manic euphoria burst into his mind. Power flowed through him, overwhelming his senses. His key sang in a maddening fit of fire and lightning. Will felt renewed. Invigorated.

Reckless.

He squared off against the reaper. With a roar, it came at him. In a single motion, Will stepped aside and drew his cutlass upward. The aerilite blade crackled electric blue with power and the rising cut took off the creature's arm. Whirling, the blade came across the reaper's neck in a lateral thrust before Will compassed himself back. Now behind his target, he brought the blade straight down, opening the creature at the collarbone and effortlessly sliding down to its hip.

Laughing with wild abandon, Will spun and threw himself into the Necrothanians.

He danced among the cultists, Flint's power surging through him as he carved through their bodies. A white shield of flame, trickling with blue lightning, spun continuously around him, charring flesh before the force of the gale ripped bodies asunder. His cutlass entered and exited bodies with hardly any resistance. When Will parried the few blows that managed to break through his shield, Flint's guard shattered the weapons. Flint was the master, the one in control. Will was but its instrument.

As din'Dael had been within the hordes of the Shale, Will was untouchable.

A boom from somewhere far off sent the ground shaking. The tremors subsided just as a large cloud of dirt and dust ejected itself from the mouth of the tunnel. There was a momentary lull in the fighting, a brief interlude where all attention turned to the burgeoning cloud. Cries sounded from within the cave.

There he is. Will smiled. He did not show any relief to the horde. To his own ears, his laughter sounded like din'Dael's. Now he understood the man. Now he could see. He was a walking god amongst a horde of ants. Empowered by the Shard of Night, he carved through flesh and bone and armor.

Pain tore through his euphoria and brought Will cascading back to the mortal plane. He cried out and stumbled. Something had taken him across the back of the leg—the same damn leg. The limb barely held his weight. Will cursed and whirled the cutlass, but the blade found only air.

Will stared up into the vacant hollows where the reaper's eyes ought to have been. The remaining skin had been shredded from its body by the force of Will's Flare. What stood before him was a hulking mass of charred grey muscle and exposed bone. *Of course, idiot.* Will snarled. He whipped his Flare back from the cultists and launched its full fury into the creature that had struck him.

He was so singularly focused on the abomination that he failed to notice the other two. Just before the walking corpse was obliterated, Will's world exploded into white, blinding pain.

He was momentarily airborne, knocked back by the force of the blow to his stomach. He looked down as he flew through the air. His injured leg was bent at an impossible angle. At the same moment, the other reaper had struck out with a large club that took him in the gut and lifted him off the ground.

Time seemed to slow. He couldn't catch his breath. The club was flying with him, seemingly stuck to him while the reaper drove it forward. Then he saw that it was not a club. It was a handle. An axe handle. The head of the axe was buried in his stomach.

Oh gods. Oh no, no no no.

Will thumped into the ground and screamed. The creature drove forward with the force behind the blow. Will pulled his Flare back farther and whirled it about him in a panicked fury. Fueled by Flint and his own rage, nothing could pass through the barrier. It severed the axe's handle and the decomposed arms that held it. But the axe head was still stuck deep inside him.

Blood filled Will's mouth. The weapons fell from his trembling hands and he grabbed at the head. Pain roared through his body. He cried out. Quivering, shaking, Will struggled at the metal wedge. His fingers were slick with blood but he found his grip. The slightest movement sent white pain scouring through his bleeding, fevered body.

Oh gods, just . . . a bit . . .

The head came free and slumped to the ground next to him. He was shaking furiously. Will fumbled with numb fingers for his blood fangs. *Rate of . . . transference.* He'd killed with them since he'd used them on his leg, hadn't he? Would it be enough?

Unconsciously, he tapped into the power and felt the flows coursing through the bloodstones. He guided them to his stomach. He spat thick blood and groaned. The world spun. Narrowed.

Oh gods, I'm going to faint.

He forced himself back to himself, to focus. The blood fangs were doing their work, he had to trust that. His hands were no longer shaking so badly. Delicately, he probed the wet surface of his stomach. It was tender, but the skin was unbroken. He'd seen pictures of axe wounds, had heard stories of the damage they could cause. He had no doubt that his guts had been a mangled mess, that the acid and bile and intestinal filth might have escaped. *Please let those damn fangs be fixing my insides as well.*

He grasped Flint and pushed himself up. He winced and nearly fainted when he tried to move his leg. He looked down and saw exposed bone jutting from his shin. *Dammit, how the hell did I miss that?* he wondered distantly. From some deep, logical place in his brain came the answer: *Shock.*

I don't have time for shock.

He grit his teeth. He was fourteen again. He was back at home with his grandfather and Madigan. Mad had fallen out of the cedar and landed on his arm, breaking it. It was a clean break. Grandda was explaining how to set it. Will had watched attentively while Mad had born down with the grim stoicism that always came to him when he was in the most pain. Grandda had set the bone. Mad's arm had healed quickly. Life went on.

Steeling himself, praying that the bloodstones still held enough power, Will reached down. This was not a clean break. Compound fractures probably took some completely separate skill set Will didn't know. He looked around wildly but could see no one that could help. Trying to remember his grandfather's every word, Will tried to set the bone.

Will was not his brother. He did not maintain the same composure. Will screamed even more than he had when he removed the axe head. Adrenaline and fear had been his allies then, dulling his senses. But now the pain struck true and deep. The world spun. His head lolled. Will collapsed back.

His head hit something soft. His head was cradled in it. His eyes flickered open and Rienne was there. *How did she get through the Flare?*

"Light's fall, Noctis. What the blazes happened?"

His words were thick. "You're supposed to be on the ridge."

"Damn the ridge. You needed help."

Despite the pain, Will smiled. There was still a little power left in the stones; he could feel it billowing lightly at his side. At his direction, it flowed over his leg, knitting bone and skin. He reached into Flint's boundless source and felt energy course back through his body. His skin tingled. His eyes felt dry and his tongue felt thick. The energy was more akin to too many cups of coffee after not sleeping all night, but it was better than nothing.

Rienne helped him to his feet. He spat out another mouthful of blood. Warily, he touched the torn, blood-soaked clothes about his stomach. The flesh beneath was healed as far as he could tell, but he stumbled when he put weight on his leg. Finding his balance and holding on to Rienne to steady himself, he took a few tentative steps. He frowned. *This is wrong. Something isn't right.* The blood fangs had knitted the bone back together as he'd set it, but whatever he'd done hadn't been enough. The leg ached.

A problem for another day. He looked around. The camp was nearly empty. He could hear the cries of battle from the tunnel's entrance. "What's happening?"

"Your plan worked, albeit with a few amendments." Rienne continued to support him while he got the feel for moving on the leg. "Jero din'Dael and Cephora led the Lightborne in a rear assault though the tunnels. The Seekers and a few of the Lightborne remained on the ridge, as you asked, to pincer them in after the trap had sprung." She shook her head and set her mouth in a thin line. "Things got a bit hairy when we saw you go down. We adjusted on the fly. The Seeker, Shyldd, he led the assault from the rear when they were focused on you. He routed the enemy into the tunnel."

"They're all in there?"

"As best we can tell. Once din'Dael launched his attack, the majority of the Necrothanians forgot all about the camp and raced for the tunnel. If the quarters are as contained as it looks, their numbers won't mean a damn thing. They'll get caught in the crossfire."

"They abandoned the camp entirely?"

She nodded. "Shyldd's crew made quick work of those who remained to fight the blaze. Now they're trapped in the mountain. We've got them surrounded."

Will winced. The air was filled with smoke and ash. The whole place was going up in flames. He let out a deep breath, beginning to feel more himself again. *The Necrothanians are trapped. Why did they retreat into the tunnel so quickly?* "That will only make them more dangerous. We need to make sure that we don't overly press them."

He stepped away from her, finding his balance and nodding to himself. *I can do this.* "You know where the others made their entrance?" Rienne nodded. "Good, get back to them and relay how things are going on our end. Keep an eye on them. Don't let din'Dael deviate from the plan. Slow and steady will get us through this."

"Agreed." Rienne gave him an appraising look. "You're better than I anticipated. I saw you go down and the storm of Flare that circled you after. I didn't expect to find much." She reached out and gave his arm a tender squeeze. "I'm glad I did."

"Me too." Will returned the gesture. "I'm glad you're here, Rienne. I owe you my life."

She gave a weary smile and nodded. “Let’s finish this and go home.”

“If there’s anything you need . . .”

“I’ll ask.” She dropped her hand and drew her weapon. “Back to it, then?”

“Back to it.”

32
LEGENDS COLLIDE

"I . . . I know I have already said it, sir. But I . . . it is good to have you back, sir."

Madigan smiled and turned. He leveled his gaze at Ynarra and shook his head slightly. "Time and time again, Ynarra. You don't need to call me 'sir,' you know that."

The sweet, playful smile that he'd begun to finally get used to danced across her face. "I . . . know." Her eyes flitted down briefly then rose to meet his own. They were a startlingly beautiful green that always caught him off guard. "It's just . . . old habits. Madigan."

She reached out and tentatively placed her index finger against his own. *Hot damn.* Madigan smiled and returned the affectionate gesture. "It is good to be back, Ynarra."

It *was* good to be back. He hadn't expected it, to be honest. His previous time in the Nordoth under the Crow's hospitality had been secluded, isolated from the world other than Will and Ynarra. But this time? Things were different. It was as though he were an honored guest. He'd dined with the Crow on multiple occasions, large, opulent feasts with all sorts of Undermyrian citizens of prominence. The commander, Shifter, had spoken to him repeatedly and, Madigan dared to say it, they were very nearly becoming friendly.

And then there was Ynarra. Madigan grinned and squeezed her finger lightly. "I appreciate your help, Ynarra."

She smiled and gave a slight curtsy, then stopped herself. She looked at Madigan in surprised embarrassment. He returned the smile and sent Ynarra into a poorly hidden fit of giggles. She turned and sped down the steps that led from the hidden entrance to the Crow's office. Madigan grinned after her, feeling light and airy, before turning and rapping quickly on the door.

"Enter," came the rough voice from within.

Madigan did as he was bid, lifting the small latch and silently entering the room. "Lord Crow," he said, inclining his head in a bow.

"Ah, Shadowborne." The Crow was seated at his desk, quill in hand. He dipped it in a nearby ink pot and did not look up. "One moment and I shall be with you."

He makes it sound like I asked him to come down here and not the other way around. Ignoring the seeming slight, Madigan entered and crossed to the decanter of wine. Pouring himself a glass, he approached the Measure that was set against the wall. The wisps of black and white within spun and whirled but never mingled. The black, though, something about it seemed different—darker—than he remembered. *Probably just my imagination.*

The Crow cleared his throat and Madigan turned just as the office door opened. One of the Crow's men, a runner Madigan had seen more of lately, entered. The Crow finished placing his seal on the document he had been writing and then handed it to the man.

"You know where this goes." It was not a question.

"Aye, my lord. I'll see it dispatched at once."

The Crow waved a hand and the man left. Madigan sipped at his wine and approached when the Crow beckoned him over.

Gesturing to the closing door, Madigan raised an eyebrow. "He seemed in a hurry. Important business, I take it?"

The Crow smiled his mirthless, toothy smile. "Very. A matter that concerns you, actually." Madigan shifted a bit at that and raised the glass to his lips. "Have a seat, Shadowborne." The Crow's tone was cool.

Madigan did as he was bid, a sudden wave of unease clouding his mind. "I hope I haven't outstayed my welcome already."

The Crow's harsh laughter grated on Mad's ears. "Far from it." The dark man leaned forward, slouching over his elbows as he peered across the table. "There is a war coming, young Shadowborne."

"That's hardly news, Crow."

The Crow sniffed and leaned back, disapproval plain upon his face. "You have grown rather familiar here, haven't you?"

"I prefer to think of it as"—Madigan smiled—"comfortable."

The Crow steepled his hands and nodded. "Yes, comfortable. Good. We shall need that."

I'm really getting tired of this man's vague mutterings. Madigan sighed. "Right. Listen, Crow. What's this all about? You've got me, alright? Fealty. It's what you wanted. So"—he spread his arms out wide—"what's all this, then? Why the wining and dining? You've never struck me as the type."

The Crow closed his eyes and shook his head. "You and your brother both have a penchant for speaking your minds without restraint."

"Yeah, well, I guess it's a family trait then."

The eyelids snapped open. "I daresay that I have taken a gamble on you, Madigan Davis. That I have assumed much of you."

"Well you know what they say about you when you assume." The Crow stared at Madigan blankly. *Or maybe you don't.* "That you make . . . never mind."

"Provisional command, Madigan."

"What? No, that's not what they say. What I meant was—"

"I know what you meant." The Crow smiled sardonically. "You were trained in battlefield tactics by your grandfather, yes?"

Madigan gave the Crow a wary eye. "To some degree, yes."

"And you are Shadowborne. One of only two known to exist at this time."

Madigan's thoughts drifted to Ileta. He had yet to receive word from her. *She's not going be happy about much of what's happened since we parted ways.* "I count three. Valmont."

The Crow ignored his words. "And you've sworn an oath. To the Thirteen. To the Nordoth. To Undermyre."

Madigan's lips drew to a thin line. He rolled his eyes. "Yeah, I hardly need reminding on that point."

"Provisional command," the Crow said again. "That was the document that was just dispatched to the war councils of Nordoth and Undermyre. You have been granted provisional command of the counteroffensive that shall be launched against Dorian Valmont and his Necrothanian horde."

Madigan paused mid-sip, his eyes flicking to the Crow's. "What?"

"The Nordoth does not sit idly while the peoples of this world suffer, Madigan." The Crow reached for his own glass of wine. "And you were bred for the battlefield, it would seem."

"You want me to lead an assault?" Madigan asked incredulously. "An assault on what? Where? None of us know a damn thing about where Valmont is or what he's planning. Hell, he's still trapped in Cascania." The Crow merely raised an eyebrow. "What, are you suggesting we go back *there* to hunt him?" Madigan shook his head. "That's insane."

"It is not your place to question, Commander. You swore an oath. It is your place to follow orders given." The Crow set his drink on the desk and let his gaze fall past Madigan to linger on the room. "Valmont will come to us."

"Why the hell would he do that?" *This day just got a whole lot more complicated. Why is everything here so goddam complicated?*

"You have much to learn about this citadel, Commander. Shifter shall see you educated, presently."

Madigan clapped his hands together. "Shifter, right, there you go. He's your man. He's far better suited for this. I mean, hell, isn't it what he already does, pretty much? Captain of the guard, or whatever?"

"Shifter will be otherwise occupied."

"With something more important than your march against Valmont?" Madigan swirled his wine in its glass, watching the legs stream down. "What the hell could that be?"

"The defense of this city, of course." The Crow stood and walked to the Measure, gazing at it. "Separate events across the world are converging, Madigan Davis. Undermyre, the Nordoth, we are at the heart of it. The battle shall be here, have no doubt of that."

Well that's just fan-freakin-tastic. "So, you're suggesting we let Valmont's force amass here—whenever that happens—and while he's distracted with the assault, I counterattack, is that it?"

The Crow traced his fingers along the glass surface of the Measure. "Something to that end. You shall see soon enough, Commander."

Madigan sighed and scratched his beard. "And I have no vote in this, I'm guessing?"

The Crow turned to him and smiled. "You swore an oath. One that I cannot say I recall you setting stipulations around."

"Not that there was room for any," Madigan muttered. "Fine. Provisional command, whatever the hell that ends up meaning."

"Excellent." The Crow turned. Madigan felt exposed beneath his gaze, a lab rat under the microscope. "Shall we, then?"

Madigan stood tentatively. "Shall we what?"

The Crow lurched toward the door and caught himself with a

gnarled fist. “It is time the people met their champion, Commander.”

What the hell? Before Madigan could speak, the door was thrown open and the Crow exited the room. The passage was framed by guards, much as it had been the day Madigan returned to the Nordoth.

What in the goddam hell is he up to this time? He had little time to ponder as he followed the dark-robed man from the chamber. When the Crow stepped into his seat at the head of the room, Madigan, who had been a few steps behind, finally understood.

The audience chamber was filled to the brim with people. Closest to the Crow’s seat were many with whom Madigan had recently dined, but beyond them stood a mass of people from all walks of life. People in ragged, worn clothes. People in mismatched plate armor and chain mail. Hunters. Bleary-eyed drunks. Children—Madigan couldn’t remember the last time he had seen children in the city. They all stared inquisitively at the raised platform upon which the Crow sat. Except that Madigan realized their eyes were not on the man who controlled the city, but planted firmly on him.

“God dammit,” he muttered under his breath.

“Good people of Undermyre.” The Crow’s voice carried across the hall. “It is now, as it has always been, the esteemed privilege of myself, as well as that of the Thirteen, to have been honored by you, charged as we are, with the defense and management of our humble home.” The Crow turned and smiled darkly at Madigan before going on. “Indeed, many things have occurred of late that have threatened our way of life. Our peace, as we have it, has been long and prosperous.”

Given the decay into which the city had fallen, Madigan was inclined to disagree.

“But ancient threats have reawakened. And, as such, ancient defenses have returned. The Borne, thought long-dead, have reemerged from the reaches of the Ways.”

A low murmur emerged from the crowd. The Crow quieted them instantly.

"It is true, the Borne live on despite the absence of their Guardians, brought low by the cruel madman, Dorian Valmont."

Another murmur raced through the crowd. The Crow let this one build, a thin smile creeping to his pale lips.

"Yes," the Crow said finally. "I speak of Dorian Valmont, for he, the trickster, the bringer of death and ruin, he is the threat of which I speak."

Madigan expected outcries from the crowd, something out of a Hollywood movie, but instead the people grew silent.

"With his mindless slaughter, his ceaseless quest to bring about the unmaking of all that is made, he will undoubtedly come to our gates. He will take from us all that is ours until he holds dominion over the peoples of Undermyre and beyond." The Crow took a beat. "Unless we stop him."

The Crow raised a hand and gestured. Again, all eyes turned to Madigan.

Dammit. Dammit, dammit, dammit. Madigan searched the crowd, but Ynarra was nowhere to be seen. Shifter stood to the right of the Crow's chair and an armed retinue of guards surrounded him. The space to the left of the Crow's seat, however, was vacant. He sighed and approached, feeling the hundreds of eyes watching him, studying him, scrutinizing him.

"I present to you Madigan Thorne, heir to the Master of Blades, defender of Undermyre, Shadowborne."

There was no fanfare, no eruption of applause, only the continued focus on Madigan. *What the hell do they want, a parlor trick?*

"The Borne live on," the Crow continued, "and they live on in service of the Nordoth. Undermyre, my friends, is safe."

"The Borne live on," came a voice from the middle of the crowd. It carried across the packed room, echoing against the walls, and yet the words were spoken softly. "You make it sound as though you had no part in their destruction."

The Crow's face, a moment ago so calm and composed, twisted in rage. Every single guard in the room tensed. Across from him, Madigan heard Shifter curse. *What's this all about?* Madigan scanned the crowd for whomever had spoken—something about the voice had seemed familiar. *Will? No, not Will. But . . .*

The crowd parted in hurried, stumbling awkwardness and the speaker stepped forward. As their attention turned to the man, the people closest to him began to tense and press against those who were moving more slowly. Madigan's hackles rose even before the man unwrapped the scarf that hid his face.

No, god dammit. No!

As ever, Dorian Valmont wore black. A long, weathered jacket with a high collar hung nearly to his knees. When the scarf was removed fully, his dark hair, flecked with blonde and hints of grey, fell to his shoulders. Mad could see the piercing blue eyes of the sorcerer even from this distance. He was armed with a sword on his hip, but what struck Madigan the most was the way the man's Shade moved with him. It seemed . . . sick. It was slow and its movements were thick—engine sludge and old oil. It bore none of the sinuous, ephemeral flow he had grown so accustomed to.

Silence followed the initial cries of dismay. The guards had all drawn their weapons, but none took so much as a single step toward Valmont. The man himself was smiling, letting his eyes linger on various aspects of the hall as he scanned it, even nodding politely to those who, by chance or sheer madness, happened to meet his eye.

Mad's throat felt tight. *Will was right. This man is evil.*

"Dorian," the Crow said in a neutral tone. His smile was polite and professional, but the look in his eyes was pure murder. *"Cth'nal feq quar'n."*

"*Cth'nal feq quar'n,* Crow." Valmont's smile was languid, lazy, and altogether unnerving. Madigan shuddered. "For now."

"Be about it, then." The tightness in the Crow's eyes had eased and now Mad could only see an impatient boredom. "Play to your audience."

Valmont's smile deepened and he stepped forward, away from the fearful mass. Madigan kept his Shade in a low cloud, pooled almost invisibly around his legs. He tensed, ready to spring as soon as he saw an opening. Valmont's gaze snapped to him and back to the Crow, and he gave a low, musical chuckle.

"This is no show of strength, old friend. My quarrel with you ended long ago. I am here but out of necessity."

The Crow waved a dismissive hand. "*Fel'naq,* Dorian."

Valmont's face fell. "As you would have it, then. My aims now are as they have ever been. It should, therefore, be no surprise to you why I've come."

The Crow sighed. "All these years and you still pursue them?" He shook his head. "You always were tenacious."

"I require the Nordoth."

Bushy eyebrows rose in amusement as the Crow eyed the man. "Do you, now?"

Valmont said nothing. His sluggish Shade bubbled and popped around him. *Gods, it's like a walking pestilence.* Mad felt disgusted just looking at it. *What the hell did this guy do to himself?*

The hall darkened and the crowd stirred nervously. *He's pulling,* Madigan realized. *The goddam bastard is pulling.* Without really knowing why, perhaps only to spite the man, Mad began to do the same.

Valmont sneered and snapped his attention to Madigan. For a second, he looked so familiar that Madigan was caught completely by surprise. *I know him. What the hell? Where from?* His train of thought was quickly interrupted, however, as the sorcerer easily ripped Madigan's control away. Valmont surged and released, sending a thunderous boom throughout the chamber. People cried out. The soldiers finally snapped to action, holding their weapons aloft and bearing down on Valmont. The man snickered and brushed his hand absently against the air. His Shade swept out and collided into the soldiers, sending every single one flying into the crowd beyond them.

Goddam, he's strong.

"Enough," the Crow barked. "I see your disregard for oaths has not changed."

Valmont raised a lazy eyebrow and spread his hands before spinning in a slow circle. "It appears to me that everyone is back on their feet." His smile held just a hint of cruelty. "There is no death to be seen." The smile widened, as though he were laughing at his own private joke. "Trust me, I would know."

"Trust you?" Madigan spat the words. *Damn you, you goddam bastard. Trust* you? *You killed my goddam grandfather.* "No, I don't think anyone here is that stupid."

The sorcerer looked once again at Mad. "Ah, the Shadowborne. I've heard just *so* much about you. I certainly hope that the stories don't disappoint."

Heard about me? Mad set his jaw and forced himself to meet the cruel blue eyes. "I've heard about you too, Bloodbane."

Valmont raised an eyebrow. "From our mutual friend, is it? No, of course not." He smiled and tilted his head. "Ah, yes. Jervin Thorne."

"Do not speak his name." *Mutual friend? It can't be.* Madigan fought to keep the quivering anger from his voice, to keep it cool and steady. *Don't let him goad you.* "You're not worth half what he was."

Dorian chuckled. "From the reports I gathered, half of him was all that remained in the end."

Madigan's rage got the best of him. His Shade roared to life. He flew down the steps and was very nearly upon Valmont before the Crow roared, "Stop!"

The force of the command drove Madigan to his knees. His

ears rang and, for the briefest of moments, he found himself struggling to move.

"*Enough*, I said!" The Crow swept his cool gaze from Valmont to Madigan. "Has it become such, with the Borne? Do you intentionally disregard your allegiances? Your oaths?" He sneered. "Another outburst, Valmont, and you shall be cast from these halls." He turned his gaze to Madigan. "And the same goes for you, Shadowborne."

Madigan froze. *There's that damn word again, cast.* He was only a short distance from Valmont. The man was even paler up close, the look of someone who hadn't seen the sun in years. He could see blue veins beneath the drawn skin. His eyes were red-rimmed and glassy. Despite his power, there was something sad about him, something detached. Madigan glared, angry at himself for the brief moment of pity. *Of course he's detached, look at what he's done to the world. Plus, he looks like a goddam corpse.* He stood down but did not drop his guard.

"Speak, Dorian. Tell us what you've come to say."

Valmont let his eyes wander from Madigan to the Crow. "I am not one to repeat myself, old friend."

"The Nordoth, is it?" Madigan said. He could feel the anger bubbling just beneath the surface, the rage building within him. "Like hell. Get the hell out of here."

Valmont snickered and shook his head. "Does this child speak for you, Crow?" The Crow said nothing. "Perhaps I need to explain further. I was not asking. I was informing." Valmont turned his smile to the crowd. "I require the Nordoth and, being gracious, am giving you fair opportunity to move elsewhere." He stepped back and walked in a slow circle as he spoke, pinning his gaze amongst those who were present.

"Hear me, denizens of Undermyre. The stories you have heard of me are false, lies spread by those who would deem themselves your master." He spread his hands out, palms up, and bowed his head. "I am no one's master. I am one of you, one of the people. And for you, the people, I grant this kindness: one year."

The liar speaks his lies. Madigan clenched his fists.

"One year, I give you. One year to recognize the error of your ways and join me in true freedom. I speak to the people as one of the people." He returned his gaze to the dais where the Crow sat silently, watching. "Take back your city from the rulers who have driven you into this state of disrepair and join me. Join me in creating a better world. Join me in freedom."

Without another word, Valmont turned and strode toward the doors and the guards who barred them. Madigan glanced at the Crow quickly. The hunched man gave him a slight nod but said nothing. The nod was all Madigan needed.

"Valmont," Madigan shouted. The figure, still being given a wide berth by the crowd, paused and turned his head back to Madigan. Mad clapped his hands together and fueled his Shade into his noctori. It crackled to life with a radiating pulse that he had never before felt from the blade. Absently keeping the blade fueled by his Shade, he surrounded himself in the rest and dropped into a ready stance. "You and I have unfinished business."

Valmont turned fully round to face him. Deep within his impassive rage, Mad felt terror course through his body as the dark man's eyes locked onto his. The Shade oozed out of him, clawing and pulling at the floor while Valmont returned to the center of the hall, his unblinking gaze fixed on the young Shadowborne.

"Another time, I think."

Before Madigan could react, Valmont's Shade surged out. Madigan stared in horror while the Shade filled the room, rising to the ceiling, pressing to the walls—coming straight for him. *It's not possible. No one has that much range.*

The vile darkness crashed into the crowded room. More than simply colliding with them, it covered them like tar. Madigan heard Shifter shouting orders. He glanced back and saw the Crow being hurried from the room by the commander. Then, the room descended into darkness. Valmont's Shade took Madigan.

Muffled screams and the sound of snapping bones turned Madigan's stomach. He couldn't see anything. He was surrounded by a darkness so pure, so absolute, that sight, light, seemed like a distant memory. Panic crept into him but he fought it down. *Not today, Valmont.*

He abandoned the noctori and drew his Shade back into him, balling up the fear and panic and rage into his center. Steeling himself, he surrounded the wild emotions with his Shade, pouring its power in on itself, folding the darkness over and over like a blacksmith working a blade.

Madigan pulled at the darkness that covered the room. It fought back at him, biting, tearing at his insides, white rapids crashing against rocks. Madigan was stuck between the two. *Dammit, Ileta, where are you when I need you?* Spurred on by the thought of his teacher, Madigan roared. The necrotic darkness was in his mouth, his nostrils. It was earthen bile, tasting of decay and sickness. Nevertheless, Madigan pulled.

A flicker. A faint crack. A black that was not so black. Some distant part of his brain, acting purely out of survival, clawed at it. He pulled and pulled more of the darkness into him and the crack widened and the faintest flicker of light appeared, blinding and terrible. Then, with a crash, the whole world came down around him.

Madigan inhaled fresh air like a drowning man surfacing at the last moment of life. The foul taste was still in the air, but the thick, oppressive darkness was gone. Every part of him hurt. It was as though his body had been sapped of its strength, leeched away by Valmont's putrid darkness.

Valmont.

Madigan's eyes shot open. He winced against the light but frantically pushed himself to his knees. He whirled, scanning the room. He was surrounded by bodies on the ground, some groaning, some weeping, some uncomfortably silent. But nowhere was Valmont to be seen.

Madigan cursed. His bones felt like they were on the verge of breaking. He coughed and doubled over from the pain. The salty, iron taste of blood filled his mouth. *What in the goddam hell was that thing?*

"One year, is it?" The Crow's words were filled with disappointment. Madigan struggled to turn his head, to find the man as he spoke. He was once again seated in his high seat with Shifter at his side. "Well. It looks like our young Shadowborne here has much to do in that time."

Madigan cursed. Or at least he meant to. Instead, he coughed once more. The room was spinning, again. The light was dwindling to a focused pinprick. Stars danced around the edges of reality.

He crashed to the ground and remembered no more.

33

THE SHATTERED WAYS

H*ow in the hell did I end up here?* Will pulled hard and drew the cutlass from the chest of a cultist before turning and using Flint to shatter the oncoming blade of another. *Is this really what you wanted for me, Grandda?*

His body ached more from habit than from true fatigue, the blood fangs saw to that. The joint line of Seekers and Lightborne was holding, miraculously. The Necrothanians were giving ground slowly as Will's forces pressed them into the tunnel. But with every enemy that fell, more arrived to take their place. The ground grew ever more uneven, corpses piling on the blood-slick ground.

Will and Rienne stood alongside the Seekers, pressing deeper into the cavern. The Lightborne, having come up far deeper within the network of tunnels thanks to Cephora, were not far off. Will could hear their assault and battle cries. They'd been right; the tunnels were key to invalidating the superior numbers of the Necrothanians. But they were running on limited time; he could also hear the fiery blasts from the Borne diminishing.

Used up. He grimaced as he took down another cultist. *The batteries are almost tapped.*

There seemed to be no end to the enemy. It was like a hive. The scouts and exterior encampment had only been the drones. Now the threat had grown, they were swarming. *We need to end this soon. We need to find out what these damn bastards are searching for.*

Shyldd battled nearby. Driving his cutlass through the chest of a cultist, Will could not help but wonder how much use he and the other Lightborne actually were to this group of death dealers. In this proximity, his Flare would have done more harm than good. And watching Shyldd battle, Will was not even certain that his grandfather could have overcome the large man. His every blow sent a body flying backward. He wielded his longsword with the control and grace of a master. He was a wall in and of himself, allowing no cultist to gain ground.

Will grit his teeth as he barely managed to parry an incoming strike. *Just have to keep pushing.* He fell back a few steps and allowed the Seekers to fill his position. The Seekers moved expertly amongst each other. They cut through cultist and reaper alike with barely a pause between targets. Watching them fight, Will was reminded of his grandfather—the speed, the seemingly omniscient deflections and counter cuts. The very walls were an asset to them, a weapon in and of themselves as the warriors launched themselves from them or sent bodies crashing into them. They were naturals to the fight.

Yet they were not impervious to damage. He saw their fatigue wearing on them, saw the blood pouring from bodies. He cursed. Despite the Seekers' skill, at least eight had fallen so far. The Lightborne seemed to have lost a similar number. It was hard to tell exact numbers in the chaos of battle. The number should have been insignificant in the wake of the death wrought by their hands, but still the Necrothanian hordes came on. The number of dead enemy did little to even the scales.

The number of dead. Will whirled and scanned the area. Enemy bodies were strewn about, bloodied and trampled in their recent deaths. *Very recent deaths.* Glancing back at the Seekers, Will sheathed his weapons and drew his blood fangs. He knelt and began draining bodies. He tugged at the flows from the bloodstones, bringing forth the energy transference stored within and sending it out amongst the nearby Seekers. Looks of surprise shone upon their faces, but none of the pain that Rienne had experienced when he used the fangs to heal her.

It's working. Gods, it's working. Will stared in awe as he wove the flows amidst the Seekers, an energizing boon. Renewed, the Seekers fought with doubled ferocity. He desperately wished he could do the same for the Borne, but to do that to them during the course of battle was to guarantee their failure. No, for now they would have to suffer their wounds.

Restoring himself amongst the flows, Will prepared to move back to the front line but then he hesitated. There were warriors aplenty, but no one could heal them the way he could. *A surgeon's toolkit, Cephora said.* He could be that. He could support them and keep them safe. *This is how we get the upper hand.*

Shyldd roared and, as one, the Seekers pressed forward and broke the Necrothanian line. The cultists scattered, scrambling back at the sudden charge. They fled around a curve in the tunnel. The Seekers chased after them. Hot on their heels, Will saw that the passage ended only a short distance away, opening up into a larger cavern. *That better be the damn place.*

He saw a flash of lightning tear through the darkness of the vast chamber. He smiled. The others had already reached the cavern. The Necrothanians were caught between them.

Nearly there. Just a little bit farther and—

"Noctis, come quickly!" Rienne shouted. "We've got them on the run!"

A torrent of blue fire tore through the cavern. Somehow, despite the fury and cries of battle, Will heard the roaring laughter of Jero din'Dael. *We're close*. Will wiped the fangs on the blood-spattered robes of a dead cultist and sheathed them. He raced to the end of the tunnel where the exhausted Lightborne filled the room with their Flares.

The battle was taking place along the lip of what seemed to be a large crater. The crater, however, ended in a sheer drop-off that had no visible bottom. A long, narrow bridge connected the edge to a small island of rock within the center of the abyss. And there, in the center of the stone island, sat an ancient door. Will paled.

"Light's fall," Shyldd cursed at his side, his thoughts obviously mirroring Will's. "That's a bloody Waygate."

The Necrothanians had found another entrance to the Ways.

He did not have time to dwell on the discovery. The Borne who had supported him up to this point were finally exhausted, their Flares expended. Steeling themselves, they drew their blades and charged alongside the Seekers into the fray. Will's gaze darted over the opposing forces. They were still outnumbered.

Will braced to leap down to the fight. But before he could move, his key screamed angrily at his chest with a force that drove Will to his knees. Will's hackles rose and he grabbed Flint. Something was wrong.

A terrible scream echoed through the cavern. Will saw one of the Borne—Letrhe, his name was—fly through the air. He'd been impaled through the chest and he crashed against the ceiling of the cavern before falling to the ground. Will was trembling, but not from the terrible death nor from the grip of his key. Whatever had impaled Letrhe had been made of pure Shadow.

"Shadowborne!" someone screamed off to the side. "There's a Shadowborne among them!"

Valmont. He's here.

Will forced himself to his feet and stared at the mass of Shade that enveloped the Necrothanian force. They poured over din'-Dael's Lightborne like a wave, cries of pain erupting from within.

His key screamed again. Will's Flare rippled along his cutlass and Flint's broken blade. He peered through the throng and followed the storm of motion to the heart of its source. *There!* He found the Shadowborne, noctori dancing gracefully and brutally through the air, cutting down all in their path without pause—Borne and Necrothanian alike.

Will's heart raced as the Shadowborne moved with brutal efficiency. *Too small to be Dorian Valmont.* Realization dawned on Will. "Aurellaine."

Pausing as though she heard him, Aurellaine Valmont whirled and met his eyes from across the cavern. Her face was covered by a shroud, her head covered by a hooded cloak. She gripped her noctori and stared Will down through wide eyes that were black as her Shade. Rage boiled within Will as he thought of the years she had manipulated his brother under the guise of the false Ileta. *No longer.*

Will Flared and stepped forward. Aurellaine held out a hand to him, fingers splayed. Despite the distance, he could have sworn that she winked. Then she closed her fist. Fire erupted. Everything touched by her Shade instantly turned to ash, friend and foe alike. The fire was black, like Shadow, but there was no mistaking the power of Radiance at work. The clouded darkness of the Shade darkened to a deep purple and black lightning spun within the shroud of death.

He had seen this power before. Will knew it. It was his. *She's like me.*

"By the Hesperawn . . ."

Will turned to see Rienne at his side, blood covering her face and arms. Will grasped her arms, forcing her to look at him. "Rienne, get out of here. Get as many of the Borne as you can and get them out of here."

She tore her gaze away from the wave of death and met his eyes. Her own were brimming with tears. "I was wrong. I said no one could be both. But I was wrong." She raised a bloody hand and placed it on his cheek. "I'm sorry."

"Rienne, you've got to—"

The roar of the blast knocked Will back a few steps. Rienne was caught by it, full force. The brunt of it took her just beneath her right arm. The lightning-laced shadow tore through her torso, blasting away armor and flesh alike. Rienne's eyes widened, and she gave a soft "oh!" before her expression grew vacant and slack. She crumpled to the ground, folding unnaturally to the side as Will cried out. Her head hit the ground hard but the vacant eyes did not even blink.

"No!" Will shouted, dropping to his knees. "No, gods, please. No . . ." He scrambled for the blades at his waist, reaching for the flows of the bloodstones, but they passed over Rienne like oil over water.

Chaos erupted in the chamber as Will hovered over Rienne's dead body. She was twisted and broken, her lifeless eyes still seeming to stare up into his own. They seemed more surprised than anything, like her last moments had been filled with disbelief rather than fear. His hand clasped at unresponsive fingers.

Another raging surge from his key sent Will spasming to the ground. For a moment he lay there, letting the pain take him. His shoulders shook, his body wracked by so much death. Yet despite everything, his eyes remained dry.

Aurellaine.

Mechanically, Will pulled himself to his feet. He'd seen the same power that Aurellaine Valmont wielded when he'd faced —*killed*—Senraks. It explained the blast of Radiance that disabled the van just before the fight. *Very well, then.* If Aurellaine was Borne of both Radiance and Shadow, then that meant that somehow, somewhere within him, Will was too.

A cracking sound from above tore him from his thoughts. He glanced up and leapt out of the way of a stone plummeting from the roof of the cavern. The huge slab slammed onto the ground where Rienne's body lay, covering her remains in rubble.

Furious anger filled Will. Hands clenched into fists, he whirled and found himself face to face with Jero din'Dael. He was bloody and his skin was ravaged, fresh wounds covering his already marred arms.

"Your fangs, use them."

"Aurellaine," Will choked out. "She—"

Din'Dael's slap cut off the words. "Forget the woman, William. The blood fangs, quickly!"

Will stared at the man in surprise but obliged him. He swept the flows over din'Dael in a wave. The Revenant cried out, wincing and recoiling against the pain, but he stayed on his feet. In a moment, the worst of the wounds had faded but din'Dael still shuddered beneath the flows.

"Not . . . me . . . you fool."

Realization dawned on Will. He spun and raced to the ledge, surveying the scene. The Lightborne were nearly in full retreat. The Seekers, exhausted and outnumbered, were slowly being overwhelmed. Aurellaine stood across the cavern from him, no longer involved in the battle. In fact, she seemed remarkably disinterested in it. She clutched something in her hands, an aged stone box.

Sliding down the slope, Will closed the distance to his allies. He neared the Waygate and, still running, tugged at the flows of the bloodstones. As soon as he got within range, he pushed out with the invisible tendrils and set his focus on Shyldd. The fierce expression of shock and renewal within the burly man was such a stark contrast to din'Dael's recent cringing that, in any other circumstances, Will would have burst out laughing.

But this was no time for laughter. He whirled from Shyldd as the huge warrior brought his great sword down through two cultists at once. Will tugged the flows from Shyldd and careened them into a nearby Seeker whose arm hung limp and bloody at his side. It twitched and stuttered, then sprang back to life. Will wasted no time, swiftly moving back and forth down the Seekers' line. The reinvigorated warriors pressed forward, their battle fury driving the Necrothanians ever farther back.

Feeling their power ebb, Will began to refill the bloodstones from the corpses of the fallen. He showed no discrimination between friend or foe when his fangs met flesh. The Lightborne, having fallen back when the Seekers pressed forward, stared at him in horror. *The lives of the fallen urge on those of the living,* he told himself. *They would want to aid their allies.*

Will brought his blades down into another corpse while the fighting raged on. Compelled by something he couldn't explain, he glanced down. He froze. He'd just plunged his fangs into Letrhe's lifeless body. The pang of loss smashed into him again, Rienne's empty eyes and charred corpse from whatever Aurellaine had done to her. *Aurellaine . . .* Will spun.

She was attempting to slip away in the chaos. The dark-clad woman stood apart from the Necrothanians save for two reapers. They towered over her, twisted, broken forms from the reaches of his nightmares. *They're guarding her,* he realized. *Her and the box.*

Dread sank its cruel fingers into Will's throat. *We need that box.*

The reapers who followed her were the only additional protection she had. Will spun, searching for din'Dael, but the Revenant was nowhere to be found. But he did see Shyldd. The large man had stepped back from the front line, dragging one of the Lightborne behind him. Will saw that the Borne was young, someone he didn't know, but the boy was missing his leg from the knee down.

Will darted to the pair, whipping the power of the bloodstones onto the boy's shattered limb. The Lightborne screamed in agony, then quickly faded from consciousness. Shyldd glanced up as Will raced toward him.

"Shyldd," he shouted over the thunderous roar of battle. "Shyldd, we've got to stop her."

The Seeker gaped at Will. "Aye, but you're a bloody sight, Davis." Shyldd propped the young Lightborne up against a rock and laid a hand on the unconscious boy's shoulder. "You'll survive, son."

"We've got to stop her!" Will shouted again. "She's trying to get away."

Shyldd stiffened suddenly and turned his attention back to Will. "Her? You mean that bloody witch? There's nothing for it. She's behind the line and those bastards are making quite the stand of it."

Will glanced back at Aurellaine. Realization dawned on him. "Behind the line and making for the Waygate."

"Damn!" Shyldd wiped blood from his forehead with his arm but only succeeded in smearing it. "Whatever it is she's clutching at, we shan't be interested in her making away with it."

Will thought quickly, eyes flicking about the battlefield. "Can you get word to Cephora?"

Shyldd eyed him. "Aye, I may be able to do that."

"She can get us there."

Beneath the bloodied face, Shyldd's flashing grin looked unnaturally white. "Aye, that she can."

Will turned to stare at the retreating Aurellaine. Rage fueled him. The air was alive with fire and static. *You don't get to win. Not today.*

34
BORNE RISING

Shyldd ran for the front line. The Lightborne had rejoined the Seekers, their Flares expended but not their strength of arms. Sending one last wave of power from the bloodstones over his allies, Will scrambled back against the crater's wall. He could see din'Dael's forces in the distance, pressing the Necrothanians back into Shyldd's path.

We're going to survive this.

Will's key went wild. A split-second later, the air crackled and boomed with thunder. Will clapped his hands to his ears and ducked, sparing only the briefest glance toward Aurellaine. Again, she had unleashed whatever devilish power it was that she wielded. But rather than aiming for the combined force of Seekers and Lightborne, she had aimed directly for the ceiling of the cavern.

Eyes widening in horror, Will stared as the roof cracked. He held his breath—*it'll hold. Come on, hold, hold*—but, in slow motion, the crack spread. Bits of stone began to rain down. Will cried out, shouting for his allies to fall back, but none seemed to hear him. The cracks spread and the roof split into giant, deadly boulders. Too late, those below realized what was happening. Stones plummeted, crushing bodies indiscriminately. A cloud of dust plumed throughout the cavern and covered the crater, obscuring the Waygate.

Will coughed and sputtered into the folds of his cloak, keeping his face buried. His ears rang from the deafening roar of falling stone. He shook his head and looked around. The dust was so thick he could hardly see anything. The eerie silence that followed was broken by pain-filled cries and the occasional trickle of stones falling against themselves. There was no movement to be seen, not from the Necrothanians or his own people. All were buried under the stones.

But not Aurellaine.

Will saw the silhouette of the woman creeping away from the rubble. Only one of her reaper guards remained with her, the other having been crushed by the falling ceiling. Fury flooded through him.

"William," Cephora's voice coughed from nearby. "Wait for us."

He spun, the power pouring forth from the blood fangs before he even laid eyes on her. Cephora breathed deep when the flows took her, letting the rejuvenating power cascade over her. She wasn't alone, Will saw. Grimy from blood and dust, she and Shyldd both stumbled toward him. But no one else.

"Shyldd, did anyone—"

"No time to worry for that now." He was bleeding profusely from the side of his face and his left eye was red and bloodstained. He spat red on the ground. "We've got to move quickly."

Will moved the healing energy from Cephora to Shyldd. Barely had the wound upon his face healed than the flow ran dry. Will grit his teeth. *Typical.* "They're empty."

"It was enough," Cephora said. Shyldd nodded at her words.

Will sheathed the blood fangs and drew Flint and the cutlass. He gripped the blade and rolled it in his hand. Flint tingled against his palm, beating in time with the pulsing of the key at his chest. He could feel Aurellaine's eyes fixed on them. "The box. Whatever she's got, we get it away from her."

"Aye." Shyldd nodded. Aurellaine made a curt gesture. The creature at her side turned toward them, putting Aurellaine at its back. "That's quite the beastly reaper she's got there with her."

Cephora's laugh quickly turned into a cough, but she smiled nonetheless. "That, Shyldd? I'm sure Will can handle it."

"No." Will's glare was fixed firmly on Aurellaine's retreating figure. Rienne's death was etched into his mind. Aurellaine's lying and manipulation of his brother fueled the rage. *She pays. Now.* "I'm going after Valmont."

Cephora's bloodied smile turned into a frown. Before she could speak, Shyldd hefted his blade and spoke.

"Aye, well. You've got the Relic. Seems we'll be on the bloody Necrothanian then."

"The Relics." Cephora cursed. "Will, I know what you're thinking. If that box *is* a Relic, whatever you do—don't take it."

Will snapped his head back around to her. "What? Why the goddam hell not?"

"Because it will kill you," said a hollow, slurring voice.

All three turned. Jero din'Dael, Revenant of Light, limped toward them. His left arm trembled, the emerald glow from his hand flickering, crushed fingers unable to make a fist. Worse, though, was his face. In his mind's eye, Will saw the man who killed his mother, saw Madigan's baseball bat colliding with his skull. Din'Dael was in much the same condition. His left cheek hung torn along his jaw and Will could see the Lightborne's teeth through the gaping wound.

"Jesus, Jero," Will said. "The fangs, they're tapped. I can't—"

"Go." Din'Dael spat a gob of blood and teeth to the ground. "Kill her, but do not let your blood touch the Relic."

"My blood?" Will suddenly remembered the lesson. *Blood will bind a Relic to a man. But attempt to bind oneself to multiple will result in the force of the powers obliterating the host.* He realized that he had no handle on which blood was his own and which was that of the cultists he'd slain or allies he'd tried to save. The power of Flint coursed through him, urging him onward. "Dammit. I'll keep my distance."

Din'Dael fell to his knees, coughing. He winced, sword clanging to the stone floor as he supported himself with his good hand. "Go, William."

"Aye, we'll pry the damn box from the fiend's corpse, shall we?" Shyldd said. His eyes hardened. He hefted his blade and took off running across the fallen stone, bearing straight for the Necrothanian.

Cephora dropped to a knee and set her hand upon the ground. Instantly, a rift appeared on the ground before them. "I'll get you as close to the Waygate as I can. Go, Will." Her tone brooked no argument. "There is little time."

Will's dread at the thought of more rifting was nothing compared to his desire to stop Aurellaine. Without a word, he stepped forward. The world became a swirling cacophony of angry wind and roaring darkness. He tumbled through the void, falling—and then felt himself slamming against stone.

His head swam. Absently, he reached for the flows of the bloodstones only to come up short. *Right. Empty.* Cephora had done it though; Will was leaning upon the stone base of the Waygate, the door at his back. With dry, scratchy eyes he saw Aurellaine Valmont a short distance away on the narrow stone bridge. Beyond her, he saw Cephora racing toward where Shyldd battled the reaper. For Will, though, there was nowhere to maneuver, nowhere to run.

"Aurellaine," he croaked, steadying himself. He forced himself upright. "Or perhaps you'd prefer that I still call you Ileta?"

She said nothing. The woman's face was hidden, but she stared at him through pitch black, furious eyes. *Shorter than I remember,* Will mused. But, then again, he'd barely had a chance to assess her before she'd betrayed them. He raised his cutlass and leveled the point at her chest. Flaring, hot lightning coursed from his body and sparked along the blade. Aurellaine took a few short steps toward him, raising her noctori.

"I owe you a death. You killed someone I cared about," Will hissed.

Aurellaine knelt and placed the box behind her, then balled the newly freed hand into a fist. Yellow crackling fire spat along its surface. Will's gaze fell to the fist. *So, she can Flare then, control them independently. Shadowborne and Lightborne both.* He smiled cruelly. "We've got something in common, you and I."

A flicker of uncertainty crossed her eyes. Then her Shade struck him hard, a brute force in the gut. Will was flung backward and slammed against the ancient door. He slumped to the ground, gasping for breath, but she was upon him. Her Shade whirling about her, Aurellaine struck, the noctori singing in her left hand. Will barely got Flint up in time to deflect the blow. Aurellaine easily rolled around the broken tip of his blade and lunged forward with her flaming fist, catching Will's exposed side.

The force of the blow drove him back again, but he had no time to worry about the damage. She was on him again—a dagger now in her off-hand—lashing out again and again. Will managed to deflect the attacks with his cutlass, the left-handed opponent robbing him of much of his usual strategy. Aurellaine did not let up, stringing her attacks together in lithe, swift movements. It was all Will could do to defend—noctori meeting Flint, dagger meeting cutlass.

Will's side roared from where her flaming fist had struck. *Get your head together, you know how to fight.* He backpedaled, Flaring and sending out a blast of lightning. Aurellaine paused her assault to deftly step out of the way of the strike, but it gave Will seconds of precious time. Removed briefly from the relentless onslaught, he quickly regained his footing and set himself to task. The years of training took over. She was left-handed and he quickly adapted to her movements, a mirror of his own. *Hanging guard against downward cut. Inside guard against her outside. Watch her point work.*

And why the hell isn't she using her Shade? Why the hell is she holding back?

He'd seen this woman obliterate a mass of fighters in the blink of an eye. Seen her blend Shadow and Radiance together into strange, terrifying destruction. A million questions suddenly leapt into his mind, but he could afford no distraction. Aurellaine pressed him again.

Holding back because her father wanted us alive, Mad and me. Alive and together. Will groaned inwardly. *Jesus, Mad was right. What the hell does he want from us?*

Will certainly didn't intend to find out. Drawing on the power within Flint, he feinted high with his blade and Flared hard. His key screamed against his chest with the power of the burst, but another bolt of lightning shot forth from the hand that held the Relic and took Aurellaine in the leg. She did not cry out in pain. She hissed in fury.

The air around them grew hazy, her Shade dissipating and filling the space. The smell of electricity filled the air. Aurellaine cast her noctori aside and the weapon winked out of existence.

Will held his weapons defensively. *She's too far to lunge at. I'd never make it.*

There was only one thing left. Staring at Aurellaine's hazy, masked face, he flung the cutlass to the ground between them.

"You didn't see Senraks fall, Aurellaine." He moved Flint to his right hand. "You were off somewhere with your father, I'm sure." She said nothing, but Will could see the smile in her eyes. He tried to calm his rapidly beating heart as he drew a blood fang in his free hand.

"If you had seen it, you'd be much, much more concerned right now."

Steeling himself, Will drew upon Flint's power with all the strength he could manage. At the same moment, he plunged the blood fang into his leg, just as he had when facing Senraks. The floodgates of pain and fiery fury burst open and filled his being. His insides became white-hot coals. Blisters popped and cracked on his blackening skin. *Not real, not real.* He cried out. The agony filled his world, but it did not distract him enough to make him miss seeing the fear take hold of Aurellaine.

Within the maelstrom, he found the power he sought. Roaring, he grabbed at it and found a fount of unyielding, maddened force. He pulled at the power and it surged through him. The darkness of the cavern evaporated. Aurellaine's Shade vanished. Channeling the power through Flint, he loosed a blast of blackened fire at the woman. The force of the outward blast, empowered by the Relic, hit Will like a truck and sent him flying backward into the door once more. The blackened, swirling blast went wide, crashing into the wall of the abyss. Sheets of rock and debris showered down into the dark depths.

What little bit of Aurellaine's face Will could see paled. She stumbled backward, all thought for killing Will seemingly forgotten. She whirled and lunged for the small chest. Will braced himself and launched another attack.

The chest, however, was open. And empty.

Will gasped and barely managed to steer the second eruption of power away from Jero din'Dael. Aurellaine Valmont stood frozen, staring at the Relic held gingerly in din'Dael's hands. Will, attempting to stem the flow of raw power within Flint, realized the delicacy of the situation. If either his or din'Dael's blood touched the Relic, it would kill them. But Aurellaine, if she was unbound . . .

"Kill us, William!" din'Dael cried out. "Take us both!"

Not another one, Will's heart pounded. *Not another—*

Aurellaine lashed out, noctori winking back into existence and thrusting for din'Dael's heart. Will bellowed and unleashed the clouded, swirling mass of power. It collided into Aurellaine just before her blade found home, but the cry of agony from din'-Dael fueled Will's rage all the more. Will raced forward, striking out again. Aurellaine whirled, her terrified eyes meeting Will's. The blast took her full on, sending her tumbling over the path into the abyss. Jero, face bleeding anew from a gaping, empty eye socket, stumbled backward and collapsed. The carefully wrapped bundle fell from his hand toward the chasm.

Fang still lodged in his leg, Will lunged. He closed blood-covered fingers around the small metal object. An astonishing roar filled his head. He heard a woman scream far below him. Furious laughter, madder than din'Dael's, drove him to the brink of insanity. His left hand shriveled and cracked around the surge of energy. Flint, a lightning rod in his other hand, set his entire arm aflame. All the while, Will's key burned into his chest, embedding himself in his sternum in a blaze of agony.

The world burned away into ash and dust. Distantly, as though from some great height, Will watched his body shrivel and wither.

This is how I die, were the last words he knew.

35

SEPARATE PATHS

"Will."

Within the void, the voice was a sinister hiss.

"Come back, Will. I know you're alive."

Something bright danced just beyond the void. He didn't want to approach it; he knew it would be painful. *Not the light. Not what's within it.* Something rough and wet was scraping against him. A foul stench was upon the air, stale breath and iron.

"Come back to me, Will. You promised."

The darkness . . . I can't. The promise though, what promise? What was the voice saying? His mind started to work, started to piece together all that had happened. *Eyes, Will. Open your eyes.*

Will did as the voice commanded. Hints of memory came back to him. With it came pain. Even in the covered darkness, the light was too bright. He shied away from it.

Hard fingers dug into his jaw. "No, you don't get to do that. Come back to me."

That voice . . .

"Morella?" His voice was a croak of dust and ash. He coughed. "Morella, where—"

"Shh, my love. You're alive. I've got you."

Will faded back into unconsciousness.

When next the world returned, it was not Morella's face that he saw. One solitary eye stared back at him. Where the other should have been sat a blood-soaked cloth, tied behind the man's short hair. Unflinching, the remaining eye held fear and uncertainty and anger. The eye dropped from his face to stare at something Will couldn't see, then returned to meet his gaze.

"What the hell are you?" the voice spat.

That voice, I know that voice. But he couldn't place it. Every thought brought a burning pain and wracked whatever consciousness remained to him. He broke out into dry, rough coughs. Something grated in his lungs, a cat shredding the tissue within.

Something tingled against his chest before fading into a warm balm, covering his limbs. Cool, soothing music filled his mind. *Just breathe,* the music seemed to say.

Will breathed.

"I think it is safe to assume that Valmont is *not*, in fact, as trapped in Cascania as the young Borne would have had us believe."

Will cracked open crust-laden eyes. The light from nearby torches was glaring and painful. He clamped his eyes shut once more. His face felt tight and thin. *Just breathe,* he repeated the mantra to himself for the umpteenth time. Who was it who told him that? He couldn't remember.

Remember . . .

Remember what? What was going on?

"Aye, well. I'd say that he was a tad bit limited in his understanding of the Ways, Cephora. Do not fault him for it."

Shyldd. He's a Seeker. He—

Memory came crashing back to Will like air pouring from a vacuum. The battle by the Waygate. The countless dead. The uncontrollable power. The fall of Aurellaine Valmont. Jero din'-Dael losing the Relic that she had been protecting.

The Relic . . .

He forced his eyes open again, mentally prepared for the torchlight this time. "The Relic," was what he tried to say, but his voice had been stolen away, replaced by a wheeze.

"Quiet, Shyldd! He's waking." There was a rustle of movement. "Send for the girl, she'll be wanting to know he survived."

Will could see snow falling from where he lay. As if an afterthought, his body began shivering and he gave a sharp inhale at the pain that accompanied it. Every movement felt like he was rolling on crushed glass. But he had to move. He had to *know.*

"Ever the astute Earth Warder," came a voice filled with spite.

Jero. Will's mind connected. He turned his head to the source and saw the battered, one-eyed man. Will nearly flinched at the look of rage that poured from him. Jero din'Dael was still covered in blood, but it had dried and cracked against his skin. His face was only inches away from Will's and the smell of the ravaged wounds on it turned Will's already shaky stomach. Jero stared at Will like he was a wild animal, ready to snap at any moment.

"How . . ." This time the word formed correctly. The rest of the thought was lost in another fit of wheezing and coughing. Reflexively, he brought up his left hand to cover his face and winced at the pain. Then he froze. Clutched within fingers stained with blood was a rectangular object with rounded corners. He could sense nothing from it, however. It seemed completely innocuous. Nonetheless, his fingers didn't respond when he tried to open them. Will's heart began to race.

"Calm yourself, Will. Here." Cephora laid a small bundle on the makeshift cot. "Your blood fangs. The stones have been replenished, to an extent. Use them."

"Carefully," snarled din'Dael. His eyes had still not left Will.

At the mention of the fangs, Will was suddenly and acutely aware of a raging pain in his leg. Triggered by the sudden return of that pain, dizziness washed over him. But within the spell he could still feel the faint flows of the bloodstones swirling nearby. He drew on them and collapsed back while the restoration took place. The pain in the leg eased. The overwhelming fatigue lessened. Gradually, the cracked, ashen dryness in his lungs dissipated. But his fingers still wouldn't open.

Will forced himself to sit up, suppressing the thought of the foreign object he held in a death grip. Absently, his fingers went to the key at his chest—but it was nowhere to be found. Panic gripped him. He scrabbled at his chest but could find no trace of it. *Burned away,* he remembered. *Burned away at the end.* And yet . . . yet it *was* there. He could feel the biting tingle of it reverberating against his breast.

Glancing down, he saw Flint lying against his side. He dropped his free hand from the absent key and closed his fingers around the hilt, taking a deep breath and allowing its power to course through him. Din'Dael leapt to his feet, prepared to strike at any moment. Within the small tent were Shyldd and Cephora as well, but no sign of anyone else. Will dreaded the question, but he had to ask.

"How many?"

"Many." Cephora was watching him almost as intently as din'-Dael. "Two-thirds of the Seekers. Three-quarters of the Lightborne."

Gods, so many. The losses hung on the air. Will saw the weight of them on the faces of those near him. *But it wasn't their plan that led us into that deathtrap. It was mine.* Will closed his eyes and fought back the wave of despair. "Morella?"

"She made it."

"Aye, she's barely left your side."

Will nodded and let out a slow breath of relief. *Not a fever dream, then.* "Aurellaine? The Necrothanians?"

"Routed." Shyldd took a step closer. "Their surviving numbers are even fewer than our own, thanks to the actions of that Borne creature. She herself took a nasty tumble into the abyss."

"Not into the Waygate? You're sure?"

"We are certain, William," din'Dael said. He looked like a cat about to pounce. "I was there."

"I know, Jero. Thank you. I—"

"Should be dead." The air crackled with static. "Should be worse than dead. Why aren't you dead, William Davis? Explain yourself."

"Leave him alone," came a frantic shout. Will turned to look but was immediately buffeted by Morella's arms encircling him and pulling him close. "Oh, Will, thank the gods."

She began peppering him with kisses and squeezing him tighter and tighter. Will recoiled at the sudden, overt display of affection. *What the hell? This isn't like her at all.* "I'm fine, Morella," he managed to say above her smothering. "Just—stop, really—I'm okay."

"It was *me*, Will. This was all my fault." She interlaced her fingers into Will's free hand and rested her head on his shoulder. "I'm so sorry."

Will tensed. "What was—"

"The Necrothanians." Cephora was visibly annoyed by Morella's display. "She thinks they knew about this place because of her."

"My research," Morella said quietly. She huddled into Will even closer. Her strange, frantic affection waning, it felt good to have her there—a small kindness against the weight of the dead. "When I was . . . taken. It has to be. They—that *woman*—must have pieced something together that I missed or . . . I don't know. But why else would they have moved now and never before?"

"Why indeed," din'Dael said. He spat on the ground and turned his feral gaze to Morella. "Blast your damn research, girl."

"None of us could have known, Jero," Will croaked defensively. "None of us could have done a damn thing."

Jero din'Dael snapped his attention back to Will. "Nothing indeed, is it? Interesting to hear from"—he waved a hand in the air—"what? What shall I call you now? What you did in there was not borne of Radiance."

"No, it wasn't." The words came from Shyldd, who had been silent for some time. "It was something different. Something unique."

Morella bristled and squeezed Will's hand. He met her eye and she shook her head. "It's nothing," she whispered softly. "I just don't like them talking about you as if you're not you, is all." He squeezed her hand back.

"Different, yes." There was a twitch in the corner of din'Dael's eye. "But unique? Hardly. The rest of you saw, same as I. The boy's power was matched by one other in that cavern." He spun to Shyldd, rage pouring from him like a physical force. "You know something of this, Seeker?" He rose to his feet, opening his arms wide and speaking sarcastically. "Please, then. *Won't* you educate the poor masses?"

"Jero, come on," Will said gently. "We all lost today."

"Bah." Din'Dael waved a hand dismissively. "But we gained so much more, young . . . halfbreed? Is that what I ought to call you?"

"Jero—"

"We recovered a Relic of Antiquity, William. The cost is nothing compared to the gain." The words were direct and harsh, but not cruel. "Had Dorian acquired it, the war would be all but lost. We have the advantage. And yet"—he cocked his head to the side—"and yet there is *you*, William Thorne. Are you ours? Are you theirs? Or are you something else entirely? What other tricks are you hiding up your sleeves, I wonder?"

Will held up the object in his hand and stared at it. *A Relic of Antiquity. We were right.* Some feeling was beginning to return to his frozen fingers, a biting tingle. A warm pulse, like a heated blanket, emanated from the Relic. His fingers twitched. Again, he tried to open them and failed, but he saw the pinky twitch. *Just a matter of time, then.*

"Enough, din'Dael," Cephora snapped. "None of us know what he is or how he's still alive. But he is." She looked over at Will and narrowed her eyes. "There are answers within the holds of Greygarde. I do not know if they are the answers to this particular query, but we shall take the boy there."

"Don't you think it would be better to investigate further here?" Will said. "At the very least, we need to know how Valmont broke into the Ways. What if he's doing it elsewhere?"

Jero din'Dael cracked his neck and rolled his shoulders back. A visible change came over the man. He stood taller and the fury seemed to leave his eyes. The maddening, lackadaisical smile returned to his face. "Then he's wasting valuable time and giving us an opportunity to regroup and kill him." He threw his head back and laughed.

What the hell? "Jero—"

Will was cut off with a sharp gesture from his mentor.

"No, William. Much as it pains me to agree with her, my old friend Cephora is correct." Jero broke out into a fit of chuckles. "My, how the world works. Our plans have not changed. The Lightborne move for the Nordoth. You shall accompany the Seekers to Greygarde and join us presently." Despite the laughter, Jero seemed strained. "Determine the cause of all these things there."

Why is he so adamant about making his stand in the Nordoth?

"Agreed," Cephora said. "We'll take the boy. We'll return to

Greygarde and retrieve what information we are able, then depart for Undermyre."

"Do I get a goddam say in this?" Will snapped. All eyes turned to him.

"No," Cephora and din'Dael said in unison. Shyldd gave a low "hmph," while Morella bristled again at his side.

"It is settled then." Din'Dael clapped his hands. "I'll retrieve the balance of my forces and we shall rendezvous with the Crow." He laughed again and shook his head. "Ah, yes. This shall be an event to remember, I'm certain."

"It's settled then." Cephora stood and brushed back her cloak. "We'll leave at once."

"Already?" Will said incredulously. "Shouldn't we—"

"Let's just go, Will." Morella sighed heavily. "They're not interested in us when it comes to their scheming. They never have been."

Will saw that neither din'Dael nor Cephora contradicted her. His gaze fell to the Relic in his hand. *It's like they've already forgotten about it.* His mouth set in a thin line, he nodded to Morella. He stood, gingerly but solid. He took Morella's hand and exited the tent without another word.

While they walked, Will began to test his frozen hand. More response came from his pinky and he was beginning to feel the slight tingling of sensation in his thumb. That they had recovered a Relic and no one seemed to question it at all was maddening. He glanced down at it. "Morella, did any of that seem strange to you? I mean, it's as if everyone—"

"Will, I . . . I can't go to Greygarde."

Will paused in his tracks. "What? Why not?"

She bit her lip and looked away from him, not meeting his eye. "It's . . . it's a long story. Just—" she rolled her eyes and spoke very quickly "—not all of my research was obtained in the most noble of ways."

A smile tugged at the corner of Will's cheek. "You stole from the Seekers?"

Morella shrugged and met his smile with her own. "Something like that. The defenses they have in place at Greygarde though, they'll know. I don't know how they'll know, but they'll know."

"I'm sure that Cephora and Shyldd would—"

"Would probably kill me on the spot if they knew."

Something in her voice gave Will pause. The memory of her rage, the furious anger that overtook her. "Dammit, Morella. You killed Seekers, didn't you?"

Her smile never wavered and her eyes showed no remorse. "Maybe one or two."

"Jesus, Morella!"

"I told you I wasn't always a historian."

Will stared at her aghast. "I can't—" He shook his head. "Look, fine. I get it. Shit happened and I don't need to know about it . . . or something. I just—" He sighed in frustration. "Dammit, Morella."

"You hardly have the right to judge me about numbers of dead."

"No, no no. It's not that. I just, gods, there's still so much I don't—" He stared at her, the words hanging on the tip of his tongue. *So much I still don't know about you.* But he couldn't find it in him to say it. He turned away. "It's just a lot to take in, is all."

"Will." She turned his face back to her. "Go to Greygarde without me. Learn everything you can. I will wait for you in Undermyre. At the Street. At *our* place."

Will was nodding despite himself. "Yeah, alright."

"And if Madigan comes, I'll let him know where you are."

Madigan. Will groaned. *How the hell did I forget about my brother?* "Jesus, I haven't even been thinking about him."

"A lot has been happening, Will."

He shook his head. "No, I know but that's not, that's no excuse. I can't believe that—"

"Stop," Morella snapped. "It's been a hellish day and neither of us need you descending into self-recrimination." Will gave a brief nod and her expression calmed. She leaned up then kissed him and squeezed his hand. "I'll stay at the Street. In our room. You know how to reach me there and"—she bit her lip and squeezed harder—"and I'll do what I can."

"Din'Dael. You'll watch him? Whatever's going on with him and the Nordoth, he hasn't let me in."

"I'm three steps ahead of you, Will."

"And if Madigan comes back, you'll get word to me, won't you?"

"Of course." She looked at him aghast. "Why would you even ask that?"

"It's just . . ." He shook his head, dropping his gaze to his frozen hand and the strange object held within. "I don't know. I don't like this, Morella. Not one bit."

She kissed his free hand and held his palm to her face. "You and your brother will figure this out. I'll watch din'Dael." Her mouth twisted in distaste. "Just don't stay away too long. I don't know if even the Crow will be able to keep that bastard's ego in check."

More feeling was returning to the frozen fingers. "I'll be there as soon as I can. As soon as I figure out what the hell this is."

"What the hell what—" She followed his gaze down to the Relic. A sudden darkness flickered across her face. Her eyes snapped back up to him, seeming to contain both anger and awe. Then it was gone. She was laughing and smiling and Will wondered if he had imagined her expression. She kissed her fingers and pressed them against his lips. "Oh, I always knew you were something special, Will. I think they're right about this course."

"I daresay I do believe that none of us care in the slightest what your opinions are on this matter."

Will and Morella both whirled. Jero din'Dael had approached and was staring at Will once more with the same earlier intensity. He looked as though he were trying to prevent himself from even blinking as his eye bore into Will's.

"Dammit, Jero. Can't you just, for one goddam minute, act like a goddam human being?"

"Come, young Burner—or whatever the hell you are," he muttered. "I require words. In private."

"Well you can bloody well have them." Morella spat at din'Dael's feet. The man did not shift his gaze to her for even a moment. Obviously annoyed by the lack of reaction, she turned back to Will and kissed him. "Find me when this putrid excuse for existence is done speaking his insanity, will you?" Without waiting for an answer, she walked away.

Will glared at din'Dael. "What the hell is your problem?"

"Stop talking," din'Dael snapped. "Do you even know how hard it is to focus on you?" He closed the distance to Will and reached out, clamping his fingers around Will's forearm. He yanked the hand holding the Relic up to eye level. Only then did he seem to relax slightly.

"What the hell, Jero?" Will tried to wrench his arm away, but the man's grip was like a vice. "Dammit, let go."

"I cannot forget, William. I refuse."

"Forget? Dammit, will you just say what the hell is going on?"

"It's impossible, but it is possible. Yes, I see it. Damn the damned Hesperawn and Velier's damn folly, I see it." His eye darted between Will's hand and face, back and forth. "Do you not understand, William? Do you not see it?" He shook his head, giving Will no time to answer. "You don't know, Burner, you don't *know*. But I see it, plain as day."

"Jero." Will struggled in the large man's grasp. "Let me go, will you? I'll listen, alright?"

"Flint, yes, it started with Flint. No, no it was before that. But it started there, Flint is proof. The binding, you should be dead. But you live and breathe. You should be dead and you are not. Bound to Flint, yes, but also to this. No one else sees it, but I see it. I remember. Do you not see it?"

"So you had the wrong information about binding, so what?" The brief sensation that had returned to Will's hand was fading in din'Dael's iron grip.

"They've *forgotten,* William. Forgotten the Relic. Forgotten that you hold it. You, yourself, may be fading from their minds. Oh, they'll remember William, or Noctis, or whatever name you may have claimed, but they won't remember *you.* You fade from memory. Do you not see it?"

Will glanced at the Relic, uncertain. *He really is mad.* "Because of this?"

"Yes!" He shook Will's arm. "Yes, because of this. Bound to Flint. Bound to *this.* Flint's power of possession was known to me, but this? Unknown, William. Forgotten. Like you." He shook his head. "I must not forget. I mustn't. You, you must learn from it. Learn to control it, William. None of us will know, otherwise."

Will finally succeeded in wrenching his arm away from din'Dael. Immediately, the Revenant tensed and bent over, staring hard at Will.

"Yeah," Will said, "that's why I'm going to Greygarde. To learn."

"Greygarde?" Jero's eye was wild with confusion. "Yes, yes of course. Learn to control it, young Burner. We need you. All of us."

"Jero." Will took a breath. "Do you really think this can help us stop Valmont?"

For a moment, din'Dael stared at him, his expression blank. A vein pulsed in his temple and his eye twitched. Then, all the strain released from his face and he took a deep breath. He looked at Will soberly and Will recognized one of the brief bouts of time where Jero din'Dael's madness abated completely. Before him stood the brilliant commander who had led the forces of Radiance during their golden age.

"William, you must listen. The world is vastly more different than you believe, than your grandfather knew. The Seekers, the Crow, our brethren within the Sapholux. They do not see it. Even Dorian, for all his foolishness, doesn't understand what is ultimately at stake here." He placed a huge hand on Will's shoulder and looked at him imploringly. "You must understand, Will, you are a great asset. But you are far from the most powerful asset the Hesperawn have to contend with."

The Hesperawn? Will looked at him askance. "Jero, I'm not trying to contend the Hesperawn, they have nothing to—Wait, what do you mean? Of course I'm not the most powerful. You and Valmont are by far the—"

"As I said, you don't truly know what is at stake here, Will. No one does. Go to the Seekers' haven. Learn what you can as quickly as you can. Do not kill yourself in the process. I need you back whole."

"Jero, I know you. I know there's something going on with you. Tell me." But it was too late. Already, Will could see the change coming over his mentor, the nearly imperceptible slouch, the gleam in his eye. Whatever voices wrenched at the Revenant's sanity had returned.

"Do not"—Jero shook his head—"Do not let . . ."

Will reached up and placed his hand on din'Dael's arm. "You're a good man, Jero din'Dael." Even as he spoke the words, he wasn't sure if he believed them. "I won't let you down."

Din'Dael threw back his head in laughter. "But of course, young Burner! For ever more, you and I shall reign triumphant!"

Will said nothing. He turned away and scanned the makeshift camp, looking for Morella. Sighting her, he walked over and stood close, din'Dael's laughter haunting his mind. "He's finished."

She snorted. “One can only hope.”

“Will,” Cephora called out. “It’s nearly time.”

Will cursed. “I’d hoped we’d have a chance to talk before I left.”

“Talk?” Morella brushed her arm against his suggestively. “Is that really what you had in mind?” She traced her fingers along his chest and he saw something catch her eye. Dropping her gaze, she peered intently at it, her eyes widening. “Well, *that’s* new.”

“What?” His hands jumped to the place she looked.

“Quite an interesting scar you have there. It looks like that key of yours left an impression.”

Tracing his fingers along the spot she looked, his fingers felt nothing. The tingling electricity, or at least the memory of it, remained. *Gone, but not completely.* “Yeah, well. Something always gets lost in these events, it seems.”

“Will!” Cephora called again.

“You’ll be safe?” Will looked deep into Morella’s eyes. “You’ll look out for yourself?”

Morella smiled and gave a slight nod. “I will. And if they try anything, I’ll kill them where they stand.”

“I don’t doubt it.” Will smiled back. “Just . . . keep a low profile.”

Morella rolled her eyes. “I don’t need you telling me how to spy, lover. I’m quite able to handle myself.”

“Of that I have no doubt.”

She squeezed his hand and kissed him once more. “Go, lover. Go save the world.”

Will smiled and shook his head, then turned back to the gathering Seekers. “I’ll see you soon enough.”

“Go, Will.”

He went.

EPILOGUE

The cool breeze of an Aerillian evening gusted through the open curtains. Ynarra shivered in her sleep and curled closer into herself, lost in her world of dreams. Madigan smiled and stroked her bare arm gently before bending down and kissing her lightly on the forehead. He watched her for a moment, then rose and made his way to the window.

The night was not dark—it never was—but Madigan could feel the quiet of sleep drifting away from Undermyre below. Time was different here than back home. He'd heard it time and time again but hadn't really known what was meant by it until he'd seen his brother. Until he'd returned to Aeril. He hadn't known what to expect, choosing instead to picture things that would have been better suited for the movies and stories back home. But that wasn't it at all.

A world of immortals and a city where the sun never fully sets. No way to differentiate one day from another. No way to track time.

It wasn't that time was different here, it was that time *didn't matter* here. How long had he lain there, curled up with Ynarra?

How many hours had passed? How many days since Valmont's appearance in the Nordoth?

One year, that bastard said. How much time has already gone?

Was a year to Valmont the same as a year to Madigan? *There was so much that Grandda never told us.*

Us.

At the thought of his brother, Madigan frowned. Time had not been kind to Will. Their time apart had created a rift between them, something Madigan didn't know how to undo.

A rift created from something that barely even exists here. Madigan stared out at the city below, to the cracked statues and decaying buildings. *Is this what happens when time doesn't exist? With no urgency, the world falls into decay? Is that what's happening to Will?*

It pained him to think of his brother in that way. Under the lasting influence of din'Dael and Morella, without the influence of someone who knew the real Will, what would happen to him? Would his mind remain his own? *Grandda tried to warn us, in his own way. He'd have known how to handle Will.*

How to handle Will. Mad felt the sour taste of the idea as a physical thing. Was Will someone who was going to *need* handling? He didn't want to believe that. But so many things had happened while they'd been separated, so much had changed. Was his brother still the same good kid deep down?

Except he's not a kid. Neither of us are.

Discontent, he pulled the curtains closed. *Maybe I'm just thinking too deeply about things. Maybe that one, stupid encounter was just that. Maybe Will's still Will. Maybe—*

"I told you not to do anything rash."

Madigan froze. The voice came from above him, up near the rafters. He whirled defensively—it didn't matter that he knew to whom the voice belonged, there was cruel anger in her words.

Mad wasn't fast enough. Her knee drove into his sternum and sent him stumbling backward. He grasped at the curtains with his hands as his Shade sought to brace the wall behind him. Only, there was no wall. There was only the city. Before he could find his footing, a second strike from Ileta sent him flying through the window.

Will was right.

His fingers closed around the curtain and he heard it tear. He slammed against the Nordoth, the thick, torn cord the only thing preventing him from plunging to the courtyard below. His hands scrambled against the stony face of the fortress. A quick glance showed him that he could make his way back up to the window easily enough if he could just get a solid grip.

"I *told* you not to do anything rash," Ileta repeated.

"What in the goddam hell are you talking about?" He grit his teeth and clung tighter to the fortress. *I can get there. I can get past her.* His thoughts jumped to Ynarra, unprotected, asleep in his bed. *If she lays one goddam finger on her . . .*

Ileta stood at the window, gazing down on him in spite. Her noctori was bared in the shape of a small, sleek dagger. "You fool, do you have any idea what you've done?"

Madigan's chest ached from her strike. He stared up at her and shifted more of his weight from the curtain to the stones. "Something to disappoint you, it would seem."

Ileta grabbed the taut curtain and, with a flick of her wrist, slashed clean through it. Madigan felt the line begin to slacken almost before his eyes registered the act. He shifted his weight entirely onto the building and dug his fingers into the stone. He shot his Shade down and angled it against the Nordoth to give him leverage. His heart slammed within his chest.

"Jesus, I must have really pissed you off," he said.

Ileta cocked her head to the side then flung the noctori down toward him. Madigan stifled a cry and braced himself for the impact, but the blade winked out of existence just before making contact. He let out a deep breath of relief, then looked back up. Ileta was standing with her hands on her hips and seemed to be wrestling internally with something.

"My master wishes to meet you."

This, like everything else in the past few moments, caught Madigan completely by surprise. He stared at Ileta and thought back to what Will had said. He thought back to Valmont's finding them in Cascania and the man's appearance in the Nordoth. "I think we're already acquainted," he grunted.

Ileta sniffed in disdain, considered a moment, then knelt and extended her hand. "Just get your ass back up here. We need to talk."

She could have killed me at any time in the past few minutes, Mad considered. *Hell, she could have killed me anytime in the past few years.* He stared at the outstretched hand for a moment, then reached out and grabbed it with his own. He kicked off the fortress and Ileta hoisted him back into the room. His feet had barely touched level ground before she was speaking in a low whisper.

"I'm disappointed."

"So I was right then," he responded dryly. "You're not subtle."

Ileta turned away from him and strode to the center of the room. She reached for a bottle of wine, unstopped the cork with her teeth, and poured the contents into a single glass. She perched on the armrest of a chair and took a sip. She raised an eyebrow. "My, my, aren't we enjoying the finer things with our new station."

Mad stiffened. *Of course.* "I take it you've heard, then."

"Everyone has heard, you idiot. I leave you unwatched for the briefest of moments and you go declaring your allegiance to the Crow?" She shook her head and took another sip. "I knew you were rash, but I didn't know you were stupid."

Mad's eyes flitted to the bed where Ynarra still lay. "He didn't exactly give me much of a choice."

Ileta set her mouth in a thin line. "I expected more from you."

"And like you said, I disappointed you."

"Do you think this was why I trained you?" She held out a

hand and gestured to the room around her. "You think that this is where you're meant to be? Shut up in a tower in a city where, by now, everyone knows your name and image? Seducing serving girls and trapping yourself for it? A prisoner of your own making?"

Madigan sought to still the roiling anger within him. "I couldn't care less about your purpose in training me, Ileta. I gave the Crow my word."

"You gave *me* your word."

"He had leverage."

"She is of the Unborn." Ileta rolled her eyes. "Slit her throat and be untethered." Madigan stared at her aghast and she chuckled. "No, of course not. That is not you. You would remain trapped." She eyed him for a moment and sipped her wine. The small silhouette of her noctori reappeared. "I could do it for you, if you like."

Madigan took a step forward. The air chilled as his Shade billowed around him. "You will not touch her."

She strummed her fingers along the suddenly frosted glass, leaving faint fingerprints on its clouded surface. "No. I will not. Regardless, my master has need of you. Valmont gave you time, yes?" She took another sip as she watched the words sink in. "It will be a quick trip. You'll be back with plenty of time to prepare Undermyre's defenses to fail against his Necrothanian horde."

She's never been so blatant. "A trip to the kitchens isn't even a quick trip, here. Where are we to go?"

Ileta held the wine to her lips and the two of them locked eyes for a moment. "To the Umbriferum." She spoke quickly and quietly then chased the words with wine.

A small stir of excitement bubbled within Madigan but he fought against it. "Your master lives in the ruin, is that it? A fine place to steal the secrets of the Shadowborne."

"Something like that."

If I do this, if it is him, I can kill Valmont in his lair. I can be the dagger in the dark that Will always set out to be. Madigan watched Ileta very carefully, searching for some deeper sense of the woman's intentions. *But I won't survive it. There'd be no escape. I'll never see home again. Never see Ynarra. Never see Will.*

But they'll be safe.

Ileta watched him patiently.

I need to know for sure. "I'll come on one condition."

"Always with the bargaining." Ileta shook her head.

"Your master's name."

Ileta pursed her lips. "He has been called many things in his lifetime."

Madigan braced himself. "One that I would know. The most common one." *Just say it, damn you. Prove to me that Will was right.*

Ileta set down her glass and rose from the armrest. "Very well. But I have conditions of my own. You will come with me now. You will tell no one, not even that sweet girl keeping your bed warm. We leave this instant, with only the clothes upon your back. And when you return, you will tell no one what occurred nor whom you met. Should you break any of these conditions, your death will follow swiftly. Do you swear it?"

I'll be dead anyway. Madigan's eyes fell back to the still form of Ynarra in the bed. A pang of sorrow went through him, yet he knew what he must do. *She'll be safe. They'll both be safe.* "I swear it. Give me the name."

Slowly, deliberately, Ileta approached him. She circled behind him, then brought her mouth so near to his marred ear that they were nearly touching. In a voice softer than a whisper, barely a breath, she spoke. "Maruq T'Aroth. He is called Maruq T'Aroth."

Realization dawned on Madigan. Before he could speak, Ileta swept her arm around his neck and kicked backward, sending the two of them plummeting through the window. Madigan's world became a black swirl while they tumbled and fell through the air, the courtyard racing up to meet them. Then he was being dragged as they raced atop walls and spires, leaping and soaring through the air, a rag doll in Ileta's arms. And over and over in his head, the words circled. The voice was not Ileta's, nor was it his own, but the voice of memory, of Jervin Thorne and the stories of his youth.

Maruq T'Aroth. Maruq T'Aroth. Aspect of Shadow. Maruq T'Aroth. Slaughtered by Valmont. Maruq T'Aroth. Maruq T'Aroth.

Madigan had no plan for meeting dead gods.

THANK YOU

Thank you for reading *Borne Rising: Beyond the Shadows* - the second books in Relics of Antiquity saga.

Please consider leaving a review—any and all feedback is greatly appreciated.

Honest reviews of my books helps to bring them to the attention of other readers. Reviews are the most powerful tool that an author has for getting attention for their work, particularly for independent authors.

WORKS BY MATTHEW CALLAHAN

Novels

Shadowborne: Book One

Borne Rising: Beyond the Shadows

Shorts

Valmont's Descent: A Tale of the Relics of Antiquity

Bottled Embers: A Tale of the Relics of Antiquity

Future offerings

Building a lasting relationship with my readers is one of the very best parts about writing. If you want to be the first to hear about news, upcoming releases, and special offers related to my work, please sign up at roguishmanner.com.

As a thank you for signing up, you will receive a FREE copy of *Valmont's Descent: A Tale of the Relics of Antiquity*.

ABOUT THE AUTHOR

Matthew Callahan is the author of the ongoing saga, *The Relics of Antiquity*. In the real world, he can be found in Portland, Oregon with his wonderful wife. In the virtual world, he can always be reached online at roguishmanner.com.

You can connect with Matthew on Instagram and Twitter at @RoguishManner, on Facebook at Facebook.com/roguishmanner, on Goodreads, and you can always send him an email at matt@roguishmanner.com

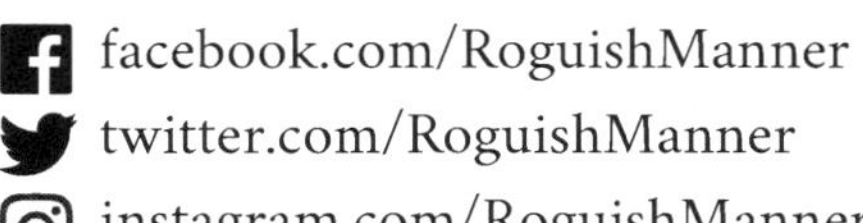

Made in the USA
Coppell, TX
17 May 2021

55843547R10240